**A M**

"I'm too old to look like a schoolgirl with my hair down," Analise said. "Millie would have a fit if she saw me now."

"Millie isn't here." His finger brushed her cheek. His voice dropped to a deep slow drawl. "It's just the two of us."

At his touch, her skin heated and warmth settled deep in her body. His face lowered to hers. Her eyelids closed of their own volition. His warm breath brushed her cheek. He groaned and touched his lips to the corner of her mouth. He smelled of the cinnamon from the cookies. Her hands fisted to keep from reaching for him, to keep from brushing her fingers along his strong neck and testing the texture of the hair on his chest, to keep from doing something they would both regret later. It had been so long since a man had touched her, kissed her, loved her . . .

# BOOK YOUR PLACE ON OUR WEBSITE AND MAKE THE READING CONNECTION!

We've created a customized website just for our very special readers, where you can get the inside scoop on everything that's going on with Zebra, Pinnacle and Kensington books.

When you come online, you'll have the exciting opportunity to:

- View covers of upcoming books
- Read sample chapters
- Learn about our future publishing schedule (listed by publication month *and author*)
- Find out when your favorite authors will be visiting a city near you
- Search for and order backlist books from our online catalog
- Check out author bios and background information
- Send e-mail to your favorite authors
- Meet the Kensington staff online
- Join us in weekly chats with authors, readers and other guests
- Get writing guidelines
- AND MUCH MORE!

**Visit our website at
http://www.kensingtonbooks.com**

# The Most Wonderful
# Time of the Year

## JENNA LAWRENCE

**ZEBRA BOOKS**
**KENSINGTON PUBLISHING CORP.**
www.kensingtonbooks.com

ZEBRA BOOKS are published by

Kensington Publishing Corp.
850 Third Avenue
New York, NY 10022

All Kensington titles, imprints, and distributed lines are available at special quantity discounts for bulk purchases for sales promotion, premiums, fund-raising, educational or institutional use.

Special book excerpts or customized printings can also be created to fit specific needs. For details, write or phone the office of the Kensington Special Sales Manager: Attn. Special Sales Department. Kensington Publishing Corp., 850 Third Avenue, New York, NY, 10022. Phone: 1-800-221-2647.

Zebra and the Z logo Reg. U.S. Pat. & TM Off.

ISBN 0-8217-7807-2

First Printing: October 2005

*To my husband, Don;*
*my children, Jeanne and Carl;*
*my grandchildren, Karissa and Kyle—*
*with much love*
*for your patience and support.*

# Prologue

The bells of Notre Dame echoed on the cold wind over the Seine. Distant strains of "Noel" from roving carolers carried clearly to the cemetery.

Analise DeLery knelt in the snow at the newly dug grave—a tiny grave the size of an infant's casket. Hot tears rolled freely down her cheeks. Alone with her misery, she hugged herself to ward off the chill in her heart. Pain cut through every inch of her body, sharper than the icy Paris wind. At one time she'd loved Christmas: a time of joy, of cheer, of miracles.

But for Analise, the holiday would always be a reminder of the time she had spent in Paris giving birth to her son. In spite of being rejected by a lover who did not want either her or their child, she loved her baby.

Etienne, whom she had named for her father, had lived only a few hours. She had been in her seventh month when she went into labor. It was too soon, he was too small, and his lungs were underdeveloped. He died in her arms.

She wished she could take him home for burial, but that was impossible. None of her family knew of his birth, or of her affair. Her father and stepmother knew only that she had come to Paris to study medicine for a year. They would be appalled to know of her indiscretions.

Besides, where was home? After her grandmother's death, she'd sold the house in New Orleans and severed all ties with her birthplace. She'd spent time in New York working at Doctor Blackwell's clinic, but she had not put down any roots in the large city.

Then there was Omega, Colorado, where her father had found a second chance for happiness. After Analise's mother had died, he had gone to Colorado to set up his medical practice. There he met a wonderful woman, who gave him a son.

Analise shoved to her feet. Her son would stay forever in Paris, and her heart would remain with him.

She lifted her gaze to the sky where a single bright star glittered in the velvet darkness of the heavens. Her grandmother had once told her that a wish upon the Christmas star was like a direct plea to the heart of God. But it was too late for her.

Tomorrow was Christmas. There would be no miracle for Analise DeLery.

*Abilene, Kansas—December 1884*

The cold north wind tore at his black wool coat as he stepped across the frozen ground. The sweet strains of "Silent Night" drifted from the church beside the cemetery. Heart weary, Tyler Morgan trudged slowly along the pathway to his goal. Tyler had traveled the world, but he returned to Abilene every Christmas Eve to mourn his dead wife and son.

Tyler knelt and gently placed the bouquet of flowers on the grave. He brushed the dirt from the headstone. ABIGAIL MARIE MORGAN, BELOVED WIFE OF TYLER MORGAN, 1854 – 1872. His gaze dropped to the next line: *Infant David Morgan, an angel returned to the Lord, December 1872.* He had buried them together—infant and mother—as they were meant to be. Only he was left behind. Tyler brushed away the tear that heated his cheek. After twelve years the pain had lessened, but he would never forget or forgive himself.

His loved ones had died because of his arrogance, and because of outlaws. He had spent the following year hunting down the bandits and bringing them to justice. Some were dead, others in prison. Tyler was in a prison of his own, with a heart full of sorrow and self-recrimination.

How different his life would be had they lived. A home, a family—it was what he had dreamed of as a child when the Morgan Players toured from town to town, state to state, country to country. Instead he had accepted Alan Pinkerton's offer and soon became a top agent, still wandering the country without roots.

He stood, and glanced at the colorful decorations on the door of the church. Inside, families gathered together in love and companionship. His gaze lifted to the heavens to a single star, brighter than the rest. It seemed to mock him, to taunt him, to remind him of the Christmas miracle nearly two thousand years ago.

However, for Tyler Morgan, there would be no miracle this year.

# Chapter 1

Tyler Morgan hunched his shoulders and leaned heavily on the battered cane. Over his head, the doctor's shingle squeaked on the rusty chain. Quelling his impatience, he knocked lightly on the door. From inside a female voice sang out, "Come in, please."

With a gentle shove, he opened the door and stepped into the waiting room. With years of training and experience, he took in the office at a single glance: a desk, several chairs, certificates on the wall, and of course, the smell of disinfectant that hung in the air. The room was very much like every other doctor's office he'd seen—and he'd seen far too many. With an effort, he quenched his distaste and smiled.

His gaze halted at the woman standing behind the desk. Her dark hair was coiled in severe braids, twisted on top of her head. Intelligent blue eyes met his. A large apron covered her dull gray gown, hiding any hint of a female figure.

"May I help you, sir?" she asked with a note of authority.

"I'm looking for Doctor DeLery. Is he in?"

"I am Doctor DeLery," she answered. Her accent, a hint of French mixed with the South, stopped him for a second. The sound brought back memories of a steamy hotel room in New Orleans and a woman with smoldering black eyes.

Tyler struggled to hide his surprise. His informants had told him about the doctor, a graying man of about fifty, with a red-haired wife of about forty and a twelve-year-old son. There had been no mention of a woman in her midtwenties. His information was never that far off.

Silence filled the room as they sized each other up. Her sharp gaze took in his appearance in a single glance. His clean but frayed black suit, crisp white shirt, and narrow black tie were exactly the expected garb of a respectable church official. The limp and cane added character to his disguise. Tyler's skin heated at her intense study. He felt as if she could see right through him into the real man behind the mask.

Fire burned behind her thick lashes, and her mouth tugged into a straight line. "If you are in need of a physician, sir, I am quite qualified to be of assistance." She stretched out a hand to a certificate on the wall. "I am a licensed practitioner."

Tyler gathered his straying thoughts. "I beg your pardon, ma'am," he answered in his meekest, mildest voice, pitched slightly higher than his normal deep tone. "I am Deacon Goodfellow, from the church headquarters in Denver. I was told to contact Dr. DeLery while I am serving the community of Omega." A little research had revealed the name of the minister and the timing of his circuit. The real preacher wouldn't return for another three weeks. Time enough for Tyler to complete his assignment and get out of town.

He removed his bowler hat and twisted it in his fingers. The stupid thing gave him a weak appearance, a look totally opposite from when he wore his favorite gray John B. Stetson.

"Oh?" She took a step back. "Then you are looking for my father. He is out making a house call, and won't be back until late this evening. He neglected to mention he expected a visitor." Suspicion glittered in the depths of her eyes, turning them as blue as the deepest ocean.

"Oh dear, I am sorry. My superiors were to contact a Doctor DeLery." On a long sigh, he set his valise on the floor and carelessly rubbed his thigh. The wound had healed long ago, but the scar and false limp were a sure way to elicit sympathy. Tyler knew good and well nobody had contacted the doctor; he had shown up totally unexpected. Sometimes surprise was the best way to get to the heart of a matter. And this matter involved murder and robbery.

"You say you're a physician, ma'am?" he asked, to draw out further information.

"Yes, I am Doctor Analise DeLery." She again pointed to the framed certificate on the wall as if to prove her identity. "Perhaps I should call my stepmother. She may have knowledge of your arrival."

"I would hate to put you to any imposition, Miss DeLery." He granted her a meek smile, one that usually garnered trust.

She squared her shoulders like a soldier ready to do battle. "It is *Doctor* DeLery." On that note, she spun on her heel and left the room.

Finding two doctors, and one of them a feisty, attractive woman, was the last thing Tyler had expected. This only added a complication he didn't need. Locating the missing payroll before the remaining Malone gang found it would take all his concentration. The agents had tracked Ace to Omega and here the trail ended. He suspected the outlaw had sought medical attention for the bullet he'd caught during the robbery. That meant one of the Doctors DeLery was the last person to see Ace Malone before he'd died, if he'd died. Tyler decided this was the place to begin his investigation. But which Doctor DeLery had treated the bandit? And did he or she know anything about the money?

The front door flung open and slammed against the wall with a bang. Tyler started, instinctively reaching for the gun tucked under his jacket. His hand paused on the weapon when a boy skid to a halt in front of him. Tyler let go of a sharp breath and backed up a step.

"Hi." The kid swiped a stray lock of fiery red hair from his damp forehead. "You looking for my papa?"

The twelve-year-old son, Tyler realized. "I suppose so. I'm Deacon Goodfellow." His heart raced as he looked at the boy. Abigail had had red hair, and if their son had lived he would be exactly this boy's age. He couldn't stop staring at the youngster. The pain he'd thought long dead twisted in his chest.

"I'm Steven DeLery." The youngster stuck out his hand. "I was named for my father. Etienne is Steven in French."

Tyler accepted the boy's handshake and forced his thoughts back to his job. "I was told to contact Doctor DeLery. I didn't expect two doctors."

"You must have met my sister, Analise. Actually, she's my half sister." He picked up a stethoscope lying on the desk and stuck it in his ears. "She's a doctor, just like Papa. I'd rather be a lawman, or lawyer, or write dime novels, anything so I won't have to look at blood all the time. I'm glad she came back. Now I won't have to sit with the sick people and help out."

The boy was a font of information. "You help your father with his patients?"

The boy listened to his own heart for a moment. "Only for a little while if he has to run an errand, and he doesn't want to leave them alone. My mom gets sick at the sight of blood and Mrs. Hennessey is always busy cooking or cleaning. Now Analise can take over."

Before Tyler could question the boy further, footsteps from the inner hallway interrupted. An attractive, full-figured woman bustled into the office, followed by Doctor DeLery—the female Doctor DeLery. The older woman smiled widely and offered her hand to Tyler. "Deacon Goodfellow, I am Mildred DeLery. It is a pleasure to meet you."

"My pleasure, Mrs. DeLery." He took her hand in a gentle grip. The wife, son, and daughter, he thought. All that remained was the doctor. "I was hoping your husband could arrange lodging for me while I am ministering in Omega."

The older woman opened her arms in a welcoming gesture. Unlike the young doctor, this woman wore a stylish afternoon gown that showed off her matronly figure to its full advantage. Her red hair was styled to flatter her, and she wore a touch of rouge. "It is our privilege to offer lodging to visiting dignitaries. You are more than welcome in our home, Deacon."

Better than he could have dreamed. "Thank you, madam. I certainly would not want to put you to any trouble."

"No bother at all, Deacon. We are delighted to offer hospitality to a man of the cloth. You can stay with us as long as you care to work in our community. Preacher Carter often stays with us."

Tyler smiled in appreciation. "I am most grateful, Mrs. DeLery. I can assure you I will prove no inconvenience to you or your family."

The pretty lady doctor stepped forward, her eyes narrowing slightly as she studied his bent posture.

"How long will you be here in Omega, Deacon . . .
um . . . Goodman?"

"Goodfellow." He bit back a grin. He would have
to watch his step around this woman. "At least three
weeks, until Pastor Carter makes his circuit. I'm here
to determine if Omega can support a full-time permanent minister."

Mrs. DeLery folded her hands in front of her chest.
"Praise the Lord. I've been praying for such a thing.
We need a regular church and a full-time pastor. Our
ladies auxiliary has been raising money to build a
parsonage."

Tyler secretly congratulated himself on his choice
of disguises. Not only did a churchman encourage
confidences, he would also be welcome in the doctor's home. If the doctor or his family knew anything
about Ace or the missing loot, Tyler had three weeks
before the minister returned and exposed him as an
imposter. He hoped to recover the missing payroll
and be long gone before then.

"What are we doing standing here?" Mrs. DeLery
gestured toward the door that led into the house.
"Are you hungry, Deacon? I can prepare us some tea
and cookies, or a sandwich, if you wish. Steven, fetch
Deacon Goodfellow's bag and take it to the corner
bedroom." She turned back to Tyler. "The guest room
overlooks our garden. It has quite a lovely view."

"Millie," Doctor DeLery interrupted her stepmother, "that room also faces the street. Perhaps the
deacon will be happier in the green room. It is much
more private, for meditation and study."

A room overlooking the street where he could
keep track of comings and goings was perfect for his
needs. "I'm sure any room would be fine. I certainly
don't want to put you through any trouble."

"No trouble at all." The older woman led the way

into the house. "We are honored to have you in our home."

Leaning heavily on the cane, his back hunched, he followed meekly behind the woman. A cloud of expensive French perfume floated behind her.

Step one, accomplished. Now, if the rest of this mission went as smoothly, he'd have the Malone gang in custody and the money safely back in Denver before three weeks were up. He glanced back at Doctor DeLery staring at him with narrowed eyes. Something told him she wouldn't be as easily duped as her stepmother.

Analise remained behind in the office while Steven carried their guest's shabby carpetbag up to his room. The bag must contain some heavy Bibles, she thought, considering Steven needed both hands to tote it. She stared at the door long after everybody else had entered the house. Deacon Goodfellow. Strangefellow was more like it. In his midthirties with skin tanned from the sun, broad shoulders, and narrowed hips, he didn't look like her idea of a church worker. Hunched over the cane as he was, she wasn't sure about his height, but she was certain he was over six feet tall. Except for his limp she would have taken him for a lawman . . . or an outlaw.

Her skin tingled as she remembered the sparkle in his gray eyes when he'd studied her boldly from behind his gold-rimmed eyeglasses. She'd seen that look before, though not from a man of the cloth. It was the same way Victor had looked at her that first morning at the sidewalk café in Paris. She shivered at the memory of how his bold gaze had heated her skin and set her heart aflutter. As always when she thought about Victor, her hands dropped to her abdomen. The ache in her heart hadn't lessened a bit after so many months.

Analise's reverie was interrupted when a young mother entered the office with a small boy in tow. Though surprised to find a female doctor, the woman allowed Analise to treat the child's scrapes and bruises.

For the remainder of the afternoon, she treated a variety of minor injuries, her patients being only women and children. The men who entered the office retreated, deciding they could wait for the *real* Doctor DeLery. As if the years she'd spent at the Philadelphia college, interning with Doctor Blackwell in New York, and the year studying under the finest surgeons in Paris were nothing.

Between patients, her gaze slid toward the parlor where perhaps Millie was entertaining the newcomer. Or had he settled in his room—the one next to hers? Was he reading and meditating? Taking a nap or preparing a sermon? Exactly what was he doing in Omega, anyway? They already had a minister, a circuit rider who ministered every third Sunday. Analise chided herself. She was spending entirely too much time thinking about a man she'd met for only a few minutes. A man who reminded her entirely too much of Victor—same black hair and eyes glittering with mystery. Except Victor LaBranche would never be mistaken for a man of the cloth. Her former lover had played her for a fool and disappeared when he learned she was penniless.

A few minutes before six o'clock, Analise locked the door and headed up the back stairs to her room. Luscious aromas wafted from the kitchen. Warm and outgoing, Millie loved to entertain. On his rotation to minister in Omega, Reverend Carter, the circuit rider, often stayed at the DeLery home. That was only yesterday, she remembered. Strange that a representative of the bishop should show up today, with no forewarning.

Her father was not only the town's beloved doctor, he also served as mayor. Analise was infinitely grateful he had found such a devoted and loving woman to marry after her mother had died. As his wife, Millie was the unofficial social leader of Omega. A soft chuckle bubbled up in Analise's throat. In the two weeks since she'd returned to her father's home, Analise had been subjected to an almost daily dose of social engagements. She'd been guest of honor at everything from afternoon teas to a dinner party and various other social gatherings. Millie felt it was her duty to introduce Analise to every eligible man in town, from eighteen to eighty.

"Would you care to share what you find so amusing, Doctor DeLery?" The soft voice came from the doorway of the room next to hers.

She glanced at the man entering the hallway. The door clicked softly behind him. He seemed taller, larger, standing so close to her. And much more handsome than she'd thought. His wide shoulders filled the narrow space. Without his spectacles, his eyes glimmered like newly minted silver coins. At her close scrutiny, he tugged the eyeglasses from his pocket and squinted before placing them on his face.

"Nothing worth mentioning, Mr. Goodfellow." She had no intention of revealing her stepmother's matchmaking schemes. "Have you settled into your room? I hope it's comfortable."

He adjusted the spectacles. "Quite. It is considerably better than many I've had in my travels."

"Oh, have you traveled very much in your work for the church?" she asked, seeking further information about the stranger in her father's home.

"Quite a bit," he answered. "I sometimes reside in

hotels or boarding houses. Occasionally I'm forced to enjoy the great outdoors. These accommodations are excellent."

"So is the food. Millie and our housekeeper are wonderful cooks. Will you be joining us for dinner?"

"Yes, thank you. First I'm going to take a short walk around town. Perhaps meet a few of the parishioners." He rubbed his thigh. "A walk will help loosen the muscles. And I'm interested in seeing the town."

She nodded. "You'll find Omega quite interesting."

"I already do."

As she watched, his shoulders hunched, and he braced his weight on the cane. Like a chameleon, he changed before her eyes. He swiped a lock of dark hair from his forehead. "I suppose I will see you at dinner." With slow, deliberate movements, he headed toward the stairs. "Mrs. Delery told me her housekeeper puts the meal on the table precisely at seven and warned me not to be late."

"And she is very unhappy when anyone is late."

His soft laughter floated from the stairs. As Analise watched him hobble down the steps, he appeared to shrink in height, turning him into an entirely different man from the one who had first approached her. A gentle shiver skittered up her spine. Whatever was wrong with him wasn't her problem. She had enough on her plate struggling to be accepted as a doctor and making plans for her medical clinic for women. Perhaps her father would have some information on the man.

Tyler learned little during his short stroll through Omega. The name of the town made him laugh. Omega: the end. The founders seemed to have been obsessed with everything Greek. Every street had a

name associated with Greece, either in place, literature, or mythology. Quite a surprise for a little town
in the middle of Colorado.

However, he wasn't interested in the town, except
as a place to look for Ace Malone and the missing
payroll. His best hope for information about the bandit was the doctor and his family.

He realized he would have to watch his step
around the pretty lady doctor. But Tyler had done
his job for many years, and in his opinion he was a
darn good actor. Once one of his disguises had even
fooled his boss, Alan Pinkerton.

By the time he returned to the DeLery home, the
older doctor had returned and dinner was being
served. He hurriedly washed up and joined the family in the dining room.

Doctor DeLery greeted Tyler warmly, like a long-
lost friend. Tyler hated being duplicitous, but it was a
necessary part of his job. "Thank you for your gen-
erosity, Doctor," he offered.

"Our pleasure, Deacon. I'm sorry we weren't better
prepared for your visit. Brother Carter didn't mention anything about you when he was here yesterday." His accent held a hint of Southern drawl and a
touch of French, much like his daughter's. As an actor,
Tyler had studied voices, and recognized the accent
as from New Orleans.

Tyler settled at the table next to Analise and across
from Steven. "I'm afraid that is my fault. When the
bishop asked me to come to Omega, Pastor Carter
had already left Denver, and I was unable to catch up
with him."

"Oh posh, that doesn't matter," Mrs. DeLery said.
"We have lots of room. Deacon, will you say the blessing, please?" She stretched out her hand to Tyler, in-
dicating that they were to hold hands around the
table. Analise offered her palm, laying it limply in his

large grip. Tyler clasped her hand firmly, enjoying the softness of her skin on his rough fingers.

For a brief second, he forgot why he was holding hands with this woman. When Millie nudged him gently, he came back to his senses.

"Oh, Lord," Tyler prayed, "bless this household, bless those who have offered their hospitality to thy servant as commanded in your Word. Bless this food to the nourishment of our bodies." He opened his eyes to see all but Steven deep in meditation. The youngster had one eye closed and the other on the platter of roast beef in the center of the table. "Amen," Tyler said abruptly.

All heads lifted, and Steven grinned. Millie whispered, "Amen? Already?"

Tyler smiled. He'd forgotten how long-winded preachers tended to be, showing off their godliness with the use of long words plus a few thees and thous thrown in for good measure. "Madame DeLery, you asked me to bless the food, not preach. If you wish, I can continue for a full hour, and this fine repast you have prepared will grow cold."

"No," Steven groaned, "sometimes I think I'll starve to death before Brother Carter gets around to saying 'amen.'"

Doctor Etienne DeLery laughed aloud. "No, Deacon, that was quite sufficient. I'm sure we'll hear a fine message at the prayer meeting on Wednesday evening."

Mrs. DeLery released his fingers, and Analise tried to pull her hand from his. For one heartbeat, he was tempted to lift her fingers to his lips and taste her instead of the roast beef. Reluctantly, he released her. "I'll be sure to prepare a special message." Thanks to being born to a family of actors, Tyler was not only a master of disguise, he also had an exceptional memory. He could memorize pages of dialogue with little effort. And he easily remembered every sermon he'd ever suffered through whenever his parents had dragged him to church.

He slanted a glance at Analise. She gazed intently at the plate in front of her, unsuccessfully trying to ignore him. Some mischief inside Tyler made him determined to see if he could rile her a bit. As the bowls were passed around the table, he managed to brush her shoulder with his. Their hands touched more than was necessary. By the time dessert was served, he felt as if his plan had backfired on him. A twinge tightened in Tyler's stomach and tingles from her touch reached clear to his toes.

Light conversation circled the table, with an occasional reprimand of Steven for one minor offense or another. He was a laughing, happy youngster, clearly well loved. The doctor had a right to be proud of his offspring. Any man would be proud of such a fine boy. As soon as Steven devoured his apple pie, the youngster asked to be excused and darted from the house. The adults lingered at the table over their coffee and conversation. After helping to clear the plates away, Analise returned to Steven's vacated chair across the table.

"Mrs. DeLery, that meal was worthy of a fine restaurant," Tyler said, meaning every word. It had been a very long time since he'd shared a home-cooked meal with a family.

"Please, Deacon, call me Millie—everybody does. Of course, I didn't do it all myself. Audrey Hennessey, my housekeeper, did most of the work." The woman smiled and patted her upswept hair with long, tapered fingers. A little on the full-figured side, the woman was quite nice looking. He wondered where the doctor had found her.

"And I would appreciate your calling me by my given name. I don't like to stand on formalities." He offered his brightest smile, and met Analise's frown across the table. Being called Deacon made him feel even more like a hypocrite than he was. "May I call you Analise?"

Her father laughed. "My daughter is accustomed to standing on formalities. People are much more formal in New Orleans, where she's lived most of her life. And she is very proud of her medical degree."

"Papa, I'm not that prim and proper." She frowned at her father.

Tyler shrugged. "How about Dr. Analise? It's at least one way to distinguish between the two Doctors DeLery."

"That will be all right with me," she said, if a bit reluctantly.

The older doctor settled back in his chair. "Tyler, exactly what is your mission here in Omega? Why did the bishop honor us with your presence?"

Here was where his acting ability kicked in. It was important that these people believe his cover identity. "I am an assistant to the bishop, going where he sends me. He believes it is time for Omega to have a regular minister, and he sent me here to see what is best for the congregation." The story came easily for a liar and hypocrite. He hated deceiving these good people, but it was necessary for everyone's safety.

"Are you a minister?" Analise asked, suspicion in her tone.

"I have not attended seminary, but I am licensed to preach and work in the church."

"Then you are more than welcome in our congregation. Omega is growing daily, and we feel we can support a full-time permanent minister." The doctor took a sip of his coffee. "Sometimes we can't wait for Preacher Carter to make his rounds when we have an emergency."

"You mean like a funeral?" he asked, seeking information about Ace, without coming right out and asking.

Millie shivered. "And we need someone to conduct our midweek prayer meeting."

"I will be happy to take over the preaching until Brother Carter returns on his circuit." He glanced at Analise. "As their doctor, you must know all of the residents in town. I would appreciate your introducing me to as many of our congregation as possible."

Analise shook her head. "I'm sorry, Mr. . . . Tyler. I'm newly arrived in Omega. I know few people. My father or Millie, or even Steven, would be a better guide than I."

There went his chance to spend time with Analise, and maybe find out what she knew about Ace Malone. He doubted Millie had seen the outlaw. That left Steven and Etienne. Of course, spending time with Analise would be more interesting, but work came first.

"Out of curiosity, how long have you been in Omega, Dr. DeLery?" He addressed his question to the older man.

He glanced at his wife. "About fifteen years. I left New Orleans after losing my first wife, Analise's mother. I met my dear Millie here, in Omega. We were blessed with a son." Love and devotion shone on the man's face. Etienne truly was a blessed man. Tyler envied a man who could settle down with a second chance at a happy marriage and family. He had long ago given up dreams of a second chance for himself. And he sure didn't believe in miracles.

"I remained in New Orleans with my grandmother to attend school, then medical college." Analise shoved away from the table.

"Our daughter also studied in Paris," Millie said. "We're very proud of her. It isn't every young woman who is so accomplished. She is not only beautiful, she's intelligent and she'll make a wonderful wife and mother someday." Millie smiled with genuine pride, as if showing her eligible daughter's attributes to a possible suitor. That unlikely suitor currently was one Deacon Tyler Goodfellow.

"Millie, please. You know I am not interested in being either a wife or mother." A glimmer of pain lurked behind her blue eyes. "I am a doctor and I have dedicated my life to building a clinic for women and children. I don't need that kind of distraction." She spun on her heel and darted into the kitchen as if the devil himself was on her tail.

Little did she know the devil was an over-six-foot-tall Pinkerton agent. In order to protect his cover, he didn't mind going along with Millie's scheme and trying to learn more about what had happened to Ace. That was his priority—spending time with Analise was a bonus.

After dinner, Tyler retired to his room on the pretext of meditation and study. The doctor had gone to his lodge meeting, Millie was visiting a friend, and Analise had locked herself in the doctor's office. Steven had run off to play with his friends. Well-honed instinct told Tyler that Steven might be a key to learning about Ace without coming out and asking the doctors directly. The less anybody knew about the missing money, the better chance Tyler had of finding it, and the safer they would all be. He couldn't have innocent people getting in the way if the bandits came hunting the money. All he had to do was get friendly with the youngster and learn what he could.

Thanks to the window overlooking the side porch, leaving the house unnoticed was a simple feat for Tyler. After climbing down the trellis, he stopped at the woodshed to change from his "preacher clothes," into those of a down-and-out prospector. After a lifetime on the stage, he'd learned the fine art of changing his appearance in mere minutes with false hair and clothing. Even his mother wouldn't recognize him.

Tyler shuffled into Blackjack Saloon and staggered up to the bar. About a dozen men loitered at the bar and at the tables. Nobody paid him any attention when he ordered a beer. Even the few women looking for companionship paid him no mind. Clearly a prospector in ragged pants and a slouch hat covering much of his bearded face was of no interest to them. He tuned his ears to the various conversations going on around the room. Most of the men were local cowboys. None met the description he'd gotten of Malone's cohorts.

He was certain the stolen money had not been found. Ace had had it with him when the gang had split up. Other Pinkerton operatives were on their trail, and he was afraid the bandits would eventually end up in Omega.

When the bartender carried away a tray of drinks through the doorway at the rear of the room, Tyler sauntered over toward the door that led to the path to the privy. He nearly laughed aloud when he caught a glimpse of the men gathered around a table covered with chips and cards. Doctor DeLery picked up a glass of amber liquid and lifted it in a toast to his fellow "lodge" brothers.

After another pass through the town, it was quite late when Tyler returned to the doctor's home. The moon was high in the sky and the night breeze ruffled the leaves. The town was very quiet, with only the sound of the night insects singing in chorus. A quick stop at the woodshed for a costume change and Tyler turned back into the respectable deacon. All that remained was to climb back to his room and slip into bed. As he approached the house, he spotted a glimmer of light from the kitchen. Somebody was up and moving about. Then there was nothing but solid darkness. He blinked, wondering if he'd merely spotted a reflection of the moon on a window.

He stepped onto the rear porch, careful to avoid the squeaking board he'd noticed earlier. Rather than take a chance on being seen by climbing up the trellis to his room, he tried the lock on the rear door. The knob turned easily in his hand. He grinned to himself. Millie had left it unlocked for when Doctor DeLery returned from his "lodge meeting."

Silent as a mouse, he crept into the kitchen and let the door click softly behind him.

"Out for a midnight stroll, Deacon?" The soft feminine voice came from the shadows.

# Chapter 2

In the darkness of the kitchen, Analise couldn't see the expression on the man's face, but she heard his quick intake of breath. She'd been right. Someone, namely Tyler Goodfellow, had been skulking around the woodshed.

"I didn't know anyone else couldn't sleep, Doctor Analise." He stepped closer, a mere shadow in the dark kitchen.

"I was on my way to my room when I saw someone in the backyard. I was expecting to find Steven out for mischief." She tightened the belt on her wrapper, aware of her state of dishabille. And of the attractive man standing close enough to smell his unique scent.

The sound of his soft laughter sent sensations skittering up her spine. "Looks as if you caught the wrong culprit. However, I assure you, I was only out for fresh air, not mischief."

Analise wasn't sure if he was mocking her or not. She wished she had turned up the lamp so that she could see his face. It wouldn't surprise her to note a twinkle in his eyes much like in Steven's when he was up to a prank. She couldn't believe she was having these thoughts about a stranger. After Millie's blatant attempt at matchmaking, Analise had made up her mind to stay as far as possible away from this man.

"I had best get to bed. Papa will lock up when he returns from his lodge meeting."

A hand on her arm stopped her. Tyler's gentle touch sent tingles across her flesh. "I'm not sleepy. Stay and talk to me for a few minutes. We didn't have time to get acquainted at dinner."

Analise wasn't sure if she wanted to get further acquainted with this man or not. He was simply too much like Victor for her peace of mind. She hesitated.

"Please."

"For a few minutes," she agreed. "Where is that lamp?"

"We don't need light. The dark is much more . . . intimate, if you will pardon my boldness." The deep, husky timbre of his voice drifted over her like a warm breeze.

He helped her to a chair at the table and sat across from her. She swallowed her nervousness. The last time she had been alone in the dark with a man had proved to be her downfall. She could lie and say that Victor had taken advantage of her innocence, but she had willingly given herself to him. And as a doctor, she knew the full consequences of her actions.

"Well, uh, Deacon—"

"Tyler."

Thinking his given name was one thing, the familiarity of saying it aloud was another matter entirely. "Tyler." She struggled to find a safe, neutral subject of conversation. "What do you think of Omega?"

"Omega. The end. I suppose at one time this was the end of the line for more than one pilgrim."

"I thought it strange the first time I heard it too. Now we're no longer the end, but somewhere in the middle, and very progressive at that. My father is trying to get an electric power company and telephone lines in town."

"Interesting. That telephone invention is really amazing. Soon the entire country will be hooked together with wires similar to the telegraph."

His voice had dropped to a deeper tone than she had noticed earlier. In the dark he seemed to be an entirely different person than in the daylight.

"I was surprised at so many Greek names in the town."

She laughed. "So was I. It's a very nice story, if you're interested."

"Tell me. I'm a naturally curious person."

She didn't doubt that one bit. "A man named Onasis founded the town. It seems he was lost out in the snow on Christmas Eve. He claimed he followed a bright star, and it led him—"

"To Bethlehem?" He laughed.

"No, to an outpost, a stagecoach station in the middle of nowhere. He believed he'd been led here by the Christmas star, and he decided this was where he was destined to remain. He built the railroad to this point and started his empire. He laid out the streets and named them for his homeland."

"What happened to him?"

"I'm not sure. I think he got homesick, sold the railroad, and returned to his homeland."

"Interesting. So Omega was founded because a man followed a Christmas star."

She shivered at the thought of the star that had shone down on her son's grave on Christmas Eve. Perhaps that same star had led her to Omega, where she could run her clinic and have a home. "Yes, it was sort of a miracle."

"I suppose everybody needs a miracle at one time or another."

Although she couldn't see him, she heard his sigh.

"Tell me about yourself, Doctor Analise. When did you return from Paris?"

Analise was thankful for the dark. She knew her emotions showed too clearly on her face. "I left Paris five months ago. I spent some time in New York, then I returned here two weeks ago. I—"

The squeak of the door's hinges drew her attention. By the stealth of the footsteps, she doubted it was her father returning home. Tyler leaped to his feet and planted himself in the path of the intruder.

"Umph, darn," the young voice muttered. He staggered back a step after running smack into Tyler's chest.

"Steven?" Analise stood and stared at her brother, her eyes now adjusted to the dark. "What are you doing sneaking in at this hour?" She reached over to the lamp and struck a match to the wick. "And look at you. You're filthy. Where have you been?"

The youngster pulled free of Tyler's grip. "I was out with the guys . . . and . . . I . . . um . . . fell." His gaze shifted from her, in her nightclothes, to Tyler, who was clad in a black shirt and dark pants. "What's going on here with you?"

"Nothing. Get washed up and into bed before your mother finds out. Papa would tan your hide if he caught you coming in this late."

Steven tilted his head. "What about if he caught you and the deacon together?"

"Touché. Looks as if we've been caught." Tyler shrugged his wide shoulders.

Steven, the little sneak, smirked. "If you don't tell on me, I won't tell on you."

"I ought to tan your hide myself." Analise grabbed her brother's arm and guided him to the stairs. "*Bonsoir, monsieur,*" she shot over her shoulder. In the dim light, she noticed that Tyler wasn't wearing his spectacles, and his hair hung loose in his eyes. A once familiar sensation tightened in her chest. No, she told herself, she was not attracted to him. Not in the least bit. Hurriedly, she tugged Steven toward his room.

"*Bonsoir, mademoiselle.*" The whisper followed her into the darkness and wrapped around her heart. How could this ordinary deacon remind her so of debonair, sophisticated Victor LaBranche? Except for their similar black hair, the men were nothing alike. It was the way he'd said good night in French, she supposed, surprised at his use of the foreign language. An all too familiar twinge settled deep in her chest. She renewed her vow to stay as far away from him as possible.


After a restless night, Tyler awoke early, determined to get Analise off his mind and concentrate on his assignment. The house was quiet when he entered the kitchen clad in his severe churchman clothes. Accustomed to fending for himself, he put a pot of coffee on the stove and waited for it to boil. His gaze shifted to the chairs shoved away from the table as he and Analise had left them the night before.

She had surprised and delighted him. Something about the lady doctor drew him like a bear to honey. And as he'd spent half of the night reminding himself, she was a distraction he didn't want or need.

He'd just poured a cup of coffee when the object of his distraction entered the kitchen. "*Bonjour, Mademoiselle Docteur,*" he said, wishing her good morning, and studied her over the rim of his cup. Today she hid her female form under a large smock. With her hair pulled into a tight twist at her nape and the collar up to her chin, he suspected she was as much in disguise as he.

"Deacon," she said, "I see you've made yourself at home."

"I hope I didn't do anything wrong. I am accustomed to taking care of myself."

She reached for a cup. "Oh, there isn't a Mrs. Goodfellow waiting for your return?"

Her innocent query cut deeper than he thought it could. "I'm sorry to say there is no Mrs. Goodfellow." He'd learned years earlier that to make a lie believable, it was important to keep it as close to the truth as possible. "My wife died before I was called." As true a statement as he was willing to admit. "Since then, I have devoted my life to working for our cause." Only he didn't tell her his cause was catching criminals as a Pinkerton agent. Taking a sip of the coffee, he continued to stare at her.

Millie chose that moment to hustle into the kitchen. "Did you just say you are a widower, Deacon?" A wide smile curved her lips. She winked at Analise, who groaned under her breath.

"Yes, and I have no children." After all the years, it still hurt to remember his dual losses. However, it might serve his purpose to let Millie consider him a potential suitor for her stepdaughter.

"If you're interested in settling down, you couldn't find a better place than Omega. I've lived here most of my life, and there aren't nicer people or a more dedicated congregation anywhere." She set a teakettle on the stove. "And, as you know, there aren't that many eligible women in this part of the country."

"I'm certain I will enjoy my stay here," he hedged, feeling more hypocritical by the moment. He hated to deceive these good people, but he had little choice if he was to successfully complete his assignment.

"Millie, Audrey must be running a little late this morning." Analise changed the subject—not that Tyler could blame her. Her stepmother certainly wasn't subtle with her matchmaking schemes.

The older woman picked up a skillet and set it on the stove. "Yes, it isn't like her. She and Oscar have been with me since I married your father, and she's always punctual, sometimes to a fault. I had better not be one minute late serving dinner or she has a hissy fit."

At that moment, the rear door burst open. The housekeeper, a fiftyish woman with gray hair, entered, out of breath. "Sorry I'm late. Oscar was having a bad morning. Down with the gout, again. Don't reckon he'll be able to help out today. I'll get one of the Johnson boys to chop wood and do the chores."

Millie waved a hand in dismissal. "Don't bother, Audrey. We'll manage. I just hope he feels better soon."

Analise turned from the stove where she had been stoking the fire. "I'll go over to your place and look in on him today. I have some medicine that should help."

Mrs. Hennessey tied on a large white apron over her black dress. "That's okay, Missy. Your papa can check on him when he gets a chance."

"I'll tell Papa when he comes down."

The downhearted look in the young doctor's eyes sent a twinge to Tyler's chest. Rejection was a hard pill to swallow.

Tyler knew better than to interfere, but he couldn't help himself. "I'll be happy to visit with your husband, since I'm trying to get to know the congregation. Doctor Analise can accompany me."

A frown pulled at the corners of the older woman's mouth. "Oscar ain't a churchgoing man. He don't take much to preaching. I've done my best to convert him, but it looks like he'll die a sinner."

Tyler pasted on his pious demeanor. "Don't give up hope. People said that about me at one time. I'll just make a short visit and try to cheer him up."

She shrugged. "The Lord works in mysterious ways. Maybe you can reach him where others can't."

Analise seemed to brighten. "We'll walk over after breakfast. Surely he won't be embarrassed with a female doctor if a man is present."

On a long sigh, the housekeeper turned and entered the pantry. "Sure do hope nobody dies today. Somebody else will have to dig the grave."

That bit of information took Tyler back a bit. "Oscar is a gravedigger?"

"All-around handyman. He does whatever needs to be done." Audrey set a basket of eggs on the table.

Millie cut thick slices of bacon from the slab. "He mostly works for us, but he also tends the cemetery behind the church. Cuts the grass, digs the graves, sets the headstones."

Interesting, Tyler thought. Another possible lead to Ace Malone. "By the way, I'd also like to see the church building." He looked directly at Analise. "Do you think you could show me the way after we visit Oscar?"

"I suppose. But I have to be back by noon for my office hours."

"I promise I won't keep you from your medical practice."

She shook her head. "Such as it is. The men don't trust a female doctor, and the women are shy around male doctors. That's why I want to open a clinic for women and children."

He reached over and patted her hand. "It takes time, Doc. Anything worth having is worth waiting for."

\*  \*  \*

The Hennessey home was an easy walk along Poseidon Creek, which ran behind town. In spite of his limp and the uneven ground, Tyler insisted on carrying her medical bag. The mid-September sunshine filtered through the trees, warming them in spite of the breeze. The path wound along the creek and through the woods. Small animals scurried into hiding as they approached. As they crossed the creek, she spotted a doe and fawn drinking farther downstream.

They spoke little, mostly about the residents in town. Analise explained that she had spent little time over the years with her father in Omega. "Most of the people know me because of my father and Millie. Before she married Papa, she ran the general store as did her parents before her. She knows everybody. Millie considers herself the social leader of Omega." Analise laughed softly. "And as you can surmise, she has made it her mission to find me a husband. So don't be surprised that you are the latest victim in her matchmaking schemes." Heat surfaced to her cheeks.

"I've met other overeager mothers. Most are happily married and want to see all their friends and daughters married. They don't mean any harm."

Analise stepped over a fallen log. "It gets a little embarrassing sometimes."

As if he too was slightly embarrassed, Tyler changed the subject. "Tell me about your practice here in Omega, Doc."

She smiled, grateful to talk about her first love. "In the short time I've been here, I've treated a few bumps and bruises, set one broken arm, and stitched a few cuts."

"Any gunshot wounds?"

"No, not yet. My papa has treated quite a few. Mostly young cowboys who get careless and shoot each other."

She laughed. "Or wound themselves in the leg or foot."

"No outlaws?" His voice quivered a little as if in fear.

She laughed. "I'm sure he's met a few over the years. They come through on occasion. The sheriff keeps pretty good track of strangers, or so I understand." She hesitated, and chuckled to share a secret that wasn't a secret. "Of course, that's when he isn't out prospecting, fishing, or courting a widow in the next county."

"I'm happy to know that there isn't much crime in Omega. That makes living here much more appealing." He hesitated for a heartbeat. "Then you've never treated a gunshot wound?"

He seemed overly obsessed with guns. Maybe he was timid and fearful. "No, but I studied under some fine surgeons who detailed how to remove a bullet and prevent infection."

"That's good to know, in case I get struck by another stray bullet." His gaze dropped to his lame leg.

"Mind telling me what happened?"

"I was in the wrong place at the wrong time and took a stray bullet. Laid me up for a while. With nothing to do, I started reading the Bible. Changed my life for the better. Now I've dedicated my life to the mission."

"I'm sorry. Not that you've repented, but that you were injured."

"Thanks, Doc."

The slap, slap of running footsteps on the hard ground drew them up short. "Hey, Lise, Deac, wait up." Steven skidded to a stop.

"What are you doing out here?" Analise asked. "You were sound asleep when we left."

"Yeah, well Mama woke me up and told me to go with you. She wants me to collect the eggs and to milk that stupid old cow." He kicked a stone and sent it skidding.

She tossled her brother's bright red hair. "*Petit*, you don't have anything better to do."

"Ha! I want to go fishing today."

"You go nearly every day, and never bring home any fish."

"They're just not biting, that's all. Anyway, school starts tomorrow, and I won't get much chance to mess around with the guys." Steven fell into step beside Tyler.

"I'll go with you, if you'd allow me," Tyler offered.

Her brother shoved his hands into the pockets of his overalls. "I might have to wait for the guys. You probably have other things to do and all."

"No," he insisted. "I want to get to know the congregation. You can introduce me to the young people. They are as important to the church the older folks. And I'll be glad to help you milk that cow."

"The Hennesseys raise chickens and keep a couple of milk cows. They make extra money by selling the eggs and milk. We're their best customers, but they also sell to the general store." Analise opened the gate of the white fence that surrounded the neat cottage. The home boasted pots of red geraniums on the porch and roses twined on the trellises. The scent of roses wafted on the air. "Let's check on Oscar, then I'll help collect the eggs."

She knocked lightly, then called out. "Oscar, it's Analise, may we come in?"

"Just a minute," a gruff voice called. After a bit of shuffling and clanging, he grunted, "Come in."

Analise shoved open the door and led the way into the immaculate little parlor. A large bear of a man, Oscar relaxed in a large easy chair, his foot propped on a hassock. "How's my favorite handyman?" She kissed him lightly on the top of his bald head.

"Hurtin', Missy. Gout. Who's the fine gentleman? Your beau?"

Tyler stepped forward, his hand outstretched. "Deacon Tyler Goodfellow."

Oscar shifted his gaze from her to the churchman. "I don't need nobody to come to my house and preach to me." With a frown, he ignored Tyler's offered hand and folded his brawny arms over his chest.

"Sir, I'm not here to preach to you. I'm new in the area, and Doctor Analise is showing me around."

"Well, she can show you out. I don't need no saw-bones poking at me, and I sure don't want to hear no preaching."

Analise ignored the grumpy older man, knowing pain made even the nicest disposition irritable. In the short time she'd been home, she had come to like and appreciate the handyman. "I won't poke you. I only want to help."

"I ain't gonna take none of that nasty medicine, and you ain't gonna stick me with no needles." He shook a finger at Analise.

She pulled up a straight-backed chair near Oscar's feet. Tyler set her black leather bag on the floor. "I'll go out and help Steven while you do your doctoring." He tipped his hat. "Good meeting you, sir."

Oscar grunted, not at all happy at being disturbed.

Once Tyler had left the room, Analise slipped her hand under the legs of the large easy chair. "What are you doing, Missy? I don't need no doctoring," Oscar snarled.

She ignored him and came up with a half-empty bottle. She removed the cap and sniffed the contents. The strong odor of liquor burned her nostrils. She reached farther and found an empty whiskey bottle hidden from view. And away from his wife. Holding it up in front of Oscar, she frowned at him.

"Medicine. It's the only thing that helps with the gout." He slunk down lower and snatched the bottle from her hand.

Analise instantly snatched it back. "This does not help the gout. Rich food and liquor make it worse. I'm going to tell Audrey to put you on a strict diet of healthy food. It won't cure you, but it should make the attacks less frequent."

He growled like an angry bear. "If this foot didn't hurt so much, little missy, I'd chase you and that fellow clear back to town. I can tolerate your papa because he don't try to tell me what to do, but you're just like any other female I've ever known. Bossy and nosy."

She laughed. "Just keep that foot elevated, and you should be better in a few days." She dropped the whiskey bottles into her medical bag and snapped it shut. "I'm going out to help gather the eggs. Behave yourself while I'm gone."

"Humph. Not much else I can do."


Tyler managed to bluff his way through milking the cow. With everything he'd done in his life, this was a chore he had never before performed. Most of his life had been spent in cities or towns, with little experience on farms or ranches. He'd chased outlaws on the prairie and mountain, but he'd never had to perform chores. He didn't want to admit his ignorance, so he simply studied what Steven did, and followed suit. The boy had the nerve to laugh at Tyler's initial clumsiness, but it didn't take him long to get the rhythm of the chore. While he carried the full buckets into the house, Steven let the cows loose into the pasture.

Oscar was still in his chair, grumbling under his breath while stretching his hand under the chair as if searching for something beyond his reach. Tyler saw this as his opportunity to find out whether it was Malone who had died—from the man who'd have buried him.

"May I help you, sir?" he asked in his most unassuming voice.

"No, da . . . darn it. That pesky female took away my medicine and won't give me no more."

From the liquor odor on the man's breath, Tyler figured out exactly what kind of medicine he had been taking. "I've met other men with gout. The inflammation usually goes down in a day or so. You should be back to your chores in a short while."

"Usually am. Reckon somebody else will have to chop the wood for the doc's house, and dig the grave if somebody kicks the bucket."

"I understand you keep up the graveyard. Do you have many funerals?"

"Not too many. Had one fellow this month. Some drifter. Didn't even know his name. Doc dug a bullet out of his side, but he died anyway. Since there wasn't nobody to claim the body, we put him in a pine box and buried him as best we could. Doc said a few words over him. 'Twas the least we could do." He narrowed his gaze at Tyler. Suspicion gleamed in his clear brown eyes. "You fixing to preach here in Omega, young fella?"

Tyler strongly suspected the stranger was Ace. "I am not an ordained minister. I work for the church investigating whether the community can support a full-time minister. Mrs. DeLery seems to think there are enough members to sustain the church. Are you a member of the congregation?"

"I ain't much of a churchgoer. I think a man can worship the Almighty just as well out in the mountains and fields as in a wood building."

"Yes, they can. However, most folks like to get together for fellowship and worship." Tyler smiled, his façade firmly in place.

Oscar chuckled. "Especially the womenfolk. Gives them a chance to get together and share a bit of gossip."

Further conversation was cut short when Steven burst into the house carrying a basket of eggs. Analise followed in his footsteps. "I'll take the eggs home with me. I have to get back to the office." She pointed a finger at Oscar. "Don't go looking for any more whiskey. I took it all." Then she turned to Tyler. "Steven will escort you to the church." She lifted the watch that hung from a chain around her neck. "Audrey serves lunch at one o'clock. Don't be a minute late, or you'll go hungry."

"What about me?" Oscar grouched.

Analise shook a finger at him. "We'll send Steven back with something for you."

The youngster set his hand on his hips. "Why me? First it's milk the cows, then gather eggs, now it's delivering food and showing Mr. Goodfellow around. I want to go fishing."

Tyler clamped a hand on the boy's shoulder. "Tell you what, after we visit the church, I'll go fishing with you."

"You won't want to get your preacher suit dirty."

"Steven, quit arguing. Show Mr. Goodfellow to the church, and you can go fishing after lunch." Analise slipped the egg basket over her arm and picked up her medical bag.

Tyler held the door as she left. "Let's get over to the church. The sooner we leave, the sooner we can catch the fish."

On a long sigh, the youngster followed him out into the yard and down the path toward town.

They reached the church on Delta Street fifteen minutes later. The sun was high in the sky, approaching noon. A low iron fence enclosed the cemetery. Tyler stepped inside and studied the various head-stones. The dates went back twenty or so years. Steven showed him the graves of his grandparents, Millie's parents, who had once run the general store. Tyler drifted toward a newly covered grave near the rear of the plot without a headstone or wooden marker.

"Who's buried here?" he asked, certain this was Ace Malone's final resting place.

"Some drifter. Got himself shot. Papa tried to save him, but he was too far gone."

"Did you see him? What did he look like?"

"I don't know. Kind of scraggy. Blond hair, beard. I found him by the creek and Oscar helped me tote him home. Papa patched him up, but he had a fever. Talked out of his head." Steven kicked at the dirt with his worn boot.

The description fit the hunted outlaw. Ace was dead, but the money was still missing. "Did you have to help your father?"

"Yeah. Papa left to take care of his other patients, and I had to stay with the guy."

Excitement rolled over Tyler. He felt himself get-ting closer to solving his case. "Did your sister help you?"

"Nah, she wasn't even here then. She didn't show up until a couple of days later."

"Then you were with the stranger when he died? Did he say anything to you? Like who he was? Or how he got shot?"

"He talked about a card game. About aces or something weird."

"What else did he say?"

"Uh . . . nothing much." Steven stepped away from the grave. "I'm hungry. Let's go home. Miss Audrey don't like us being late for lunch." The boy ran to-ward the road and home.

Tyler followed more slowly. He was definitely on the right track. Steven knew more than he was telling. Being the last person with Ace before he died, the youngster may very well be the key to finding the money. Obviously, the outlaw had hidden the loot before he collapsed from his injuries.

What about Steven's sister? A niggling of suspicion settled in Tyler's mind. Did she know something about the outlaw? He didn't believe in coincidences. It seemed a little too convenient that Analise had arrived in Omega at about the same time as Ace. Was she the reason he had set his sights on the out-of-the-way town, instead of one of the larger cities, or Mexico? Tyler could hardly believe the lovely lady doctor would have anything to do with the outlaw, but stranger things had happened. If she had been an accomplice, he'd soon learn the truth.

Nobody and nothing would stand in the way of Tyler Morgan completing his mission.

# Chapter 3

By three o'clock Analise grew bored from sitting behind her desk waiting for patients who never came. Her father had gone to the bank, then planned to make a few house calls. It seemed that nobody in town was sick or injured. That made for a lonely doctor's office.

She gave up waiting and wandered toward the kitchen. Millie and Mrs. Hennessey were elsewhere in the house or out running errands. She poured a cup of tea and meandered to the rear porch. The sharp clump of an axe striking wood drew her gaze toward the woodshed. With Oscar laid up she wondered who had come to split the firewood.

Curiosity got the best of her, and she stepped off the porch, strolled through Millie's prized rose garden, then headed toward the woodshed. The roses had finished blooming for the season, but would burst into their glory next spring.

"Ain't we got enough yet?" Steven whined loudly, his young voice carrying on the breeze.

"Just a few more. Set that log on the stump," returned the deep male tones.

"Oh, man," her brother grumbled. "Milk the cow, get the eggs, chop the wood. I'll sure be glad when Mr. Oscar gets better."

Tyler's laughter was followed by another crack of the splitting wood. "We went fishing for over an hour and didn't catch anything. After we finish here, you'll be free as a breeze."

Analise stopped at the corner of the house, surprised at the sight before her. Partially hidden behind a large oak, she watched Tyler and Steven work together as a team. The boy set a log on the stump while Tyler swung the axe with expert precision.

Tyler had removed his coat and rolled up the sleeves of his white shirt. Without a stiff collar, his open shirt revealed a thick neck and a smattering of dark hair on his chest. The man wielded the axe as if it was no heavier than his cane, which rested against another stump. His biceps flexed and the muscles in his back and shoulders strained against the thin cotton shirt. Sensations fluttered in her chest at the sight of the muscular man. Tyler Goodfellow didn't look like any church official she'd ever seen. Come to think of it, he didn't *act* like any deacon she'd ever met. Again she wondered, just who was Tyler Goodfellow?

In spite of feeling like a peeping Tom, she continued to watch Tyler split the wood. She had seen enough of the male anatomy to know that Tyler was an exceptional specimen of masculinity.

The more she saw of him, the more she realized he was the opposite of Victor, whom she'd once thought the epitome of male beauty. Tall, slender, and aristocratic, Victor was extremely handsome and sought after by any number of women. Analise shuttered to think that she had been so flattered by his attention that she had forsaken her ethics and moral principles to become his lover. She squeezed her eyes shut to close off the bitter memories.

"Say, Doc. A glass of cold water would sure taste good about now."

The sound of Tyler's voice snapped her out of her reverie. Caught spying on him, she felt her face heat with embarrassment. "I'll run and fetch one for each of you hard-working men." Needing the time to bring her thoughts under control, Analise dashed back into the house.

Moments later, she carried two tall glasses of water outside. Tyler sat on a stump, while Steven slumped on the grass. Tyler brushed his arm across his forehead to wipe away the perspiration. His shirt clung to his wide chest, defining well-formed muscles.

"*Merci, Mademoiselle Docteur,*" Tyler said. His fingers brushed hers as he took the glass from her hand. A sweet sensation skittered up her arm at his touch.

"*Parlez vous français, monsieur?*" she asked, noting his perfect enunciation. She tucked her hand in her pocket to savor his touch.

He swallowed the cool water, then wiped the drops from his lips with the back of his hand. His mouth curved in a smile. "Those were the full extent of the few phrases I picked up in my travels. I am barely literate in English."

Somehow Analise doubted that. From what she'd seen and heard, she believed he was far better educated and intelligent than he pretended. Without his coat Tyler looked more like a lawman than a churchman.

"Can I go fishing again?" Steven downed the water and stood. "I've done everything you wanted."

Tyler patted the boy on his shoulder. "You've done a fine job. Go on. Have fun with your friends."

Steven darted into the woodshed and came out carrying a shovel. Before Analise could question him, he dashed between the trees and disappeared into the bushes.

She laughed at her brother's antics. "He's in such a hurry, he forgot his fishing pole."

Tyler's deep chuckle warmed her heart. "Perhaps one of the other boys will have a line for him." He eased to his feet and stretched his arms over his head. "I'm a little stiff from lack of exercise."

Her gaze followed his every move. From the look of his biceps, she would have thought that chopping wood and performing other physical chores was a common activity for him. He glanced at her, catching her staring openly at him. His gray eyes sparkled behind his spectacles. She hurriedly turned away.

"I'll carry some of this into the kitchen." He leaned over and filled one arm with wood. After taking one step, he reached down and picked up his cane. "Don't want to trip and fall on my way into the house."

Analise picked up the two empty glasses and followed closely at his heels. "Deacon, no one expects you to do chores. You are our guest. We'll get someone to chop the wood."

"Sorry, Doc. The Word tells us that if any would not work, neither should he eat. And I do enjoy eating. Especially the fine meals your stepmother puts on the table."

Tyler loaded the wood into the box near the stove. Too many times he'd almost given himself away. Analise had distracted him enough that he'd nearly forgotten the cane and his limp, along with his meek voice of a church officer. Speaking French, a language in which he was quite fluent, had slipped out unintentionally. Then when he'd caught her staring at his body with desire in her eyes, he'd nearly doubled over. Her gaze affected him in the most elemental way. If he'd known he would have to live with such an attractive woman, he would have chosen a different disguise and taken a room at the hotel. He sincerely prayed that he would find the stolen money and leave before he gave in to temptation. He also hoped she wasn't involved with the outlaws.

While Tyler washed up, Analise returned to the office. He wondered why Steven had hurried off. She'd been right: the youngster said he was going fishing, yet he carried a shovel. Tyler straightened his shirt and slipped into his coat. He was certain Steven was digging more than worms. All kids dreamed of finding buried treasure. The possibility of finding Ace Malone's hidden loot had sent the kid scurrying away.

Tyler left the house quietly. He'd learned tracking from an Apache scout, and following Steven was as easy as if he'd left bread crumbs in his wake. Near the creek, Tyler heard grunts and the sound of a shovel digging into the soft earth. He slipped behind a tree. Steven was about fifty feet ahead, putting all his strength into digging a shallow hole. The boy dug around, then flung down his shovel and flopped to the ground. He let out a string of epithets that would turn his mother's ears blue and get his mouth washed out with strong lye soap in the process.

"Digging for worms?" Tyler asked, stepping out of the shadows.

Steven groaned and covered his head with his arm. "Sorry, sir, I didn't know you were there."

"Just wanted to know if you needed help digging those worms."

The boy looked surprised, probably wondering why an adult would take so much time with him. But Tyler enjoyed being with the youngster. He was reminded of what could have been with his own son.

"Nah, I'm through for today. Guess I'll go home and see if Mama has anything to eat."

Steven surged to his feet. The boy filled up the hole and slung the shovel over his shoulder.

"We'll dig some more worms tomorrow, and maybe you'll remember to bring your fishing pole." Tyler glanced around, wondering if Ace had told Steven the exact location of the hidden loot. Looked as if he would be following the kid around until they both got lucky.

On Thursday morning, Analise entered the kitchen to find Oscar enjoying a cup of his wife's coffee and a large plate of eggs.

"Feeling better, I see," she greeted the handyman warmly.

He grunted an answer and stuffed another biscuit into his mouth.

"Good as can be expected," his wife replied from the stove. "He's still complaining about that diet you put him on. Especially since you took away his 'medicine' and the chili peppers from his food."

Analise settled at the table and nodded her thanks at the cup of tea Mrs. Hennessey set before her. "It's for his own good." She glanced around at the empty chairs at the table. "By the way, where is everybody?"

Audrey shrugged. "The missus ain't up yet, neither is the doc or Steven. Mr. Goodfellow left a while ago. Took a bit of bread and cheese with him. Said he'll be gone most of the day. Reckon he wants to get out alone with the Almighty." She handed Analise a plate of eggs and biscuits. "That was a mighty fine sermon he delivered last night. Better than most preachers I've heard."

Analise had been surprised at the inspiring and heartfelt sermon Tyler had delivered. She was mesmerized by his sincerity and professional delivery of the Word. He was a talented speaker and had gotten more than his share of amens from the congregation. After the service, she had returned home, while

Tyler had been invited to the home of Mr. Winters, the bank president, and his wife. The couple just happened to have a daughter of marriageable age. Analise shoved aside the twinge of jealousy. He was free to see whom he would, being fair game for every matchmaking mother in Omega.

Oscar pointed his fork at Analise. "Mind you, Missy. You ought to be looking closer at that man. He's a fine specimen of manhood, if I must say so myself." The older man puffed out his chest. "Reminds me of myself just a couple of years ago."

Audrey laughed as she refilled his coffee cup. "Oscar, you ain't never been as fine looking as that young man. Why, I'd look twice myself if I was ten years younger." She patted her tightly coiled gray hair.

"*Ten* years?" Oscar laughed aloud. "Add a few to that one, Audie."

Analise finished her breakfast to the older couple's banter. Tyler was a handsome man, and probably a fine catch for some woman. But not for Analise. How many ways did she have to tell her family that she was not interested in "catching" a man?

When she carried her plate to the sink, she glanced out the window. Early morning sunlight glittered on the leaves of the big oak in the rear yard. The flower garden was fading, and many of the vegetables in the kitchen garden were ripe for harvest. It was a shame to spend such a lovely day indoors waiting for patients who might never come. She had been studying about medicinal herbs and plants, and decided it was a fine day for gathering herbs and planning her experiments, plus getting Tyler Goodfellow off her mind.

A few minutes later, Analise left the house, her head covered with the large straw hat Millie used for gardening, and a basket on her arm. Mrs. Hennessey insisted she carry a jar of lemonade and a couple of sandwiches made with fresh bread and ham. "And if you run into the deacon," she'd said, "I added extra sugar cookies to share with him."

Since Analise had no idea where that certain man had gone, she planned to eat all the cookies herself.

For several hours, Analise hunted through the undergrowth of the wooded area that edged the stream. She'd located quite a few of the plants she had been searching for. Her hands were dirty from digging at the roots, and her stomach growled with hunger. Yet, she wasn't ready to go home. Being out in the woods was both pleasant and invigorating. Quite a contrast to the cities in which she had spent so many years.

Though Omega couldn't begin to compare to New Orleans or Paris, it had a certain charm of its own. Mainly in the beautiful trees and meadows, and the mountains in the background. Analise approached the stream where a small waterfall tumbled over the rocks. A breeze wafted across the water, cool and refreshing. She glanced around, making sure she was alone. The splash of the water and the song of birds and insects were her only company. A large frog croaked at her from the other side of the stream. Wanting to cool down after the exercise of the morning, she tossed aside the hat and released her hair from the confines of the hairpins. She ran her fingers through the long chestnut tresses, lifting the mass from her neck to the cooling breeze.

Feeling like a carefree child, she removed her walking boots and rolled down her stockings. She set both aside, along with the long-sleeved smock that protected her white shirtwaist and black skirt. As inviting as the water looked, Analise did not have the nerve to disrobe and plunge into the cooling depths. A dunk of her feet would have to do, as would unbuttoning her high collar to cool her throat. She leaned over to wash her hands and splash her face with the clear water. Carefully she sat down and dangled her feet in the water. She reached into the basket and took a long drink of the lemonade. A loud sigh of contentment escaped her lips.

"Mind sharing the contents of that basket with a hungry stranger?"

Analise started, and nearly dropped the jar of lemonade. Long fingers snatched it up before it hit the rock. She clasped her hands to her chest.

"*Mon Dieu, monsieur*, you nearly frightened me to death." She lifted her gaze and met Tyler's silvery eyes. How had a man who walked with a limp been able to approach as silently as an Indian?

"*Pardon moi, mademoiselle*. The water must have drowned out my approach." He eased down onto the rock beside her. "And you looked so charming and relaxed, I was reluctant to disturb you."

Embarrassed at being caught in such an indecorous manner, heat spread from her cheeks to the open neckline of her blouse. "Really, Mr. Goodfellow, you could have called out."

"It's Tyler, remember." He removed one boot and tossed it aside. A sock followed.

"What are you doing?" she shrieked, surprised at the sound of her own voice.

"Getting comfortable. That water looks too cool and refreshing to pass up." The second boot and sock landed in the grass behind him.

"Don't. It's unseemly." Her gaze locked on his bare feet, long and perfectly formed. He wiggled his toes as if to wave at her.

"Why? As a doctor, I'm certain you must have seen feet before." She heard the smile in his voice. "Oh, and look. You have two of your own." He rolled up the legs of his trousers and stuck his into the water.

Analise shook her head. "You certainly have liberal ways about you. My grandmother would turn over in her grave if she saw me now. Not only am I showing my limbs to a man, but he is showing his to me."

"When I get to heaven, I won't mention a word to her."

Analise laughed, feeling more carefree than she had in ages. "Is that a promise?"

His deep laughter joined hers. "Cross my heart. Tell me about this grandmother."

After a second's hesitation, she sighed. "*Grand-mere* was a very special lady from a wealthy German family of merchants and shipbuilders. She met my grandfather in Paris when he was on his grand tour of the Continent and fell madly in love. They married and returned to New Orleans where his family lived. The DeLery family had been in Louisiana since before the American Revolution. Unfortunately, my grandfather died of the yellow fever, which is one of the reasons my father wanted to become a doctor." She took a deep breath and shared the warm memories in her heart.

"Grandmother ran the businesses better than any man. Unfortunately, the war came along and she lost most of the money. She was very strict Protestant, though most of New Orleans was Catholic. She took me in after my mother died and I stayed with her when Papa moved west. *Grand-mere* believed any place west of the Mississippi was the wilderness. She sent me to a fine academy for young ladies, as was befitting my station in life. The headmistress would faint if she saw me now." She laughed softly at the memories.

"Was she very strict with you?"

"*Mais oui.*" Analise reached into the basket for a cookie and took a bite. "Once on a trip to the park, I walked away while she was conversing with friends. I wandered to a fountain where other children were playing. The girls sat on the side with their feet in the water while the boys were splashing and running in the pool. It looked like so much fun, I couldn't resist. I pulled off my shoes and stockings, and joined them." She kicked her feet in the water. "My grandmother nearly had a seizure. After she berated me in at least two languages for an hour, I was punished for a week for showing such scandalous behavior. A DeLery has a place in society, and I must remember who I am at all times."

"What did she think of your becoming a doctor?" Tyler kicked his feet, splattering them both with drops of cool water.

"In some ways, she was very forward thinking. She believed I had the right to choose my own path in life. And that if I had the intelligence and stamina, I could be anything I wanted to be. You would have liked her."

"I'm sure I would have." He picked up one of the cookies. "Do you mind?"

"Not at all. Mrs. Hennessey said I should share them if we happened to meet up."

"I'll remember to thank her when I return to the house." He took a swig of the lemonade. "What else do you have in that basket? I'm starved, and it looks as if we've both missed lunch."

Analise emptied the basket's contents. They ate quietly, sharing the food and lemonade. Neither spoke until the food was gone and the jar empty.

Tyler leaned back on his elbows and splashed his feet. His shirt was open at the neck and his sleeves rolled up to the elbows. Again she was struck by his bold masculinity, so unlike the persona he projected.

"What are you doing out here alone, Doc?"

She kicked, splashing him in return. "I was hunting herbs and plants for my medical practice."

"Isn't it dangerous for a woman to be out in the woods by herself? What with wild animals and outlaws." His voice trembled slightly.

"No more dangerous for me than you."

"I have protection."

She laughed. "What? Do you intend to fight off an angry bear with your Bible?"

He reached out a hand to the back of her head and twined a loose curl around his finger. "Not exactly. I suppose I could preach until he got so bored, he would fall asleep."

His sense of humor sent sweet sensations all over her. The man was certainly not what he appeared on the surface. There were depths to Tyler Goodfellow she would love to explore. "Nobody got bored last night at church. I believe that if you decide to stay, the congregation would vote to keep you."

Behind his eyeglasses, she caught a glimmer of sadness. "We'll wait and see what the bishop has to say on the matter. I suppose they would prefer to send an ordained minister, not just a lowly deacon." He stroked her hair between two fingers. "You have lovely hair. You should wear it loose more often."

Caught up in their banter she had forgotten her state of dishabille. His gaze dropped to her lips, then lowered to her bare throat. She swallowed down her nervousness. "I'm too old to look like a schoolgirl with my hair down. Millie would have a fit if she saw me now."

"Millie isn't here." His finger brushed her cheek. His voice dropped to a deep slow drawl. "It's just the two of us."

At his touch, her skin heated and warmth settled deep in her body. His face lowered to hers. Her eyelids closed of their own volition. His warm breath brushed her cheek. He groaned and touched his lips to the corner of her mouth. He smelled of the cinnamon from the cookies. Her hands fisted to keep from reaching for him, to keep from brushing her fingers along his strong neck and testing the texture of the hair on his chest, to keep from doing something they both would regret later. It had been so long since a man had touched her, kissed her, loved her. Common sense hit Analise like a cold towel. She turned her head and jerked her feet from the water.

"I really have to get back to the office. I may have patients waiting for me." Her voice trembled. She scooted away on the rock, leaving Tyler staring at her with surprise on his face, as if he couldn't believe that he had actually kissed her. Grabbing her shoes and stockings, she hurried behind a large shrub for privacy. Her heart pounded in her chest, and her breath came in short gasps. How could she let herself get carried away again? Hadn't she learned her lesson in Paris? How pathetic she must be. How lonely and pitiful. She tugged on her stockings and shoes, then buttoned her blouse to her chin. Was there some terrible flaw in her character that she would throw all her moral upbringing to the wind whenever a man paid the least bit of attention to her? Tears burned behind her eyelids. Was she some awful wanton? A loose woman?

"Analise," Tyler called from the other side of the bushes. "Are you all right? I'm terribly sorry, I didn't mean to upset you."

She pulled herself up to her full height. "It's past time I returned home." Stepping around the bushes, she found Tyler, now wearing his socks and boots, watching her. She picked up her smock and hat. He stretched out a hand and offered the hairpins she had so carelessly discarded. "Thank you," she mumbled. Hurriedly, she twisted her long hair into a chignon and tucked it under the wide straw hat.

Together they gathered the remains of their lunch into the basket with her plants. "I'll walk back to the house with you," he offered, picking up the basket.

Analise snatched it from his fingers. "No. What would Millie think if she saw us returning together?"

He pried her fingers from the basket and set it on his arm. "Your stepmother will think that her plans and schemes are working. She will be quite happy to see us together."

"No." She set her hands on her hips. "I do not want any gossip going around about me. It is difficult enough to be a female doctor without rumors about my morals. And we certainly don't want anybody talking about you—a man of the cloth."

He shook his head. "Analise, nothing happened between us that the whole world can't know about. It would be very rude and ungentlemanly not to escort you to your door."

Tyler had a stubborn streak that she would never have guessed. It was clear that he would not be dissuaded. "Let's hurry. My father makes house calls in the afternoon, and I must tend the office."

He gestured to the narrow path that led back to town. "Then let's be off. We don't want to keep any injured people waiting."


Tyler clutched the basket in one hand and the cane in the other. It took all his self-control to keep from tossing Analise on the ground and making love to her until they were both sated. He didn't understand how he'd been so quickly smitten by this woman. In his travels he'd met many beautiful women, but few had affected him like the fascinating lady doctor. Thankfully, she had stopped him before he totally gave himself away. He'd wanted to kiss her as much as he wanted to breathe. Once more, he regretted his choice of disguises. A respectable church official was expected to remain celibate until after marriage. If he had any sense, he would leave Omega and turn the assignment over to another agent.

He carefully made his way over the uneven ground.

Tyler wasn't a quitter, and he was too close to reaching his goal to give up now. He'd been searching the hollowed-out trees, digging holes, and struggling to discover where a wounded man would hide a satchel of money. When he'd spotted her at the pond, he'd hidden his coat and sidearm. He would retrieve both when he was alone.

"Slow down, Doc. With this bad leg, I can't keep up." Another lie to spend a little more time with her.

"Sorry." She slowed her pace and walked beside him where the path was wide enough for two. "Does it bother you much?"

"Only when the weather changes. I'm like an old woman with arthritis. I can tell when it's going to rain."

"Be thankful this is dry country. We don't get too much rain. But when it rains, it's a downpour. You would have suffered in New Orleans where it's always rainy and damp."

The path narrowed and she walked a few steps ahead of him. Without her loose smock, he had a fine view of the feminine attributes she kept carefully hidden. Their splashing in the stream had dampened her shirtwaist, making the thin batiste transparent in spots. The fabric clung to her skin, outlining the fullness of her breasts through her camisole. He clutched the basket and cane tighter. If he didn't get his libido in check and his mind off this woman, he was in for a tough few weeks and would risk blowing his disguise.

"Do you miss New Orleans? New York? Paris?" Tyler had been to all three, but it was best to keep that to himself.

"I miss my grandmother. She passed away while I was in college in Philadelphia." She slowed and fell into step beside him. "New York was crowded. I believe I'm going to like living in Omega."

He noticed she had omitted talking about Paris. Most people who had been to the beautiful city enjoyed sharing their experiences. "I've always wanted to go to Paris. Is it all they say?"

She shrugged. "I suppose." Her voice trembled slightly. "I used the last of my inheritance from my grandmother to study under some of the finest surgeons available. I wanted to learn all I could."

Her answer wasn't what he would have expected from a woman recently returned from Paris. Tyler decided to dig further and learn more about the illusive lady doctor. "I've heard that Paris is a very romantic city. How did a beautiful woman like you avoid the amorous Frenchmen?"

She ignored his query and hurried a few steps ahead of him. "I really must get home."

Clearly she had no intention of sharing her experiences with him. That made him think something had happened in Paris she didn't want known. Or was there another reason for her secrecy? Like she'd returned from Paris sooner than her family knew, and had somehow become involved with Ace Malone.

"We're almost there, I believe." He glimpsed the DeLery woodshed through the trees.

Analise stopped and turned to him. "I'll take the basket into the kitchen, if you don't mind."

He nodded, certain she didn't want anybody to see her returning with him. "Here you are. I shall return in time for dinner. Please thank Mrs. Hennessey for the cookies and lunch."

"Yes." She took the basket and scurried away.

Besides Steven he would have to keep a closer watch on Analise. It was possible she too was searching for the hidden loot, not only herbs and plants.

He turned toward the railroad station. It was time to send a telegram to one of his associates in New York and learn more about the pretty lady doctor.

# Chapter 4

That evening, Tyler noted big grins on the faces of Mrs. DeLery and Mrs. Hennessey. The doctor greeted him warmly and patted Tyler's shoulder, welcoming him to the dinner table. Steven appeared his usual impatient self, waiting for his mother to allow him to begin eating. Analise's chair was the only empty one at the table.

Something was up, and he had a pretty good idea what. The women had learned he'd spent most of the afternoon with Analise, and they were making the most of the situation.

"How was your day, *mon ami?*" the doctor asked, a jovial smile making his mustache quiver.

"Quiet," Tyler answered, not sure how to respond. "I spent most of the time admiring God's creations and meditating." After leaving Analise he had gone to the telegraph office and sent a wire to the associate in New York. He needed information on exactly when Analise had left the city and headed west. The coded wording would keep his message from being read by every nosy telegraph operator from Colorado to New York. When the Omega operator asked about the strange words, Tyler lied, replying that he was sharing Latin scripture with an associate.

Afterward, he returned to his search for the hidden loot and retrieved his gun and coat. After school let out, Steven had continued his own search, with Tyler secretly at his heels. Again the search proved fruitless. Later, Tyler had met with another agent for news of the Malone gang. The news wasn't good: he reported that before the robbery Ace had been seen in Denver in the company of a dark-haired woman. Without more information, Tyler didn't want to speculate on the identity of the woman. The outlaws now appeared to be following Ace's path, leading directly to Omega. More than ever, Tyler needed to find the money first.

"How did you enjoy the cookies and lemonade that Analise shared with you today?" Millie studied him openly. "She was rather quiet when she returned, and she didn't mention your encounter by the brook."

Tyler forced his mouth not to gape. The woman had more spies and informants than Pinkerton. "The food was delicious. I asked Doctor Analise to offer my appreciation."

Doctor DeLery waved a hand in dismissal. "Don't be upset, Millie, *chèrie.* Analise must have forgotten. When she gets involved with a patient or a new medical journal, she loses track of time and place. All she can think of is that medical clinic she wants to open."

Millie glared at her husband. "Etienne, they were alone down by the brook, and Analise returned with her clothing damp and rumpled, and her hair . . ."

The good doctor laughed. "Don't get your dander up. Analise is a grown woman, and Tyler is a man of the cloth. I'm certain she was perfectly safe."

Millie slanted a glance at Tyler. He didn't miss the

speculative gleam in her brown eyes. "You're right."
She turned to her son. "Steven, go into the office
and remind Analise that dinner is served."

Tyler bit back a groan. The doctor and his wife
had more confidence in him than he had in himself.
A few more minutes alone with Analise that afternoon, and they would have been after him with a
shotgun.


Dinner passed with the usual banter and conversation. Steven ate as if it was the last meal for a
condemned man. Millie chatted happily with a self-
satisfied smile on her face. Analise groaned at her father's obvious interest in Tyler's and her activities of
the day. As for Tyler, he seemed to touch her more
than was necessary in passing bowls and reaching for
his glass and utensils. After placing the meal on the
table, Mrs. Hennessey winked and nodded as if sharing a private joke.

Overall, dinner was miserable—for Analise, that
is. No one else seemed to notice her discomfort.

Each time Tyler touched her, she remembered his
heat from that afternoon. That memory could only
get her into trouble. After coffee and dessert had
been served, Analise offered to wash the dishes to
free Millie to spend the time with her husband.

Millie smiled at the offer, as she had insisted the
housekeeper leave after serving the meal to be with
Oscar at her own home. As usual, Steven rebelled
when Analise tagged him to help. Grumbling under
his breath, her brother toted a large tray of dirty
dishes into the kitchen, then disappeared through
the rear door. Analise stared dumbfounded at his de-
sertion.

"Steven," she called to his retreating back.

"I sent your brother on an errand," Tyler said from

over her shoulder. "I'll take his place." He gave her a sly smile.

Something about that look reminded her of a wolf trying to lure a rabbit into his lair. "That isn't necessary. I can handle the dishes. Mrs. Hennessey has already cleaned the pots and pans."

Tyler lifted the heavy kettle of hot water from the stove and filled a large basin. "I insist. It is the least I can do to repay my hostess for such a fine meal, comfortable accommodations, and . . ." He paused. "Wonderful company."

Sensing his determination, Analise gave up arguing. She turned away to shave off soap into the hot water. Long arms snaked around her waist. "What are you doing?" she asked, startled at the touch.

"Surely you don't want to get your clothing wet." Tyler's warm breath tickled her ear. "Again."

Before she could protest further, he tied an apron at her waist. Even through layers of clothing, she felt the tingles of his touch. She swung her gaze to him, ready to berate him for taking such liberties. But he had already stepped away to remove his jacket. He rolled up the sleeves of his shirt and picked up a large cloth.

"You wash. I'll dry," he said.

After several minutes, Tyler broke the silence that hovered between them. "We work well together."

Her heart skipped a beat. She hadn't expected him to flirt so openly with her. Had he gotten caught up in Millie's plot to snare a husband for her? Analise wanted no part of it. It took all her time and energy to build her medical practice and make plans for opening the clinic. She knew how fleeting a relationship with a man could be. One broken heart in a lifetime was enough, *merci beaucoup*. She'd gotten over Victor; the heartache of losing the baby would remain with her forever.

With the last of the dishes clean, she wiped her hands on her apron. Instantly, Tyler was behind her loosening the ties. His face was very close to her neck. His warm breath tickled her skin. Analise took a deep breath, inhaling the scent of male and of lye soap from the dishwater. For a moment she remained as still as a marble statue. Her skin heated, and her heart raced. Her mouth watered for something other than food.

At the click of footsteps from the dining room, Tyler jerked back a step. Analise twisted her fingers in the apron. Past Tyler's shoulder, she spotted her father and Millie.

"Analise, Millie has a ladies' meeting of some kind and I have to meet with the town council about the telephone exchange." He kissed her lightly on the cheek. "Tyler, if I get home early enough, I'll take you up on that chess game."

Tyler nodded his head. He slipped into his jacket. "Doctor DeLery, may I have your permission to walk out with your daughter?"

Etienne smiled widely. "Of course, *mon ami*. It is a lovely night for a walk. Analise spends too much time with her journals and plans for her clinic."

"Thank you, sir. I'll have her back home early."

Millie caught her husband's arm. "Etienne, surely Analise can't walk out with a man unchaperoned? It isn't seemly." In spite of her protest, Millie had a speculative gleam in her eyes.

"If we can't trust the deacon with our daughter, who can we trust?" He caught his wife's arm and urged her from the room. *"Bonsoir, chère.* Have a good evening."

Analise gritted her teeth against the audacity of her parent. She was twenty-eight years old, a spinster, and quite capable of making her own plans for the evening. With her father and stepmother out of earshot, she turned on Tyler. "I am too busy for a leisurely stroll." She folded the apron and set it aside on a shelf.

Tyler glanced out of the window. "It is a lovely night, and I thought we could get better acquainted."

She laughed. "We don't need to get better acquainted."

"You can tell me about your clinic." Tyler offered his arm in a gallant gesture.

Civility and good manners urged Analise to accept his offer. Her grandmother instilled in her good manners. A lady was never rude, no matter the circumstances. He took a shawl from the pegs near the door and draped it over her shoulders. She set her hand lightly on his arm and allowed him to escort her from the kitchen.

Usually when on assignment, Tyler focused totally on the mission at hand. He could justify his desire to spend time with Analise on the speculation she was involved with Ace. But his own well-honed instincts refused to accept his suspicions. He would simply wait for an answer to his inquiry to be sure. Meanwhile, he would enjoy the company of a lovely woman and see what he could learn. Tyler had to admit he liked being near her; he enjoyed talking to her. His body tightened with desire. He loved touching her and he wondered how her lips would taste when he kissed her. There was no *if*, it was *when* he kissed her.

They strolled slowly along the wooden boardwalk that fronted the businesses and shops on Alpha Street. Most were closed for the night, the shopkeepers home with their families. He carefully avoided leading her past the saloon, where raucous noise spilled onto the street. At the corner of Athena, she turned toward a residential area. They passed several small homes and a few larger ones. Lamps glittered behind lace curtains, and a dog barked when they passed a picket fence.

"Look at those stars," he said, lifting his gaze.

"The sky looks like black velvet strewn with diamonds. See, that one star is brighter than the others."

A strange feeling of peace washed over him. "Do you suppose that's the star that guided your Mr. Onasis to Omega?"

"He claimed it was the Christmas star. And Christmas isn't for another three months."

Tyler shrugged. "Well, he started a very nice town."

"Yes. Papa was lucky to find a home here. Millie is a gem. And he always wanted a son." A hint of pain turned her voice slightly husky.

"Didn't he appreciate having a beautiful daughter?"

She laughed. "Of course. I followed in his footsteps. But Mama was ill after I was born, and she couldn't have another child."

"So when he married the present Mrs. DeLery, he was able to have a son." And a second chance at happiness, he thought. Tyler wondered if the stars had a second chance in store for him.

"I'm only now really getting acquainted with Millie. I've been so busy with my studies, my visits with her and Papa have been few and far apart. I understand why Papa loves her. She's a wonderful lady."

Tyler smiled. Etienne was a lucky man—having a lovely wife, a beautiful daughter, and a healthy son. A band of envy tightened around Tyler's chest. The doctor had it all. At one time Tyler had thought the same about himself. He'd forgotten the words from Proverbs: "A man's pride shall bring him down." And Tyler had hit rock bottom because of his arrogance and pride.

Analise stopped in front of a large but empty house

at the end of the street. No lights shone behind the windows, and the large lot backing up to the woods was badly overgrown. "I believe they would like to have another child while Millie is still able."

He opened the gate to allow her to enter. "What about you, Analise? Do you want children?"

In the pale moonlight, he spotted the strain on her face. "No. I do not intend to marry. I plan to devote my time to the clinic."

There was more to this than she seemed willing to admit. She climbed the steps onto the porch and peered into the dirty window. "Are you interested in living here?" he asked.

She wiped the cracked pane with her palm. "Sort of. This would make a perfect place for the clinic."

"So, you're serious about opening a clinic."

She glanced over her shoulder at him. "Did you think I was joshing? Of course I'm serious. Women and children need a safe place to get good medical care. Especially women who are expecting a child."

He pressed closer to the window, his chest pressed to her back. She smelled of roses and a hint of disinfectant. On her it wasn't at all unpleasant. A unique combination that was Analise. He braced a hand over her shoulder on the window sash. "Why this house? Why not at your father's place?"

She turned slightly, her face inches from his. "There isn't enough room for his work and mine. I want a place where women can stay after delivery, where they can gain their strength back before having the responsibility of a new baby. I also believe in complete prenatal care. Too many women don't see a doctor until the minute they deliver. With proper medical care, I believe we will save more mothers and children. And it is large enough for me to have living quarters upstairs. I'm quite old enough to be on my own."

"By the passion in your voice, this means a lot to you."

"It does."

"What's stopping you?"

"Lots of things." Moisture glittered in her blue eyes.

He brushed a finger along her soft cheek.

"Mostly money. This house originally was built by Mr. Onasis several years ago."

He laughed. "Hence, the Greek Revival façade."

She nodded. "When he returned to Greece, he sold it, then the next owners defaulted, and the bank foreclosed on this house. I'm trying to talk Mr. Winters into renting it to me by the month. Then there's equipment and furnishings to buy. My father will give me the things he doesn't need, but I still have to remodel the house."

"Do you have available funds?" He brushed his lips across her forehead. His heart beat double-time. He wanted nothing more than to take her into his arms and sate the needs that engulfed him whenever she came near. But he had to learn whether she had a connection with Ace and the stolen money. For such a noble cause, would she consort with outlaws to make it a reality? It hardly seemed possible.

"I still have a few pieces of my grandmother's jewelry. I'll sell them when the time comes."

His fingers dropped to the pulse in her neck. She drew a sharp intake of breath. Heat sizzled between them. In the shadows of the porch, they were virtually unseen from the street. Tyler tightened his grip on his cane to keep from crushing her in his arms. To give in to his needs would be totally out of character. He couldn't afford to blow his cover. He swallowed hard and forced himself to step away.

"When . . . when do you plan to open the clinic?" His voice cracked like an adolescent's.

"As soon as the bank agrees to rent the house."

"You have noble goals, Doctor." He dropped his hand to his side, guiding her the way they had come. Tyler couldn't help admiring the woman for her zeal for helping others. If she had been around for Abigail, things might have turned out good instead of the nightmare he'd lived through—events that had left both Abigail and his baby buried in the Kansas cemetery.

By Monday afternoon frustration burned in Tyler's gut. He was no closer to finding the hidden payroll than he'd been the week before. He'd followed Steven for days, rutted in hollowed-out trees, and dug holes along the streambed. Analise seldom left the house or office, except to run errands into the heart of town. It was only a matter of time before the remainder of the Malone gang reached Omega and sought out the doctor—or Analise. He hoped he was wrong. Either way, he couldn't let that happen. He'd already wired for reinforcements of other Pinkerton men. However, it would be another week before they would arrive.

The previous day, he had performed his duties as the substitute minister to perfection. So far, no one showed any sign of suspecting him of being a complete fraud. He'd preached a sermon, sung the hymns, and been invited to have dinner with one family, then supper with another. He wasn't surprised that both families had daughters of marriageable age.

He hadn't seen Analise since leaving the church after the service the day before, and he felt the strongest need to seek her out. He'd missed her at breakfast, as he'd left the house before sunrise to hunt for the loot. Now he wanted to see her, if only for a moment or two.

He entered the doctor's office, where she was again

seated behind the desk. "Afternoon, Doc." Taking a few halting steps forward, he smiled down at her. "No patients today?"

She closed the journal she was reading and brushed a stray lock of dark hair from her forehead. "No, the few who came said they would wait for Papa to return."

He propped a hip on the corner of the desk. "He mentioned a trip to Denver to get more information about the telephone lines. Did Mrs. DeLery go with him?"

"Millie wanted to do some shopping. They'll only be gone a few days. Steven was disappointed he couldn't tag along with them."

Tyler laughed. "I suppose they needed a little time alone." The thought crossed his mind how much he would like to spend a few days with Analise in Denver, at a fine hotel, one with room service. Far away from the impending danger in Omega.

"By the way, how—" Her query was cut off when the office door flung open and banged against the wall.

Steven skid to a halt, tugging a small boy by the neck of his shirt. The youngster was barefoot with tattered pants. He pulled against Steven's grip and let out a string of Spanish.

"I was on my way home from school, when I found this injun kid. He said he wanted to see the doc. I tried to tell him Papa wasn't here." Steven dropped his grip on the boy.

"*I* happen to be a doctor, Steven. You shouldn't be so rude."

"I couldn't hardly understand him. Didn't want him to cause any trouble." Steven set his hands on his hips and glared at the smaller boy.

"I must see doctor," the strange boy muttered. "Polly hurt."

Tyler knelt down to eye level before the boy and clutched his arms. "Slow down, son. Who are you?"

The child was about seven or eight with tanned skin and black shaggy hair touching his collar. He trembled wildly. "I am Manuel Gonzales. Alex send me for doctor. Polly very sick. She hold belly and squeal like pig."

"Why didn't he bring her into town?" Analise asked.

Tears rolled in tracks down the boy's dusty cheeks. "Wagon is broke, and Polly too sick to ride horse."

"Sounds like she could be having a baby, or she is very ill. We had best hurry." Analise stood and shot a glance at Steven. "Run over to the livery and fetch Papa's buggy."

Fear paralyzed Tyler for a moment. A woman in labor with no help but her husband. He shoved aside his painful memories and jumped to his feet. "Go," he ordered when Steven hesitated. "I'll check with Mrs. Hennessey while you get your supplies ready."

Analise rose quickly and reached for her medical bag. "I know what I'll need. I'll only take a few minutes to get ready."

Ignoring the cane and his pretense of a limp, Tyler rushed into the kitchen where Mrs. Hennessey was busy at the stove. The housekeeper went into action. She packed a basket of food, then pulled out a stack of clean towels, sheets, and blankets. She explained that Doctor DeLery always carried clean linens when he went to deliver a baby.

By the time Steven returned with the rig, Analise and the boy were in the kitchen. Mrs. Hennessey had given the youngster a large glass of milk and some cookies. Tyler and Steven loaded the supplies behind the seat while the young boy mounted his horse.

Analise stepped up to the buggy, and her face turned white. "Oh, dear," she said.

"What's wrong?" Tyler helped her into the high seat.

"I've always lived in the city. I don't know how to drive a buggy."

"Not to worry. I'm going along with you. I'll drive."

Her eyes widened. "You can't."

Understanding that time was of the utmost importance, he climbed up beside her. He truly believed that the time he'd lost getting medical help for his wife had cost her life. "Analise, I'm going with you. That woman needs your help. Isn't that why you spent all those years studying?" He picked up the whip and snapped it over the horses' heads. The boy was already ahead of them, leading the way out of town.

Whether she liked it or not, Tyler refused to allow her to venture out alone—or with Steven. Not with outlaws possibly nearby. While Mrs. Hennessey had gathered supplies, he had retrieved his cane and gone to his room for a pistol, which he tucked into his waistband under his coat.

The boy followed the road for several miles before turning off onto a trail that was only a rut through the tall grass. Tyler pulled his hat low on his forehead against the glaring sun and dust kicked up by the team. Beside him, Analise remained silent, her lower lip caught in her teeth.

"Can't we go any faster?" she asked, gripping the seat until her knuckles turned white.

"Not if we want to reach that woman in time. We don't want to have an accident and not make it at all. This isn't the city, Analise, with brick or cobblestone streets. These roads are little more than cow paths."

"Then pray. Pray we get to that woman in time."

"I've been praying, Doc. Have faith."

The road turned, and Analise swayed against him.

She caught his arm for balance, pressing against his side. Her touch sizzled through his coat like the heat from a branding iron. Tyler forced himself to concentrate on driving, not on the woman at his side. They slowed to cross a small stream. The horses' hooves splashed them with the cool water. "I have to give your papa credit. This is a fine buggy. He must have had it specially made for travel on these roads."

"I suppose I'll need one of my own, if I'm to visit my patients. After I learn to drive." She loosed her grip from his arm. "Thank you for coming with me."

The sun was dipping low in the sky by the time a small homestead came into view. A tiny log cabin was surrounded by several outbuildings and a corral containing a single horse. A small herd of cattle grazed in the pasture.

Tyler tugged the reins and slowed the horses at the door of the cabin. The door flung open and a man stood in the doorway, a rifle in his hands. "Who are you?" he asked, with a touch of a Spanish accent.

Tyler set the brake and carefully lifted his hands where the man could see them. "This is Doctor DeLery and I'm Deacon Goodfellow. Manuel said you needed a doctor out here."

A loud squeal came from inside the cabin. The man looked over his shoulder, then back at Analise. "I am Alexandro Gonzales. I sent for a doctor for Polly. She is having a baby and I think something is wrong." He lowered the rifle and stepped aside.

Tyler hopped down from the buggy, then helped Analise to the ground. She shook out her skirts and moved toward the man. "I'm a doctor. Help Mr. Goodfellow unload the buggy while I check on my patient." Taking charge as if she had been issuing orders all her life, she grabbed her leather medical satchel and marched into the cabin.

Alex propped the rifle against the door and hurried to the wagon. "Is she a real doctor?" On closer look, Tyler saw how young the man was—not much over twenty and clearly of Mexican or Indian heritage.

"Yes, she's a very good doctor." Tyler grabbed a load of blankets and followed Alex into the cabin. Mewing sounds came from corner. Memories of Abigail writhing in pain trying to deliver their child stopped him dead in his tracks. He dropped the blankets and towels and signaled Manuel. "Let's get the horses unhitched and watered." The kid looked scared to death—not that Tyler could blame him. They could hide out in the barn until this was over.

"Tyler." Analise signaled him closer. "I need you here—you and Alex. Please hurry."

"I take care of horses," the young boy said.

Not wanting to appear the coward he was, Tyler swallowed down his own trepidation and glanced around the cabin. The large single room was clean, but poorly furnished. To one side was the kitchen area with a stove, dry sink, wooden table, and two benches. A rocking chair and battered davenport faced the fireplace. On the opposite wall, a curtain set off the bedroom area. Soft whimpers came from a bed in the corner. Analise stood at the bedside, rolling up her sleeves. She slipped a large apron over her frock. Without looking up, she issued orders. "Fill every pot and bucket you can find with clean water, and set them on the fire. I want each of you to wash your hands, then get over here."

Tyler removed his coat and placed it on a chair, his sidearm hidden in the folds. Moans and whimpers continued, interspersed with an occasional scream. Analise scrubbed her hands and arms with lye soap from her bag. Tyler instructed Alex to do the same. The young man trembled so badly, he splashed water all over himself—not that Tyler was much calmer.

"Tyler," she called, "I need one of you to lift Polly so I can put these clean sheets under her." She turned to the young woman and spoke in soft tones. "It will be over soon, sweetheart."

For the first time, Tyler took a good look at the woman. His heart leaped into his throat. Long damp blond hair clung to her cheeks. Except for the distended stomach, she was extremely thin. "How old is she?" His words lodged in his throat. Both the age and the girl's coloring surprised him. It was rare to find a white woman married to an Indian.

"Seventeen."

Tyler grew faint. Abigail had been only eighteen. The sorry excuse for a doctor couldn't save Abigail. Was Analise any different? Could she save this girl's life? And the baby's? He wanted to believe in her—but memories had his stomach churning and his hands shaking.

"Do you think you can lift her?" Analise asked, all business.

"Yes." Carefully, he slipped one arm under the woman's knees and the other under her back. "Easy, sweetheart," he whispered. "We'll just do whatever Doctor Analise says. She'll get you through this."

The young woman screamed and twisted as another spasm hit her. At the sight of the blood that oozed from between her legs, Tyler's knees grew weak. It took all his willpower and strength to remain upright.

With quick, efficient movements, Analise stripped the bloody sheet and placed a clean rubber pad and sheet on the bed. Gently, he lowered Polly to the bed. Analise draped a clean sheet over her for the examination. Tyler swallowed down the bile in his throat.

Analise looked under the sheet that provided a bit of modesty for the young woman. "She's fully dilated, but something must be wrong with the baby. Tyler, hold her legs apart, while I work with her. Alex press her shoulders to the bed. I don't want her moving."

Girding his strength, Tyler did as instructed. Too many memories of Abigail bombarded him. Her screams, the pain that sliced through him as much as through her. His skin grew cold and clammy, his face paled. He would rather be horsewhipped himself than watch a woman endure this torture.

"Don't you pass out on me," Analise warned, her voice strong and determined. "I need your help, and Polly definitely needs you."

"Yes, ma'am," he whispered around the lump in his throat. While Analise continued her ministrations, he turned toward Polly. This young woman needed him, and he wasn't going to let her down as he felt he had let Abigail down. He started praying, reciting every prayer, scripture, poem, and hymn he knew to keep both his mind and Polly's off what was happening under that sheet.

When she called for it, Alex brought hot water for Analise to rewash her hands. Then he sat at his woman's head and wiped the perspiration from her forehead. Alex looked as frightened as a deer facing a hunter's rifle. Manuel remained outdoors with the horses. The youngster didn't need to see this. It took all of Tyler's strength to keep down the nausea.

"Good job, Tyler. Just keep talking. It will help her relax. We're almost there. I'll tell her when to push."

"Is Manuel your son?" Tyler asked, to keep his mind occupied.

Alex shook his head. "No, Manny is my brother. Our mother died when he was born. I take care of him."

Tyler didn't need another reminder of the danger of childbirth. Alex's mother and Abigail—neither survived their ordeal. His heart sank at the possibility of what could happen to Polly.

Analise lifted her gaze. "Did you bring her into town to see the doctor when you found out she was expecting?"

"No. We have no money. Besides, last time I was in town the sheriff told me to stay away. He did not much like that a half-breed would take up with a white girl. Our neighbor, Mrs. Daniels, is a midwife, and she said she could take care of Polly just fine." The young man's voice quivered. "When Polly started getting the pains, I went over to fetch the midwife, but she is down with her back. Cannot move out of the bed." Tears flowed freely from his eyes. "Polly was hurting too bad to get into town, so I sent Manny to fetch the doc."

"You did the right thing," Analise said. "She probably wouldn't have survived the trip. The baby is breech, which means it is turned the wrong way. Hold her for a few more minutes, and I'll have it turned."

Tyler's stomach clenched, but he focused his gaze on Analise. Damp tendrils of hair had pulled loose and clung to her neck and cheeks. The concentration on her face was a thing of rare beauty. Moments later, she stood.

"Let her go for a minute to rest. The baby is in position. It won't be long now."

Perspiration rolled down her forehead. Tyler picked up a clean cloth and his hand trembled as he wiped her face. "Alex, will you light the lamps for us? Doc has to see what she's doing."

The young man did as requested. At the next loud scream from his wife, he returned to her side. "Can't you give her something for the pain? I don't think she can stand much more."

"Later, after she delivers." Analise looked under the sheet and nodded to Tyler. He again took the girl's knees in his hands. "Polly," she said softly, "when I tell you to, take a deep breath and push."

Over the next minutes, the young woman did as she was told. She breathed and she pushed at Analise's instructions. Her cries tore from a throat sore from her screams. Tyler wondered how any woman had a second child if they endured this for the first. His own heart felt torn from his chest.

"That's it, almost there. One more good push and I'll have it."

"I can't," Polly grunted.

"Sure you can, sweetheart," Tyler said. "Just do what Doc says."

"Yes!" Analise shouted. "It's a girl. A beautiful, perfect girl." A loud squeal came from the red, moddled, squirming bundle in her hands. "Let go, Tyler, and come help me. I need you to cut the cord."

This time he forced his hands to remain steady as he followed her instructions.

When the baby was wrapped in clean swaddling, Analise set the child in the mother's arms. "Here's your fine, healthy daughter." Tears poured from Analise's eyes.

At that moment, she was the most beautiful thing he had ever seen. Without jewels or silk, her hair mussed, her skin damp, real love and beauty shone in her face. How could he suspect this doctor, this saver of lives, of being involved with outlaws like Ace Malone? He had to be mistaken. It was probably only coincidence that Ace had ended up in Omega at about the same time as she.

"I thought I was gonna die," the young woman whispered.

"Not with Doctor Analise around. She wouldn't let you." Tyler spoke with conviction from his heart.

Analise smiled at the young mother. It truly was a miracle. If Abigail had gotten this kind of care, his life would have turned out a lot differently.

When she finished with the mother, Analise sat on

the edge of the thin mattress. She reached over and took the baby from the sleeping woman. "You can hold her, Tyler, while Alex and I put Polly into a clean gown and change the sheets again."

He trembled when she placed the child in his arms. The baby was bald, her face red and squinched up. She was a miracle. Nothing had ever touched his heart more. His child had been a boy. Yet, Tyler imagined, he would have looked a lot like this infant— had he survived the doctor's bungling. He wiped away the tear before it touched her head, then gently pressed his lips to her tiny cheek.

# Chapter 5

Analise finished ministering to the mother, then took the baby from Tyler's arms. Moisture glittered in his eyes that the spectacles couldn't hide. "She wants her mother to feed her." She smiled up at him. "You can hold her later."

He placed the tiny baby into Analise's arms and seemed reluctant to let go. She weighed next to nothing, a burden so light and fragile, yet the most precious thing in the world. Love filled her heart, both for this child and the one who had never had a chance.

"I'll go out and help with the chores and stable our horses for the night. I don't believe it would be safe to try to return to town this late."

Analise nodded. "I want to stay and keep watch over both the mother and child for at least twelve hours. I don't want any complications." She set the baby in Polly's arms, where the tiny mouth nuzzled for the mother's breast. "Could you please fetch the basket Mrs. Hennessey packed for us? We can all use some supper about now."

Tyler brushed a finger along her cheek, wiping

away her tears. "You were magnificent, Doc. You saved both their lives."

Her skin tingled from his touch. "Not me. Your prayers gave us all strength. And you were a wonderful assistant."

"Don't give me credit. I was scared to death."

Analise longed to slip into his arms and let her tears flow. Not that another ocean of tears could wash away the ache buried deep in her heart. She glanced over her shoulder at the baby making slurping noises at her mother's breast.

"I'll fetch that basket. I'm getting mighty hungry for some of Mrs. Hennessey's fine cuisine." Tyler left quickly.

Moments later, he set the basket on the rough wooden table in the kitchen area of the cabin. Tyler signaled for Alex. "Let's get those chores done, so we can eat." He slipped his arm across the young father's shoulder. "You'll have plenty of time to be with your baby when her crying keeps you up all night."

Analise smiled. Seeing Tyler with the baby in his arms had sent strong emotions through her. He had come through like a trooper. She reached for the jacket he'd left on a chair. Her hand stilled. She realized at that moment that she was falling in love with him. Falling in love was definitely not part of her plan. It was best for all that she bury these feelings under the pain of the past.

She picked up his jacket to hang it on a peg. A large, heavy object fell from the folds and banged onto the floor. She jumped back a step. A frightening-looking handgun lay at her feet. A big handgun. Like the one the sheriff wore on his hip. Like an outlaw would carry. With trembling hands, she picked up the gun. The dangerous-looking weapon was not something one would expect a churchman to carry.

She studied the smooth handle and long black

barrel. The more she learned about Tyler Goodfellow, the less she knew about him. She tucked the gun into the bottom of her medical bag for safekeeping and hung his jacket on a peg near the door.

By the time the three males returned to the cabin, Analise had a meal on the table. Thanks to Mrs. Hennessey's foresight, they had a loaf of bread and sliced ham. Analise had found a basket of eggs and had scrambled up a batch.

"Can I see the baby?" Manny raced across the room to Polly's bed. "Can I hold her?"

"After you wash up real well," Analise said.

The boy scrubbed his hands, face, and feet, then showed off to Analise. She nodded her approval and followed the child to the bed. The young mother was sleeping with the baby tucked in her arm.

"Sit on that chair, and I'll put her into your arms."

Manny settled on the chair that had held Tyler's coat. Tyler glanced at the coat on the peg, then shot a questioning glance at Analise. She ignored him and picked up the baby. Wrapping the tiny girl in a warm blanket, she knelt beside the chair and placed the baby in the child's arms.

"She's littler than a pig," the boy said. "How come she don't got no hair?" He brushed a small finger across her head.

"It will grow in. Give her time."

"Was I ever this little?" he asked, lifting his gaze to his brother.

"No, you were a bigger than a little pig." Pain glittered in Alex's dark eyes.

"You said my ma died when I was borned. How come Polly didn't die?" With little knowledge of death, the youngster had no idea of the pain his words caused. The baby opened her eyes and made a tiny noise. "Look," the boy said, "she likes me, but she smells funny."

"Of course she likes you," Analise said. "But I think she needs her nappy changed. I'll take care of her while you eat your supper."

While Alex and Manny ate, Tyler hovered over Analise as she changed the baby's diaper. "Did you move my coat?"

She looked up from the squirming baby. "Why? You missing something?"

He lowered his voice for her ears only. "Yes, where is it?"

"In my bag."

"You can give it to me later. We may need it on the road."

"Do you believe that you need to help the Lord protect us?"

"My faith wavers, and I feel it best to take precautions rather than be sorry later." He glanced over at the others at the table. "We'll talk some more."

"We certainly will." Tyler Goodfellow owed her an explanation.

She returned the baby to her mother's arms, then went to the table. After the excitement of the afternoon, she felt like a deflated balloon. She sagged onto the bench beside Tyler. He reached over and filled a mismatched plate for her. "Did you fix the eggs?" he asked.

"Yes." She took a small forkful.

"They're good. I didn't know you could cook."

She laughed. "The full extent of my culinary skills."

When the food was gone, Alex returned to sit at his wife's side. Polly had eaten a little, and was sleeping from exhaustion. Analise learned that the young woman had been in labor for over twenty-four hours. She shivered at the thought that Polly and the baby might have died if she and Tyler hadn't arrived in time.

Tyler and Manny offered to wash the dishes while

Analise examined the baby and again changed her diaper. Polly had a few gowns and supplies ready, but somebody would have a lot of laundry to do in a few days. From the way he looked at his wife, she had no doubt that Alex would pitch in and help wherever needed. Love for both child and mother shone brightly on his sun-bronzed face.

With their chores finished, Manny cleaned up and climbed up to the loft to sleep. The youngster was clearly exhausted from his day's work. For such a young child, he showed bravery and courage far beyond his years. Manny had as much to do with saving Polly and the baby as had Analise and Tyler—not that they could take all the credit. Analise had been tended by the finest doctor in Paris, and her child had not lived more than a few hours.

"I'm going to make a pallet on the couch, so I can be near my patients," she informed Tyler, feeling more humble by the minute. "I feel it is important to be on guard against complications."

Tyler nodded. "I'm going to bed down in the barn. Walk out with me for a minute."

She glanced back. Alex had fallen asleep reclining on the bed with his arm around his wife. The baby was safely nestled in a blanket-lined basket. "All right. I want to stay close in case they need me."

He paused at the doorway. "May I have my gun, please?"

"It's in my bag. I'll get it."

Carefully, she retrieved the sidearm from her medical bag. What a contrast. Her bag contained medicines and equipment to save lives; the gun was meant to take lives.

"Thank you." He tucked the revolver into the waistband of his trousers and slipped on his jacket. They stepped outside together into the chill wind.

"Never know when I might encounter some wild animal out in the barn."

The simple explanation did little to satisfy her curiosity. "I didn't know men of the cloth carry weapons, except for their Bibles."

"The smart ones are always prepared. I can't very well beat off a bear with my Bible, can I? But, one shot fired in the air will send him scurrying away."

That made sense. Yet something about him still bothered her. An air of mystery seemed to hang over him.

He stopped a few feet from the cabin and smiled down at her. His eyes glittered silver in the moonlight. He brushed a loose tendril of hair behind her ear. "Did I tell you how magnificent you were today?"

Her eyes met his. Emotions flooded her. Pent-up fears and anxiety burst forth. "I was so scared. I don't know what I would have done if we hadn't made it in time."

He tugged her into his chest, wrapping his arms securely around her back. "It worked out perfectly. You knew what to do and you did it. There isn't a better doctor in the world."

"You're just saying that because you don't know many doctors." She nestled closer. Her fears dissipated in his embrace. His warmth made her feel safer, more secure than she had in ages. Since long before Paris.

"I've met quite a few." His voice turned cold. "There aren't many like you and your father."

Analise thought about his leg. Had poor medical care left him with the limp? "I've met some who should never have gotten a license." He kissed the top of her head. "Doc, have you delivered a lot of babies?"

She tightened her grip on his back. The gun at his waist bit into her stomach. "Yes, but it was in the city, where I didn't have to travel these distances to reach my patients, and other doctors were available. That's one of the reasons I want to open the clinic. I can give the women good prenatal care and a sterile place to deliver their children. And I can look after them to prevent childbirth fever or other infection. Plus, I can look after the babies for a while."

His warm lips dropped to her forehead. "Noble goals, Doc."

"Nothing hurts like losing a child." Her voice cracked. It would take a lot longer than a few months to ease her private pain, but nothing would make her forget. As much as she enjoyed being in Tyler's arms, she knew the danger of getting too close. She was vulnerable, her feelings at the surface. "I had best get back to my little patient. I'm not sure Alex knows how to handle a baby."

Tyler laughed. "He raised Manny. I believe he has an idea of what to do." As if reluctant to move, he stepped away. "I'll be in the barn if you need me. We should try to leave early tomorrow. Mrs. Hennessey will be concerned about you."

Analise nodded. "As soon as I make sure mother and daughter are doing well, and I leave instructions, we can go."

"Goodnight, Doc. I'll get up early to help with the chores, then we can be on our way."

"*Bonsoir,* Tyler. And thanks for everything."

She watched him walk away, tall, strong, and without any hint of a limp. Another thing she didn't understand about the man. Maybe the leg didn't bother him all the time. Perhaps it depended on the weather, like people with arthritis. As a doctor, she could ask him about the problem, but as a woman, she realized it was none of her business.

\* \* \*

During the long night, Tyler realized how many times he had given himself away during the previous day. From forgetting the cane, the limp, and slumped shoulders, to letting Analise find his gun—his actions were totally out of character for his current role. He had let his emotions overrule his plan. He hoped he had given a plausible explanation. However, Analise was far from stupid. Sometimes he thought she saw right through him.

The next morning, after Tyler fed the horses, Alex showed up with two mugs of coffee. "Sir, can I talk to you for a minute?"

"Certainly." Tyler warmed his hands on the cup and propped against the corral rails. "Is everything all right with the baby and your wife?"

Alex removed his battered hat and slapped it against his leg. The chill morning breeze whipped at his hair. "That's just it. Polly is not my wife. Not legal like."

That surprised Tyler, considering the devotion Alex showed to the woman and child. "I'm sorry. I just assumed . . ."

"I know. My *madre* was Apache and Mexican and my *padre* was a soldier. He never even knew I existed. Without a man we were forced onto the reservation. She took up with the government agent. That was how we got extra blankets and food. When he learned she was expecting a baby, he sent us to another reservation. She died right after Manny was born. I did not want Manny to grow up on that miserable reservation, so I took him away."

The young man shifted his gaze to the pasture where a small herd of cattle grazed on the grass. "We ended up here on this ranch. I worked for Polly's paw until he died about a year ago. She wants to keep the ranch, so I stayed on to help her. I know it was wrong, that a breed has no business fooling around with a white girl, but we were both lonely, we could not help it." He bent his head and stared at his battered boots. "I really love her. I do not know what I would have done if she had . . . if it had not been for Doc Analise. And you."

In spite of his tough exterior, brought about by a hard life, the young man had more integrity than most men Tyler knew. "Is that why you were reluctant to take Polly into town?"

"I am not welcome. Most folks know that we are living out here alone, and last time they were mean to Polly. Think what they would have done if they knew she was having my baby."

Tyler had seen more than his share of prejudice and bigotry in his travels. "Doctor Analise isn't like that, and neither is her father. You'll have to swallow your pride and get good medical care for your baby."

"I know. That is why I need your help. Doctor Analise said you are a man of God. Can you marry us before you leave? I do not want my baby to be called a bastard because I was not man enough to marry her maw."

Pain arched through Tyler. He was caught between a rock and a hard place. Since he wasn't a minister or even associated with a church, he had no authority to perform a marriage ceremony. He couldn't reveal the truth, yet he certainly didn't want to deceive the young couple, who deserved a legal marriage. Well, a half truth was better than total deception.

"I wish I could help you, Alex."

He turned on Tyler, his hands clutched in fists. "You mean you will not marry a breed with a white woman. You are no better than the rest of them."

"Hold on, son. That isn't what I mean. If I had the

authority, I would be honored to perform the ceremony. However, I'm not authorized to marry or baptize. I can only preach and visit the members of the church until I get ordination papers." That was as good a story as any. He hated to deceive the young man, but this time it was necessary. "When Reverend Carter returns to Omega, I'll see that he performs the ceremony. Doctor Analise will handle everything in case I've already gone." Which he hoped was soon.

"You believe he will do it?"

"If he won't marry you, I'll find somebody who will. Until then, we'll just let people think you've been married for a year."

Alex settled his battered hat on his head. "I know Polly wants to make it legal although she never complains or anything."

Tyler scanned the small homestead. "You're running this place by yourself?"

"Me and Manny. Polly wants him to go to school, but I do not think he will be accepted. She is teaching him how to read and write."

"From what I see, you're doing a fine job. The buildings are in good shape and the cattle look healthy."

The younger man laughed bitterly. "Not bad for a lazy, good-for-nothing breed. Is that what you mean?"

Tyler draped an arm across the man's shoulder. "No, I can see you're a hard worker. Help me hitch up the rig. I want to get Doctor Analise back to town."

The few chores done, Tyler and Alex ambled back to the cabin. The young man had a hard road ahead of him, but from what Tyler had seen, Alex was up to the challenge. And Tyler would definitely see that a preacher came out and married the couple.

They entered the cabin to find Analise sitting beside the bed speaking softly to her patient. Manny was at the table, eating a slice of bread. Tyler joined him, smearing several slices of bread with jam.

"Are you ready to get on the road, Doc?" he asked, swallowing a large glass of fresh milk. "If we leave right away, we should beat those storm clouds on the horizon."

Analise glanced up at him. "And get home in time for lunch."

"Of course. Mrs. Hennessey hates it when we're late."

"I'm ready." She turned her attention back to the young parents. "I want you and the baby to come into my office in a month so I can examine both of you. It is important to get regular checkups. However, if anything unusual happens—a fever, rash, anything— please either send Manny for me or come into town."

"Doctor," Polly said, smiling down at her daughter. "I can't thank you enough for what you done for me." She looked over at Tyler. "You, too, Mr. Goodfellow. When we come to town, I want to bring Anna to the church for you to dedicate her."

Alex opened his mouth to protest. Tyler realized how important it was for Polly to believe her daughter would be accepted in town. "You've named her Anna?"

"Yes, sir. For Doctor Analise."

Analise brushed away a tear. "That is very sweet. I'll look forward to seeing her grow into a fine lady. Maybe she'll grow up to become a doctor."

Alex frowned. "Those are grand plans for a poor rancher's child."

Tyler picked up Analise's bag. The fine leather satchel had her initials engraved in gold. "Don't be surprised what a woman can do when she sets her mind on it. And with the new century coming up, anything is possible."

"I don't have cash money, doctor, but I want to pay

you. We have lots of eggs, and I've got a calf I'll give you as soon as it's weaned. We'll bring it when we come into town." Alex stood, proud and tall—a mature man in spite of his young age.

"Thank you, Alex. But why don't you keep it here for me? I really don't have any place to keep a calf in town."

"Yes, ma'am. Manny, if you can quit eating long enough, put a dozen eggs into the doc's basket, then get on with your chores."

The boy filled the basket with the eggs and carried it out to the buggy at the door. "Did you say your neighbor is down with her back?" Analise asked.

"Yes, ma'am," Alex said. "The Daniels's place is about two miles north of here. But, ma'am, you might not want to go there."

Analise set her medical bag in the buggy behind the seat with the blankets Tyler had fetched from the house. Most were clean, unused. He had tied the dirty linens into a bundle. "Why not?"

The young man removed his hat and shoved his fingers through his hair. "The Daniels's are colored folks. They're real friendly to us, but most of the white people don't have much to do with them."

Analise lifted her chin. "I am a physician. I do not look at the color of my patients' skin. We can go over there on our way home."

Tyler glanced up at the sky where storm clouds gathered in the west. "It's really out of our way, and the weather is acting up."

She glared at him with fire in her blue eyes. "I took an oath. If you don't want to go with me, I'll go alone."

"No, you won't. I'll take you there. If we hurry, we might be able to get home before the storm breaks."

"Thank you." The ice in her voice could have chilled hot water.

Alex assisted Analise into the high seat. "May the gods go with you, Doctor." He stretched out a hand to Tyler. "Thank you, sir."

"God bless you, son. And your family." Tyler joined Analise on the seat and picked up the reins. He shook the lines and the horses took off at a trot.

Analise sagged against Tyler's shoulder, exhausted and drowsy in spite of the uncomfortable ride. She'd gotten little sleep the previous night worrying about Polly and the baby. Her concern extended to the entire young family scraping out a living on the small homestead.

They located the Daniels's place, and spent about an hour visiting with the family. It was no wonder Mrs. Daniels was down with her back with six children under the age of ten. Analise could only imagine the amount of laundry, cooking, and work involved in keeping the family going. Analise offered advice and gave her a vial of laudanum to relieve the pain, with instructions to be careful with the dosage.

By early afternoon they headed south toward Omega. The sun drifted behind the gathering clouds, and the swaying buggy made her sleepy. Tyler's wide shoulder made a perfect pillow. He slipped his arm over her shoulder, offering safety and security. She loved feeling his arm around her. She loved Tyler.

The thought startled her awake. No, she did not love the deacon or whatever or whoever he was. She could not fall in love, not again.

She shoved away from him and glanced at his face. Worry lines creased his forehead. The clouds hung low, and lightning flashed in the distance. Thunder rumbled, loud and threatening. A chill wind whipped at her shawl. The horses started to bolt, but Tyler managed to control them. She lifted her gaze to the sky as the first large raindrop splattered on her face.

"I don't think we're going to make it to town before this breaks," he said, urging the team faster.

"What are we going to do?" She wiped away the cold drop with her gloved hand.

"On our way out, I spotted a cabin not too far from here. We can stay there until this blows over."

As they raced across the narrow path, the rain fell harder and the thunder rumbled closer. A loud crack sounded, and lightning split a tree in half. She shivered with fear at being caught out in the open during a thunderstorm. "How much farther?" she asked, her teeth chattering.

"I see it up ahead, past those trees. Doesn't look like much, but 'any port in a storm.' And that is our port."

He guided the team over the rocky terrain to the dilapidated cabin. Tugging hard, he halted the team and set the brake. At another bolt of lightning the horses reared up. Tyler leaped down and grabbed the bridle, calming the frightened animals. "Get inside while I unhitch the team and get them to safety."

Analise hurried to obey, her wet hair now plastered to her face. She grabbed her medical bag, her most valuable possession, and an armload of clean, dry blankets. The door to the shack hung on one leather hinge and opened easily. Her footsteps stirred the thick layer of dust, and cobwebs hung like curtains from the ceiling. Broken pieces of furniture littered the floor, along with animal droppings.

"Any port in a storm," she reminded herself. Another blast of thunder shook the walls. She jumped back and nearly tripped over her own feet. Indeed they were very lucky to find even this bit of shelter in the isolated countryside. From the condition of the room, it was evident no one had occupied the cabin in a long while. She set down her bundles and returned to the door. Tyler was struggling to move the excited horses toward the rear of the cabin. Not knowing how to help him, she rushed to the buggy, and retrieved the basket from under the seat. At least they would have something to eat. She had left most of the food with Alex and Polly, but a partial loaf of bread remained, as well as the dozen or so eggs Manny had given her.

Back inside the cabin, she shook off as much of the rain as she could from her clothing. Her wool shawl was soaked through, as well as her shirtwaist. She shivered against the chill. Wind and rain whipped through the open doorway. While waiting for Tyler, she searched for some way to make a fire. The stone fireplace was in sorry shape, and she hoped starting a fire in it wouldn't burn down the entire place.

Seconds later, Tyler came through the doorway. He shoved a shoulder against the door and managed to get it closed, and latched. "This might hold, unless the wind worsens."

Analise glanced up at him. "You're soaked to the skin," she said, noting the way rivulets of water rolled down his face and neck. Earlier he'd placed his eyeglasses in his pocket. He removed his hat and set it on a peg on the wall.

"Looks like this is home until the storm lets up." He scanned the room. "I've been in worse."

"What about the horses? Are they safe?"

"I hope so. I tied them to the lean-to away from the wind. Unless they become frightened and break free, they'll be safe until morning."

"Morning?" Analise gaped at him. "Do you think we'll be here all night?" The idea had both interesting and frightening possibilities.

He removed his coat and placed it on a nail sticking out of the wall. "Looks that way. Even if the storm passes over quickly, it will be too dark to take a chance traveling back to town." He shook his head like a dog, spraying water all over Analise. Without his coat, the gun stuck in his belt looked even more menacing than before.

"We can't stay here." She covered her mouth with one hand.

He shrugged, the damp cotton shirt clinging to his wide shoulders. "Can't help it, Doc. These roads are too dangerous at night for somebody unfamiliar with the terrain."

"What about my reputation?" she asked. *What about my heart?* she thought.

"Like your father said, if he can't trust his daughter with a man of the cloth, who can he trust her with?"

She turned toward the cold, empty fireplace. It wasn't him she didn't trust. It was her own needs and emotions she didn't trust. "Let's see if we can start a fire. I'm freezing."

He moved behind her, resting his hands on her shoulders. His touch warmed her through the wet clothing. "You're soaked. Get out of those wet things, and wrap a blanket around your shoulders." She stiffened. "Don't act shocked. Your undergarments should still be dry, and the blanket will protect your modesty."

"You're right. I need to get dry, but so do you."

"As soon as I get the fire going I'll get my own blanket." With quick, sure movements and no hint of a limp, Tyler circled the room, picking up broken pieces of wood and setting them into a pile. "Go on, I won't watch." Minutes later, the fire had caught the dry wood and a weak flame flickered in the fireplace. He knelt down and blew on the kindling, urging a fire to life.

Quickly Analise removed her wet shirtwaist and skirt. Her camisole and petticoats were relatively dry, so she kept them on. Following suit, she hung the garments on other nails sticking out from the walls. She wrapped a towel around her wet hair and a blanket around her shoulders. "You can look now," she said.

He shot a glance over his shoulder. Even in the dim light, she didn't mistake the heated look in his eyes. Without the spectacles, his eyes glittered with emotion. "Come over here where you can get warm."

She moved closer, and hunkered down in front of the fire. Another blast of wind shook the walls. Sparks flew from the fireplace. "This is like a hurricane."

Tyler stood and grabbed a dry towel from the small stack they had brought from home. He wiped his face and hair, then tugged his shirt over his head. "I suppose you experienced a few storms in Louisiana."

Analise forced her gaze back to the fire, struggling to ignore the flame that burned inside her at the sight of his body. "A few. We also endured quite a bit of flooding since New Orleans is so low." Not daring to look at him again, she heard when he shucked his trousers and moved closer to her. The thought of being isolated with a nearly nude man brought shivers not at all associated with the chill air. "I've heard that in Colorado during bad storms, the streams and rivers in the mountains become torrents."

With a blanket around his shoulders, he hunkered down beside her. "I've seen flash floods that washed away everything in their paths."

"Do you think we're safe here?"

"This little sanctuary is on a rise. The water will drain away from us. We might have to cross swollen streams on the way back home, though."

Eyes wide, she stared at him. "Will that be a problem?"

He shrugged. The blanket had slipped. Her gaze dropped to his wide shoulders and broad chest. Tiny drops of rainwater clung to the black hair that covered his well-muscled torso. With skin bronzed by the sun, Tyler clearly had not spent all his time sequestered in churches with his Bible. Callused hands and honed flesh came from hard physical labor outdoors.

"Could be. If the current is too fast, we could be swept away like driftwood." He reached out a hand and tugged the towel from her hair. "We'll have to find a safe place to cross, or wait until the water recedes."

"Wait?" She tugged the towel from his grip. "Tyler, I can't be gone another day. With Papa in Denver, I'm the only doctor in town. And Mrs. Hennessey will be frantic that I'm gone." And she would be alone even longer with a man she had problems keeping her hands off. She bit her lip to keep her feelings bottled inside.

"She knows you're with me, and I won't let anything happen to you. I promise to get you home tomorrow, if I have to carry you across the streams on my back."

She groaned. If word got out that she and the attractive man were marooned together, her reputation would be in shambles. As would his.

Tyler reached over, and plucked a hairpin from her already mussed hair.

"What are you doing?" She reached up and stopped his hand.

"That mass of hair will never dry bundled up like that. You'll have to let it down to dry." Pin after pin plinked on the wood floor. Analise shifted and tightened her grip on the blanket. His fingers combed through the tresses, fanning her long hair across her shoulders. "That's better. You know you have beautiful hair. It glimmers with rich highlights in the firelight."

Her breath caught. "Tyler, this is terribly inappropriate." But she couldn't deny how good his touch felt.

He stroked her hair from scalp to the ends. "Everything about this is inappropriate. Being here, alone, together. Partially clothed." His words faltered. "Sheltered together like shipwrecked survivors on a deserted island."

Heat sizzled from her head to her inner female parts. Needs surged through her, needs she'd suppressed since Victor's deception. Tyler's deep voice lulled her into the fantasy. "And having to depend on each other for survival."

"Like the only two people in the universe." His arm slipped across her shoulder, drawing her closer to his side. A sudden flash of lightning and loud blast of thunder jolted her to her senses. She surged to her feet. Her pulse beat double-time. She was playing a dangerous game with her heart. "I'm starved. Let's see if we can find something to eat in that basket."

# Chapter 6

Analise stumbled on the long blanket. Nature had saved her. It was a sign to Tyler to keep his hands to himself, and his emotions under control. Again he regretted this subterfuge. He ducked his head, resting his forehead against his knees. Usually when on assignment, he got into the role as if he were on the stage. This part should have been no different to him than playing Hamlet, Macbeth, or dozens of other characters in his former career. Once again, he regretted his choice of disguises. Most of all, he regretted lying to Analise. He couldn't deny his attraction to her. Under normal circumstances he would already have made love to her. As a church leader he was restricted to holding hands, if she allowed it.

He surged to his feet, careful to keep the blanket around his lower body. Evidence of the way she affected him would embarrass them both. "I'll try to catch rainwater in that jar from the basket." He stuck his arm out the door, letting the chill air cool his needs. It didn't take long to fill the jar with water. The fury of the storm seemed to be easing, but it was still too dangerous to get on the road.

"If we had a pan, we could cook these eggs. I don't believe I can eat them raw." Analise had spread out a towel and set out the bread and slab of cheese.

Looking around at the debris on the floor, he spotted a tin can. "I think we can boil some eggs in this." He reached out into the rain and caught more water. "This will make them a sight better than raw." He sat in front of the fireplace and set the can and eggs on the fire.

"You're certainly skilled for a man of the cloth." Analise glanced over at the gun he'd set aside, but close within reach. "Do you know how to use that?"

"Well enough to protect both of us." The lies nearly choked him. She wouldn't believe a mild-mannered deacon could be a crack shot with both a pistol and rifle, as well as an expert in fisticuffs and other forms of hand-to-hand combat. "As I explained before, this is dangerous country. A man has to be prepared."

"Have you ever had to use the weapon? I mean to shoot at someone?"

How could he tell this saver of lives that he had taken lives? "Not often," he hedged. She was getting too close to learning the truth about him. "I had better go check on the horses again."

"But it's still raining and cold."

He snagged his trousers and tugged them on. "I won't be long." Only long enough to get his thoughts and needs under control. She affected him in the most elemental way. With her, he forgot about charades, about missions, about lies. He thought only of the desire to be with her, to hold her, to make love, to throw off the robe of Deacon Goodfellow and become Tyler Morgan, a man of passion, more of a devil than a saint.

He rushed through the doorway, closing it tightly behind him. Lifting his face to the sky, he let the cold rain wash over him. A woman hadn't affected him this way since he was a youth, sporting with every pretty girl in the acting troupe. Unless he got his libido under control, he would have a very long, uncomfortable night alone with an appealing woman.

Analise stared into the fire long after Tyler left. The man was such a mystery. One minute he was gentle and mild-mannered, almost helpless, then he switched, revealing unusual abilities and accomplishments. Which man was the real Tyler Goodfellow?

When he'd run his fingers through her hair, and sat close enough to her to feel the heat from his body, she wanted to wrap herself into his warmth and become one with him. She shoved the dangerous thoughts away. No good could come of her giving in to her baser needs. Growing close to him would only complicate their lives. Neither of them needed that kind of distraction. And she certainly didn't need to get involved with a man, any man.

Thunder roared off into the distance. The storm was letting up. On a deep sigh, she shoved aside her needs. She couldn't deny she was drawn to him—a man so like Victor, yet so different. One very important thing she had to keep in mind: he would be gone from her life in a few weeks. Just as Victor had rejected her, she had no doubt that Tyler would disappear, not leaving a wisp of smoke behind.

Images in the flames brought back bittersweet memories. It had taken all of her willpower to keep her emotions under control as they worked together to deliver Polly's baby. Analise had assisted in dozens of deliveries, but each was special in its own way. This time they'd had two lives at stake. Little Anna was her first delivery in the West.

Without Tyler's help, it would have been nearly

impossible to save both mother and baby. Although he'd appeared queasy at first, he had come through the ordeal with strength and purpose—as if he had done this before. Another mystery about him to solve. He'd mentioned once being married. Did he have children? Had he assisted in childbirth in the past? Tyler was a man of many talents as well as surprises.

Using two sticks, she removed the can with the eggs from the fire. The meal on the floor wasn't up to the usual standards of her father's home, but it was more than adequate in an emergency. Behind her the door opened, and Tyler entered, again soaked to the skin. She pulled the blanket more securely around her.

"The eggs are ready. Are you hungry?" she asked, her voice husky.

"Yes. The horses are okay, and the cabin seems secure for the night. The rain should end soon. We can head for home at first light." He again shucked his trousers and wrapped a blanket around his shoulders before he settled beside her on the floor.

With the rain easing, and the thunder and lightning drifting into the distance, they sat quietly in front of the fire sharing their meager meal. Sparks flew from the fire. Sparks sizzled between them.

Analise watched him from the corner of her eye. The man was an egnima. From the first she had wondered about the man behind the severe black suit and eyeglasses. In church, he fit the part of a man of the cloth to perfection. A saint would praise him. But out here, away from people, he changed like a chameleon fitting into his environment. Tyler was all man, strong, capable in many ways—a dangerous man. To the world he was soft-spoken, educated, mild-mannered. Yet there was something about him that didn't quite fit. His penetrating gaze noticed everything, not missing the tiniest detail.

"Who are you, Tyler Goodfellow?" The sound of her voice surprised her. She hadn't expected to speak aloud.

For a long moment, she wondered if he'd heard her. He drew a deep breath. "Just a pilgrim and a stranger," he whispered.

"Have you worked for the bishop long?"

He shook his head. "Not long."

His short, clipped answers surprised her. She had expected a longer dissertation on his profession. "What will you do when you leave Omega?"

"I'll give my report, and go on to my next assignment."

Sorrow touched her heart. There seemed to be a restless spirit in Tyler. Something that prevented him from settling in one spot for long.

"Did you mention you were married at one time?" She could have bitten off her tongue at her audacity.

After another long pause, he whispered, "Yes, when I was very young."

Curiosity prompted her to delve further into what was none of her business. Except that she needed to know. Needed to understand his restlessness and a sadness that all his bravado could not disguise. "I realize it's none of my affair, but do you mind telling me what happened?"

Again he hesitated as if gathering his thoughts. Perhaps he still loved his wife, and talking was difficult. For her part, Analise had never told anyone about Victor and their affair. Or about her child.

"I don't mind telling you. Abigail died in childbirth."

Pain laced through Analise at his loss. "I'm sorry."

He poked a stick into the fireplace. "She was young, not much older than Polly. Abigail was a small woman, but we were thrilled to be having a baby." His voice cracked with emotion.

She reached out and touched his arm. "You don't have to tell me if it's so painful."

Tyler covered her hand with his. Her touch offered comfort and encouragement. Other than his parents and Alan Pinkerton, few people knew the details of his past. Somehow, he felt the need to confide in her, to share some of the pain that gnawed at him daily. "It was a long time ago." Yet it seemed like yesterday.

He took a sip of rainwater from the Mason jar to clear the lump from his throat. The events of the day before had brought back so many memories—both bitter and sweet—and they threatened to choke him. "We were traveling through Kansas by train. She was in her seventh month, so we thought we had weeks before her time." His voice hardened.

"When we neared Abilene the train came to a sudden stop. It was a holdup." He surged to his feet, clinging to the blanket like a lifeline. Emotions, feelings he'd hidden under his many disguises, spewed forth like a geyser. He wanted Analise to know, to understand. For twelve years the pain had festered and churned inside him. It was past time to heal the wounds.

"Gun-wielding bandits boarded the train and demanded our valuables. Abigail and I had little worth stealing. When they tried to take her wedding ring, she resisted. I stood in front of her, and one of them aimed a pistol barrel at my head." He paced the floor behind her. "I suppose I should be grateful he didn't shoot me." His voice dropped to a whisper.

"When they finished, they rode off and Abigail went into labor. We knew it was too early for the baby. I wanted to get her to a doctor, but the tracks were blocked by a fallen tree. It took an hour to clear the tracks. Meanwhile Abigail was suffering and crying for me to help her." He returned to stand in front of

Analise. Her gaze moved from his bare feet to his legs, encased in cotton drawers. He tossed his blanket beside her and sank to her side. He rested his arms on his updrawn knees and dropped his head to his arms.

She reached out a hand to his face. With one finger she brushed the dampness from his cheek. "I realize how difficult that must have been."

"Analise, do you know what it is to love someone and not be able to help them? I had insisted we take the train to St. Louis. Abigail wanted to wait until after the baby came. I still blame myself for what happened. By the time we got to Abilene, she was hemorrhaging. I found a doctor, such as he was. He was a sorry excuse for a man, let alone a doctor."

He swallowed down the lump in his throat. "I worked with him to deliver the baby. But our child was small and blue—stillborn. The doctor made excuses. Abigail was too young, she was too small, it was too early. Excuses. Not reasons for her to die and my son to die."

She wrapped an arm around his shoulder offering a comfort he felt he didn't deserve. "Don't beat yourself up, Tyler. There was probably nothing you could have done."

"I tell myself that every Christmas when I visit their graves in Abilene."

He studied her. She closed her eyes as if fighting her own pain. "If you had been her doctor, Analise, she might have stood a chance. I saw you with Polly today. Without you, she and her baby would have died. It was like seeing Abigail in that bed, screaming for help."

She cupped his face with her hands. "Tyler, I know it's difficult, but you can't go back and redo the past. You've made a new life for yourself, a life of service and dedication."

A life of lies and deceit was more like it. He bit his lip to keep from revealing the truth about himself. After he'd buried Abigail and the baby, he set his purpose to preventing this from happening to another family. He hunted down the train robbers and brought them, one by one, to justice. He had known Alan Pinkerton for years, and had worked for him on occasion. With Abigail gone, he joined Pinkerton's forces full time. He hated withholding the truth from Analise, but she was better off not knowing. Besides, in spite of the goodness he saw in her, he wanted to be certain she'd had no association with Ace Malone.

"Analise, have you ever been in love?" Tyler wasn't sure what had prompted that bold question. "Surely a woman as lovely as you has had her share of beaus."

She laughed, a bitter sound lacking humor. "Many times. I was the belle of the ball in New Orleans. Every young gentleman of Creole and American descent wanted to court me. But I had already fallen love with medicine. I wanted to be a doctor above all things."

"There was no special man? Not even in Paris?" Probing for information had always been his specialty as an agent. But these personal things in her past were none of his affair. Yet some inner devil prodded him on.

Her voice grew soft. She wrapped her arms around her updrawn knees. "Yes, I thought I was in love, but it was just a foolish woman's dream."

"I would never call you 'foolish.'" Tyler reached out and brushed a stray tress behind her ear.

"Everybody falls in love in Paris, and I was no different. I thought he loved me too, until he learned I was as penniless as he."

"He was after your money?" He reached over and twined her fingers with his.

"Money that I didn't have. He was an impoverished French aristocrat looking for an American heiress." She squeezed his hand. "At one time the DeLery family was very wealthy, but most of our property was lost in the war. I inherited when my grandmother died, but after paying the debts, not much was left. I used my inheritance to support my education, and I used the last of it to study in Paris."

Sensing her need for comfort, Tyler shifted closer. "How did you become involved with a gigolo?" Tyler couldn't hide the disgust in his voice. He hated men who used women, and this Frenchman had clearly hurt Analise badly.

"I met him at a sidewalk café. He was handsome, debonair, and sophisticated. I couldn't believe such a worldly man could be interested in me. Because I wore nice clothes and jewelry, he mistakenly thought I was wealthy. When he learned . . . ." her words faltered, "otherwise, he disappeared. I heard he had gone to Italy with another woman. An older, experienced widow." Her voice trembled as she blinked back tears.

"He was a fool." Tyler touched her gently on her cheek, but he couldn't hide the note of distain in his voice.

In the dim light, their eyes met and held. Pain glittered in her eyes. "I was a fool to trust him."

"Love often makes people do foolish things. Did you come directly from Paris to Omega?" he asked, ashamed to use her distress to probe for information.

"I left Paris when I finished my studies, spent a few months in New York working with Doctor Blackwell, then I came to Omega to be with my family. I hadn't seen them in two years."

"I'm sure they were glad to see you."

She sighed. "Steven certainly was happy. He hates

staying with the injured or sick patients for Papa. The last patient he'd tended died in front of him."

*Ace,* Tyler thought. "Weren't you there to help?"

"No, I was still in New York. I didn't arrive until after the man had been buried."

It sounded as if he had been barking up the wrong tree, and that she'd had no contact with Ace. The very idea of suspecting this woman made him feel like a fool.

Her long eyelashes hid pain she couldn't express. He lowered his face to hers. His lips feathered across her mouth. "Would you mind if I kissed you?"

His boldness caught Analise off guard. "I don't know."

"Maybe we should find out."

His lips brushed hers in a kiss as tender as a baby's touch. She set her hands on his chest. His skin was warm in spite of the cool air. Delicious sensations surged through her. Such a small kiss, a bare brush of his lips to hers. Gently, he circled her neck with his fingers. His touch sizzled down her spine like the thunder that crashed in the night. Her heartbeat sped up and her breath caught in her throat. Tyler rained tiny kisses on her mouth. His tongue stroked against the seam of her lips.

The kisses were so sweet, so tender, she felt as light as a butterfly on the wing. She moved her fingers to his jaw, roughened with a day's stubble. It was so deliciously male, she couldn't resist stroking his skin. He smelled of rainwater, he tasted of passion.

With infinite care, he increased the pressure on her mouth. His lips were warm; exquisite tingles flowed over her like a warm summer rain. His tongue nudged at her lips, seeking entrance. Analise welcomed his invasion, accepting the touch of his tongue to hers. Pleasure surged through her, pooling deep in her abdomen.

His fingers tangled in her hair. She tugged at Tyler's shoulders, pulling him down on top of her. His body was hard and unyielding. She had never felt like this before. Even Victor's most ardent lovemaking hadn't affected her this way. A voice deep inside warned her to be careful. Another voice urged her to throw caution to the wind and enjoy the moment.

Tyler groaned, ending the kiss. He lifted his head and brushed a finger over her lips. "Do you know how delicious you taste?" He nuzzled his nose into her hair. "How wonderful you smell?"

The warmth of his breath brushed her ear. "I smell like disinfectant."

"No, like sunshine."

Outside the rain pattered gently on the roof. Inside the fire burned within her body. Beside her, Tyler's touch warmed her heart. "It's raining outside."

"The sun is shining in here."

His face was close, his body pressed to hers. Through their thin underclothing she felt every inch of his maleness. Her soft breasts pressed into his hard chest. It was heaven. A heaven that could only get her into trouble. Like her weakness had gotten her involved with Victor with disastrous results.

The realization of who they were and what was happening slammed through Analise like a rifle shot. She shoved against his chest. "We can't do this."

He sat up, taking her with him. "I know. I would never do anything to compromise you."

Taking a deep breath to gain control over her nerves, Analise tightened her hands into fists. "I'm afraid I'm the one who corrupted you."

With a wry laugh, Tyler lifted the blanket and wrapped it around her shoulders. "That should prevent further temptation."

She tightened her grip on the rough wool. "I'm sorry."

"Don't be sorry. I started it, and I am definitely not sorry."

Her face heated at his bold statement. "Honesty, neither am I."

For a long moment, he stared into her eyes. The expression on his face was unreadable in the dim light. "You aren't sorry because you tempted me, or because you enjoyed the kiss?"

Analise wasn't sure who had tempted whom. "Both. I am not a young maiden unaware of relations between men and women. As a doctor, I know the dangers of letting my emotions override my good sense." As a woman she knew firsthand what happened to a woman who could not control her emotions.

On a deep sigh, he wrapped his own blanket securely around his shoulders. "Let's get some sleep. As soon as the rain stops, we'll head for home." He wrapped the spare blanket into a pillow for her and urged her to lie down. After checking the fire, he shifted to her side and lay down on the floor. From lowered lids, she watched him pick up his gun and set it within reach. Only then did he close his eyes.

Analise studied him while he slept. Who was he? she wondered. Saint or sinner? Man of the cloth or a man with a secret? She fell asleep not sure what to believe. Her last thought was that even though she did not really know Tyler Goodfellow, she would trust him with her life, if not her heart.


Due to swollen streams and nearly impassible roads, it was late afternoon when Tyler pulled the buggy to a halt at the rear porch of the DeLery home. As expected, Mrs. Hennessey and Oscar rushed out to meet them. A thousand questions bombarded them before he could hop down from the vehicle. Tyler was surprised that Oscar wasn't holding a shotgun on him.

The older man shot an angry glance at Tyler as he helped Analise down. She sagged in the big man's arms, clearly exhausted from their long ordeal.

"Where ya been, little missy?" he asked, leading her gently into the kitchen. His wife remained behind, glaring at Tyler like a mother hen at a fox about to get her chicks.

"I'll explain everything, as soon as I have a cup of tea." She glanced back at Tyler. "I'm certain Mr. Goodfellow could use some too. Along with something to eat. We finished the last of our food this morning."

Tyler followed more slowly, carrying an armload of blankets and the empty basket. It was time he returned to being Deacon Goodfellow, a rather modest and unassuming fellow—a man just a little on the helpless side. He had revealed too much of his true nature to Analise, and further revelations could be dangerous to all of them.

"This has been quite an ordeal." He sagged onto a chair, sighing heavily. "Doctor DeLery was magnificent. She saved the lives of a mother and child."

Mrs. Hennessey hovered over them, pouring tea and setting a plate of fresh biscuits on the table. "I'll have supper ready after a bit. Your papa and Miss Millie will be in on the evening train. When you didn't come home yesterday, I sent them a wire." She clucked her tongue. "That worthless sheriff wasn't anywhere around to get help from him. Oscar was about to get up a search party to look for you. Why, anything could have happened to both of you out there alone."

Analise patted the older woman's hand. "Audrey, we were delayed by that storm. We had to find shelter for the night, and then today the roads were nearly impassable. We were forced to detour miles around overflowing streams."

"Humph. Too bad we don't have those new-fangled telephones out here. We were worried sick." She set a cup of steaming coffee in front of Tyler, knowing he preferred the strong beverage to tea.

"Thank you, ma'am," he said.

Oscar glared at Tyler. "You been alone with Missy for two days and nights?" Not giving Tyler a chance to explain, the older man poked a thick finger at Tyler's chest. "If I was her paw, I'd have a shotgun at your back, deacon or not."

Tyler glanced at Analise. Her cheeks had pinked, and a horrified expression showed in her wide eyes. "It was all perfectly innocent, I assure you." Except for that devastating kiss they'd shared. If the man knew how Tyler had nearly given in to temptation and made love to Analise, Oscar would surely either blow him away, or run him out of town tarred and feathered. Deacon or not.

"Please, Oscar, listen to me." Analise grabbed the big man's hand in both of hers. "We had to deliver a baby. The woman was in very bad shape. Another hour and she and the baby would have died. Mr. Goodfellow helped in the delivery. He was wonderful."

Oscar swallowed. "It ain't right for menfolk to watch something like that."

She sighed. "My papa is a man, and he's delivered hundreds of babies."

"But he's a doc. Not a man."

Tyler remained silent. Let Analise deal with her protector. Anything Tyler could say would only get them deeper in hot water.

"He prayed for us the whole time. He was a wonderful help."

"Who is this young woman?" Mrs. Hennessey asked, refilling his cup from the pot on the stove.

"Polly Gonzales. Her husband is Alexandro Gonzales."

Mrs. Hennessey gasped. "You mean that Dawson girl who kept that run-down ranch after her parents died? She took up with that half-breed and now she had his baby? Disgraceful."

"Mrs. Hennessey!" A look of horror passed over Analise's face. "What an unchristianlike thing to say. They are young and in love. Alex is a fine young man. He works very hard to take care of Polly and his little brother. He'll make a fine father to little Anna."

The housekeeper glared right back at Analise, not backing down an inch. "They've been out there living in sin. What do you think, Deacon?"

Tyler wasn't surprised at the woman's reproach. He'd seen too much self-righteous prejudice in his lifetime. Using his meekest demeanor, he lifted his hands in surrender. "The Word tells us to 'judge not, lest ye be judged,'" he said, evading the subject. "I believe that they are good people, and they are struggling to support themselves on their ranch." He needed to defuse the woman's outrage. "My dear Mrs. Hennessey, you would have fallen in love with little Anna, the same as we. They named her after Doctor Analise."

The woman's eyes softened. "Well, I suppose the Lord don't hold the children responsible for what the parents do."

"I instructed them to bring the baby to the church so we can welcome her into the Family of God. We should rejoice when a new soul is born both into the world and into the Kingdom." He hoped he sounded pious and religious enough to ease the woman's misgivings.

Analise sipped her tea. "We spent the first night at the ranch to make sure the mother and baby were healthy. Then we visited another family before we started for home." He noticed she didn't mention the name of the other family they'd visited.

Tyler picked up the story. "We were caught in the storm and had to seek shelter. Thank the Lord, He led us to an abandoned shack to protect us from the weather."

Oscar again puffed out his chest like an enraged rooster. "I don't care if you are a church fellow, you're still a man, and you spent the night alone with Missy. I don't think her papa is going to like that."

"What won't her papa like?" Millie DeLery stepped through the doorway into the kitchen. She was an imposing figure with her chin held high and her eyes blazing with indignation.

Tyler's stomach dropped to his feet and he groaned inwardly. Dealing with the housekeeper and handyman was one thing, an irate father and mother was another. He jumped to his feet. "Mrs. DeLery, Doctor."

The doctor entered behind his wife. "We received a wire that said Analise and Mr. Goodfellow were missing. They seem to have been found."

Millie stepped toward Analise, surveying her from head to toe. Only then did Tyler realize how wrinkled and travel-worn he and Analise were. Mud splattered their clothing, Analise had managed a single, rather ratty braid down her back, and they both needed baths. Tyler swiped his hand over the thick stubble on his jaw. Overall, they were a sorry pair.

"Etienne, look at them. I have never seen a more bedraggled couple. We have only been gone two days, and look what we return to find. What has been going on since we left for Denver?" The doctor's wife set her hands on her hips and tapped her foot on the floor. She was quite a contrast to her daughter. Millie's green travel suit was immaculate, her hat perched at a jaunty angle on her head, and her white gloves spotless.

Analise shoved away from the table. "Millie, Papa, both Tyler and I have had a very hard few days. We delivered a baby, tended a woman down with her back, and, thanks to Mr. Goodfellow, we survived a terrible storm." She lifted her shoulders and tilted her nose into the air. "Now, if Oscar will carry some hot water to the bathing room, I would like a bath." With a swish of her skirts she marched from the kitchen, her back straight, her nose in the air.

"One minute, young lady," Millie called after her. "That was not a satisfactory explanation."

"Then ask Deacon Goodfellow what happened. He can explain everything." Analise's footsteps faded up the stairs.

Left to face irate parents, Tyler decided that sometimes the best defense was a delaying tactic. "Your daughter is a wonderfully dedicated physician. She saved several lives while you were away, and proved to be a great asset to the community." He picked up his ugly bowler hat. "Now if you will excuse me, I will return your buggy to the livery, and repair to the barbershop for a shave and bath."

"Young man, when you return, we will meet in the parlor and discuss this . . . this indiscretion," Doctor DeLery ordered in no uncertain terms. Tyler could see the shotgun being loaded and pointed at his back. It would take some fast talking to get out of the mess he'd gotten into. The thought bounced around in his brain: did he want to get out of it?

# Chapter 7

Analise leaned back in the large claw-foot tub, mentally thanking her stepmother for the bathing room she had installed in the house. She sank into the water, letting the warmth wash over her. Closing her eyes she thought about Tyler, and the kiss they had shared the night before. Her toes curled as tingles spread throughout her body.

A tiny smile arched her mouth. Tyler Goodfellow could handle horses, make a fire, deliver a baby, preach a sermon, and he really knew how to kiss. She wondered just how far his talents extended. He was certainly an enigma.

"Are you ready to tell me exactly what happened while you and Mr. Goodfellow were stranded in that cabin?"

Startled by Millie's voice, Analise sat up and splashed water over the sides of the tub. Her smile quickly faded. Lost in her own thoughts she hadn't heard her stepmother enter the room. She sank lower into the bubbles for a bit of modesty.

The older woman pulled a stool closer and handed a bar of her special French-milled soap to Analise.

"It's one thing to have a story for your father, but I've been around the block a time or two. I know women. And I know men."

Analise gasped with surprise. "Millie, you're talking about a man of the cloth."

"A man is a man. I saw the way he looked at you. And I saw the way you looked right back at him. You reminded me of two hungry cats eyeing a saucer of milk." She picked up a pitcher of water and poured it over Analise's soapy hair. "As far as I know, only Roman Catholic priests are forced to remain celibate. Protestant ministers marry. A deacon is a layman, so there are no restraints against his marrying."

Analise sputtered, not only from the water running down her face. "I am not interested in marriage. Neither is Mr. Goodfellow."

Millie stood and held up a large towel for Analise. "The two of you spent a night alone."

"He was a perfect gentleman." Analise stood and wrapped the towel under her arms and around her body. With another towel, she squeezed the water from her hair.

"Ah, *petite*, there are gentlemen and there are *gentlemen*. As a doctor, you should realize that men have . . . uh, certain needs. And I'm not ashamed to admit that women have needs also."

"Nothing untoward happened." She hid her face in the towel to hide her embarrassment. She knew all too well about needs. After a minute, she dropped the towel.

Millie picked up a hairbrush and tugged the bristles through Analise's long hair. "By now everybody in town knows about your little, shall we say, escapade. We know how people like to gossip. Think about your reputation."

She laughed. "Millie, people have been talking about me all my life. In New Orleans, they talked when I followed Papa on his rounds to see his patients and when I volunteered at the charity hospital. And when I danced all night at the Mardi Gras balls. Then I went from my debut to medical school. My grandmother's friends wanted her to lock me in a convent—and we weren't even Catholic."

"Well, if you aren't concerned about your reputation, what about Deacon Goodfellow's reputation? He's a representative of the bishop here in Omega. He must be aboveboard and have a sterling character."

"Are you blaming me for ruining his character?"

"Of course not. I understand that he offered to escort you, and you had no way of knowing about the storm. I understand completely. But I'm not so sure about your father. He still thinks of you as his little girl. And he may insist that the deacon do right by you."

Mouth agape, she glared at Millie. *"Do right by me?* Please believe me, Tyler did not compromise me, nor I him. His virtue is as intact as before we left town." Of course she refused to admit that the kiss they'd shared had sorely tempted her. Nor did she mention that her own virtue had been compromised over a year ago. "You cannot force us into a marriage neither of us wants!" She grabbed the hairbrush from Millie's hand and slammed it down on the dresser. "I have to devote my time to my clinic. I cannot get married."

Millie set her hands on her hips, as always, determined to have her own way. "You may not have a choice."

"There is always a choice. I am a twenty-eight-year-old woman, not a child. I can make my own decisions, just as I've done for the past ten years. I will do as I please."

Her stepmother shook her head. "You are a

woman. But we both know you aren't free to do as you please. As a spinster, you are under your father's protection. That is one of the reasons I am fighting so hard for female rights and women's suffrage. Once we get the vote, and pass a few laws, we won't have men lording it over us."

"And I won't be forced to marry against my will."

Millie laughed. "In spite of all I've said, and what your papa wants, I believe that nobody can force you to do anything you do not want. But are you sure about Tyler Goodfellow? He is both handsome and intelligent, and I'm sure he would make you a fine husband."

"Millie, you never give up." Analise picked up her wrapper.

The older woman shrugged. "Tenacity is one of my most endearing qualities, much to your father's dismay." With a flip of her skirts, Millie left the room. But her words lingered long after her footsteps died away.

In the bathhouse behind the barbershop, Tyler sank into the large tub of hot water. All he lacked was a glass of good whiskey and a Cuban cigar. But it would be out of character for a deacon—he snickered at the title—to indulge in drink and smokes. Still, the bath did much to revive him. He closed his eyes and let the heat soak clear to his bones, much like the heat that had flooded him when he'd kissed Analise. That woman could start a fire on an iceberg. He still tingled from their kisses.

Not to mention the effect on his heart. The cold dark corners that had filled his chest when he'd lost Abigail were slowly being replaced with warmth and light. All thanks to Doctor Analise DeLery. Seeing the miracle of a new life come into the world re-

*Jenna Lawrence*

newed his faith as nothing had in years. Maybe there was a miracle for him after all. If only he could get rid of the niggling suspicion linking her with Ace.

Memories of their single night together made him lethargic. His eyes closed, letting him relive every delightful minute of his night with Analise. She had snuggled into his arms, pressing her soft body to his. He doubted she knew that her blanket had fallen away, and all that separated their bodies were her thin chemise and drawers and his own underclothing. It took all his willpower to keep his hands on her back and not on the other inviting parts of her body. Just thinking about her was again having an embarrassing effect on his manly parts.

Tyler was drifting off to sleep when a commotion on the other side of the curtain shook him awake. Automatically, he reached for the gun he'd set on his clothing beside the tub. He held it out of sight.

"That church fellow in here?" a husky male voice shouted.

"Get out of here. He's taking a bath," the proprietor roared.

"I'm a sinner. I has got sins to confess afore I croak."

Tyler relaxed, recognizing the voice. "Let him in. I'm always ready to help a sinner."

The man staggered into the room, and dropped to his knees beside the tub. He wore dirty denim pants and a ragged plaid shirt. His battered hat sat low on his forehead. The sight of the man's disheveled appearance brought an amused grin to Tyler's face. Leroy King was one of most fastidious agents in the field. This disguise tickled Tyler.

"I been a sinner, deacon. I need you to get the Lord to forgive me." Leroy was nearly as good an actor as Tyler. In fact, Tyler had recruited the actor from another traveling troupe to work for Pinkerton.

"Tell me, son, what did you do that was so terrible?" Tyler choked out the words around his desire to laugh aloud.

Leroy leaned closer to Tyler's ear. "Quit laughing, Morgan. Heard you spent a couple of days and nights with that pretty lady doc." He waggled his eyebrows suggestively. "You might be the one needing forgiving."

Did everybody in town know about his business? Tyler lowered his voice. "What have you got for me?"

"The Malone gang is on the move. Looks like they're headed here. I spotted a stranger in the saloon. Young guy, Southern drawl, asking a lot of questions about the doc."

"Damn," Tyler muttered. "And I still haven't found the loot. If they start snooping around, they could cause trouble." He lifted his voice. "The Lord will forgive you. Just stay out of the saloon, quit drinking and swearing, and come to church on Sunday."

"You really know how to play a part, Morgan. I'll keep my eyes open and let you know if I hear anything." Leroy glanced around to make sure nobody was listening. "Another thing. Word came about the lady doc. Seems she didn't leave New York until after the robbery, and Ace was on the move. That Doctor Blackwell vouched for her." Louder he said, "Thanks, Deacon, I'll surely try to walk the straight and narrow."

The day that that Pinkerton agent toed the line, Tyler would take a vow of celibacy. The chances of that were nil to none. Leroy exited the bathhouse, leaving Tyler alone with his thoughts. Relief flooded him. Analise had been telling the truth. It was highly unlikely she knew Ace or anything about him. She was innocent and exactly what she appeared to be, unlike him, an imposter and a liar.

At least he knew backup was nearby if he needed

assistance. Tomorrow, he would question Steven about the money. Tyler had a feeling the boy knew more than he was telling. With the Malone gang closing in, Tyler had to concentrate on locating the money and keeping the outlaws away from town.

He finished his bath, got a shave, and set off to the DeLery home to face the good doctor. He and Analise had committed a serious social blunder by spending the night alone together. But it couldn't have been helped. They had had to either seek shelter or drown in the storm. Surely her father was reasonable enough to understand, though Tyler wasn't so sure about Mrs. DeLery's tolerance. He could find himself betrothed to the beautiful woman who set his blood on fire. Things could be worse.


Tyler timed his arrival at the DeLery home to coincide with the family's suppertime. He entered through the kitchen door and was surprised to find the room empty. Usually the housekeeper and her husband were bustling with last-minute preparations. A ham sat on the table along with several covered bowls. The aroma of fresh bread filled the air. Where was everybody? He wandered through the dark, deserted dining room into the parlor. His chest tightened with fear. Had something happened to the family? Had the Malone gang come calling?

Always cautious, he reached for the Colt revolver hidden under his coat. Soft voices came from the parlor. Easing around the door frame, he studied the group gathered together as if for a Sunday social. Doctor Delery sat in an overstuffed easy chair, his wife at his right on a fragile-looking Queen Anne chair. Analise paced back and forth, wearing a hole in the carpet. The clock in the hall chimed seven times.

Analise turned to her father. "Can't we just have

supper? There's no need for this interrogation. I've already told you everything that happened."

Tyler wondered just how much she had confessed. Did she mention that devastating kiss, or the way she had cuddled up to him all night long? He doubted it. He didn't see a shotgun on her father's lap.

"As soon as Deacon Goodfellow arrives, we will settle this problem. Then we can sit down to our meal." The doctor tapped his fingers on the arms of his chair.

On a long sigh, Tyler returned his gun to the holster. He'd designed the apparatus to fit snuggly under his arm so that it wouldn't be noticeable under a jacket but an easy draw when necessary. They were all waiting for him. He straightened his coat, leaned on his cane, and prepared to give the performance of his life.

"Sorry to keep you waiting." He adjusted the spectacles on his nose and slumped over his cane. "My watch is one minute slow." Back in character as the mild-mannered deacon, he nodded to the doctor, and bowed to his wife. "As lovely as ever, madame." He swung his gaze to Analise, where she paused at the window.

"Let's get this over with." Analise glanced from her father to her stepmother. "I know you're upset over what occurred between Mr. Goodfellow and me over the past few days, but I assure you that nothing untoward happened."

"Analise, I will handle this situation. Please sit down." Her father gestured to the small settee opposite him. "You too, Deacon."

Analise obeyed without protest. Tyler looked around and decided that since they were both on trial, he might as well sit beside the other defendant. With a brief nod, he sat down, his right leg straight out in front of him. He rubbed the muscle, as was his habit.

Doctor DeLery steepled his fingers and stared at Tyler and his daughter over his fingertips. Millie didn't try to hide the twinkle in her eyes. The doctor cleared his throat. "Deacon Goodfellow, I am sure, as a man of the cloth, you realize a man's obligation toward his family. Analise is my only daughter, and although she believes she is beyond my authority, I take my obligation to her seriously."

"Papa, is this necessary? You're embarrassing Mr. Goodfellow." Analise twisted her fingers in her lap. "And me."

Tyler had never seen her so nervous. During their days and nights together she had been as strong as a rock. Now, facing her father, she was as shaken as a leaf in a windstorm. He covered her hand with his. Millie caught the gesture and smiled that secret smile women used when they had the upper hand. "I am not embarrassed. We didn't do anything wrong."

"I believe both of you, Deacon. However, as mayor and a leader in the church, I have a certain reputation in this town. As does my entire family. And you, sir, cannot afford to have a single stain on your name if you wish to continue working for the bishop. But we all know how people will talk. In order for Analise to establish her practice and especially her clinic, her reputation must be aboveboard. I'm afraid people are already whispering about her morality. You are unmarried people in your prime, and you spent two days and nights alone."

"We were alone only one night," Analise groaned.

"One night, two nights, people talk, Analise," Millie added. "Now we have to decide how to remedy this situation."

Tyler remained quiet. Somehow, he found himself enjoying the banter going on around him. This was better than a show on the stage.

Millie touched her husband's arm. "I believe the

only solution is for us to announce the betrothal of our daughter to Deacon Goodfellow."

"What?" Analise leaped to her feet, shocked at the odd turn of events. "This foolishness has gone far enough. I told you I do not want to marry." Actually, she could not marry. There was no way she could let a husband know that she was not a virgin—that her virtue had been compromised by another man. A good man like Tyler would be appalled. He would demand an annulment, and her reputation would be soiled forever. Nobody would want a disgraced doctor as their physician.

There had to be a way out of this predicament. Tyler rose to stand beside her. Thank goodness he was willing to offer a solid defense. More than anybody, Tyler knew the whole thing was ridiculous.

"Doctor DeLery, I would be honored to have your daughter as my wife."

His words sent another shock wave through Analise. She had expected him to be on her side—to refuse her hand. "What? You plan to leave in a few weeks. You can't marry me."

He caught her hand and carried it to his lips. "Please, Analise, let me finish. You are right. When my work is completed, I plan to leave Omega. As fond as I am of you, I do not believe a woman should be forced into a relationship she doesn't want." Still clutching her fingers, he addressed her father. "I am willing to announce our betrothal to save Analise's reputation and my good name. This is her home, and I have my duties to the church, which require me to travel far and wide for the time being." He locked gazes with Analise.

She could not believe what he was saying. "What do you mean?" she asked, confused.

"I say we let the people believe that we are engaged, then after I leave, you can say I was sent out of the country as a missionary, and you were not allowed to go."

"Do you mean a pretend engagement?" Millie gasped in horror. "Why, that would be a sham on the institution of marriage."

Her father tugged on his mustache. "That sounds rather dishonest, especially for the clergy."

A tinge of pain caught in Analise's chest. He didn't want her, but he was willing to lie for her reputation. She didn't know which was worse: not being desired or becoming engaged for real. Still, this could be the solution to their problem.

"I believe Tyler has an excellent idea. It really isn't anybody's affair but ours. If we call off the marriage after he leaves, we can blame it on his vocation." Analise tugged her fingers from his. She immediately felt oddly bereft without his touch—just a tiny hint of how she would feel after he was gone from her life.

Millie narrowed her eyes at the couple. "I do not like to lie or deceive my friends. I do not see any reason why this cannot be a betrothal for real. Mr. Goodfellow is unmarried, as is Analise. He can remain here and Analise can have her clinic all right here in Omega."

Analise knew that Millie wouldn't give up so easily: she had set her sights on getting a husband for her stepdaughter, and the best prospect so far was agreeing to a pretend engagement. The pain behind Analise's eyes had now turned into a pounding headache.

Tyler reached for Millie's hands. "My dear Mrs. DeLery, I fully agree with you. I would like nothing more than to settle here with your lovely daughter. However, I must be about the Lord's business and go where the bishop sends me. If he allows it, I can stay until then, I must do as I am directed."

Analise stared at him, astonished by the way he had manipulated the situation. The man could talk his way out of a hangman's noose, and this was nearly as bad. "I'll accept a pretend engagement for the next few weeks. After Mr. Goodfellow is on his way, I don't want to hear any more about betrothals or marriage."

The idea of him leaving Omega brought a bit of sadness to Analise. She shoved away the feeling. It would do her no good to think about this man—or any man, for that matter.

"Fine." Millie stood, clearly out of sorts. "But we will do this properly. I will throw a party this Saturday at the town hall to announce the betrothal of our daughter to Deacon Tyler Goodfellow. The entire town will be invited, and I expect the pair of you to act as if you are madly in love and ready to marry." She paused and pointed a finger at Tyler. "We must make sure that everyone understands that Analise is not at fault when she ends the betrothal. I will protect her reputation at all costs. I hope we can stop the gossips."

"Or start more talk." Analise mumbled under her breath. She felt as if she was caught in a whirlpool, unable to swim her way out.

She glanced up at Tyler. A hint of amusement glittered in his eyes that even the spectacles couldn't hide. He seemed to be taking the bizarre turn of events much better than she.

At that inopportune minute Steven darted into the parlor. "I heard the clock, how come we ain't eatin' supper yet?" As usual, her brother's primary concern was for his stomach.

"We are ready to sit down to supper, now that our business is settled." Millie caught her son by his nape and guided him toward the kitchen.

Steven spotted Analise, rooted to the floor. "What's wrong with Analise? She looks like she just took a bite out of a sour apple."

"She's fine. Analise and Mr. Goodfellow are getting married."

Steven ducked out of his mother's grip. "Married? Yuck. Does that mean we'll have a preacher in the family?"

Analise knew better than to reveal the truth of the sham engagement to her brother. There were no secrets with a twelve-year-old. "Yes, but it will be months, maybe years, before we can marry."

Tyler stepped forward and tossled the boy's hair. "Your parents are throwing a party for us on Saturday. I'm sure you'll be there to congratulate me."

"Will there be cake and punch?"

"Of course," Millie said. "And music, dancing, and decorations."

The youngster shrugged. "Guess I'll be there, if the rest of the guys are invited too."

Millie marched into the kitchen. "The entire town will be there."

The entire town. Analise would have the devil of a time breaking off an engagement if the entire town was involved. "Millie, do you think a party is wise? I'm really busy trying to get the clinic started."

"Oh, posh." Millie waved her objections away like swatting at a fly. "We must have a party. It's our obligation. After all, your father is mayor of Omega. Our friends would be disappointed if we didn't throw a gala event." Her son and husband followed her into the kitchen.

Left alone together, Tyler sidled up to Analise. He caught her fingers in his. "Don't worry, Doc. It will all work out for the best."

"Is that the deacon spouting scripture, or a man who's caught like a fly in a spider's web?"

He carried her fingers to his mouth and touched his lips to the knuckles. "I suppose I'm an optimist, and I do have faith." His tongue lingered for a moment, sending delicious sensations up her arm. "And would an engagement to me be so horrible? We seemed to be very compatible last night in the cabin. This engagement should be quite interesting."

Her gaze locked with his over their hands. Interesting was a weak word for what she felt. His eyes glittered with what she could only name as passion. It was the same way he'd looked at her that night before they had kissed. Needs surged within her like a flower looking for rain. His touch had awakened desires she'd tried to bury for over a year.

"I blame myself for what happened in the cabin. I put you in this situation." A tear gathered in the corner of her eye.

Tyler bent his head and touched his lips to the tear. "Don't blame yourself. I knew what I was doing. Sometimes the flesh is weak, but we did not break any of the commandments." He smiled at her over their hands. "Let's go eat. I'm starved."

He tucked her arm in the crook of his elbow and gestured to the kitchen with his cane. Analise laughed. "Just like Steven. Always worried about your stomach."

"Considering the fine meals Mrs. Hennessey puts on the table, I believe I will enjoy this engagement immensely."

"Then you had better enjoy them while you can. In a few weeks you'll be gone and no more meals."

"That is a very sad thought."

Analise agreed. His departure would leave a very big hole in her life, and in her heart.

# Chapter 8

Tyler waited at the foot of the stairs for Analise. Her family had gone ahead to the town hall, to assure that the preparations were complete for the "engagement party." To make the farce believable, he had gotten his suit pressed, his shirt starched (so stiff it scratched his skin), and his black necktie precisely knotted. He also vowed to put on a performance that would make all of the Morgan Players proud, that of a smitten swain. He'd played Romeo on the stage more times than he could count. To him, this would be just another act in the play.

He'd seen little of Analise over the past few days. His time had been consumed with searching for the missing money, while Millie had enlisted Analise's help with plans for the party. The entire town seemed to be involved in making the gala the social event of the year. Millie and her cohorts had arranged an affair that would put a larger town to shame. They had moved across town like a swarm of locusts, devouring anything and anyone that stood in their way. It would be interesting to see what they could accomplish with more lead time—and for a wedding.

A wedding. That was the next step in a natural progression. He hoped they wouldn't be too disappointed when the wedding did not take place. That thought seemed a little sad. Falling in love, becoming engaged, marriage, children—all were natural for most men. But not for Tyler Morgan. He shoved the idea of marriage out of his mind. He had taken a wife once, fathered a child, and lost them both. His heart could not stand that kind of pain a second time. It was best to remain a bachelor, and avoid the heartbreak.

At the sound of footsteps on the stairs, he lifted his gaze. He'd known that Analise was a pretty woman; he'd seen more of her luscious body than was good for his libido. But the vision descending the stairs took his breath away. He blinked, to keep his eyes from bulging from his head.

"Close your mouth, monsieur. You are going to catch flies." She slowly descended the stairs, an embroidered silk shawl over her arm. "Surely you've seen a woman in a ball gown before."

"*Mais oui.* But none so lovely." He wasn't exaggerating. The gold gown clung to her shoulders, dipping low onto the tops of her breasts. The waist narrowed into a point, emphasizing her womanly shape. The short sleeves topped her slender arms, with long white gloves reaching past her elbows. In its simplicity, the gown was stunning; the woman in it was magnificent. Her everyday gowns of gray and black hid any hint of her stunning womanly figure.

She met him at the foot of the stairs. "I haven't worn this gown since the last ball I attended in New Orleans. It's outdated, but I've always liked it." She tugged on the low neckline. "I've also gained some weight since the last time I wore it." She laughed. "Millie had to stuff me into a corset so it would fit." Taking another few steps she twisted at the waist. The movement made the tops of her breasts jiggle provocatively. "I hate corsets. They are the bane of womanhood—restricting the breath and crushing the ribs. Women ought to stand up and burn these instruments of torture."

Tyler smiled at her tirade, but he couldn't speak for the effect she had on him. It wouldn't take much encouragement to carry her back upstairs and strip her of the gown and undergarments.

He took the shawl, embroidered with gold thread, and set it on her bare shoulders. His hands lingered for a moment, enjoying the warmth of her flesh. Her hair was piled on top of her head, leaving loose tendrils touching her cheeks. "You smell as delicious as you look."

Husky laughter bubbled from her throat. "You're quite a flatterer, Mr. Goodfellow. Are you ready for our little charade?"

"As I'll ever be." The shawl did little to hide her natural feminine assets. If the engagement had been real, he would never have let her out of the house looking so desirable. He could well believe she had been the belle of every ball in New Orleans.

Tyler set Analise's hand on his arm. He fortified himself for the show. His performance as a churchman had come easily, and he'd acted the devoted swain numerous times on the stage. Combining the two different personas would take all his acting abilities. His best course of action would be to act the cow-eyed lover while remaining meek as a lamb. A strange combination.

The town hall was in the center of town, surrounded by a large grassy lawn. A space had been left to build a courthouse and new jail when the town raised the funds. Several couples greeted them on their way to the gala. Millie was right. She had invited all of the townspeople and those from surrounding farms and ranches. Children dashed past them, hurrying to find the refreshments. Analise trembled slightly as they approached the lawn, decorated with colorful Chinese lanterns.

"Doc, you're going to your engagement party, not the gallows." He tugged her closer to his side.

She hugged the shawl tighter against the evening chill. "Is there a difference? I feel as if we're both being railroaded into something neither of us wants." A shiver racked her body. "I hope I can get through this evening. I'm not sure I can pull off this charade. What if somebody wants to know when we will be married?"

"You'll be fine. We can say we will be married after you establish your practice, and I complete my commitment to the church." Or complete his assignment for Pinkerton, he thought. The idea of marrying Analise had interesting possibilities. Tyler shoved away the ideas as fast as they assailed him. "Pretend you're attending a Mardi Gras ball." He paused outside the open doors of the town hall. "Put on your brightest smile, Doc. Here we go."

Inside the hall, Analise released her grip on the shawl, giving him a glimpse of the deep cleavage displayed by her gown. He was tempted to turn around and take her home to change into one of her awful high-necked shirtwaists and black skirts. Instead, he did the gentlemanly thing and hung the shawl along with his hat on a wall rack.

Doctor DeLery and his wife approached with wide smiles and open arms. Around them the crowd parted like the Red Sea for Moses, allowing them to pass through.

A smattering of applause and female giggles rang through the gathering. A few oohs and ahhs came from behind open fans in ladies' hands. The men stood a little straighter, and like roosters, stuck out their chests. A feeling of what could be considered jealousy lashed through Tyler. He didn't like other men lusting after his woman. He considered removing his jacket and covering her, but with his gun in the hidden holster, he couldn't take a chance on anybody seeing it and asking questions he didn't want to answer.

Tyler smiled and tightened his grip on his fiancée's arm. His. She belonged to him. That thought caught him by surprise. For the first time since Abigail's death, he felt as if he belonged somewhere and with someone, and that a special woman belonged to him. Little by little, sunlight was creeping into the dark corners of his heart. All because of the pretty lady doctor on his arm.

He could settle here in Omega, with these people who had gathered to congratulate him on his engagement. Good people, caring people. A genuine smile curved his lips—not an expression learned and perfected on the stage, one from his soul.

Of course when word of his deception came out, these same people would probably ship him out of town on a rail. With Analise DeLery carrying the tar and feathers.

Tyler shook hands and accepted the congratulations of the men. The women smiled and nodded as he and Analise made their way to the small platform where a trio of musicians had set up. Doctor and Mrs. DeLery followed at their heels. The doctor stood on the dais and raised his hands for attention. The crowd quieted.

"Ladies and gentlemen, friends and neighbors. Thank you for attending this gala affair." He reached for his wife's hand. "My wife and I are delighted to welcome you to share this joyous moment with us."

Tyler waited as the doctor paused and smiled down at him. He entwined his fingers with Analise's. Her forced smile was almost comical. He could just about hear her teeth grinding together. He widened his smile.

The doctor gestured to Tyler and Analise. They stepped up together onto the platform beside her parents.

"You all know how proud we are of our daughter, *Doctor* Analise DeLery. It is our pleasure to announce that the Deacon Tyler Goodfellow has requested the hand of our daughter in marriage." The crowd nodded in agreement. He shook Tyler's hand vigorously. "We have given them our blessing. Welcome to the family, Mr. Goodfellow. You have gotten our jewel."

A round of applause filled the air. Tyler had the inclination to bow, out of habit. Millie kissed his cheek, and the doctor kissed his daughter. Tyler wished he could reveal his true identity. He felt more like a hypocrite than ever.

"Thank you, sir, madame," he said. "I am truly blessed to be welcomed into your family. Before God and these witnesses, I promise I will only do what's best for your lovely daughter." Even if the best for her was leaving in a few weeks. He lifted Analise's hand to his lips. "Thank you for accepting my suit."

Analise glared at him over their hands. "Thank you for choosing *me*, sir." She grounded the words between her teeth.

"Smile, *chérie*," he whispered for her ears only. "We're in love."

"Pretending."

Only Tyler didn't feel as if he was acting. The emotions she instilled in him were entirely too real. "May I have the first dance?"

"I would be honored." She curtsied. "Are you able?"

"I'll manage."

Looking for all the world like a cat that had swallowed a canary, Doctor DeLery instructed the musicians to begin playing.

Tyler dropped the cane on the platform as he assisted Analise to the dance floor. He executed an awkward bow. In keeping with his masquerade, he used the waltz as his opportunity to lean heavily on Analise. He circled her waist with his arm, while catching her hand in his. Allowing her to lead in the dance, he enjoyed the feel of her body pressed to his. Pretending to dance with a limp was more difficult than executing the most intricate step. Actually, he had been dancing since he was a boy.

"You're such a wonderful dancer, Doc, it's a shame you are stuck with such a clumsy partner." He swung her in a circle and stumbled enough to pull her flat into his chest, while making sure he didn't step on her toes.

She laughed. "I suppose after one revolution of the floor, we should check out the refreshments and leave the dancing to the others."

"And greet our guests." The music ended, and he offered his arm to lead her to the refreshment tables.

The night passed quickly. Analise danced with her father and nearly every man in the room. Tyler gritted his teeth to keep his temper in check. Those men had no business dancing with his fiancée. If it wasn't for his desire to complete his assignment successfully, he would throw off his disguise, shoot a couple of cowboys, and sweep Analise off her feet.

Instead, he smiled and acted the besotted swain who was betrothed to a beautiful lady doctor. At about nine o'clock, Tyler stepped outside onto the lawn for a breath of fresh air, and used the opportunity to calm his temper. The last man to dance with his woman had been a young cowboy from a local ranch. The guy was good-looking, cocky, and he held her a little too closely. Rather than make a scene, totally out of character, he chose to calm his nerves with deep-breathing techniques. He paced back and forth, forgetting about the cane in his hand. Music flowed through the open doors and windows. Young boys and girls raced across the lawn as if they had all the energy in the world.

"Morgan."

He stopped in his tracks at the husky whisper from the shadows at the corner of the building. Tyler glanced around to make sure nobody was watching him. "What have you got, Leroy?"

The agent sidled up to Tyler's side, ducking his head to hide his face. "Having a good time with the lady doc?" Leroy laughed. "We'll have to talk to Alan about this. I hear you're drinking punch and eating cookies with a beautiful woman, while I'm drinking warm beer and rotgut whiskey with a bunch of smelly cowboys."

"That's the luck of the draw, King. What's the latest on the Malone gang?"

"Spotted about twenty miles west, and moving toward Omega. They keep a few miles ahead of us. Watch your back." He lifted his gaze past Tyler's shoulder. "Give my best to your fiancée." The agent slipped away into the shadows as if he had never been there.

Without turning his head, Tyler knew that Analise stood a few feet behind him. "Who were you talking to?" She stepped to his side.

"Just one of the kids." He caught both of her gloved hands in his. "What are you doing out here?"

"I came out to see the stars."

He laughed, lifting his gaze to follow hers. "Isn't that the star we spotted the other night? The one you claim led Onasis to safety?"

"I believe it is. And I like to think it's my special star."

"Then I give it to you." He lifted her hands to his lips and pressed kisses to the tops of her gloves. "And whenever you look at it, remember this night. And me."

"If you promise to remember me." Her soft voice drove deep into his heart.

Although he would soon leave, Tyler knew he would never forget her. "I promise." He tugged her closer into his chest. "Would you mind if I kissed you to seal our bargain?"

"I think I'd like it," she admitted, more to herself than him.

Tyler tugged her deeper into the shelter of the building. Across the lawn he spotted shadows under the trees, lovers seeking a moment away from the prying eyes of family and friends. Music drifted from the open doors, and light slanted through the windows. Shouts of children enjoying a late night outdoors sang in the air. But here, in the darkness, they were the only people in the world.

His mouth settled completely on hers, sipping gently, sweetly. Her fingers clutched his jacket, tugging him closer than was decent. He groaned deep in his throat, she answered with a moan of her own. The kiss devastated her senses. Analise couldn't think or consider what was happening.

A little voice deep inside reminded her about the last time she'd slipped off into the shadows and was swept off her feet by a man. That had been the beginning of her affair that had left her broken and shattered. Her poor heart remained scarred from Victor's deception. It couldn't stand being broken again.

She had to remember that this was all make-believe, like a play on the stage. The engagement wasn't real, and the kisses were only part of the masquerade. At least she already knew how this one would end. Locking her emotions away, she pushed gently on his chest. Hard muscles flexed under her fingers, and his heart pounded like thunder.

She stroked her fingers along his jaw, and the stubble of dark whiskers added to her fantasy. "I'm not so sure it would be wise to let Millie or my father catch us out here. He does own a shotgun, you know."

"Then I suppose we had better return to the party. People will start looking for us."

"Yes." She stepped away, only to be pulled back into his arms.

He planted a light kiss on her mouth. "Let's go face the music. But don't dance with any more cocky cowboys."

She smiled, surprised at the hint of jealousy in his voice. "I'm certain they mean no harm."

"*Petite*, you don't know cowboys."

"I can't be impolite. What excuse would I use?"

"Just tell them you're engaged to marry a dangerous man." His smile was just a touch too serious to be a jest. She remembered that at times he carried a gun, but she suspected he was more dangerous to her heart than to any brash young cowboy.

For the remainder of the evening, Tyler remained pressed to Analise's side. When she was approached by a young man to dance, he spirited her away, taking her for an awkward spin around the dance floor. By evening's end, Analise was left wondering how much of his behavior was for show—or if any of it was real.

She lay in her bed that night recalling their banter and the kisses they had shared. A part of her wanted it all to be real, while the realist in her knew it was only pretend. Just for a little while, she would enjoy the attentions of a handsome man. Experience had taught her that it would end all too soon. But this time she would have her clinic and her work to occupy her mind. And she vowed to keep her heart intact.


Analise sat at her desk Monday afternoon trying to study the latest medical journal from back East. It seemed she spent more time studying about medicine than practicing her skills. An earlier visit to the bank had proved fruitful. Mr. Winters had been certain that he could convince the bank officers to rent the Onasis house on Athena Street for the clinic. They would prefer a buyer for the foreclosed property, but she did not have the funds for purchase. Her little cash would have to go for equipment and furnishings. Unless the bank received an offer to purchase, the house would be hers.

She shoved aside the journal, and as usual, her thoughts drifted to Tyler Goodfellow. A delicious shiver raced over her. She recalled how tender he'd been when they'd looked up at the star together. It was true: no matter where or when she would look up at the stars, she would always remember him. In her heart, she'd whispered the wish she couldn't voice aloud. A wish for the miracle of love.

But Analise DeLery didn't deserve love. Everything in her life was a farce, a lie. She wasn't the pure virginal lady doctor she portrayed so effectively. Even the engagement was a lie. She wasn't engaged to be married, she was engaged to be rejected.

She wondered about Tyler. Over the past two weeks, she'd seen him set his jaw a time or two as if controlling a temper, and she knew he carried a gun on occasion. He was a mysterious man who kept his own counsel. He'd mentioned little about his past, except about losing his wife and baby. Never had he told her of a previous occupation or where he was from, if he had family—parents, siblings, relatives. This man was as mysterious as an Egyptian tomb.

She hadn't seen Tyler since Sunday night supper. After they had eaten, Tyler and her father had retired to the study for a game of chess. Millie had sidetracked Analise into talking about the wedding as if it was really going to take place. As usual, Tyler had conducted the church service. Maybe it was curiosity about their engagement, but the congregation was more crowded than usual. Even Oscar Hennessey had attended with Audrey.

That morning, Tyler had left the house before she had risen, as was his custom. She often wondered what he did all day. Where did he go? It seemed strange that he spent so much time in the woods alone, or with Steven.

As if conjured out of her thoughts, her brother raced into the office at a full run. The boy never walked when he could run. He skidded to a halt and tossed his schoolbooks on her desk. His hair was damp, and his overalls hung by one strap. Steven kept the housekeeper busy sewing buttons on his clothes.

"Steven, quit running. Your mother warned you about running in the house."

"Yeah, yeah, I heard it all. This time it's important."

"What is it? What did you do now?"

He swiped his hair out of his eyes. "It ain't me. It's some guy. I was on my way home from school when he stopped me. He said he needs a doctor."

Her spirits lifted. "Papa is making a house call, so since I'm the only doctor here, I'll take care of it."

"Are you sure?" Her brother lowered his voice. "He looks kind of rough, like an outlaw or something."

"Is the man injured?"

"He said it's his friend. The hombre is real bad off. Fell from his horse and can't be moved. He wants the doc to come with him and take care of the guy."

"Where is he?"

Steven glanced around to see if the fellow had followed him. "I told him to come in, but he said he's too dirty. Said he'll meet us behind the woodshed."

She thought for a moment about the situation. "Run on down to the livery and tell Horace I need a wagon and horses." She thought for a moment. "Is Mr. Goodfellow handy?"

"No, neither is Mr. Oscar. I can drive you out there. I can handle a team as good as anybody." Again he took off at a trot.

Analise bit her lip. Going off with some stranger wasn't the smartest thing to do. But last time things had worked out fine and she had saved two lives. She girded her strength. As a country doctor, she would be called on many times to go out into the countryside. Papa seemed unconcerned and did this every day. Here was her chance to prove her worth as a doctor to her father and to the community.

By the time she had gathered her medical supplies and closed her bag, Steven was at the rear porch with the team and wagon. Millie was at one of her meetings, so Analise left a note informing her and Papa that she and Steven were on a mission of mercy.

Her brother guided the team out of the yard, where they were met by a man at the rear of the property. She shivered at the sight of the road-weary man. His clothing was covered with dust, and he appeared to not have bathed or shaved in days. A shiver raced up her spine.

"Where's the doc?" he growled, approaching the wagon.

"I am the doctor," she informed him in no uncertain terms. "What's wrong with your friend?"

His gaze touched her from head to toe, his eyes dark and wild. "He's got a broke leg, and maybe his arm too. Let's go," he ordered with a strong Southern drawl.

Like the last time she went out on a call, they followed their guide. The route appeared familiar—the streams, meadows, winding road. After a while, she realized they were headed toward Alex and Polly's place. Then they turned west and neared the cabin where she and Tyler had spent their night together. Strange that this man should be leading her toward a deserted cabin. A bead of perspiration rolled down her back. Fear followed. She wondered if she had made a mistake in trusting this stranger.

"This is where Mr. Goodfellow and I spent that night during the storm," she whispered to Steven. "It's deserted."

"Not any more," her brother answered. He gestured to the three horses tethered at the door.

Steven tugged on the lines and stopped the team. Their guide leaped down and raced toward Analise. The door of the cabin burst open, and three rough-looking men pointed rifles at her.

"Where is the injured man?" she asked, studying the trio, who were armed to the hilt. Instinct told her to turn around and race back to town. The physician in her told her an injured man needed assistance. Ignoring the urge to cut and run, she jumped down from the high seat and picked up her medical bag.

A man who appeared at least ten years older than the others stepped forward, his face an angry mask. "What's wrong with you, Davis? You go to fetch the doc, and come back with a woman and kid. We ain't got time for no woman. We got to get the money and head to Mexico before those Pinkerton men catch up."

The one who had led them there, Davis, growled in his Southern drawl, "Harv, she said she's the doc."

"I am the doctor. Now where is the patient?" she asked, putting on a brave front in spite of her trembling knees.

Harv struck out and and grabbed Analise by the arm. "Let's get inside."

Davis shoved Steven toward the cabin. "Hey, leave me alone. I'll wait out here. I hate blood." Her brother tried to loose the man's grip.

He twisted the boy's arm. "Move, or the blood will be yours."

"What's going on?" Analise asked. "I'm here to help you."

He pushed her into the dirty cabin. She tripped and caught her balance before she fell.

Analise studied the men. They all stood straight and strong. There was nobody else in the cabin. Fear washed over her. "What do you want with me?" Heat drained from her body. While working at the clinic in New York, she'd seen the broken bodies of women after a gang of men got through with them. These men meant harm. And she and Steven were their victims.

"The money. Where is it?" The one called Harv approached Analise. Matted graying hair hung to his shoulders, thick whiskers covered his lower face, and his clothes were travel-worn and filthy.

She backed up a step and collided with the stone fireplace. "I don't have any money. If you've kidnapped us, our father doesn't have much, but he'll give you all he has." Now she wished she had carried a gun. She understood why even a gentleman like Tyler carried a weapon.

"Don't act stupid, lady. We want the money that Ace Malone had with him before he died." It was the other man who spoke. Shorter than the others, he resembled an angry bull.

Three men closed in on her. Confused, she shook her head to clear away the nightmare. "I don't know what you're talking about. I don't know any Ace Malone."

Harv reached out to slap her. She ducked and he caught the side of her head. Bells rang in her ears. "We want that money. Ace was my brother and those guards shot him. He's dead and we want it now."

Steven tugged free of his captor. "Leave her alone. She don't know nothing."

Analise rubbed her aching head. These men were killers. She read it in their eyes. Cruelty, hatred, and evil hovered like a fog around them. "Steven, no."

"What about you, kid? What do you know about the money?" Harv stepped forward as the leader.

"N . . . nothing."

"Ace had a bag full of money with him when he got away. But he was wounded. Did you see it? Did he give it to the doc?"

The boy cowered away from the outlaw. "No."

"I think you're lying, kid." He moved toward Analise. "This your maw?"

"I'm his sister," Analise said, struggling to hide her fear.

"You know how much a broken arm hurts? If I break your sister's arm, she won't have nobody to help her." He leaned into Steven's face. Her brother looked as if he were about to vomit. "You want that to happen to her? Or do you know what a man can do to a woman? There are four of us here." His face twisted into a grimace. "When we get through with her, ain't nobody gonna be able to put her together again."

Nausea roiled in her stomach and threatened to choke her.

"Let us go, and I'll get the money for you." Steven grunted.

"Steven, what do you know about this?" she asked, her voice too much like the croak of a frog.

"I found the bag."

"What do you mean?"

Her brother ducked his head. "I was with that man when he was dying. He told me he hid the money out near Poseidon Creek. I found it a couple of days ago."

Analise shook her brother by the shoulders. "Steven, how could you not tell anybody?"

"I don't know."

The man with the Southern accent grabbed Steven's arm. "Tell you what, kid. They'll keep the lady here, while me and you go get the money. When we come back with the money, we'll let her go good as new."

"Okay, I'll do it. If you hurt my sister, I'll kill you."

They laughed, an evil sound that sent shivers up her spine. "We're scared. Get going, kid. And don't go to that sheriff. We'll be watching every move you make."

Steven nodded. He looked at Analise, an apology in his gaze. Tears dampened his cheeks. Fear twisted like a snake around her heart.

Davis grabbed Steven's arm. "Let's go, kid. I'll make sure you don't tell the sheriff or some Pinkerton man."

"What do you mean, you're going with him?" Harv stepped between Davis and Steven.

"Somebody's got to keep an eye on the kid," Davis stated, setting his hand on the gun at his hip. "We don't want him telling the sheriff."

"Yeah. And when the kid hands the money over to you, what's gonna stop you from running off and forgetting about us?"

Davis spun on the other three men. "What are you talking about, Shorty? I wouldn't do that."

"How can we be sure?" The fourth man, the one

with a knife in his hand, spoke up for the first time. Of them all, he was the most frightening.

"Joe, Shorty, Harv, don't you trust me?"

"Why don't all of you go with him? Steven can give you the money, and you can be on your way," Analise offered.

"So you can run away, and your brother can notify the law?" Joe flicked his knife at her. "That won't work."

"You can tie me up, and be on your way with the money."

Harv considered the situation for a minute. "Tell you what. We'll let the kid go, but we'll keep the woman here. If he's not back by dark, we'll kill her. But if he notifies the law, we'll kill her real slow."

Analise cringed. Being alone with these outlaws was a fate worse than death. Harv caught the frightened look on her face. "Don't worry, lady. All we want is the money. If the kid comes back, we'll let you go. Until then, you're safe with us." He shook a finger at Steven. "Until sundown."

"Hurry, Steven," she whispered.

"And, kid, if anybody follows you, both you and your sister are dead."

# Chapter 9

Frustration burned like molten lava in Tyler's gut. Not only had he failed to locate the stolen money, he also ached to be with Analise. To hold her, to make love to her.

After another morning spent in a fruitless search for the money, he was tired, hot, and out of sorts. By afternoon, he was ready to give up the search and return to the house. With Steven in school, he had continued his search on his own. On his way back to the house, Tyler walked slowly along the edge of the creek, keeping his eyes open for disturbed grass. Spotting a footprint in the dirt, he stuck the end of his cane into the bottom of a dead tree. The cane struck something soft. On hands and knees, he reached into the hole and felt a bag. A cloth satchel.

Excitement sizzled through him. He tugged the bag free. Wells Fargo was stamped on the bag in big black letters. He'd found it. Expectations high, he hurriedly opened the bag.

Empty. He turned it over and shook it. The bank

notes and silver coins were gone. Tyler sank to the ground and banged his cane against the bag. All his work for nothing; somebody had gotten there before him. The outlaws? He studied the area around the tree, spotting only one set of footprints and a button. A button like one missing from a boy's overalls. Like the ones Mrs. Hennessey was continually sewing on Steven's overalls. The scamp had found the bag and emptied it.

Taking the bag as evidence, Tyler raced back to the house. It was time for the young man to come clean and tell the truth. The money belonged to Wells Fargo and the Sunshine Mining Company. By recovering the stolen payroll, the boy was entitled to a reward, at least a ten percent reward. Quite a handsome sum for a youngster.

The house was quiet when he entered through the kitchen. A strange wagon was parked outside the gate. A note on the table from Analise said she was off on a mission of mercy, with no mention of where she had gone. The hair on the back of his neck stood on end. Had she really been foolish enough to go off with only Steven? He shook his head. Surely she could have waited for her father or Oscar.

He wondered if the DeLery family had company. No voices came from the parlor or the doctor's office. Silently, Tyler climbed the stairs, ready to search Steven's room for the stolen money.

He opened the door and stepped into the boy's room. Overall-clad legs stuck out from under the bed. Tyler sat on the bed and waited until Steven shimmied back out. "Looking for something?"

Steven jerked upright with a burlap sack clutched to his chest.

"What do you have there?" He snatched the sack away before the boy could react.

"It's mine," Steven grunted. "I found it. Finders keepers."

"And was it originally in this bag?" Tyler held up the Wells Fargo satchel.

Steven's face turned white. "Yeah. Give it to me. I've got to have it."

"You know this doesn't belong to you. It belongs to the Sunshine Mining Company. It was stolen over a month ago by that outlaw Oscar buried behind the church."

The boy's face turned white. "I know. But I got to have it."

"Sorry, son. This money is going back to the rightful owners. I'll see that you get a reward for returning it."

"You don't understand." Fat tears streaked down his grimy cheeks. "I got to take it to them. They'll kill my sister if I don't."

His words hit Tyler like the kick of a bull. "Who? What are you talking about?"

"Bandits, outlaws, they said one of them was hurt and needed a doctor, so Analise and I went out to help. They captured her and said that if I don't bring them this money by sundown, they'll kill her, or worse."

A thousand fears bombarded Tyler. The Malone gang had Analise. How did they know about her? Had he been right all along, and she'd been somehow involved with Ace? It hardly seemed possible that a saver of lives would be mixed up with killers. None of that mattered. Those were dangerous men and he couldn't let anything happen to her.

"Where are they?"

"In some deserted cabin. Analise said it was where you spent that night together in the storm." He reached for the sack. "You got to let me go. They're waiting for me. Said if I tell anybody, they'll hurt her bad."

Anger sizzled through him like lightning. He knew what men could do to a woman. They couldn't be trusted not to harm her or to let her go. He swore under his breath that if a hair on her head was touched, he would personally skin them alive.

"Okay. Take the sack, and go back. Don't worry about a thing. You'll both be okay." It was a promise he would keep, or die trying.

He watched from the window of his room as the youngster mounted the wagon and took off. Tyler quickly strapped on his gunbelt and holster. He also checked the ammunition in the gun in the shoulder holster. He grabbed his rifle and saddlebags with additional ammo and set out for the livery on a run. His horse had been stabled there for the past few weeks, ready for this action when the time came. He couldn't afford to take the time to look for Leroy or any of the other agents who might be in town. Analise and Steven were in danger and he would handle this mission on his own.

With the wagon, Steven was forced to stay on the road, while Tyler, on horseback, was able to cut across country. He was also familiar with the terrain around the cabin. He'd studied it in detail when he'd walked in the early morning to control his passion after spending the night with Analise in his arms.

The very idea that these outlaws might hurt her urged him to take chances to beat Steven to the cabin. He already knew where he would hide to keep watch. If the bandits kept their word and released both Analise and Steven upon receiving the money, he could wait until the pair were safely out of sight before approaching the cabin and capturing the outlaws. Or, he would wait until they came out and pick them off, one by one. Then he would settle with Analise.

He reached the knoll above the cabin as Steven approached the doorway. The sun had dropped behind the nearby hills. The deadline given by the bandits was almost up. With care to stay down and out of sight, Tyler stretched out on his stomach, his Remington rifle in his hands. Summoning a patience he didn't feel, he waited for the tableau below him to unfold. It was like watching a play on the stage.

Steven drove the wagon up to the door. Two men raced out to meet him. They dragged the boy from the seat and snatched the bag from the floor of the wagon.

"It had better all be here," the taller of the men said. Even from a distance Tyler recognized Harvey Malone, Ace's brother. The Pinkerton office in Denver had sent drawings of the men believed to be part of the gang. Harv glanced around, studying the line of trees where Tyler hid. "You tell anybody?"

The youngster shook his head.

"Were you followed?" Harv shoved Steven toward the door.

"Where's my sister?" Steven struggled against the strength of the outlaw. "I brought you the money, let us go."

Voices carried far in the dry cool air. The laughter of the men sent a chill down Tyler's spine. He had no idea how Analise had survived her ordeal, or if she was still alive. Even if she'd been involved with Ace, these were dangerous men. There was no guarantee they wouldn't hurt her. Pain twisted in his chest. He tightened his grip on the rifle.

The men shoved Steven into the cabin and disappeared inside. Impatience gnawed at Tyler like a dog with a bone.

From his distance he heard nothing from inside. A thin wisp of smoke came from the chimney—the only sign of life. Four horses were tethered where they could munch on the grass.

He waited, then a shadow moved in the trees far to his right. Another outlaw? One keeping watch?

Tyler slipped behind a tree, careful to stay hidden. The shadow disappeared. He strained his eyes and spotted a place where the tall grass was flattened. Taking his time, Tyler carefully slipped behind a man lying flat on his stomach, a bare shadow in the growing darkness. As if sensing his presence, the man jumped to his feet, and spun to face Tyler, a rifle in his hand. They faced each other armed and ready. The man stared, his long black hair lifted in the wind.

"Alex?" Tyler whispered.

"Deacon?" The answering whisper carried on the wind.

Relief surged through Tyler. An ally. A man he could trust.

Not wanting to be seen or heard from the cabin, he gestured toward the copse of trees behind them. Safely hidden, he turned to the younger man. "What are you doing here?"

"The same as you, I guess. Looking for the lady doctor." Alex glanced through the trees to the cabin with only a dim light coming through the rag that covered the window. "Manny was out chasing rabbits when he saw some men grab the doc and a boy. He got scared, so he came for me. I was trying to figure out what was happening when you found me." He looked at Tyler with a sense of awe. "For a white man, you are a great tracker. Few men would have spotted me."

"I almost didn't see you. But I was watching for the unexpected. You weren't."

"Is the doc in there? Is she in danger?"

"Yeah. They're outlaws after a payroll that was stolen over a month ago. They have her, her brother, and the money. I've been tracking the gang for weeks."

"You? Tracking outlaws?"

Tyler sighed and wiped his damp palms on his trousers. "I'm a Pinkerton agent. That's why I couldn't marry you and Polly."

Alex shook his head. "I thought you were different from any church fellow I ever met." He gestured to the cabin. "How many?"

"Four, I believe. They're all inside with her."

"What's your plan?"

"We wait. If we rush in, they might hurt the doc or the kid. When they come out, we can pick them off one by one. But we'll do it quietly. No sound. No gun shots. We don't want to give any warning."

They dropped to the ground and waited.

After what seemed like an eternity, the door opened. On alert, Tyler sighted with his rifle, ready to pull the trigger.

One man exited. Alone. He moved to the wagon and unhitched the horses. He led the team toward the other horses and tied them there.

Tyler's heart sank deeper when the outlaw returned to the cabin. Clearly they were not going to release Analise and Steven. He prayed as he'd never prayed before for the safety of two people he cared for.

Darkness descended quickly in the hills. The moon was a thin sliver, but the stars shone brightly—one brighter than the others. He uttered a silent prayer for their safety.

With no sign of either Steven or Analise, he was unable to stand the suspense. Tyler signaled Alex to wait in hiding while he crept toward the cabin. He ran from tree to tree, and crawled through the tall grass on his stomach. Not making a sound, he sidled up to the cabin. Pressing his back to the wall, he approached the single window. Loud voices came through the walls.

"You said we're going to get equal shares." The harsh voice was full of menace.

"Look, Ace died, so as his brother, I should get his share."

"Harv, are you nuts? There's four of us. Four shares."

Tyler eased closer to listen. Through the torn rag that covered the window, he tried to see inside. The only light was from the small fire in the fireplace. All he could make out were the forms of four men squatting on the floor, the burlap sack in the middle.

"You said you would let us go when you got the money." Steven's voice rang over the noises of the outlaws.

"Shut up, kid. We decided to take you and the woman with us. You're our protection against the law."

"You promised," Analise said. Her voice was strong and authorative. So she was alive, not injured or too frightened to argue.

He listened for any hint that she knew these men or was involved with them. They clearly weren't cutting her in on their loot.


Analise pulled her brother to the corner, where she huddled away from the men.

"Are you all right?" Steven asked.

She refused to admit how frightened she'd been alone with these men. Now, in the darkness, with only the dim fire for light, the men were even scarier. "Yes. They made threats, but they didn't hurt me." She whispered to Steven. "What were you doing with all that money?"

"I found it. That outlaw that died told me he hid it. So I've been looking for it," he whispered softly.

"Is that where you've been going every day when you said you were fishing?"

Steven ducked his head. "Yeah."

"Why didn't you turn it over to the law or Papa?"

"I wanted to keep it for myself. And look what I did. I got you mixed up in this."

"Hey, you two, shut up. We're trying to count." Harv shot an angry glare at them.

"Don't worry. We'll get out of this." She prayed they would. These men were very dangerous, and wouldn't hesitate to kill them both.

"*Monsieur Bon Homme* knows," Steven whispered.

Analise stared at her brother. He never spoke French, and his translation of Mr. Goodfellow's name came as a shock. He had told Tyler. They had a chance. If Tyler had notified the sheriff or other lawmen, help could be on the way.

"What did the kid say?" Shorty growled at them.

"He said he wants to go home."

Harv laughed. "He'll go, when we get through with you."

Analise cringed. So far they hadn't abused her or misused her. But there was no telling what these evil men had in mind for a woman and boy.


Under cover of darkness, Tyler worked his way toward the horses. He needed to get the men outside, one by one. The easiest way was to cause a commotion with the horses. Picking up a stone, he tossed it toward the animals—close enough to spook one of them. Then he let out a howl like a coyote, a skill he'd learned from an Indian scout.

The sound echoed through the hills, carried on the breeze. An answering howl came from the trees where he'd left Alex. The horse whinnied and reared up. The other horses joined in raising a ruckus.

Tyler pressed against the wall as the cabin door opened. Harv stuck his head out. "Something spooked those horses. Shorty, go see what's out there."

"Go yourself. I don't want you to cheat me out of my share." The voice came from inside.

"It's all divided up, take your share with you."

A short, stubby man exited the cabin, carrying a sawed-off shotgun.

Tyler waited, not even daring to breathe. The outlaw moved toward the horses, walked around them, then cursed the animals for disturbing him. Satisfied that there was nothing to fear, he propped the shotgun against the wall. He slowly unbuttoned his trousers and relieved himself.

Tyler almost laughed at the way the man was making things so easy for him. Like a wisp of smoke, he eased up behind the man, and anchored his arm around the bandit's neck. For a brief second, he considered killing the man. Instead, he chose to disable him by applying pressure to the neck. Without a sound, the outlaw slumped to the ground. Alex appeared out of nowhere. With his help, Tyler removed the man's weapons, and quickly and efficiently tied him up with his own belt. He shoved the outlaw's dirty kerchief in his mouth and pulled him deep into the shadows. One down, three to go. Alex drifted back to the trees while Tyler crouched under the window.

"Shorty, you got lost out there?" Harv shouted from inside the cabin.

When no answer came, the outlaw stuck his head out the door. "Dammit man, what are you doing?"

"I gotta go out," another man said. "I'll see what's keeping Shorty." He eased through the doorway and headed away from the cabin toward the trees beyond the horses.

Perfect, Tyler thought. These fools were like sitting ducks in a rain barrel, waiting to be picked off. Moving from shadow to shadow, Tyler crept up behind the second outlaw. This time he wasn't as lucky. One of the horses made a sound, catching the man's attention. He glanced over his shoulder in time to spot Tyler a few feet away. Before he could shout and alert his comrades, Tyler leaped on his back, tumbling him to the ground. Taken by surprise, the man had little time to fight back. Somehow the outlaw managed to get in one hard sock to Tyler's jaw. The taste of his own blood and the thought of Analise in danger fired his strength. Tyler rolled over on the bandit and pressed his arm against the man's windpipe, cutting off his breath. He forced himself to stop before he killed a man who deserved to die. But he would let the law punish this one.

"Need help, Deacon?" Alex whispered.

Tyler shrugged. "Tie him up and take him and two of the horses into the trees." With quick efficient movements, the younger man did as instructed. He dragged his captive into the shadows of the trees.

While Tyler crept back to the cabin, Alex untied two of the horses and moved them into the trees, far out of sight. If it weren't for Analise and Steven being in danger, Tyler would be enjoying the contest of wills and cunning.

Little noise came from the shack. He still couldn't see anything inside. Footsteps from inside grew louder. He slunk back just in time as a hand shoved the rag aside from the window.

"It's so dark, I can't see a thing out there." The curtain fell. "Where the hell are Shorty and Joe? How long does it take?"

Another man grunted. "Don't know. They're so stupid, they must have got lost finding their way back."

"Or they left." Analise's voice was a weak whisper.

"They took their money with them. They must have taken off before the law got after them."

"Shut up!"

Tyler recognized Harvey Malone's harsh voice.

"The law's been after us for weeks, and they ain't caught up yet."

"Nothin' we can do about them. Let 'em go. We can travel faster without them. All we need is the woman and kid. They're our safe passage to Mexico."

*Come on,* Tyler thought, *send out another man.* Already the odds are even. Two to two, the bandits didn't stand a chance. However, he couldn't rush in and put Analise and Steven in danger. He would continue to bide his time.

Analise wondered what had happened to the two outlaws. Her gut instinct told her that they hadn't run away. If Steven had told Tyler, he may have gotten help and was even now out there with the sheriff.

If she could help them, then nobody would get hurt, especially Tyler. He wasn't a lawman. What could he do against armed outlaws? In the corner, she carefully opened her medical bag and slipped her hand in. Both men were at the small window, looking for their missing companions. She closed her fingers on a small bottle of laudanum and slipped it into the pocket of her apron. All she needed was the chance to slip a few drops into the whiskey they had been drinking all evening.

"Stay here," Analise whispered softly as she stood and stretched.

Davis, the man with the slow Southern drawl, turned to her. "Where do you think you're going, woman?"

"Nowhere. I'm just stretching." She took a step toward where they had been squatting on the floor to

divide up the money. She picked up the whiskey bottle they had been sharing.

"What are you doing?" Harv shot an angry glare at
her.

"I'm thirsty. May I have a drink?"

They seemed distracted by the missing men. "If
you can stand it, go ahead."

She picked up the half-empty bottle. Turning her
back on the men, she opened the small vial of the
drug and poured the contents into the whiskey. Then
she pretended to sip from the bottle. She coughed
and gagged as if she had really sampled the strong,
smelly drink. She returned the vial to her pocket and
wiped her mouth with her apron. Analise replaced
the liquor where she had found it.

"You think we ought to go out and look for them?"
Davis asked. "Something just ain't right. Me and
Shorty was gonna head for New Orleans to spend
our money." He shot a glance at Analise. "She reminds me of those gals I met that time I went down
along the levee. She even talks like them."

He moved from the window toward her. "The whore
even had hair this color." A dirty hand snaked out
and tugged on a loose tendril of Analise's hair. "She
talked all that Frenchy talk. Really got me going." He
stroked the hair between his fingers. "Say something
Frenchy to me, darlin'."

*"Allez vous faire voir."* In honeyed tones she told
him "go to hell."

"That sounds nice and sweet. Like you're ready to
throw up your skirts for me." He twisted his fingers in
her hair. "How about you and me, sherrie? I got lots
of money to spend on you."

He grabbed her upper arm, dragging her to her
feet. "Let's you and me go outside. I'll show you what
that sweet talk does to me."

"Let go of her!" Steven yelled. "She's my sister!" The boy leaped on the man.

In one easy swing, Davis shook Steven off like an annoying insect. "Stay out of it kid, or I'll cut you into pieces with my bowie knife."

Analise stepped in front of her brother. "Leave him alone, he's just a boy."

The man laughed. "Hell, I wasn't much older than him when I killed a carpetbagger back in 'Bama."

She cringed. The man was truly dangerous. "Why don't you just have a drink? He can't hurt you."

Harv marched over to them. "I'm thinking we ought to head out like the others. No use hanging around here until morning. Somebody might start missing these two, and come looking for them."

Davis took a long swig from the whiskey bottle. "This stuff gets worse every time I drink it." He passed the bottle to Harv. "I'll hitch up the wagon for me and the woman. You take the boy on my horse."

"How about I take the woman on your horse, and you take the boy in the wagon." Harv stood over Davis as if challenging him to defy his authority. "I got plans for her myself. Those Comancheros in Mexico will pay a pretty penny for a white woman. And her being a doc makes her even more valuable."

Fear raced up her spine. Sell her? In Mexico? She prayed that somehow Tyler had gotten help, or better still, that they would both drink the doctored liquor and pass out.

"Isn't it dangerous to try to go at night, especially if you're not familiar with the territory?" She fought to keep the tremor from her voice. They needed to stay until daylight. By then help could come, or they would fall asleep from the drug. She picked up the whiskey bottle and pretended a sip then passed it on to Davis. He took a long swig, then corked the bottle and shoved it under his arm.

Harv snatched the bottle away from Davis. "Take the kid and go hitch up the wagon. Me and her will be right out." After taking a swallow, he spit out the drink. "I ain't never tasted anything this bad. With all the money I got, I should have the best bourbon they make in Kentucky, not some rotgut that burns holes in a man's stomach."

Analise ignored him and picked up her medical bag. "You aren't going to get far, you know. Especially with a woman tagging along. You should just leave Steven and me behind. There's no way we can do anything to you."

He caught her arm. "I said you're going with me to Mexico. Nobody's going to take a shot at me if you're in front of me."

"Only a coward would hide behind a woman's skirts."

"I'd rather be a live coward than a dead hero." He shoved her toward the door.


Tyler watched from the shadows as Davis and Steven left the cabin. If he moved too fast, either Steven or Analise could get hurt. But he had to stop the men before they got away.

He'd heard their plans for Analise, proof she wasn't part of their schemes. They were in for a few surprises. When he got through with the men it would be a long time before they kidnapped another woman.

Davis shoved Steven to the horses and grabbed the reins of the team. Occupied with hitching up the horses, Davis didn't pay attention to the boy. "Give me a hand, kid," he shouted. "Hey! Where ya going?"

As if the boy could read Tyler's mind, he dashed into the thicket of trees. Let Alex take care of the boy. Tyler had plans for the man. Staying away from the door of the cabin, Tyler circled and came face to face with the outlaw. In the darkness, Tyler, clad all in black, was nearly invisible. Davis stopped and reached for his gun. Tyler couldn't allow a gunshot that would warn the man who had Analise, but he knew more tricks than a magician on a stage. He pivoted on one foot, swung around, and kicked the gun out of the outlaw's hand. It landed with a thud on the ground. The man yelped in pain. In another quick movement, Tyler's foot connected with Davis's jaw. The man went down like a fallen tree.

Like a shadow, Alex was again at his side. "You're having all the fun. You should have saved him for me." Alex quickly and efficiently tied up the outlaw and dragged him away.

His heart thumping in double-time, Tyler moved toward the horses. The excitement had them tugging at their tethers and squealing in fear.

Harv raced from the cabin, tugging Analise behind him. "What's going on here? Davis, where are you?"

Tyler stepped out, his rifle held loosely in his hand. "He's kind of tied up right now. You'll have to deal with me."

"Who the hell are you?" He tugged Analise in front of him like a shield.

"I'm your worst nightmare."

"Tyler," Analise breathed his name.

"Let her go, Harv. This is between you and me."

In the dim starlight, he caught the flash of metal. Harv pressed the knife against Analise's throat. "It's between me and the lady. You come closer, and she's gone."

"You hurt one hair on her head and I'll skin you alive with that knife."

"Big man talking. I've got the woman. Put down your weapons and get out of my way."

"You're not going to get away, Harv. Ace didn't get away, and you won't either." Tyler tossed down the rifle and unhitched his gun belt. He dropped it to the ground. "See? No weapons. Let's handle this like men. Just you and me."

Harv laughed. "I'm getting on my horse and taking her with me. You're staying here." He shoved Analise toward the horses. As he got closer, both horses galloped away.

The outlaw momentarily dropped his guard. She slammed the heavy medical bag against his legs. He yelped, and loosened his grip. She spun away from him and raced toward Tyler.

"Run, Analise!" Tyler yelled, diving at the outlaw. Harv dodged the onslaught and came at Tyler with his knife.

Harv slashed, and Tyler sidestepped out of his reach. Analise stood frozen to the spot, unable to tear her eyes from the scene unfolding before her. In the starlit night, the knife flashed as the outlaw swung at Tyler. She prayed that the man she loved would survive the fight. Harv was an outlaw, an experienced fighter—a ruthless man who knew no mercy. Tyler was a kind, gentle man, a preacher accustomed to using words, not weapons. However, the man grinning at the outlaw like a wolf on the prowl showed no sign of fear or misgivings. And no sign of the timid man she'd come to love.

"Come on, Harv, let's see what you can do with that knife," he taunted. Tyler leaped from side to side, avoiding every lunge of the outlaw's knife. He slipped off his jacket and dropped it on the ground, along with his shoulder holster and gun. The man staring death in the face was neither timid nor meek. He faced the outlaw's assault with boldness and recklessness.

She sensed movement at her side and spotted her

brother watching wide-eyed at the action. Alex slid from the shadows and relaxed against a tree. So Tyler had brought help. "Help him," she shouted.

Alex shrugged. "The hombre can handle himself."

Analise stared, mesmerized by the action. She felt as if she was at a theater, watching a strange dance unfold on the stage.

The outlaw shifted the knife from hand to hand, as if to show his expertise with the weapon. "You won't be laughing when I cut out your heart."

"We'll see about that."

This time when the knife flashed out, Tyler hesitated a heartbeat too long, and the blade slashed across his upper arm. Blood spilled out, soaking his shirt. Analise bit back a scream. Tyler spun away, and glanced down at the blood as if he hadn't even felt the wound.

Again Harv dove at him, knife extended. Tyler sidestepped, caught the outlaw's wrist and twisted until the blade dropped to the ground. Again the outlaw managed to get loose. Blood ran down Tyler's arm, soaking his hand. Tears poured down Analise's cheek. She loved him so much, and she was about to lose him.

Steven snatched up the rifle from the ground. "I'll shoot him! Move away!" the youngster shouted to be heard above the grunts and moans of the combatants.

Alex snatched the weapon from the boy's hand. "This is between men. A man with right on his side does not need help."

Tyler shifted from foot to foot. "Guess I'll quit playing with you, Harv, and finish the job."

With a flash of movement, Tyler pivoted like a ballet dancer, and with the heel of his boot caught the outlaw on the side of his head. The man dropped to the ground, shaking his head. Tyler knelt on the outlaw's chest, and pressed his elbow to the man's throat. "One move, Harv, and I'll crush your throat."

Alex moved toward them, the rifle extended. "I've got him covered. He won't get away."

A huge bruise spread across the man's jaw. He moaned.

"I think you broke his jaw," Analise whispered, still shaken from what she'd seen.

"He'll live. Until the law hangs him." Tyler got to his feet and took the rifle from Alex. "I'll cover him while you get a rope and tie him up." He pressed the rifle to the outlaw's heart. "Now, Harv, tell me about your plans for the lady."

The outlaw tried to talk, but his words came out as a string of angry curses, barely understandable.

Within minutes, Alex had the man's hands tied behind his back. "Where are our other prisoners?" Tyler asked.

"Under the trees."

"Good work, Alex." Tyler dropped his hand to Steven's shoulder. "You did a great job taking care of your sister, son. You'll make a fine lawman someday."

Analise continued to stare. The sight of Tyler's blood dripping down his arm brought back her alarm. "You're hurt. Let me look at that."

He glanced down at his arm, as if noticing the injury for the first time. "You're right. Good thing there's a doc handy."

# Chapter 10

It was over.

Tyler had captured the four outlaws, he had recovered the money, and Analise and Steven were safe from harm. Now he had to deal with his relationship with Analise—if they still had a relationship after she learned the truth about him.

By the time Tyler, Alex, and Steven had loaded the trussed-up men into the back of the wagon, the pink-streaked sky was chasing away the darkness of night. He sent the bandits with Alex and Steven into town, while he stayed behind with Analise. They would follow on the horses with the sack of money. He wasn't taking any chances on losing it again.

Alone with Analise, it was time to face her with the truth. Tyler didn't fear men, or many things in life, but he was scared to death of Analise's reaction—of hurting her. How was he going to explain his lies and deception? Plus his own doubts about her integrity. That would be her toughest medicine to swallow.

"Will you please let me look at that cut before it becomes infected?" Analise dragged him to the damp, cold ground where she had set her medical bag.

"Don't get upset, Doc. It's only a scratch and the bleeding has already stopped." By the expression on her face it was better not to argue. She had shown so much strength and courage during her ordeal, he knew it was best to settle down and do as instructed. He slipped out of his coat. Her eyes widened at the sight of the shoulder holster with the gun under his arm. He ignored her questioning glance.

With scissors from her kit, Analise cut off the sleeve of his shirt. The cut slashed across his upper arm was long but not deep. Analise dipped a clean cloth in alcohol and patted the injury.

"Ow, that burns worse than the cut. Be gentle, Doc, I'm a hero."

"Deacon Goodfellow, you are an idiot. What did you think you were doing?"

"Rescuing you and your brother."

"Ha! I didn't need rescuing. I already had a plan in place."

He looked at her with skepticism. "What kind of plan?"

"I laced their liquor with laudanum. A few drinks and they would be sound asleep. Didn't you hear Davis snoring in the back of the wagon?"

"You thought you could drug the men and escape? What if they didn't drink the whiskey? What then?" He stuttered at the thought of her foolhardy plan. "You're just lucky they didn't . . ." Tyler couldn't say the word of what could have happened to a woman in the hands of lawless men. "Abuse you."

"They were too involved with making sure they received their share of the loot. They mostly ignored us."

"I overheard Harv say he planned to sell you down in Mexico. I saved you from a fate worse than death."

She shivered. "I suppose you did. What I don't understand is how you did it all. There were four of them."

"Four to one. The odds were in my favor. I just picked them off one at a time. And I had Alex to back me up."

"You were unarmed against a man with a knife. An outlaw who's probably killed before." She rubbed harder than necessary to remove the dried blood.

He bit his lip to keep from laughing. Mocking her would only make her angrier. Her touch did more than soothe his cut. Her caring manner touched his heart as nothing had since he'd lost Abigail.

"Analise, believe me, I knew what I was doing."

She patted an ointment on the cut, then wrapped a clean bandage around his bicep. "Where did you learn to fight like that?"

"Finished doctoring me?"

"Yes." She snapped the medical bag shut. "For goodness sakes, Tyler, you're a . . . a, whatever, not a gunfighter." She paused, and stared into his eyes. "Or are you? Who are you? What are you?"

Tyler took a deep breath. With the vulnerable look in her eyes, he couldn't lie to her. It was past time for truth. "I'm a Pinkerton agent. My name is Tyler Morgan."

Her eyes grew wide. "I don't understand. You aren't a church official at all, or a deacon? Or anything?"

He ducked his head, ashamed of his lies and deception. "I've been on the trail of the Ace Malone gang for weeks. I used the cover to get information."

"You lied to me? About your identity? About everything?"

"Doc, let me explain."

"I really don't want to hear what you have to say." She started to stand. He caught her hand and tugged her back to the ground.

"You're going to listen to me. It's important."

She shrugged away from him, huddling in her shawl against the morning chill and against him.

Regardless of how much it would hurt her, he had to tell her the whole truth. "Over a month ago, Ace Malone and his gang stole a huge payroll going to the Sunshine Gold Mine, hundreds of miles north of here. They killed the Wells Fargo guard and a Pinkerton agent." He lifted his gaze to the skies, where the day was gradually gaining on them. Yet there it was, still shining in the dim daylight—their star, as if it were watching over them. He watched as it disappeared. "The agent was a friend of mine, a friend with a wife and two children."

Analise listened without speaking. Sympathy glittered in her eyes.

"In the holdup, Ace was wounded and another bandit killed. The posse chased them until another outlaw was shot. They scattered after that. We recovered the gold and silver, but Ace got away with a bag of bank notes and silver coins. Alan Pinkerton sent for me and I started tracking him. Since he was wounded, we thought he would have sought medical attention. His trail led to Omega. That's why I looked up the doctor in Omega, your father. I didn't know about you at the time. When Steven told me about the stranger who had died, I knew it had to be Ace."

Tyler paused to gather his thoughts. "I guessed he'd told Steven about the money, so I started looking for it."

"Steven didn't tell Papa or the sheriff." Analise was clearly shocked at her brother's duplicity. "Or me."

"He's a kid. Kids do stupid things. It was like a treasure hunt for him. He located the money, and he was willing to give it to the outlaws to save your life."

"Yes, he was very brave. He would have fought them all for me." Analise met Tyler's gaze, still questioning him. "But Tyler, why didn't you simply tell us who you were? That you were after a bandit. My father, we all would have done our best to help."

He sighed. Now came the hard part, the part that would hurt her worse. For the first time, he questioned his methods. "I didn't know who I could trust, so I decided not to trust anybody. I didn't want anyone to get involved and possibly get hurt. Look at what happened when the outlaws suspected you knew about the money."

"So you chose to lie to us."

After all that had happened, his reason seemed lame even to him. "It could be that I like wearing disguises, like I'm on the stage. Truth is, I didn't know who to trust. I didn't know your father. He could have been in cohoots with Ace, the reason that Ace came all the way to Omega to get treatment."

She glared at him. "My father is the most honest man I have ever met. He can't even tell a little white lie to save face."

"I know that."

"Tyler, what else did you think?" Her eyes grew wider. "You suspected me too, didn't you?"

He removed his hat and raked his fingers through his hair. "Analise . . ."

"Do not continue to lie to me. You thought that somehow I was involved with murderers and thieves." She jumped up and stomped away from him.

In a few long strides he caught up with her. "Listen, please. I had good reason to suspect everybody."

She set her hands on her hips and glared at him. "Everybody? I'm so glad I'm not alone. Did you think Millie would associate with those evil men? Mrs. Hennessey? Oscar? Or only Steven, Papa, and me?"

He caught her upper arms and shook her slightly. "Am I going to have to kiss you to keep you quiet?"

"You would kiss a woman who would consort with outlaws?"

Tired of arguing, he did what he'd wanted to do for hours. He pulled her hard against his chest and settled his lips on hers. The kiss was hard and demanding, filled with the need to know all was well, that the danger was past, and she was safe where she belonged—in his arms. She didn't struggle against him, neither did she give in. When her tears moistened his mouth, he ended the kiss, but he couldn't let her go. He snuggled her face into his neck and held on like a drowning man holding a life ring.

"Sweetheart, I didn't want to believe it. But I thought it too much of a coincidence—your arriving in Omega at about the same time as Ace." He spoke softly into her hair, pulled loose and falling down her back. "My informants told me he'd been seen in Denver a few days before the robbery with a dark-haired woman."

She gasped, and shoved against his chest. He let her go. "I suppose that's overwhelming evidence against me. Considering nearly half the women in the world have dark hair."

He reached out and brushed a tear from her cheek.

She slapped his hand away. "Why did you choose to pretend to be a deacon of all things?"

He shrugged. "People tend to trust church workers, and I had a better chance at learning the truth than coming as a lawman. If word had gotten out about Ace and the money, it would have started a treasure hunt and somebody could have gotten hurt. Look what happened to your brother."

"So you thought it was best to lie, to me, to everybody—about everything." Her voice broke, and he could hear the pain in her words. "You slept in my father's bed, you ate his food, and you deceived all of us. We trusted you."

"Analise, it's my job. I didn't want to lie. I'm very fond of you. In fact . . ." He paused just short of telling her that he was falling in love with her. Her feelings were too raw for her to understand. "Let's get back to town, and we can discuss our situation after we change and get something to eat."

"Yes, and I'm certain you have to finish your job."

"I have to see that those outlaws are properly locked up, and let Alex get back to his family." He followed at her heels to the horses.

"By the way, how were you able to enlist Alex in this mission?"

He picked up her medical bag. "He said that Manny was chasing a rabbits when he saw them hustle you into the cabin. Manny told Alex, and so Alex came to see what was happening." They moved to where the horses were tethered. "If I hadn't shown up, no doubt he would have rescued you."

"I told you, I had plans to escape."

He ignored her response. "Let's get back to town." He gathered the reins of the outlaws' horses. "Do you ride, Doc?"

She looked at the horses. "I took lessons when I was a girl, but that was sidesaddle. I've never ridden astride."

He walked around the animals and selected a gelding with a gentle manner. "This one should be okay. We'll leave the rest of them here. Harv and his gang won't be needing horses for a while, and Alex can make good use of them." He examined a stallion and a mare. "This pair could help him on his ranch. This will be his reward for helping capture the outlaws."

"Can you do that?"

"These horses were probably stolen. I can't locate the owners, and I don't want them running wild. Alex will give them a good home."

"That's one way to rationalize it, but then, you're very good at rationalizing everything."

Grabbing Analise by the waist, he lifted her onto a

gelding. She settled in the saddle and tucked her skirt around her legs for modesty. Still, a goodly amount of shapely leg showed above her low boot. He adjusted the stirrups, resisting the urge to slide his fingers up her legs. There was time enough for that later, when their misunderstanding was settled. In his favor, of course.

Tyler moved the remaining horses where they could munch on the grass and water from the small stream that flowed through the woods. He mounted his own horse and moved beside her. Analise clutched the reins with white knuckles, but she sat straight and tall without a single complaint. He tied her medical bag to her saddle horn.

"We'll take it easy, so don't be afraid," he said.

"I am not afraid. I want to go home."

The only thing Analise wanted was to soak in a hot tub and wash away the past twenty-four hours. So much had happened to her, it would take a river to wash away the anxiety of the kidnapping and the pain from Tyler's deceit. His lies and duplicity had cut her heart like a scalpel.

They spoke little during the ride. Analise concentrated on keeping her seat on the horse, struggling to avoid thinking about Tyler and the pain that clutched at her heart.

As they rode into town, Analise wondered whether the residents were waiting for a parade. Men, women, and children were lined up along Alpha Street, staring and pointing as they passed. As she and Tyler approached the town jail, her father raced out into the street.

The doctor grabbed at Tyler's hand. "Deacon, Steven told me you're a hero. He said you captured four dangerous outlaws and rescued my daughter. *Mon Dieu.* I want to hear all about it."

"Later, sir. Right now, I have to get Doctor Analise home and see to the prisoners at the jail," he said, shooting a glance at her.

"You go see to your prisoners. I'll escort my daughter to the house. I'm sure, like her brother, she's ready for a good meal and hot bath." He laughed and his eyes glittered with love for her. "Not that my son wanted a bath. When you finish your business, come and have dinner with us."

"Yes, sir. And I have to talk to you. It's very important."

Analise wondered how her father would accept Tyler's confession. She believed her father had hoped for a real engagement between them, and then a marriage. This deception put an end to all his plans.

Tyler hadn't come to Omega looking for a wife or to work for the church; he had come hunting outlaws. She didn't want a man she couldn't trust, and who didn't trust her.

She squared her shoulders and urged the horse forward. Her back ached, her legs felt stretched in an unnatural way, her stomach growled, and her head pounded like a kettle drum.

"I'll see you in a little while," Tyler said to Analise. "I still have things to discuss with you."

What more was there to say? she wondered. He'd lied about his identity, about his mission in Omega, about everything. Like Victor had lied, from the beginning. How could she let herself fall into the same trap a second time?

From the corner of her eye, she watched the crowd gather around Tyler. Several men, armed men she didn't recognize, came forward and spoke softly. He disappeared into the jail with the men. The crowd milled on the boardwalk, talking and whispering among themselves. If Analise and Tyler had been the target of gossip a week ago, today they would be headline news.

At the house, Oscar rushed out to help her down and take the horse away. Millie and Mrs. Hennessey hovered over her like mother hens. Analise shook off their concern, and went directly to the bathing room. The tub was filled with hot water, and Millie had set clean clothes out for her, plus a tray with tea and sandwiches.

For a long while she soaked in the tub, her mind in turmoil. As noble as Tyler's intentions were in his attempt to apprehend felons, he had lied. He had deceived her, lied to her, tricked her into loving him, just as Victor had. Now he too would leave her. Tyler would be moving on to his next assignment, building trust in others to achieve his goal. How many other women had he seduced and left brokenhearted?

She dropped her hands into the water and covered her abdomen with her palms. Tears gathered in the corners of her eyes. At least he'd had the decency not to make love to her.

Bittersweet laughter choked her. He was safe from one transgression, at least. Analise could not become pregnant again. She could never have another child.

It took hours to settle the affairs before Tyler was able to leave the jail. He'd secured his prisoners, interrogated them, and locked the money in the bank vault. Several agents had arrived that day to assist in the mission. Now, Pinkerton men stood guard at the jail and at the bank.

He'd made arrangements to board the train the next evening with the prisoners and money, and return to Denver for the trial. He'd sent telegrams to Wells Fargo, Sunshine Mining, and Alan Pinkerton.

He had gotten little rest, but he was able to bathe and shave before meeting with the DeLery family. It was time to come clean to the good people who had taken him into their home and offered their hospitality, kindness, and trust. And he especially owed Analise an apology and would beg her forgiveness. He cared for her, and hated that he had deceived her. She didn't deserve to be hurt.

If he hadn't been so focused on his job, he would have realized that a woman who would fight to save lives could never associate with a criminal like Ace Malone, no matter the circumstances.

Shortly before seven o'clock he arrived at the DeLery home. After bathing, he had dressed in a clean shirt and a decent suit from the trunk he'd stored at the hotel, along with the gray Stetson hat he wore on his freshly cut hair. As usual, his gun was neatly tucked in the shoulder holster. Although there had been a lot of questions and speculation, he'd kept his dealings with the Pinkerton men confidential. The people in town still referred to him as Deacon Goodfellow. He wanted the DeLery family to be the first to know the truth.

Tyler knocked on the door. He twisted his hat in his fingers, as nervous as a boy courting a girl for the first time.

Mrs. Delery opened the door wide and offered her brightest smile. "Our hero is here. Come in, Mr. Goodfellow. We're expecting you."

He looked around for Analise. She sat ramrod straight on the small settee. Tonight she wore her usual severe white shirtwaist and dark skirt. He had shed his disguise, he wondered when she would shed hers. Their gazes met and locked across the room.

Obviously she hadn't revealed his identity to her parents.

"Thank you, ma'am." He entered the parlor. Oscar and Mrs. Hennessey hovered in the doorway to the dining room.

Doctor DeLery stood and greeted Tyler with a solid handshake. "Did those Pinkerton men take care of the outlaws?"

"Yes, sir. We'll take them to Denver tomorrow for trial."

Millie caught his arm and guided him to the settee where Analise had spread her skirt and had plopped in the center of the small sofa. The contrast between the women was startling. Whereas Millie wore bright colors to enhance her femininity, Analise did her best to hide her womanly attributes. "So you will have to go to Denver with the bandits? Are you leaving us?"

"Please take a seat, madame. I have to explain something to you. This will take a while, but I want you to fully understand what's going on." He nodded at Steven, who sat tall and proud of his part in capturing the outlaws. The local newspaper had already published a special edition praising the youngster and Tyler for the arrests. Alex's name was barely mentioned at all.

After word spread about Tyler's real identity, the editor would certainly publish another special edition tomorrow. First he had to confess the truth to the DeLery family. He owed it to them, and more.

Analise folded her arms across her chest and stared up at him. Her stiff white blouse was buttoned clear to her chin, as if she had put up a shield against him.

Millie fanned her face with her hand. "I can't tell you how upset we were when Analise and Steven didn't return home last night. Then when we learned you were missing as well, we became concerned for all of you."

"I'm sorry to worry you and Doctor DeLery. I'm aware I should have left a note informing you I was on their trail. I just didn't want to take the time," he said. Actually, the thought didn't cross his mind to inform the doctor. Tyler was accustomed to acting on his own.

"When Steven and Alex returned to town, I'd gone to the sheriff's office to enlist his help in searching for all of you." Doctor DeLery returned to his favorite chair. "Good thing you were on the job. That sheriff never did show up."

Tyler wasn't surprised. The local lawman spent more time away from town than in it. He took a deep breath and surged ahead. "First, I want to apologize to all of you. I am not a man of the cloth, as I led you to believe when I came to your home. My name is Tyler Morgan and I'm a Pinkerton agent."

Millie slanted a sly glance at her husband, then dropped into a chair and covered her chest with her hands. "Impossible. You preach such inspiring sermons. And everybody loves you."

Not everybody, he thought, with a quick glance at Analise. If looks could kill, he would join Ace Malone behind the church.

Doctor DeLery nodded. "You told us you had come to determine if we can support a full-time minister. That was a lie?"

"One of many," Analise put in with a sneer.

Tyler stood up and paced behind the settee, not wanting to see the anger and pain in Analise's eyes. "Yes, a fabrication to gain access to your home and any information you had on the bandits."

"But we didn't know anything about outlaws. We are law-abiding people, churchgoing, God-fearing people." Millie's outrage cut right to his heart. He hated what he'd done to these innocent people.

"I am aware of that. Let me start from the beginning." He took a deep breath to clear his thoughts. Where to begin? "I work for Alan Pinkerton and I often use disguises in my assignments. To gain your confidence, I chose to come to Omega as a church official. I'm sorry I had to deceive you."

The doctor leaned forward shaking his head. "Why did you come here, to us? To my home?"

"Over a month ago, Ace Malone and his gang robbed a payroll going to the Sunshine Gold Mine. They killed a Wells Fargo agent and a Pinkerton man. Ace got away with the money, but he was wounded. We tracked him to Omega, and we thought he might have seen a doctor. I had to find out if you had treated him, and where he had gone. Steven told me about the stranger who had died. I deduced he was Ace, and that he had stashed the stolen money near Omega. I had to find the money before the remainder of the gang showed up. I've been searching for the money, but Steven found it first. My fears were justified when the outlaws kidnapped Analise and Steven. They used Analise as a hostage to get it from him."

The doctor stared at his son. "Steven, you knew that money wasn't yours. Why didn't you turn it over to me or to the sheriff?"

The youngster ducked his head. "I don't know. I guess I wanted to keep it for myself."

Tyler felt he could defend the boy, since he too had lied. "He gladly gave it up to save his sister's life. He told me that the outlaws had her in the same cabin where we had spent our night together." He smiled for the first time since entering the house. "The night that got us into trouble."

"Forget about that . . . Mr. Morgan, is it? Or is that another alias?" Analise snapped.

"Morgan is my legal name." He returned his gaze to the doctor and his wife. "I suppose you know the rest. I followed Steven, then Alex Gonzales and I were able to capture the outlaws and rescue Analise."

The doctor drummed his fingers on the arms of his chair. "I appreciate what you've done. If I had known my children were in danger, I would have moved heaven and earth to save them. I can only thank you for putting yourself in danger and bringing them safely home."

"Humph." Analise drew his attention. "I had a plan to escape. Steven and I would have been all right on our own. I laced their whiskey with laudanum, and it was only a matter of time before they all fell asleep."

Tyler shoved her skirt aside and dropped onto the settee beside her. She hurriedly moved to make room so as not to touch him. Her best efforts to avoid him weren't going to work. He caught her icy fingers in his hand.

"That might not have worked. What if they hadn't drunk enough?"

"I would have thought of something." She snatched her hand away.

"I don't doubt it. You've proved to be resourceful."

"Can I suppose that to be a compliment?"

"Of the highest order."

Steven stirred, getting restless with the conversation. "When are we going to eat? Mrs. Hennessey baked a special chocolate cake for me."

Millie stood. "She also prepared a lovely supper for the . . . I'm sorry, Mr. Morgan. I'm not sure I can get used to that. It all seems so strange."

Her husband joined her. "Let's go into the dining room. We can continue our conversation there." He offered his arm to his wife. "We don't want our son to starve to death."

Steven raced into the dining room to the table. Tyler moved more slowly. He offered his arm to Analise.

She lifted her gaze to his. "I do not need assistance to stand." Ignoring his help, she surged to her feet.

Tyler stepped in front of her. "It's the gentlemanly thing to do."

She glared at him. "A gentleman does not lie and deceive his host. And you haven't told my father the whole truth. You left out how you suspected us of working with the outlaws. Or that you supposed I was Ace Malone's lover."

"I never accused you of being his lover." Pain arched through him at the very idea. He snatched her hand and set it into the crook of his arm. "I admitted to being a scoundrel. But I am begging you to forgive me."

"When hell freezes over." She fell into step at his side. For a second he considered tossing her over his shoulder and kidnapping her. Or spiriting her on that train tomorrow. He nixed the idea. If she came to him, it had to be of her own free will. First she had to forgive him. He hoped his full explanation would defuse her hostility, as well justified as it was. She deserved the full story.

Mrs. Hennessey bustled in from the kitchen, a large platter in her hands. Oscar carried another tray and plopped it on the table. He shot Tyler an angry glare. Disappointment glittered in the housekeeper's eyes. Tyler had hurt far more people than he had intended. Not only had he hurt the DeLery family, but the good people of the church as well. He'd hoped to slink out of town when his assignment ended with nobody realizing that he'd fooled them all. It was too late for that. His true identity would spread overnight.

Holding the chair for Analise, he moved his hands gently to her shoulders, feeling the need to touch her. She shivered under his touch. He took the chair at her side, inching it closer to hers.

As the family settled at the dinner table, they reached out to hold hands.

"Let's bow our heads," the doctor said. While Tyler had been their guest, Deacon Goodfellow had been called on to pray. But now, since the deacon did not exist, the head of the household took over that responsibility.

Tyler tightened his grip on Analise's hand and bowed reverently as the doctor prayed. He would miss this when he left. The comradeship, the closeness, the family he almost had.

Not that his own family ever sat down to supper together on a regular basis. It was usually a quick bite before a performance or late snack after.

The prayer ended and Analise slid her fingers from his. They passed the bowls of fried chicken, mashed potatoes, and fluffy biscuits—Tyler's all-time favorite meal. Once he'd mentioned his preferences to Mrs. Hennessey. She had prepared the special meal for a man she had thought a hero. That man eating the meal was a liar and fraud.

Steven took a big bite of a chicken leg and wiped his mouth on his napkin. "Deacon, sorry, guess I should call you Mr. Morgan."

"Tyler would be fine."

"How'd you get to be a Pinkerton man? I read all about detectives hunting down outlaws in my dime novels. I like the ones about lawmen, like Texas Rangers and Pinkerton agents who solve crimes. How'd you get in?"

This was his chance for full disclosure. "It's kind of a long story, you sure you want to hear it?"

Analise glanced at him, curiosity in her gaze. "We are all interested in your past, aren't we, Papa? I'm sure it's quite colorful."

"Let's hear it, Tyler. I want to understand why you felt the need to dupe us."

So the doctor had his doubts too. "I'm from a family of performers, actors on the stage. Morgan Players performed all over America and Europe. We were in Washington on April 14, 1865, performing at Ford's Theater with John Wilkes Booth. We watched him shoot the president."

Analise gasped, Millie grabbed her chest, and the doctor simply stared.

"You saw Mr. Lincoln get shot?" Millie asked. "You must have been just a boy."

"Fourteen," he answered. "I was devastated. I believed that I could have stopped the assassination. If I had been a little bit closer, if I had been faster, I might have stopped Mr. Booth from firing the shot." He took a drink of water. "That's where I met Alan Pinkerton. We became friends."

Oscar and Mrs. Hennessey had moved closer to listen to the story. "I continued with the troupe, with my parents, but I kept in contact with Alan. From time to time I took a few cases from him, investigating a variety of crimes. I enjoyed the detective work. As an actor, I knew all about makeup and disguise. I got very good at being an undercover agent, but I'm also a very fine actor."

"We know," Analise said. "You fooled all of us."

He shrugged. "That couldn't be helped."

"The Morgan Players. That sounds familiar. Did you play Romeo in Denver about, oh, twelve years ago?" Milllie asked.

Tyler nodded. "I suppose so." How could he forget? It was their last performance before Abigail died.

"You were magnificent. Etienne and I attended several performances that winter. I believe it was your father who played Hamlet. Where is he now?"

"My parents moved to Europe. They feel more appreciated on the Continent."

Millie clutched her hands to her chest. "Your Juliet was the most beautiful woman I've ever seen."

Pain tightened his chest. "She was my wife, Abigail."

"I believe you mentioned you'd lost your wife. Was that another lie?" Millie asked, her voice hard.

On a long sigh, he confessed his past. "No, I lost Abigail only a year after we married. We were expecting a baby, but I insisted we leave Denver and go to St. Louis. Abigail wanted to wait until after the baby came, but I didn't want to pass up the opportunity to star in a new production of *Taming of the Shrew*. Outside Abilene, we were caught in a train robbery. Abigail went into labor. She died and the baby died."

Millie reached over and touched his hand. "You have our condolences. We're truly sorry for your loss."

Tyler nodded. He didn't want pity, but the sympathy in Millie and the doctor's eyes brought warmth to the chill in his heart. These people truly cared. "I blamed the outlaws who had stopped the train and kept us from getting medical help. I spent the next year tracking down the outlaws. Then I signed up with Pinkerton as a full-time operative." He couldn't admit aloud that his arrogance and selfishness were as much at fault as the outlaws for the deaths of his wife and child.

"You gave up your career on the stage?" Millie asked, awed by the story. "You were such a fine actor. It is quite a loss to the theater."

"I'm still an actor. Only on a different stage. Occasionally, I take a role, just to keep up my skills."

Millie grinned. "All the world's a stage, and all the men and women merely players."

Analise added, "They have their exits and their entrances—"

"And one man in his time plays many parts." Tyler shrugged. "As I have done."

He lifted his hands in surrender. "I'm very sorry I had to involve your family in the charade. At the time, I felt it was the best way to locate Ace and recover the loot. I didn't know Analise and Steven would become involved. I didn't want anybody to get hurt."

He shoved away from the table. "I'll have my things out of your house within the hour."

"Sit down, Tyler," the doctor said. "There's no need to leave so soon. You're still welcome here, and you don't want to miss Mrs. Hennessey's prizewinning chocolate cake."

Surprised at the man's kindness, Tyler dropped back into his chair. "Thank you, sir. I don't deserve your kindness." It was amazing how these people had forgiven him and still welcomed him into their fold. Except for Analise, of course. He would have to take his time and make it up to her somehow.

"You certainly don't," Analise mumbled under her breath.

The housekeeper set a large cake on the table. "I hope you enjoy it, Mr. Morgan. I made it for you."

"Say, I thought you made it for *me*," Steven groused.

"You can have a piece," his mother assured him.

"I was a hero. I want two pieces." Steven reached for a plate and held it up for his share.

For the first time that evening, Analise smiled. "You're my hero, Steven. You can have my share."

Tyler laughed. "I'll take a big piece. Chocolate is my favorite."

Mrs. Hennessey handed him a slice of cake. "I'll

make a larger one for the wedding." She frowned. "Or has that changed too?"

"Yes," Analise said.

"No," Tyler declared at the same time. The words had burst from his mouth before his brain caught up. As soon as he'd spoken, he realized he meant it. More than anything, he wanted to marry Analise and make a home with her. After years of hopelessness, hope blossomed in his heart. Now, to convince her that he was sincere. That would take a miracle. As far as he knew, he was fresh out of miracles.

Analise shoved back her chair. "As you all know, the whole thing was a farce, just a ruse to protect the 'deacon's' reputation. And mine. We had no intention of carrying it through." She stood and threw down her napkin.

Tyler surged to his feet. "At first it was a ploy, but now I realize that I want to marry you." He caught her arms and stared into her eyes. "I want to make it real."

She shook him off. "I do not want to marry you. Or anybody. I didn't take any of it seriously." Stepping back, she turned to her father. "If you will excuse me, I am going to my room. I am still exhausted."

"Analise," her father called after her, "do not be so rude."

With a toss of her head, she continued toward the front stairs. Tyler didn't know what had gotten into him to want to make the engagement real—to actually go through with the marriage. Until that moment he had agreed that the whole thing was a sham, a way out of a tricky situation. Now he felt that losing Analise would be as great a loss as when he'd lost Abigail. Watching her lift her skirt to ascend the stairs as regally as a queen, he felt a stirring in his chest. The woman had broken down the barriers he'd erected around his emotions years before.

With her, he felt alive and vital. It would take work and cunning, but he wasn't going to let her go. He loved her. That thought struck like a blow to the stomach. He loved her, pure and simple, and he wanted to make a life with her.

He returned to his seat at the table. "It's a shame to waste this cake. Mrs. Hennessey, I believe you have outdone yourself. Thank you." All eyes on him, he took a large bite of the chocolate cake. The others continued to stare. "Doctor, would you like to continue our chess game after dinner?"

"Yes, Tyler. That would be fine."

# Chapter 11

Analise fumed all the way to her room. Tyler Morgan, or whoever he called himself, certainly had nerve—claiming he wanted to go through with the engagement and marriage. He was entirely too good at breaking his word. He'd agreed to the pretend engagement, and now he claimed to want to make it real—or was that a lie too? He'd come to work in the church, only to reveal he wasn't a church official at all. She didn't believe anything he said. It was possible that he wasn't a Pinkerton man, either, but a bounty hunter out for the reward.

As a matter of fact, he was such a consummate liar he may be an outlaw. One of the Malone gang looking to keep the money for himself.

That would explain everything. He was a liar and a cheat—a fraud who didn't care who he hurt or whose heart he broke. She shouldn't believe a word that fell from his honeyed lips. Falling in love with him had been a mistake she'd promised she'd never allow to happen again. Tyler was more like Victor than she had believed. Both men were deceivers, liars, and cheats. Brothers in their handsome flesh. Wolves in sheep's clothing, and Analise was the lamb who'd been fleeced—twice. Both knaves had stolen her heart and stomped it into the dirt. She doubted that Tyler cared, or had even noticed how much she loved him. This announcement about wanting to go through with the wedding was just another deception to him.

She removed her clothing and slipped a wrapper over her chemise. Wallowing in self-pity, she sat at her dressing table and stared at the damp-eyed woman looking back at her in the mirror. How pathetic and naive she must seem to him. Tyler had fooled her completely. Victor had taken her virtue; Tyler had stolen her heart and trust.

She tugged the hairpins from her hair and picked up her brush. "One, two, three," she said, counting the strokes as she tugged her silver-handled hair-brush through her long hair. When she reached one hundred, she shook out her hair and lifted the heavy tresses in her hands.

"Maybe I should cut it off," she remarked to the image in the oval mirror.

"Don't. It's very beautiful."

At the sound of Tyler's soft voice, she turned on the stool. Her eyes widened at the sight of the man with his back pressed to the door. He'd removed his coat, and his shirt was open at the neck.

"I know I locked that door." Anger streamed through her like a tidal wave in a storm.

He shrugged. "Guess you didn't."

Gritting her teeth to keep from yelling, she hauled back and flung the hairbrush at his head. He ducked to the side and the heavy brush slammed against the door.

"Nice throw. You almost got me." Bending over, he picked up the brush.

"Go away, *s'il vous plaît*." She turned back to her reflection in the mirror, appalled that the blush on her face extended down her neck to the tops of her exposed breasts.

"Your grandmother would be very proud how politely you ordered your fiancé from your room." He moved silently across the floor to stand behind her.

"And my papa would be after you with a shotgun if he knew you hadn't gone quietly."

He dropped his hands onto her shoulders and shifted his fingers under her hair. Lifting the heavy tresses to his face, he inhaled deeply. "Smells like roses."

Their gazes met in the mirror. He let her hair fall to her back. Gently, he touched the brush to her scalp and pulled it slowly through her hair. "Like silk," he whispered.

Mesmerized, Analise simply sat and stared. His shirt, open at the neck, showed the hair-covered expanse of his chest. He opened his mouth, then shut it. Analise tried to protest, but no words came. It was unseemly, outrageous, completely improper.

But it felt too good to demand that he stop. His touch was more powerful than the strongest drug in her bag. It was like an opiate, robbing her of her will, of her voice, and her power to resist. Sensations sizzled through her. He again pulled the brush through her hair in the intimate gesture—something a lover would do—a lover setting the stage to seduce, to entice, to wear away the will to object.

But Analise didn't want him to stop. She wanted to feel, to know she was really alive. For over a year, she'd been only half-alive, half a woman. His simple action brought healing to her scarred heart and hope to her tortured soul.

He lowered his face and his whisker-roughened cheek pressed next to her smooth skin. An intriguing smile curved his mouth. "I'll do this every night after we're married," he whispered. His warm breath tickled her ear. "Then we'll go to paradise together."

Together? Married? Her blood ran cold. Memories of her past assailed her. Analise stiffened. Tyler Morgan was an actor, a liar, and a fraud. He'd played a lover onstage, and she didn't know how many women had been seduced in their boudoirs by his performance.

As if waking from a stupor, she trembled with fury. "Didn't you hear me at dinner? There will not be a marriage, and I will not go anywhere with you, even paradise." She snatched the brush from his hand. "Get out before I yell for my papa."

He stretched to his full height and grinned down at her. "That would only force your father's hand. He'll have us married by the local justice of the peace before morning." Stepping back, he gestured to the door. "Or should I call him myself?"

"Get out of my room. Get out of my life. Get out of this town."

With a shrug of his wide shoulders, he marched to the doorway. "I won't cause a scene, so I'll go, for now. But this isn't the last you'll see of me. I don't know how long my business in Denver will take, but you can bet your bottom dollar I'll be back."

"Do you know, monsieur, I liked you much better when you were pretending to be a gentleman than when you're acting the rogue."

He laughed, and took a few long steps toward her. "Good night, good night. Parting is such sweet sorrow, that I shall say good night till it be morrow." Without warning, he caught her arms and hauled her hard into his body. Her breasts flattened against his chest, and his mouth crushed hers in a kiss meant to conquer and subdue. His hands slid behind her back, her palm pressed against his chest. Their hearts pounded as one. The kiss lasted only a few blissful seconds before Tyler set her away from him.

"That was so you would remember me while I'm gone."

Stunned she stared at him as he slid like a shadow through the doorway. "No, Tyler," she whispered, "that was so you would remember me. I'll never forget you."

News of Tyler's identity as a Pinkerton man spread faster than ticks on the back of a dog. By morning, the newspaper had published another special edition, detailing his background and exploits. He wondered how they had gotten so much information so quickly. Most Pinkerton men were closemouthed for safety's sake.

Morgan tossed the newspaper onto the battered desk in the sheriff's office. There were no secrets in a small town. He and the operation were big news in a town where little exciting happened. When he'd revealed the truth to the DeLery family, he knew they would spread the news as quickly as the words fell from his mouth. In fact, Millie was best friends with the editor's wife. The editor was on the town council and was one of the doctor's poker buddies.

Loud voices from the street alerted Tyler to a disturbance outside the jailhouse. Picking up his rifle, he and Leroy moved to see if the other agents needed assistance.

"What the devil is going on here? Who are all you people?" A man of about fifty, dressed in rough clothing, stood toe to toe with a Pinkerton agent nearly twice his size. "Get out of my way," the man demanded.

Tyler shouldered his way to the boardwalk. He recognized the wayward town sheriff who'd been off courting a widow in the next county. And was nowhere to be found when needed.

"Sheriff," he called, "come in, I've been waiting for you."

"Goodfellow?" he looked from Tyler's face to the rifle in his hand. "I was out taking care of personal business." The sheriff rubbed his hand over his bristly jaw. "What's going on here? Who are these men?"

The men parted, allowing them to enter the office. "We're Pinkerton operatives. We have four outlaws locked in your jail." Tyler picked up the newspaper. "This should explain everything."

The older man glanced at the headline, then shifted his gaze to the solemn men behind the iron bars of the jail. "Gosh darn. I'm gone for one day, and all hell breaks loose." He sank into the chair behind the desk. "You're not really a deacon?"

"No, I am here on a Pinkerton assignment. We've been on the trail of the Malone gang for weeks. We'll have them on the train this evening, and you can have your jail back."

Plucking a pair of eyeglasses from his pocket, the sheriff studied the newspaper story. Tyler stepped outdoors, needing a breather from the smell of unwashed bodies, stale coffee, and the cheap cigar Leroy insisted on smoking. People gathered on the sidewalk in front of stores and businesses as if waiting for a parade. He sighed. The parade would begin at six o'clock when they marched the prisoners down Alpha Street and up Olympia to the train station, and carried the iron chest with the money safely locked away.

Tyler glanced toward the end of town where the doctor and his family lived. After his escapade the previous night with Analise, he hadn't slept a wink. If he'd been half the man he thought he was, he'd have spent the night in her bed, and made sure she knew she was his woman. Somehow, the noble part of him won over the carnal, and he'd spent the night in the jailhouse with outlaws and rogues.

The need to see Analise again, once more before he boarded the train, propelled him toward her home. However, with every few steps he took, he was stopped by one person, then another. By the time he reached the DeLery home, his fingers ached from so many handshakes.

As was his custom, he circled to the rear door and knocked softly. Mrs. Hennessey flung open the door. "Welcome, Mr. Good . . . Morgan. I just can't get used to you not being Mr. Goodfellow." She hustled to the stove and filled a cup with coffee. "We missed you at breakfast. I fixed a nice plate for you, but you were already gone."

"Sorry, ma'am. I spent the night at the jail."

"Then sit down. I have some chicken left from last night and fresh biscuits." She set her hand on his shoulder, like a mother ushering her child to the table. "You're probably starved."

The meal looked too good to pass up, and what he'd gotten from the café down the street could barely pass for food. The housekeeper hovered over him, refilling his cup every time he took a sip. Finally, he held up his hand to stop her.

"Thank you, Mrs. Hennessey. I'm going to miss you when I get to Denver."

"You're coming back, aren't you? For the wedding?"

He caught her hand and drew it to his lips. A little charm would go a long way. "If Doctor Analise won't marry me, I'll spirit you away from Oscar."

The housekeeper giggled like a schoolgirl. "You are a rascal, sir. And I will give your proposal my full consideration."

He laughed. "Speaking of my fiancée, is Doctor Analise in the office?"

She cleared the dishes from the table. "No, she left a while ago with her father. She mentioned wanting him to escort her to the Dawson place to check on her patient."

"The Dawson place? Did she say when they'll be back?"

Millie entered and answered. "They won't be back

until supper or later." She picked up a cup and filled it with coffee.

Suppertime. The evening train left at six. Unless the train was delayed, he wouldn't get to say good-bye. Anger gnawed at his gut. Analise could have waited one more day to call on Polly and the baby. She'd purposely planned the visit to avoid him. He started to rise, when Millie signaled him back to his seat.

"Stay for a moment, Tyler. I was hoping for a chance to speak with you privately." Millie settled at the table opposite him and nodded to Mrs. Hennessey. The housekeeper promptly left the kitchen.

From the gleam in her eyes, he knew he was in for an interrogation or worse. "I really have to get back to the jail."

"This won't take long." She eyed him carefully over the rim of her cup. The woman studying him wasn't the soft, motherly wife of a country doctor—she was a formidable opponent, who knew the ways of the world and of men. "Don't think you fooled me for a minute, Tyler. You had all the outer trappings of a churchman, but you couldn't disguise that appreciative gleam in your eyes every time you looked at Analise. I've seen that look many times before, and I knew it was entirely too carnal for a man of the cloth."

Tyler chuckled softly. "I suppose I'm not as good an actor as I thought."

"Oh, you're very good. But I had seen you in several plays in Denver, and I never forget a face, especially a handsome man's." After taking a sip of coffee, she continued. "Etienne and I checked with the bishop in Denver, and found he had never heard of Deacon Goodfellow."

Shocked, Tyler stared at her. He'd been caught when he'd thought he'd been safe. "Why didn't you say something? Confront me?"

"I also have friends in law enforcement, who identified you as a Pinkerton man. They advised us to keep our own counsel for a while. For your safety as well as ours. They vouched for your honesty."

He slumped in the chair. "And you didn't tell Analise?"

"No, we knew she was falling in love with you, and we hoped you felt the same for her." With one long fingernail, she tapped on the side of the china cup. "Tyler, I don't want to see her hurt. We don't know what happened to her in Paris, but she came back with a broken spirit. She is only now recovering. I do not want to see that happen again."

The warning in her voice hit him square in the heart. "I don't want to hurt Analise. I offered to marry her."

"And she stubbornly refused you. She's afraid of being hurt again."

"I think she needs a little time to digest everything that's happened. When I return from Denver, I'll court her properly, like a real gentleman."

"Her father will be happy to hear that. Can you come for supper?"

He shook his head. "I have to be on the evening train."

She stood and offered her hand. "Sometimes the evening train is hours late. Consider the invitation open, just in case."

He took Millie's hand in his and bid her good-bye. Millie's words echoed in his head. She was right, about everything. A plan in mind, he headed back to the jail. If Analise thought he would give up so easily, she had better think again. Tyler had a few more tricks up his sleeve.

"We're late for supper. Mrs. Hennessey will have a fit." Etienne tugged on the lines and slowed the team. "I'll take the rig back to the livery and be home in a few minutes."

At the porch, Analise hopped down from the buggy. "Thank you for going with me today, Papa. I knew you'd love little Anna as much as I." Her father had reluctantly agreed to the house call, but Analise had needed to get away from town and away from Tyler. His visit the previous night had left her unsettled and out of sorts. Visiting the baby had lifted her spirits as she'd known it would. "I'll tell Millie you'll be back in a few minutes. Supper will be waiting for you."

She entered through the kitchen and dropped her medical bag on the table. The housekeeper stood at the stove ladling gravy into a bowl. "Sorry I'm late. Papa will be along in a few minutes."

"It's all right, Missy. We held it for you. Go clean up. It will be on the table when you get down."

Laughter and voices came from the parlor. Millie, the social butterfly, must have company or another of her meetings, Analise thought. She hurried up the rear stairs to her room. After washing her face and hands, she slipped on a clean shirtwaist.

Studying her image in the mirror, she removed a few hairpins and loosened her hair from the tight confines. She tugged a few strands free and let the curls touch her cheeks and neck. Millie was always after her to change from her usual severe braids or chignon. Yes, she thought, much better. Tyler would like it. She frowned at the woman staring back at her. Her scalp still tingled from his touch. And her body heated every time she thought about the outrageous things he'd said and done the night before. She slammed down her hairbrush and stalked out of the room. Time to put him out of her mind, as he was now out of her life. The train to Denver had left over an hour ago, with Tyler on it.

Her stomach growled at the luscious aromas wafting from the dining room. "Sorry I'm late," she said, rushing to her usual seat.

She stopped dead in her tracks. A tall man stood behind her chair as if waiting for her. Tyler Morgan, looking as much like an outlaw as the Malone gang, smiled at her. He wore his usual black suit, but this time he didn't try to hide the gun holstered at his hip. His eyes glittered with mischief.

"What are you doing here?" She grunted. "Why aren't you on the train to Denver?"

"The train is running late. Seems it was delayed down the track. I decided to take Mrs. Hennessey and Millie up on their generous offer to join you for supper." He held her chair. "I didn't want to miss this opportunity to bid my betrothed good-bye."

"I am not your betrothed," she said between gritted teeth.

"Analise, quit acting like a petulant child and sit down," Millie ordered in a voice she seldom used. "We've been waiting for you."

Analise allowed Tyler to seat her as he'd done nightly for weeks. This time, he planted a quick kiss to the top of her head.

Across the table, Steven snickered and shook his head. "Oh, brother," he grumbled.

Millie flashed a knowing grin, and her father dipped his head to hide his smile.

Embarrassed, Analise snapped her napkin and set it on her lap. She didn't know what kind of game Tyler was playing, but she wouldn't allow him to get away with mocking her openly. "Shouldn't you at least be at the jail guarding your prisoners?"

"The other agents can look after them until the train arrives." He reached out his hand to take hers while her father said the blessing. After the "amen," Tyler tightened his grip and pulled her hand to his lips for a quick kiss. Sensations swept over her. First her head, then her hand—the man was entirely outrageous and unsettling.

"How are Polly and the baby?" he asked.

"Fine."

"I'm very proud of my daughter. The young couple sang her praises, and yours, Tyler. And Alex said something about thanking you for the horses." Her father gestured with his water glass.

"It was the least I could do for his help with the outlaws." Tyler again smiled at Analise. She buried her hand in her skirt to keep him from grabbing it again.

Moments ago, she'd been starving, now Analise couldn't swallow a single bite—nor could she engage in the light banter around the dinner table.

At the exact moment Mrs. Hennessey entered the dining room carrying a golden-crusted apple pie, the long, sorrowful whistle of the train echoed from the other side of town.

Tyler frowned and pushed back his chair. "I'm sorry I'll have to leave before enjoying that delicious-smelling pie. Will you please excuse me? I don't want to miss the train."

Etienne stood and offered his hand. "We understand. Take care of yourself, Tyler."

Mrs. Hennessey set the pie on the table. "I'll bake one especially for you when you return."

"*If* he returns," Analise grumbled under her breath.

With a finger crooked under her chin, Tyler lifted her face to his. "Never fear, Doc, I will return to claim my prize."

She slapped his hand away. "You'll soon learn I'm no prize. I'm opinionated, stubborn, judgmental, domineering, assertive—"

"Beautiful, intelligent, courageous, kind, everything I desire in a woman. Life with you certainly won't be dull."

A hard knock on the rear door interrupted the

discussion. "That'll be one of my men. I have to go. Thank you, Doctor, Mrs. DeLery, and Mrs. Hennessey for your hospitality." He glanced across the table to her brother. "Steven, want to come with us and watch the procession? Looks like half the town is out there to get a look at the outlaws."

"Save me a piece of pie," Steven said. He darted from the room and out the rear door.

Tyler caught Analise's elbow and lifted her from the chair. "How about you, *mon coeur*? Want to give me a proper sendoff?"

Embarrassed at his impropriety in front of her parents, she shook off his hold. "No. Good-bye."

To her surprise he released his grip. "Don't you even want to escort me to the door?"

"I believe you can find the way."

Millie shot an angry glare at her. "Analise, do not be so rude. Where are your manners? Tyler is your betrothed. You should treat him with more courtesy."

She pasted a false smile on her face. "*Adieu*, monsieur."

He caught her fingers and lifted them to his lips. "*Au revoir, mon amour.*" The kiss was short, polite, and appropriate. "I don't want to miss my train. I'll be in touch."

Another loud knock and Tyler shrugged in apology. He picked up his wide Stetson hat from the peg at the rear door, and disappeared into the night.

Mrs. Hennessey was the first to regain her senses. "I believe I will go down to the depot and watch the excitement. Oscar left a while ago." Setting the pie on the table she returned to the kitchen. Seconds later, the rear door slammed shut.

Millie stood. "Etienne, let's go and watch. After all, Tyler is a hero, and he's going to be our son-in-law."

"Not if I have anything to say about it," Analise groused—like Steven when he was in a snit.

Her father straightened his shoulders. "*Chère*, you've already had your say. Now come with us and wave good-bye to your fiancé."

She plopped back into her chair. "I believe I'll have a large slice of pie, and enjoy the quiet."

Millie grabbed a wrap from the hall coatrack. "Etienne, your daughter is the most stubborn woman I have ever met."

Etienne laughed. "About as stubborn as you, *ma petite*."

The house was deadly quiet with everyone gone to the depot. They considered Tyler and Alex heroes. As if Analise couldn't have escaped and helped to capture the outlaws without their assistance.

She took a large bite of pie. But truth be told, she had never been so relieved as when she'd seen Tyler with that rifle in his hand come to rescue her and Steven.

The pie caught in her throat. Tyler was leaving. He'd promised to return. But with all the lies he'd told, how could she believe anything he said? The whistle of the train shrieked loud and long—a sound as lonesome as her heart without Tyler.

She shoved aside the plate, along with her stubbornness, and rushed to the front door. She grabbed a shawl, then dashed into the street. Lifting her skirt, she raced to the depot. Just one last glance at him. That was all she wanted. He wouldn't even know she was there. Only one final look to last a lifetime.

Scores of people thronged the station's platform. She stood at the rear of the crowd watching the shackled prisoners climb into a private car. She recognized several of the lawmen from the day before. Finally, Tyler climbed the steps, with two armed men carrying an iron chest beside him. He paused to look over the spectators. Leaning over he whispered to one of the guards. Then he leaped down and started through the sea of people. The curious parted before him. Fascinated at the show, Analise followed his progress, wondering where he was going with such a determined stride.

He was about six feet away when she looked around, and realized that she was his target. She tried to turn and run, but was stopped by a surge of bodies. By then he was beside her.

"I didn't think you would come, *chére*. I'm grateful for a proper farewell." Without a by-your-leave, he wrapped his arms around her and hauled her hard into his chest. His mouth caught hers in a kiss meant to attack her senses, conquer her protests, and proclaim his victory. Around them people cheered, but to Analise, she and Tyler were the only people in the world. Emotions swirled around her. Her legs grew weak. If not for his strong embrace, she would have sunk to the ground. There, in front of the entire throng, he staked his claim on her heart.

The long whine of the train whistle was joined by the slow chugging of the wheels. Tyler abruptly released her. "You'll have to wait for the rest, *petite*," he whispered against her kiss-swollen mouth. Then he vanished. The crowd closed around him, hiding him from her sight.

Analise pressed her fingers to her lips, hoping to hold in the delicious heat and sweet taste he had infused into her. The train was moving and Tyler raced to the rear platform. He grabbed a railing and swung aboard. Even as the train pulled out of the station, she felt his gaze on her. She watched until only a whiff of smoke drifted back to her and the loud whistle echoed into the night. With the back of her hand she wiped away the tears from her eyes. It was the smoke and cinders, she told herself, not sadness that he was gone.

## Chapter 12

A month later, Analise and Tyler remained the topic of local gossip. October had come and gone, with no word from her so-called fiancé. It was early November and not a day went by that somebody didn't stop her on the street and question her about Tyler.

When was he coming back? How was he? Had they set a wedding date? My, wasn't he handsome? Wasn't she lucky? Would he give up being a famous Pinkerton detective? How easily he had been forgiven for his duplicity. Even Millie was talking about him celebrating Thanksgiving with the DeLery family.

Well, Analise wasn't quite so forgiving.

She had not received a single word from her illusive betrothed. Not that she considered him her fiancé. For a man who had made such a show of kissing her and putting on such a fine performance, he hadn't bothered to contact her. It was just as well. She didn't have time for him, anyway.

Getting the clinic started took all her time and energy. Her patient base had grown. Now patients accepted her as their doctor, rather than wait for her father.

She'd also learned to drive a buggy. Until she was able to purchase her own rig, she either used her father's or rented from the livery. Analise loved the freedom of being able to drive into the countryside on her own, and feeling the wind blowing through her hair.

She'd even driven out to see Alex and Polly at their place. With Steven at her side, they had spent several pleasant afternoons visiting with the small family. Both Polly and little Anna were well and thriving, and Manny had accepted Steven like a big brother. Thanks to Alex's hard work, the ranch was looking better all the time.

As thanks for helping in her rescue from the outlaws, she'd given Manny a real grown-up hat of his own. The boy was thrilled. For her namesake, Analise had brought a lovely lace shawl for Anna's upcoming dedication. Reverend Carter had agreed to perform both the wedding and Anna's dedication ceremony the following Sunday. Since Alex was reluctant to enter the church, the ceremonies would take place in the DeLery's parlor.

Analise had agreed to stand up as godmother for the baby and witness for the wedding. Too bad Tyler hadn't returned, as he'd promised the young couple to stand up for them. But that couldn't be helped. Nobody knew when or if he would return to Omega.

Not that she cared. Analise had more important issues on her mind—her clinic. She was ready to face the bank president and get her plans in motion.

With determination in every step, Analise DeLery braved the wind whipping at her cloak and marched boldly down Alpha Street. She was a woman on a mission, determined to get her clinic up and running early in the coming year. Wanting to look and feel her best, she wore her nicest suit with a pretty lace-trimmed blouse. Millie had dressed her hair in a flattering chignon topped with a stylish hat. As a professional woman, she knew the importance of making the proper impression. Enough time had been wasted already. Once Mr. Winters at the bank realized the importance of the clinic to the town, he would willingly rent the Onasis House to her.

Every day she had gone past the Onasis House—her house. Once, she'd found the door unlocked and had gone inside to inspect the building. The house was in good condition, with only minor repairs and renovations needed. She planned to divide the front parlor into a waiting room and office. The dining room could be partitioned into two separate examining rooms, giving the women complete privacy. The former library would make an excellent nursery for the children who had to wait for their mothers. With four bedrooms upstairs, she could use three of them as wards for patients who had to stay for an extended period of time. The other room would be her private space.

She had taken the time to measure and draw out a floor plan to present to the bank manager. With his approval, she could get started immediately on her dream. All he had to do was rent the house to her until she could afford to purchase it outright.

Millie had agreed to lend her the necessary money to begin the repairs until she got to Denver and sold her grandmother's jewelry.

Analise approached the bank with strong determination. The clinic was important to her and to the women in town. She crossed her fingers and said a silent prayer for strength and favor with the banker.

The bank was a large stone building set on the corner of Alpha and Hercules. Mr. Winters had been president since the day it opened, about fifteen years ago. The banker and his wife had been close friends with Millie and her papa ever since he'd come to town.

Analise hoped to use that friendship as leverage to encourage him to rent the Onasis House to her.

She entered through the heavy wooden doors and paused to look around. Two tellers waited behind the long mahogany counter protected by iron bars. Mr. Winters had made the bank virtually burglar-proof. She approached the man at the end.

"Good morning, Miss DeLery, how may I help you?" The clerk ran his fingers through his thinning hair and flashed a wide smile. James Henry had been one of the bachelors Millie had invited to tea as a possible suitor. He was a very nice man, but not at all suitable for Analise. Not at all like Tyler.

Annoyed that again she was thinking about *him*, she forced a smile. "I'm here to see Mr. Winters. Is he in?"

"Yes, I'll tell him you're here. Please have a seat." James tugged at the sleeves of his black suit and hurried to the office at the rear of the building.

Too nervous to sit, she twisted the ties of her reticule and paced. Several ladies waiting in the other teller's line glanced at her and whispered behind their gloved hands. She double-checked her hands to make sure that her gloves were sparkling white. Her grandmother had always told her that you could tell a lady by her gloves. Thanks to Mrs. Hennessey, they were as white as new-fallen snow.

Moments later, Mr. Winters exited his office and greeted Analise cordially, in spite of the fact that she had little money in his bank. He unlocked the security door that separated the tellers, offices, and vault from the lobby.

"Miss DeLery, how nice to see you. Please come into my office so we can talk." The tall, slender man took both of her hands in his. Even through her gloves, she felt the perspiration on his palms. "Let me take your cloak," he offered.

She loosed the tie at the neck and allowed him to

take her garment. "Thank you for seeing me, Mr. Winters."

He gestured to the chair in front of his imposing oak desk. "Please have a seat." The banker returned to his large leather chair and sat down. "Do you have any idea when Mr. Morgan will be returning? That was quite some excitement, with him apprehending those outlaws and recovering the payroll. He locked it in my vault for safekeeping, you know. Over a hundred thousand dollars." His voice was as reverent as if he was discussing the Almighty.

She gritted her teeth. Was that all everybody had to talk about? Didn't they realize that after a month's absence without a word, it was clear he was not returning? "Yes, he's quite the hero."

The banker leaned back in his chair and steepled his fingers in front of his face. "Now, to what do I owe the honor of your visit?"

"You'll remember that I approached you some time ago about the Onasis House on Athena and Delta streets. The bank had recently repossessed it, and I mentioned I want to rent it for a clinic for women and children. I'm ready to offer a fair rental, until I can raise the funds to purchase the building."

He dropped his hands and drummed his fingers on the desk. "Miss DeLery, I'm not sure how to tell you this. I know you had great expectations for that house. And I'm aware that your goals are commendable. We all know how important proper medical care is in the community. Your father is doing an excellent job and I know he's very proud of your accomplishments."

She could hear the refusal in his tone. He wasn't going to rent the Onasis House to her. "You said you would speak to the board of directors. Did they refuse me?" A rope tightened around her chest. He was trying to let her down easily. But there was no easy in this situation. She tugged her sketch from her reticule. "Look, I drew up these plans to renovate the house into offices, examining rooms, and even a nursery for children." She blinked back the tears that threatened to pour like a fountain down her face.

He gestured in surrender. "I'm very sorry, Miss DeLery. There is nothing I can do to help you. We had an offer to purchase with a handsome profit for the bank."

Shocked, she was momentarily speechless as her dream slipped away. "Who . . . who bought my . . . the Onasis House?" Her throat tightened against unshed tears.

"I would tell you if I knew. However, the transaction was handled by an agent. He didn't reveal the name of the buyer. He wired the funds, and I am preparing the deed."

"You do not know the buyer? And you did not give me the chance to make a counteroffer?" Not that she had the money, but he could at least have given her time to get some resources together.

"It happened quickly, Miss DeLery. The board jumped at the chance to dispose of the property at a profit. The buyer demanded immediate possession."

"He's here? He's already moved in?" She stood, ready to seek out this illusive owner.

"I don't know. The agent didn't give any other details."

Analise's heart sank. Unless she could convince this mysterious buyer to either rent or sell the house, her clinic would be nothing but a fleeting dream. There wasn't another suitable property in Omega either for sale or rent. Her only other choice was to find an empty lot and build from the ground up. With her lack of funds, and the time involved in building, she would be an old woman before her dream came true.

"Thank you for your help, Mr. Winters. If another piece of property becomes available, please let me know."

He got to his feet and escorted her from his office. Gently, he set her cloak on her shoulders. "I'll certainly keep you in mind. I'm sorry."

The banker wasn't at all sorry, she thought. His goal was to make as much money as possible, no matter who he had to swindle out of their clinic.

As they reached the outer door, a gentleman entered the bank. He paused, as if startled by their presence, then he tipped his hat. "Good afternoon, madam, sir," he greeted with a guttural German accent.

Mr. Winters stretched out his hand to the stranger. "Mr. August. How good to see you again."

The stranger nodded. "It is *Herr* Agg-gust," he corrected the pronunciation of his very German name.

Analise stared at him for a long moment. Tall, but on the paunchy side, his beard and mustache hid most of his face, and gray streaked his dark hair. A very large overcoat did little to hide his extended belly. Yet something about him struck her as familiar.

"Sorry, this is Miss DeLery. Miss DeLery, this gentleman is the agent who purchased the Onasis House for his client." He gestured to Analise. "Miss DeLery is interested in renting the residence."

*Herr* August nodded. "*Guten Tag, fräulein.* Pardon me, good day—I must remember to practice my English. You wish to rent the house?"

"Yes," she replied. "I would appreciate the opportunity to present my case to your client. Will he be coming to Omega soon?"

The man shrugged. "I am not privy to that information. However, I would be delighted to discuss the situation with you and present a proposal to my employer."

For the first time since entering the bank, Analise felt a ray of hope. If she could charm this man into accepting her proposal for the clinic, she had hope of making her dream come true.

"If you are free now, we can walk over to the property and I will show you what I have in mind. I am sure that when you hear my plans for the house, your client will be very receptive to my ideas."

Mr. August offered his arm. "Let us stroll to the Onasis House, and I will be delighted to listen to your ideas."

Analise took his arm and allowed him to escort her from the bank and down the boardwalk. A strange shiver raced up her arm from his touch. She'd felt this way only a time or two with a man. He shuffled slightly as they strolled down Alpha toward Athena.

"This is an interesting town. So much Greek," he said, his accent so heavy, she barely understood his words.

They reached the Onasis House, and he opened the gate for her. "This is a rather large house," he noted. "Why would an unmarried woman require such a grand residence? Are you planning to marry, and have a large family?" His voice had the hint of a smile. He seemed a rather pleasant man. *Herr* August unlocked the front door and gestured her inside. "Or do you have other plans for the, uh, upstairs rooms?"

It took a moment before his insinuations sank in. "Absolutely not, sir. I plan nothing immoral or illegal for this house."

"Then what are your plans, if I may ask? My client is an upstanding citizen, and he would not want to promote any immoral behavior."

"Sir, I am a physician. I wish to set up my practice here. I propose a clinic for women and children. A place where I can provide excellent medical care, and if there are complications in childbirth, I can safely deliver the babies here."

"A *doktor*? That is an admirable goal, *liebe* . . . my dear. But do you have the necessary funds to carry out such a noble plan?"

"I am now raising the money." Excitement bubbled in her heart. At least he hadn't turned her down without listening to her proposal. She dug into her reticule and pulled out the paper with her plans. "I have sketched out what I have in mind for the house."

He unfolded the sheet of paper and squinted while he studied it for a long moment. "Very interesting." He paced the various rooms without comment. "If you will allow me to keep this sketch, I will present it to my client with your offer."

Hope took wings in her chest. "Yes, that would be fine. I do appreciate your help. This clinic is very important to me and to the town."

He folded the paper and shoved it into his coat pocket. Again, he nodded. "Good. I wish you well, *Fräulein . . . Doktor* DeLery." He bowed in the old-fashioned manner and caught her hand in his large gloved one. "If you will excuse me, I have other business to attend. *Auf Wiedersehen.*"

He straightened and gestured her from the house. They parted at the corner, she to go home, and he to the center of town.

Strange, she thought, as she watched him shuffle away, she hadn't seen him around town, nor had Millie or Mrs. Hennessey mentioned a stranger. With the gossip mill in full force, it was unusual that nobody had mentioned the stranger staying at the hotel.

Analise shrugged. It wasn't unusual that she wasn't privy to the latest gossip. Her medical practice kept her too busy to even listen when Millie related news of one kind or another.

Unless it concerned her or Tyler, she didn't hear. On a sigh, she realized how much she missed him. She turned on her heel and started after *Herr* August. Why did he seem so familiar? She laughed at her own imagination. This man looked nothing like Tyler, even though he was as tall, and wide shouldered. But he had fooled her once with a disguise; could he do it again? Determined to learn more about the man, she hurried after him on the boardwalk.

"*Herr* August," she called. Lifting her skirts, she ran in the direction he had gone. He turned onto Alpha Street. By the time she reached the corner, she saw no sign of him. He had disappeared into thin air, or into one of the doorways of the various businesses along the street. She set her hands on her hips. How could a man who shuffled so slowly move so quickly?

She continued down Alpha to the only hotel in town. If he'd only recently come to town, he could be staying at the Olympia Hotel. She entered the lobby and studied the various men sitting on the sofas and at the small tables. None was *Herr* August.

The desk clerk, Mr. Anderson, smiled when she approached. "What can I do for you, Miss DeLery?"

Did anybody respect her as a physician? Few people addressed her by the title she'd earned. "I'm wondering if you have a *Herr* August registered at the hotel?"

He glanced at the large hotel register. "Yes, he came in yesterday on the train from Denver."

"From Denver? Did he say anything about his business in Omega?"

Mr. Anderson shrugged. "He asked for directions to the bank."

"Did he mention how long he'll be staying in town?"

"He didn't say. Would you like to leave a message?"

She sighed. "No, but thank you for your help."

"By the way, have you heard from Mr. Morgan?"

"I understand he's busy with the trial and conducting business. It may be quite some time until he returns." Not that she was expecting him to ever return to Omega. Soon people would quit asking about him, and she could just forget they had ever met.

She squared her shoulders. "I must get back to the office. Good day, Mr. Anderson."

"Good day, Miss DeLery. I'm sure I'll see you in church on Sunday."

"Yes, Sunday."

Hidden behind a stack of overalls, Tyler watched the street through the frosty mercantile store window. He'd barely made it into the store when Analise marched past. He breathed a sigh of relief and wiped a sheen of perspiration from his forehead. The fake whiskers and makeup itched, but it safely hid his identity. His gaze followed her across the street to the Olympia Hotel, where he was currently registered as *Herr* August, the German agent.

Taken by surprise when he'd bumped into her at the bank, he'd barely stopped himself from tugging her into his arms and kissing her senseless. Instead, he'd taken her arm and escorted her to the Onasis House. He'd expected to retain his anonymity with the disguise while he dealt with the bank. *Herr* August had an easier time conducting business than Tyler Morgan, with his notoriety. But to run into Analise had thrown him completely off-kilter. He'd needed only a day or two to get the ball rolling on the project. This was one disguise, one masquerade he planned to keep to himself. He doubted she would understand why he'd again fooled her. But his motives were all good. He wanted to give her heart's desire to her as a gift. He only hoped he could keep his distance until Monday.

Monday seemed a year away.

# Chapter 13

Sunday dawned bright and sunny in spite of the chill wind from the mountains. Analise awoke filled with anticipation. It was more than just the upcoming wedding and dedication of a baby. Deep in her heart, she felt as if something significant, something important, was about to happen.

She could hardly sit still during the church service. Reverend Carter delivered an inspiring sermon, though not as eloquent as the ones Tyler had delivered. Analise couldn't enter the church without thinking about the illusive and mysterious Pinkerton man—the actor who had duped her. Actually, everything reminded her of him. Even the impending wedding and christening brought thoughts of him. After all, he'd helped to bring little Anna into the world.

Millie had been as excited as if the celebrations were for her own family. She loved to entertain, and the thought of a wedding had her in titters. She'd even gotten Mrs. Hennessey involved. The housekeeper had baked a large cake and set out a cold dinner for the guests.

After the final hymn rang with "Amen," Reverend Carter again mounted the pulpit. Analise groaned. Surely he wasn't going to begin another dissertation.

"Friends," he began, "I have some exciting news for you. I have greatly enjoyed my circuit here in Omega, and especially the hospitality of Doctor DeLery and his family." The minister patted his stomach to show how much he had enjoyed the meals. "But as I'm getting older, pastoring three churches on my circuit is becoming difficult." The entire congregation groaned. The minister was well liked. "The bishop in Denver realized that you need a full-time minister, and that the congregation at Omega is able to sustain such a person. This will be my last Sunday with you, unless you call me for a revival or special service." He chuckled softly. "That was a broad hint, folks."

The people began to whisper among themselves. Even Analise was shocked. Had Tyler followed through on his promise and solicited a minister for them? Did he have that kind of influence?

Mr. Gabriel, the blacksmith, stood up and raised his beefy hand for attention. "Who is going to be our new preacher?"

"I am happy to announce that a young minister, fresh out of seminary, with a lovely young wife, will be arriving soon. I'm sure you will make them as welcome as you have me."

One person after another bombarded him with questions, voices overlapping one another. Preacher Carter raised his hands to quiet the congregation. "That is all I know. Our bishop will send a wire to inform you of when the new pastor will arrive. Now, I've talked enough. Return to your homes and enjoy the rest of the Lord's Day."

For a long while after the service ended, the congregation gathered on the lawn, gossiping among themselves and giving the minister their best wishes. It was nearly two o'clock when Analise and her family returned to their home. They entered through the front door where Millie had decorated the parlor with streamers and greenery.

Analise wondered when Alex and Polly would arrive. Then she noticed movement on the rear porch. Opening the door, she found her guests waiting patiently on the rockers. Manny darted to Analise the instant he spotted her.

"Doctor, doctor." The boy wrapped his arms around her waist. "I get new boots. Look. And my hat. I grown up now. I take care of Anna."

She smiled at the boy's childish antics. How proud he was to have something new. These were probably the first new items he'd ever received. The child wore clean but faded denims and a plaid shirt. Instead of a coat, he was wrapped in a thick blanket. He was scrubbed clean and wore shiny new boots. She wondered when Alex had come to town to purchase the shoes. "You're very handsome."

Alex stood and helped Polly to her feet. Both looked shy and embarrassed. "Come in and meet my family. Millie is dying to get her hands on Anna."

Both wore neatly pressed and clean clothes, if slightly faded. Polly was lovely and Alex a handsome man. Hesitantly, they entered the kitchen. Once inside, Analise took the baby from the young mother.

"Come into the parlor. Everybody is waiting for you. The minister is here, and ready for the wedding."

Alex looked as if he was about to bolt and Polly dragged her feet. Manny raced ahead and found Steven. Her brother dropped his hand affectionately on the child's shoulder.

Once in the parlor, Analise made the introductions. The young couple barely spoke, as if expecting to be ordered to leave. Being part Indian, Alex had

endured more than his share of prejudice in his young
life. Etienne and the minister shook the young man's
hand as they would a close friend.

Millie hugged Polly and snatched the baby from
Analise. She then moved to the stairway. "Polly, come
upstairs with me and Analise. I have a surprise for
you." She turned to the waiting group of men. "We'll
only be a minute or two. Have a cookie or something.
Dinner will be served following the ceremonies."

On the way up the stairs Millie played with the
baby. Analise had no idea what her stepmother had
in mind, but the smile on Millie's face said she was
proud of herself. "In here." She gestured to the bedchamber she shared with her husband.

Polly glanced to Analise for help. "I ain't never
been in this fine of a house before," she whispered,
afraid to enter the chamber.

"Go in. Millie is harmless."

Millie handed the baby back to Analise. Her christening present of the lovely lace shawl was wrapped
around the infant. "You take care of this angel. But
be careful of her head."

Analise laughed. "Millie, I am a physician. I know
how to hold a baby."

"But you aren't a mother."

Pain arched through Analise. Millie did not mean
anything hurtful. She didn't know about the baby
Analise had lost, or of the fact that she could never
have another child. Her stepmother's greatest hope
was for grandchildren. Hence her determination to
get a husband for Analise.

"Sit down, Polly." Millie led the girl to the vanity
stool in front of her mirror. With a few deft movements, she tugged the braids from the girl's hair and
ran her brush through the blond tresses. "You have
beautiful hair, like spun gold. You are so lucky." Millie

continued to chat while dressing her hair. "Here I am stuck with this red hair."

The young woman looked up at Millie with adoration in her eyes. "Oh, no, Miz DeLery. Your hair is like the sunrise, all bright and pretty."

Millie laughed, clearly pleased. She pulled the girl's hair into a high chignon, leaving long tendrils trailing down her cheeks. Then she set a ring of silk flowers on top of her hair. "You're too young for a hat. These flowers enhance your youth and beauty."

When Millie finished, she turned the girl to the mirror. "Is that me?" Polly asked in awe. Tears gathered in her blue eyes. "You shouldn't have gone to so much trouble for somebody like me."

Millie caught the girl's face in her hands. "Somebody like you is a lovely young woman. You are getting married to the man you love. This is little enough to do for you."

The young woman wiped away her tears. "I don't know how I'm going to thank you. I'll do your laundry or your mending to pay you."

"You don't owe me anything. We are delighted to do this." Millie lowered her voice. "This is practice for Analise's wedding to Mr. Morgan."

*Not again*, Analise thought. Millie wouldn't give up. She couldn't accept the fact that Tyler wasn't coming back for any reason, marriage being the last thing on his mind.

"Let's get downstairs," Analise said. "We've kept the men waiting long enough."

"Not yet," Millie said. "Your turn, Missy."

"Millie, I'm already dressed." She turned the baby over to the mother.

Not taking no for an answer, Millie set her hands on her rounded hips. Analise shrugged. If she didn't do exactly as her stepmother ordered, they would never get to the ceremony. "I'm only going to do little adjustments to your hair." She tugged on the curls in Analise's hair, letting them caress her cheeks and neck. "At least you wore a nice gown. This rose is lovely on you, it brings out the glow in your complexion. However . . ." Millie picked up the scissors from her sewing basket.

Eyes wide, Analise stared at the older woman. "You aren't going to cut off my hair?"

"No, I'm going to make a little alteration to this dress. The collar is entirely too high. I want you to look like a woman, not a nun."

Too stunned to resist, Analise watched in the mirror as her stepmother trimmed away the lace yoke of her favorite afternoon gown. Millie tucked the loose edges under, leaving Analise's chest and neck bare. "There, just right," Millie declared, satisfied with her handiwork. "Just a hint of cleavage, enough to look interesting."

"Millie, I can't go out like this." Analise splayed her hand across her bare chest.

"Posh. It isn't nearly as low as the gown you wore to your engagement party. Let's get downstairs." Millie again took the baby. "I'll hold her during the wedding. Then I'll give her back to the godmother for the dedication."

There was no use arguing with the determined woman. Millie always had her way—with her husband, with her family, and with her friends. Analise locked arms with Polly as they descended the stairs. Male voices and laughter came from the parlor. Millie marched in first. "Here comes the bride," she announced.

Analise stopped and released the young bride. Polly entered slowly, twisting a lace handkerchief in her fingers. She looked at Alex, smiling widely. The young man walked toward his bride as if in a trance. Analise stepped into the room and stopped in her tracks.

A tall man, dressed in a finely tailored black suit with a crisp white shirt and shiny boots, stood with an elbow propped on the mantel. He smiled and Analise's heart leaped into double-time.

Tyler Morgan, as big as life and twice as handsome, met her gaze from across the room.

"What are you doing here?" she asked.

"I heard there's going to be a wedding. A wedding needs a best man and a baby needs a godfather." He gestured widely with his arms. "Here I am."

Tyler watched Analise enter the parlor. It took all his self-control to remain at the mantel and not sweep her up in his arms. He'd missed her, more than he'd ever thought possible. His gaze drifted slowly over her. She was lovelier than ever. He ached to slip his fingers into her hair, to stroke her pink cheeks, and drift lower to discover the female curves that tempted his resolve. Her rose-colored dress enhanced her complexion, and drew his gaze to the deep scoop and the fullness at the top of her breasts.

Tamping down his lascivious thoughts, thoughts that had made for many sleepless nights, he moved away from the fireplace and offered his arm. "May I escort you to a wedding, Doctor Analise?"

While the others focused on the young couple about to be wed, he couldn't tear his gaze away from the beautiful woman who had invaded his life and thoughts from the moment he'd seen her.

Keeping away from her for the past days had been torture. He'd known when he'd returned to Omega that it would be impossible to avoid her, and even harder not to reveal his identity and sweep her into his arms. But Herr August was leaving the next day, and Tyler was staying. Forever.

Analise placed her hand on his arm. Unable to help himself, he tucked her arm close to his side and covered her cold fingers with his warm ones. "I've missed you," he whispered. "Did you miss me?"

"No, I was much too busy getting things in order for the clinic."

He laughed softly, not wanting anybody to notice them. The others gathered in front of the minister to begin the ceremony. "Soon that will be us in front of the preacher."

"Not if I have anything to say about it."

"That's just it, *chérie*, you don't have anything to say about it. You've already accepted my proposal."

She stiffened at his side. "I happen to be engaged to Deacon Tyler Goodfellow, who does not exist."

"I'll change my name, if that will satisfy you."

By then they had reached the end of the parlor where the minister and young couple waited.

"Shall we begin?" Pastor Carter asked, opening up his Bible.

Alex caught Polly's hand in his. Both looked scared enough to dart from the room. Doctor and Mrs. DeLery stood to the side, Millie holding the baby securely in her arms.

Polly looked very young and fragile. Yet Tyler knew she had a strength many older women didn't possess. Alex clearly loved her, and from their conversations, he knew his young friend intended to do his best for his family, or die trying. The outlaws' horses would make a good start for a horse ranch.

The ceremony went smoothly. Even little Manny and Steven stood quietly and respectfully.

When it came time for a ring, Alex dipped his

head. Before he could respond, Tyler pulled a small gold circle from his pocket. "I have it right here," he said.

Alex stared at him as if Tyler was handing the young man a dead rat. "I . . . I . . ." he began.

"Asked me to hold it for you. Take it. Everybody's waiting."

"Thank you," he whispered. At the minister's instruction, Alex slipped the ring onto his bride's finger and lifted her hand to his lips. Tears flowed freely from this man who put up a tough front to the world.

"I now pronounce you husband and wife," the minister announced. "You may kiss the bride."

Polly lifted her face and Alex pressed a chaste kiss to her lips.

Tyler leaned over and whispered for Analise's ears only. "May I kiss you too?"

"No." She stepped away from him.

Reverend Carter smiled. "I believe we have another important ceremony to perform. Bring the little one to me. Our Lord said to bring the little children, and he blessed them." He reached out and took Anna gently into his arms.

The traditional ceremony went smoothly, each speaking when it was their turn. Analise and Tyler promised to see that the child grew up in the Lord. Tyler always took his vows seriously, and his heart swelled with purpose. From the moment little Anna had drawn her first breath, he had fallen in love with her. She would be forever a part of his life. He glanced at Analise and could read the same promise in her eyes.

So much love flowed over him, Tyler's heart pounded like a thoroughbred's hooves in a race. Analise, the baby, new friends, and soon a new family. It was all a man could want. All he had to do was convince her that he was sincere. That he loved her. His heart sank. Given her reaction to his presence, he might as well ask a pig to fly.

After hugs and kisses, handshakes, and congratulations all around, Steven set his hands on his narrow hips. "When are we going to eat? My stomach thinks my throat's been cut."

Laughter and joy filled the house. The small crowd entered the dining room and sat at the table. As always, Mrs. Hennessey had outdone herself.

The food was delicious and the conversation lively. Polly excused herself to feed the baby, and Anna fell asleep soon after. They toasted with punch and sliced the cake. All during the party, Polly stared at her ring, as if she couldn't believe it was hers.

When the clock chimed six, Alex notified them it was time to return to the ranch. It was over an hour's drive in the farm wagon.

After good-byes all around the young family returned to their home. Before they left, Mrs. DeLery filled a basket of the leftovers so Polly wouldn't have to worry about cooking the next day. Steven took a book and went to his room. Millie excused herself to retire to her boudoir, while the minister and Doctor DeLery went into the study for a game of chess. They invited Tyler to join them. But he had other plans for his evening.

"I believe I'll go upstairs also," Analise said. "Mr. Morgan, thank you for everything." She turned toward the stairs.

Tyler caught her arm. "Come out on the porch with me, sweetheart. It's a beautiful evening, and too early to go in."

She stared up at him, studying his features. "Yes, thank you. I believe we have a few things to discuss."

Discuss? He was certain she wanted to argue with him or give him a really good set down. He had other activities in mind. Tyler picked up a woolen shawl from the coat rack at the door and draped it over her shoulders. His hands lingered, and he couldn't stop himself from touching his lips to the top of her ear. "You always smell like heaven."

She shivered. "I usually smell like antiseptic. Millie insisted I use her soap."

"And was the gown Millie's idea also?"

"It belongs to me, with a few alterations by my stepmother."

He dropped his gaze to the low neckline. "You look lovely, more beautiful than I even remembered. And believe me, my dreams were very vivid."

Pink touched her cheeks and drifted down her chest. He stepped away, afraid that he wouldn't be able to control his needs. He loved her, and he wanted to make her his, his forever. Until they married, he would have to control his desires. He respected her and her family too much to compromise her reputation.

Dusk had fallen, and the moon spread its light over the garden. The roses had long faded and the bushes cut back. He took Analise's arm and guided her away from the wicker chairs to the railing.

"Look, there's our star. It's getting closer all the time. Every night that I was away, I looked up and thought about you." He wrapped his arm around her, pulling her close to his side. "Did you look up and think about me?"

She lifted her gaze to the heavens. "I was much too busy to think about you."

"I'm never too busy to think about you."

"Ha." She laughed. "I haven't heard from you in over a month, and you didn't even let me know when you were coming back."

"Sorry." He brushed his fingers along her shoulders. "I had a million details to take care of. Alan even called me to Washington. But look, I'm here now."

"How long have you been back?"

"Not long."

"You've been to see Alex. That's how Manny got the new boots, and you bought the ring. But you were too busy to come to see me?" She let out a bark of laughter. "And you claim to want to marry me."

He shrugged. "It was the least I could do for them. Manny needed nice shoes to go with that fine hat you gave him."

Analise laughed. "He is such a precious child, he deserved to feel special."

"They are all special. I've become very fond of that little family."

"So have I. Anna is my first baby here in Omega."

"And my first godchild." He dropped a kiss to the top of her ear. Lord, she smelled good. Now that he was back, he didn't know how he had survived the past month.

She shifted slightly. "When do you leave for your next assignment?"

"I'm not. I've decided to make Omega my home."

She stared at him. "Here? What will you do?"

"I'm investigating new opportunities. And if I can't find anything, I'll stay home with the babies, and let my doctor wife support me."

"I have told you time and again, I am not going to marry you."

"What will it take to change your mind?"

On a long sigh, she shook her head. "Nothing. Let's change the subject. That one is getting tiresome. I read in our *Omega Herald* that the outlaws were sent to prison."

Tyler nodded. "They'll be there for a very long time."

She shivered.

"Cold?" Wrapping both arms around her, he pulled her into the warmth of his chest.

"No. I suppose I'm just now realizing how much danger I was in. I am grateful to you. Harv was the most dangerous of them all. He wanted to sell me in Mexico."

He touched his lips to her temple. "I never would have let that happen. You belong to me. I would have moved heaven and hell to keep you safe."

"Tyler, sometimes I believe you're the most dangerous of them all."

He nuzzled his lips into her neck. "Not nearly as dangerous as you."

"I'm not the one carrying a gun hidden under my coat, nor am I skilled at fisticuffs." She moved her hand to his cheek and stroked lightly on his growth of whiskers.

"You're even worse. You've stolen my heart and run away with it." Tyler knew that if he didn't move away, he was going to kiss her—and there was no telling where that would lead.

"Tyler, I believe you've played Romeo and Don Juan too many times on the stage. You've memorized the dialogue and turned into a seducer."

"Can I seduce you, Doc?" He lowered his face until his lips were a hair's breath from hers.

"You're doing a very good job of it already."

"Does your father still have his shotgun?"

"Loaded and ready. Do you want to take a chance?"

"For you it would be worth a load of buckshot."

His tongue snaked out and touched her lips. She drew a sharp intake of breath. "I'll dig it out of you."

"This is getting more interesting all the time." His mouth closed over hers, tenderly sipping at the sweetness that was all Analise.

Her fingers snaked into his hair, and sweet sensations slithered clear down to his toes. This was dangerous. With any other woman, he could stop and set her away. But Analise had such a profound effect on him, he doubted he could stop if they went even one iota further.

To his surprise, she opened her lips and invited his quiet invasion. He didn't dare increase the pressure. With how much he loved her, he couldn't wait until they married. No matter how much she protested—they would be wed, and soon.

Tyler ended the kiss and pressed his forehead to hers. "I had better stop, or we'll be starting the honeymoon right now."

She breathed in a soft laugh. "I told you there won't be a wedding, hence no honeymoon."

On a long sigh, he set her away from him. "We'll discuss that situation later." Giving her a gentle push toward the door, he opened the screen and gestured her in. "I'll be back tomorrow. We can talk then. It will be much safer with Millie and your father present."

"Safer for whom? You or me?"

"Both of us, I believe. I'm not too fond of buckshot in my rear."

He caught both her hands in his and carried them to his lips. "*Bonsoir, chérie.*"

She slipped away and entered the house, leaving him alone and adrift with his thoughts. Tyler dropped down from the porch and headed for the hotel. Nothing had changed, everything had changed. Whether she liked it or not, the wedding would take place.

He never gave up when pursuing a wanted man, and he wouldn't stop until he captured his woman's heart.

Glancing up into the sky, he imagined the star was winking at him. Was it encouraging him or mocking him? He wished he knew.

* * *

The next morning, Analise awoke with a new resolve. She wanted her clinic. More than anything she wanted to open her clinic to save lives and give quality medical care to the town. Her heart went out to women and children who were often too timid or poor to ask for help.

Determined to follow through with the project, she dressed carefully in a smart navy suit with a stiff white blouse. Her first stop was the Onasis House. She stopped at the gate and stared at the house. A row of columns stretched across the front, reaching to the high roof. The graceful façade reminded her of the Greek Revival façade of many homes in New Orleans's Garden District. That could be why she'd been so drawn to this house.

A load of lumber lay on the ground and two men wearing overalls were tearing away rotten wood from the porch. The new owner was already at work renovating the house that should have been hers. Fury rose up in her chest. She walked around to the back and spotted *Herr* August, speaking to a man sitting on the high seat of a wagon.

"*Herr* August," she called out, ready for a confrontation.

Either the man was deaf or ignoring her. She made her way across the overgrown lawn to the rear entrance. The wagon pulled away, but when she looked again, *Herr* August was nowhere to be seen. She made her way into the house and called again. "*Herr* August, are you in here?" Entering the open door, she walked through the empty rooms. The only sound was her echo, and the sound of ripping lumber from the porch.

A long shadow fell across her path. "*Doktor* DeLery, how nice to see you again." *Herr* August stepped through an open doorway.

She stared up at the illusive agent. Something about him bothered her, but she couldn't put her finger on it. "I would like to know if you have contacted your client about renting the house to me?"

He shrugged and shook his head. "I am sorry, *Doktor.* He has not made a decision."

"Do you know of his plans for the house?"

"I am afraid I do not. He simply asked me to contact workmen, and he would provide the plans."

"Do you think there is hope he will consider my offer?" She glanced around the room where she planned to put her office.

"There is always hope. Have faith, *fräulein.* Anything is possible. My client is a reasonable man. He is also very kind and known as a philanthropist." He bowed and stepped away. "I must go. I have a train to catch."

"Well, thank you for any help you can give me. Please inform me when you know the answer, yes or no."

"I certainly will, *Doktor.* Now I must be on my way." He shuffled toward the door. "May I escort you home?"

She shook her head. "No thank you. Do you mind if I stay here for a while and look around? I have so many plans for my clinic." Tears gathered in the corners of her eyes.

The man noted the moisture and handed her a handkerchief. "Do not be upset. I will do all I can to help you."

With a forced smile, she took the offered handkerchief. "Thank you. You are too kind."

With another nod to her, he left her alone in the parlor. Her dreams were here, the dreams of her clinic. Analise touched the handkerchief to her eyes. The fine linen smelled of man and a touch of cologne. A familiar cologne. Where had she smelled this before?

She closed her eyes and let the aroma drift over her. Tyler. The handkerchief smelled like Tyler. The way he'd smelled last night on the porch when he'd kissed her.

"*Herr* August," she whispered. He was as tall as Tyler, as wide-shouldered, but with his eyes hidden behind his thick spectacles, the color was indiscernible. Tyler was an actor, a master of disguise and makeup.

She'd been duped. Royally duped. Again.

What kind of fool did he take her for?

Well, this time he wasn't going to get by with his deception.

As she marched down Alpha Street toward the Olympia Hotel, Analise wished she had a gun. All she had to do was catch him in the act and expose him for a fraud. It was about time somebody called his bluff. And she was just the woman to do it.

She entered the hotel lobby and boldly strolled up to the desk. "Afternoon, Mr. Anderson. What is *Herr* August's room number?"

He flashed her a sly grin. "He's in room two-twelve. Mr. Morgan is in two-ten."

So they were registered in different rooms, adjacent to each other. Ha, she thought. If she was right, he was paying for one room too many. She turned to the stairs.

"Miss DeLery, you can't go up there. It's unseemly."

She paused. "Mr. Anderson, I am a physician. I received word that *Herr* August needs medical assistance. Please, bring the key and let me in."

"But he seemed fine when he came in a while ago. In fact, he said he had to pack and catch the evening train." The clerk hesitated.

"Mr. Anderson, if he dies, it will be on your head," she declared.

The man shrugged. "I guess it won't hurt to check on him. I don't want anybody to die in my hotel."

Together they climbed the stairs. At room two-twelve, she paused and listened. She heard footsteps across the floor. "Please unlock the door," she whispered.

"Shouldn't we knock first?"

"No. He may be lying on the floor unconscious."

Reluctantly, the man slipped the key into the lock. It clicked, and she turned the knob. The door jerked open in her hand. She gasped, and fell forward. Mr. Anderson stood in the hallway and stared.

Analise found herself looking down the barrel of a very large gun in the hand of the man she recognized in spite of the beard on his face.

"Exposed for the fraud you are, Mr. Morgan."

# Chapter 14

Tyler tugged Analise by the arm and slammed the door shut behind her, blocking out the desk clerk. "Get lost, Anderson," he called through the closed door. He returned the gun to the shoulder holster and backed up a step.

His stomach dropped. Analise stared at him as if he was the lowest worm on the planet. And he couldn't blame her one bit. What had ever made him think he could fool her a second time?

"How should I address you? You're wearing *Herr* August's whiskers, but without the pillow in your trousers, you look amazingly like Mr. Morgan. Or is it Goodfellow? Strangefellow would suit you better." She folded her arms over her chest and tapped her foot.

He lifted his hands in surrender. He'd really done it this time. "You caught me red-handed. What can I say?" He grinned, in a futile effort to defuse her anger.

"You can tell me why you put on a masquerade. Why you chose to hide your identity from me. Why you saw fit to dupe me again." She shook a finger at him. "On Friday, when *Herr* August was so polite, and again today, when he . . . you made me feel like a complete idiot." Color rose in her face. "*Fräulein,* my client is very kind and he is a philanthropist," she said in a harsh and very fake German accent. "If I had a gun I would shoot you."

"You'd only have to dig the bullet out and patch me up."

"I'd let you die."

"Didn't you take an oath?" He moved past her to the mirror that hung over the washstand, using the time to gather his thoughts. He should have expected her to see through his disguise. Carefully he caught the ends of the beard and slowly removed the false facial hair. "You're too good a doctor to let a patient die." Next, he brushed the graying powder from his hair.

Looking more like himself, Tyler turned to face a woman with fire in her eyes. Heat sizzled all the way to the male parts of his body. Damn, she was like an avenging angel out to right every wrong in the world.

She was magnificent.

"I'd make an exception for you."

He laughed. "Analise, I can explain everything."

"I'm sure you can. You seem to have an explanation for every one of your transgressions." She paced across the floor and picked up his oversized jacket. "You never should have given up the stage. You're a very good actor. I can honestly say I was royally and sincerely duped. You must think I'm the biggest idiot in the world. How stupid do you think I am?"

"Analise, I don't think you're stupid at all. I think you're the most intelligent and beautiful woman in the world."

Anger streamed from her like the rays from the sun. "Oh, you are good. If I didn't know better, I would believe you."

"I don't blame you for being angry. But I didn't mean any harm. If you'll let me explain, we can

straighten this out, then we'll laugh about it together."
He moved toward her, lifting his hands in supplication. She slipped past him before he could catch her arms.

"Laugh at me, you mean."

"I didn't mean to hurt you, and I would never laugh at you. Please sit down, and let me explain."

She moved to the door. *"Monsieur, allez vous faire voir."*

He bit back a grin. "Your grandmother would be appalled at your telling your fiancé to go to hell."

Gritting her teeth, she glared at him. "You are not my fiancé. You are a liar and a cheat. I do not want anything to do with you."

That did it. He caught her arms and pulled her hard to his chest. "I've heard enough, Analise. You will listen to me if I have to tie you to that bed." She struggled against his hold. "That has interesting possibilities."

"Let go of me."

"Not until you listen to me."

"There's nothing you can say that will justify lying to me or deceiving me with your masquerade. You didn't see fit to contact me when you returned. It was only by accident that I encountered *Herr* August— you. Still you kept your identity hidden, laughing up your sleeve at the naive country doctor."

"Analise—"

Frantic pounding on the door stopped him cold. "Mr. August, Miss DeLery? Are you in there?" Male voices rumbled through the door.

"Analise, are you in there? Are you all right?"

Of all the impossible situations. The sheriff and Doctor DeLery had chosen a heck of a time to interfere.

"They think I'm hurting you. Will you please say something and get rid of them?"

"Papa, I'm here." Through gritted teeth, she ordered, "Open the door."

On a string of curses in three languages, he turned the key and flung open the door. "Come in. Everybody is welcome. We're having a party. Let's invite the entire town."

Gun drawn, the sheriff led the way into the room. Tyler hoped the incompetent man wouldn't shoot himself or anybody else with the firearm shaking in his hand. Doctor DeLery followed while the desk clerk watched from the hallway with half a dozen men.

Setting his hands on his hips, Tyler stared down the mob. "What do you want?"

The doctor studied Tyler, his daughter, and the bed. Analise faced them, her cheeks pinked. Her hat was askew and her jacket mussed. It wasn't hard to get the wrong impression. Tyler gritted his teeth at the absurdity of the situation.

"Analise, what's going on here? Mr. Anderson sent for the sheriff and for me. He said an outlaw with a gun had killed Mr. August and captured you." Etienne glanced back at the desk clerk, now easing away.

"I saw it with my own eyes. He pointed a gun at us, and he grabbed Miss DeLery, then he locked the door. I heard her yelling like he was hurting her." Anderson dug his finger under the tight collar of his shirt. The other men in the hallway stretched for a better view of the commotion in the room.

"As you can see, August is gone. My fiancée and I were having a small lover's quarrel."

Analise shoved past him, past the sheriff, and turned to her father. "Papa, I am going home." She tugged the hem of her jacket. "You have my permission to shoot Mr. Morgan." With a swish of her skirts, she pranced down the hallway.

Bewildered, the doctor stared after his daughter.

The sheriff looked so flustered, he didn't know what was happening. "Mr. Morgan, do you need help?" asked the sheriff.

Yes, Tyler thought, with the woman he loved. But it was a problem he would handle on his own.

"No, it's all under control." He stared at the crowd in the hallway. "You can go home now, the excitement's over." They grumbled among themselves, upset that nothing had happened. Of course the gossip about Analise being in his hotel room would race through Omega like lightning in a storm. "Doctor, I'll explain everything later. Can you meet me in your parlor in an hour?"

Always cordial, the doctor nodded, but fire gleamed in his eyes. "Yes, I believe we have business to discuss."

"Please have your entire family present. I have some important news for all of you."

After the uninvited and unexpected visitors left, Tyler sank to the bed. In his effort to do good, to give Analise what her heart desired, he had made a mess of the situation. He would be lucky if she didn't have a shotgun waiting for him at her father's home. He just hoped that what he had to tell her would turn the tables, and open her heart.

How many times would she allow him to make a fool of her? She didn't know whether she should be angry or hurt. How could she be so stupid to be duped again and again by men? First Victor, now Tyler. Analise paced the parlor and glanced out the window. It was past time for a confrontation. One that Mr. Tyler Goodfellow August Morgan, or whomever, deserved more than he knew.

Through the window, she spotted him marching toward the house. For a second she didn't recognize him. This man exuded confidence and he looked as dangerous as any gunslinger. For today's confrontation he had shed his suit for tight-fitting denims and a chambray shirt. His long black coat danced in the wind—revealing the leather holster that hung low on his hip, holding the large revolver he had shoved into her face earlier that day.

The very thought of his audacity burned in her gut like Louisiana hot sauce. Behind him trailed a small horde of boys, led by her own traitorous brother, Steven. They worshiped the imposter as if he were some kind of hero, not the charlatan who had deceived her and her entire family.

Steven raced ahead and slammed into the parlor, trailing mud on the clean wood floor. "Papa, Mama, Analise—Mr. Morgan is here."

Analise gritted her teeth. "Steven, wipe your feet. Mrs. Hennessey will have your hide."

Her brother returned to the door and held it open for his hero, ushering him in like an honored guest. "Wait outside, guys, I'll be back after a bit." The youngsters flopped on the chairs and steps of the porch.

Tyler entered, removed his wide-brimmed Stetson, and placed it carefully on the rack in the foyer. His black coat followed.

"Please remove your gun before entering our home," Analise ordered in no uncertain terms. She glared at him with her hands propped on her hips exactly as her grandmother had done when she had chastised Analise for unladylike behavior.

With a wide grin, he obeyed, adding the offensive weapon to the rack. "Don't want to take a chance on your grabbing it and shooting me."

His mocking grin only made her angrier. "Not to worry. Blood is very difficult to remove from a wool rug. And Mrs. Hennessey would have *my* hide."

He advanced on Analise, not stopping until he stood toe to toe with her. Determined to face him like a woman, she didn't dare back up a step. Nose to nose, they stared at each other. Heated silver gleamed in his eyes. "Analise, please let me apologize—"

His words hovered in the air as her father and Millie entered the room. Having come directly from seeing a patient, Etienne had left his jacket behind. He carefully rolled down the sleeves of his white shirt. From the confrontation that morning, her father was clearly agitated.

"Let's get this little problem settled," he said. "I have patients to see this afternoon."

For her part, Millie took her usual seat and smiled at the deceitful visitor. "Good afternoon, Tyler. You should make yourself comfortable, since you'll soon be part of the family."

Analise glared at her stepmother, who had never given up her campaign to get Analise wed. "Mr. Morgan is not here to court me or anybody else. He asked for an audience with Papa to explain why he felt it necessary to once again dupe me with yet another disguise."

Etienne settled in his easy chair. "Analise, please let me handle this. Sit down, both of you."

This time Analise took the single chair beside the fireplace. Tyler dropped to the settee and Steven flopped on the floor.

"Doctor, Mrs. DeLery, I owe all of you an apology for my behavior. I explained before I left that with bandits on the loose, I felt it best that no one know about them or the money. It was my way of protecting you and the townspeople."

"Humph!" Analise snorted, her heart torn apart by his pretense at caring for them. Would the pain ever end? "You told us that. What I don't understand is the present deception. Why disguise yourself as

*Herr* August when you returned to town? Why didn't you want us to know you had returned? Do you continue to suspect us of being criminals?"

"I have the utmost trust in your honesty and integrity. It was simply that I had some business to conduct, and I didn't want all the commotion that would occur if I returned as myself. As you can see, I'm being followed everywhere I go."

"My, my, the price of fame and notoriety."

He ignored her sarcastic remark. "I have some important news for you. Especially for Analise and Steven. I could have told you yesterday, but I thought it best to let Alex and Polly have their special day."

Her brother brightened up. "Hey, I'm a hero too, you know."

"Let's hear what Tyler has to say," Etienne said, in his usual calm manner. Her father seldom passed judgment or made a diagnosis without having all the facts. It was a trait that made him a very good doctor.

"You may not know that there was a bounty on the heads of the outlaws and a reward for the return of the payroll." He glanced at Analise, then at Steven. "I was able to collect the bounty for Alex since he assisted in the capture of the bandits."

"Wow," Steven's eyes grew wide. "A reward."

Analise couldn't hide her surprise. "He certainly can use it. That will be a huge help in building his ranch and supporting his family."

"At first he didn't want to accept it, but I convinced him that he deserves it, and he can save part of it to educate Manny and Anna."

Analise's heart swelled with compassion. Maybe some good had come out of the whole sordid situation. "That was very kind of you," she admitted, if a bit reluctantly.

"There's more. The reward for the return of the money goes to Analise and Steven."

That announcement took her breath away. All around the room gasps rang out. "Me? I didn't recover the money. Steven did."

"You were instrumental in recovering it. I'm sure your brother won't mind sharing the reward with you."

Steven was the first to react. "How much money? Am I rich?"

"It was ten percent of the payroll—ten thousand dollars. Your share will be five thousand." Tyler reached into his shirt pocket and pulled out several sheets of paper. He handed one to Analise and one to Steven. "The Sunshine Mining Company and Wells Fargo thank you for your help. The reward has been transferred to the Omega Bank in your names."

For a long moment she stared at the letter. Surely it couldn't be true. She handed it back to Tyler. "You should keep it. You chased down the outlaws and recovered the money."

He lifted his hands in refusal. "You were the one in danger. Besides, I was amply rewarded with a substantial bonus from Pinkerton."

"Then give the money to Steven."

Her father reached for the letter of transfer. "This is a tidy sum, Analise. It will go far in opening your clinic."

"Yes, dear," Millie added, "don't look a gift horse in the mouth. Be thankful that your dream can come true. Now you can buy the Onasis House and open the clinic."

"If I want to open the clinic, I'll have to look for other property. The bank sold it to . . . *Herr* August bought it for . . ." She stared at Tyler, disbelief in her eyes. "You bought it. You're the new owner. You stole my house right from under me. Snake in the grass, you stole my clinic from me." Unable to stop herself, she stood, grabbed a crystal vase from the table and flung it at him. He ducked, and the vase shattered on the fireplace hearth. "You really are a low-down skunk. Take your reward, go back to Denver or to h——."

Millie gasped. "Analise, calm down. That is no way for a lady to talk." She glared at her stepdaughter. "And please do not destroy the entire house."

Analise shot a glance at Millie. "I will not calm down. Not only did he dupe us, and make us look like idiots, he stole my house."

To her surprise, Tyler grabbed her wrist and tugged her down on his lap. He wrapped both his arms around her, stilling her. "I did not steal your house. I bought it for you."

That silenced her. Held tight against his wide chest, she gaped in shock. "For me?"

"Yes, for you and for the people in the community. I've already begun renovations according to your own plans."

"The layout I gave *Herr* . . . you."

Her father cleared his throat. "Tyler, unless you want a shotgun at your back, I would advise you to release my daughter."

Millie laughed. "Oh, Etienne. Don't be such a fuddy-duddy. I think it is very romantic."

Tired of being the brunt of his deceptions, Analise shoved at Tyler's chest. "I'll be the one with the shotgun." Abruptly, he cupped her face in his big hands and kissed her. Full on the mouth. In front of her father. With her stepmother watching. And her brother. His hands held her captive and his tongue snaked between her lips. It was a kiss to quiet her, a kiss to subdue her, a kiss to make her forget who and where she was.

The spell the kiss held over her vanished when her brother made sickening noises.

"Yuck," Steven groaned. "I don't want to see any spooning and sparking in broad daylight." He leaped to his feet. "I'm going to tell the guys I'm not only a hero, but I'm rich too."

Analise jerked away from the reprehensible man and stood. "Just when were you going to tell me about the house?"

Fire flashed in Tyler's eyes. "I wanted to give it to you as a wedding present."

The day held one shock after another. "A wedding present?' She turned away from him more conflicted than ever. If she was a young innocent woman, she would jump at the chance to marry him. In spite of his penchant for disguises and secrecy, he was kind and generous. And so handsome her heart leaped every time she looked into his silver eyes.

It hurt to refuse, but it was best for all that she remain a spinster. That nobody knew about her past indiscretions. "I already told you that I will not marry you. Or *Herr* August, or Deacon Goodfellow, or Romeo, or Don Juan, or whoever you want to pretend to be."

Again, her father cleared his throat. "Analise, we still have a problem." With a glance at his son, he ordered the boy out. "Steven go play with your friends. Tell them about your reward, and go to the general store and buy candy for all of you."

"Wow. You mean it, Papa?" he asked.

"Yes, and charge it to me."

With a grin at his father, Steven dashed from the house, shouting for his friends to follow him.

"What problem, Papa?" Analise asked, concerned about the stubborn look on her father's face.

He stood and paced the floor with his hands locked behind his back. "For the second time, you and Tyler have been caught in a compromising position. My dear, that was two times too many."

She sagged onto the chair by the fireplace. "Papa, neither time was my fault. And nothing happened either time."

"Hmm, Analise," Tyler interrupted, "it depends on what you mean by 'nothing.'"

Eyes wide, temper rising, she glared at him. "Nothing immoral or unseemly happened. I conducted myself as a lady and as a physician. And Mr. Morgan was a perfect gentleman."

Millie laughed, a soft ladylike twitter. "I told you, dear, there are gentlemen, and there are *gentlemen*."

A deep growl escaped Analise's throat. The grin on Tyler's face escalated her temper a notch.

To add fuel to her fire, he said, "Analise, would you call the kisses we shared 'nothing'?"

Her father stopped pacing. "Kisses? I don't believe I want to hear any more." His face florid, he turned to his wife. "Millie, get with the 'happy' couple and set a wedding date. Whatever you think is the proper length of time for an engagement. I will not have the DeLery name sullied by my daughter and the man who ruined her."

Both Analise and Tyler spoke at once. *"Ruined her?"*

Tyler faced her father as if he was a bandit with a rifle pointed at his chest. "Sir, I did not ruin your daughter. Her virtue is and was safe with me. I respect you and Analise too much to dishonor her like that."

*Ruined*. Heat drained from Analise, leaving her icy. She'd been ruined, but not by Tyler. That distinction belonged to Victor LaBranche. To Paris, and a romantic who should have known better.

"Papa, you can't be serious." Her voice dropped to a whisper.

The French stubbornness of Etienne DeLery made him look a foot taller than his five feet ten inches. "I most certainly am serious. You will not dishonor my family by flaunting your indiscretions. You and Mr. Morgan will be married at the time society dictates. My wife will assist in the arrangements."

Like Louis XIV, who expected his dictates to be obeyed, Doctor Etienne DeLery turned on his heel and returned to the sanctuary of his medical office. Behind him two people stared openmouthed at his abrupt departure, while his wife grinned like a satisfied cat.

Millie smoothed the skirt of her afternoon dress. "I'll go consult Mrs. Hennessey on the proper time schedule for the planned celebration. After all, we've already had the engagement party and official announcement. "I'll make a list of things we must do." She turned toward the dining room, where the housekeeper waited in the shadows. "Audrey," she called, "we have a lot to do. Let's get started."


Tyler felt as if he'd been poleaxed. Never would he have expected the mild-mannered Doctor DeLery to assert his authority over his daughter and Tyler. Not that Tyler objected. No, he was getting what he wanted, or rather who he wanted. He'd wanted Analise from the moment he'd spotted her in the medical office. Only he was not accustomed to being railroaded as the good doctor had done.

Clearly, Analise was furious. And he knew where that fury would fall—flat on his head. With her stepmother out of earshot, and her father safely in his office, she rounded on Tyler.

An unexpected and welcome flutter settled in his chest. He loved her and he wanted her. Things couldn't be better. Now he just had to convince her that she needed and wanted him. Another thought shot across his mind. He'd been accused of compromising her, he'd admitted to kissing her—why not take advantage of the allegations and enjoy himself? She opened her mouth to berate him. Having taken all he could for the day, he caught her upper arms, dragged her to his chest, and silenced her with a kiss. A little compromising would go a long way in getting what he wanted.

Aghast at his audacity, Analise struggled against his hold. Her mouth opened in protest, and he took advantage by slipping his tongue between her teeth. The fight went out of her at the first touch of his tongue. Her hands slipped up his chest, to rest on the front of his shirt. He moaned deep in his throat, and thrust into her mouth.

Lost in the wonder of the taste of her, lost in the sensations that surged through him, he relaxed his hold. As if she suddenly gained superhuman strength, Analise shoved against his chest at the same time that she stomped her heel on his instep.

Stunned, he staggered backward, and grabbed his injured foot. He bit his tongue to keep from howling.

"Next time you try to manhandle me, I'll bite your tongue clean off," she declared. "And give you a knee in a very vulnerable spot of your male anatomy."

She spun on her heel and marched toward the stairs with the same haughtiness her father had displayed moments earlier. Tyler hobbled after her, catching her arm as she mounted the first step.

"Listen, you little hellcat, like it or not, we are going to be married, even if I have to compromise you right here in your father's parlor."

Eyes wide, she glared at him. "You wouldn't dare."

"Don't bet on it, *chère*. I'm determined to marry you, and I now have your father's full approval. Not only his permission, but his mandate as well. I'll call on you this evening at six o'clock. We'll have dinner in the Olympia Hotel dining room, where we will discuss our plans for the future."

"I will be busy this evening."

On a long sigh, he shook his head wearily. "Analise, *mon coeur*, don't make this more difficult than it need be. We can talk about plans for the clinic." That got her attention. Her face brightened for a moment. Then, to convince her he was serious he added, "If you aren't ready at six, I'll toss you over my shoulder and drag you to my hotel room for all the town to see, and quite thoroughly compromise you."

She opened her mouth, once, twice, three times, but only a tiny squeal came out.

He turned toward the foyer and glanced over his shoulder. "And, sweetheart, wear something nicer than that dull gray skirt and blouse. That pretty frock you wore to the wedding yesterday would do nicely."

Knowing it was time to strike a hasty retreat before she recovered her equilibrium, he hurried to the door, grabbing his hat, coat, gun, and gunbelt on the way. A glass object shattered against the door the instant it closed behind him.


The clock in the hall downstairs chimed six times. Analise started, shocked at how fast the last few hours had flown. She had hidden in her room to pout, refusing to speak to either her father or stepmother.

"Analise." Millie knocked on the door, drawing Analise to the fact she had run out of time. "Tyler is here. Are you decent?"

Pasting a false smile on her face, she got up from her vanity and unlocked the door. "I'm always decent," she growled. "Not that you or Papa believe me."

Millie pushed her way in, not at all disturbed by Analise's show of temper. "Of course we believe you are a decent, respectable woman, dear, and a very handsome gentleman is awaiting you in the parlor." A few steps inside the room, Millie stopped and gasped.

"Analise, you aren't going out looking like that, are you?"

Analise squared her shoulders and glared back at Millie. "What is wrong with the way I look?"

Setting her hands on her hips, Millie stared her down. "You look like something the cat dragged in. That is the ugliest dress in your wardrobe, and your hair is pulled so tight, your eyes are slanted." As if Analise was a child without a will of her own, her stepmother proceeded to loosen the buttons on the front of her dress.

"Millie, stop." Analise swiped her hands away from her bosom. "I am going like this."

"Oh no you aren't. You will be the perfect fiancée, gracious and beautiful. You will honor your father's wishes." The women glared at each other in a battle of wills—two stubborn people determined to win. Millie narrowed her gaze, and Analise knew it was time to retreat.

"All right. I'll change. Go down and keep Tyler company before he comes banging on my door." She tilted her chin at Millie. "And if he does, I might decide to invite him in and shock all of you."

"Fix your hair first, and put on some perfume. Men love to bed a sweet-smelling woman." With that declaration, she strolled from the room, closing the door gently behind her.

Never in her life had Analise lost so many battles. It seemed everybody in her family was conspiring against her. Surely, she had thought, Millie would understand, or her very own father. But, no, they were bound and determined to see her wed. And with Tyler so set on marrying her, she didn't stand a chance. If she had the nerve, she would run away and join a circus or something.

The thump of heavy footsteps on the stairs and into the upstairs hallway alerted her to the fact that

Tyler meant every threat he had made. She hurriedly set the lock an instant before he pounded loudly on the door. "Analise, it is after six o'clock. Do you need help?"

Oh, she bet Millie was enjoying this. "Sorry, master," she said between gritted teeth, "I will be ready in just a second. Please wait for me downstairs."

"I'll wait here in case you need assistance with all those tiny buttons women like." His voice was soft, with a hint of seduction.

Analise couldn't stop the thrill of excitement that sizzled up her spine. "You really do want a shotgun wedding, don't you?" As she spoke, she threw off the ugly gray dress and hurriedly slipped on a lovely afternoon gown she'd bought in New Orleans. The green gown was simply cut, with sleeves that puffed to the elbows. Since she refused to wear a corset, the waist nipped in tighter than when she was younger, and pushed her bosom slightly above the scooped neckline. Tugging a few pins to loosen her hair, she pulled a few stands from the chignon, and pinched her cheeks. Analise was ready to face the impatient man waiting outside her door.

With an angry growl, she opened the door to face her fiancé. And her entire family. Tyler leaned against the far wall, his feet crossed at the ankles, arms folded over his wide chest. Millie linked arms with Etienne, and even Mrs. Hennessey and Oscar stared at her.

After the initial shock wore off, she narrowed her gaze and shot disparaging looks at her entire welcoming committee. "Where's Steven? Did you forget to invite him to my coming out?"

"He's out with his friends," Millie answered, unable to hide the laughter in her voice. "You look lovely, dear. We just wanted to be handy in case you needed help dressing."

"If I had needed help, I'd have called on my betrothed. He offered his assistance with all these tiny buttons. I don't doubt that he is quite experienced in such matters." Only Mrs. Hennessey appeared shocked at her declaration. The others simply snickered under their breaths.

Tyler surged away from the wall and offered his arm. "I'm sure our meal won't be as fine as the ones Mrs. Hennessey prepares, but if I'm to properly court you, I want to do it right."

Knowing it was time to give up, she set her hand on his arm and allowed him to guide her to the stairway. "I see no reason why we can't eat here with the family."

"That's not possible, dear. Your father and I have been invited to the Winters's home for dinner, and Steven is going home with the Hennesseys." Her stepmother sounded awfully pleased with herself. "Have a lovely dinner. We may be out quite late, so don't wait up."

At her side, Tyler shook with silent laughter. "Thank you, Doctor DeLery, Mrs. DeLery. I will see that your daughter returns home safely." He leaned over and whispered, "With her virtue intact."

# Chapter 15

Analise DeLery was not a happy bride-to-be. She didn't look happy, she didn't act happy, she didn't feel happy.

She was sick of poring over books of fashion designs for a wedding gown. The idea of wearing white—virginal white—made her stomach hurt. She was as big a fraud as Tyler Morgan had ever been. But he had confessed his sins, revealed all. She continued to hide hers from him and the world. If he had the slightest inkling of her deception, he would reject her as surely as the sun rose in the morning.

The way Victor had rejected her.

The only bright spot in the whole horrid situation was that she would get her clinic. Or would he take that away when he learned the truth about his bride?

By the end of the first week of their official engagement, Millie had the plans rolling like a steam engine going downhill. She had sent announcements to the *Omega Herald*, the *Rocky Mountain News* in Denver, the *New Orleans Daily Picayune*, and even the esteemed *New York Times*. She was in her glory as the mother of the bride, and wanted the world to know that Doctor

Analise DeLery, the daughter of Doctor and Mrs. Etienne DeLery, was engaged to marry Mr. Tyler Morgan of the famous Morgan Players. She had even sent an announcement to Europe, hoping to catch up with Tyler's parents on their tour.

For his part, Tyler had turned out to be invaluable in the planning and renovating of the Onasis House for the clinic. He agreed that they would live in the upstairs rooms until they could build their own house.

More than once, Analise had offered him all of the money from her reward to purchase the house outright. He refused, insisting the clinic was his wedding gift to her.

If there was to be a wedding.

At the Onasis House, Analise moved around the workmen, looking for Tyler. He usually could be found on a ladder, wielding a paint brush, or doing anything else that was needed done. They wanted to open the clinic before their wedding, which Millie planned for February, Valentine's Day. Millie's words rang in her head: "It is absolutely the earliest date I can arrange a proper ceremony. What with Thanksgiving and Christmas coming up, even that is pushing things. June would be much better."

When both Analise and Tyler protested, Millie and the housekeeper had taken over the preparations with more strategy than Napoleon planning a campaign against Wellington. Analise had no doubt that if the Little General had had Millie as his advisor, he would have soundly defeated the British and taken over England.

She shoved aside her anxiety and inspected the renovations. The clinic was shaping up nicely. Thinking Tyler might be working on their living space, she climbed the stairs, careful not to snag her skirt on an exposed nail or loose board. Renovations hadn't begun on these rooms, but they had discussed the layout. She wandered into the room they had selected as their private bedchamber.

Closing her eyes for a moment, she imagined what marriage to Tyler would be like. A shiver, both of delight and dread, passed over her. Surely as a man of the world he would realize she wasn't a virgin the instant they consummated the marriage. Her heart ached every time she remembered the past. She had to tell him. She had to give him the opportunity to call off the wedding. An inner voice whispered that if she really didn't want to marry him, this was her way out. The band tightened around her chest. From the first, she'd felt a pull toward Tyler, no matter what he called himself, or professed to be. Since they had worked to deliver little Anna and spent that night together, she'd fallen deeply in love with him. That love continued to grow with each of his kindnesses, his kisses, and even his stubborn determination.

"Daydreaming about me?" the husky whisper tickled her ear. "I thought we could put the bed right there, where we can watch the sunrise together every morning." Tyler dropped his arm over her shoulder. "And at night, we can make love with the moon giving its blessings and our special star smiling at us."

A shiver raced over. Here was the perfect opportunity to confess her sins. The words caught in her throat. At that moment, she realized she did want to marry him. To be his wife, to bear . . . he realization of the truth of her situations struck her like a hammer. She groaned and almost doubled over. Tyler had never mentioned children, but she knew he would want a family. He'd sounded devastated whenever he spoke of the son he'd lost. And he loved little Anna, Manny, and Steven.

"*Chère*, what's wrong? You're as pale as a ghost." He pulled her into his embrace, but his touch did little to relieve the shivers that racked her.

She screwed up her courage. "Tyler, I have something to tell you. It may change everything."

"I doubt anything you say can change my plans." He kissed the top of her head.

On a deep breath, she rushed ahead. "I can't have children." Hearing the words fall from her lips was like a shot to her heart.

He stiffened. "How do you know?"

"How could I not know? I am a physician, and I was examined by the best doctor in Paris." There was no way she could reveal the entire truth of the situation, of how she had lost her baby and had learned that she could never carry a baby to term. Some things were best kept buried in her heart. Like her love for her child. She pulled away, turning her back to him.

This was it. He wanted a wife and family; surely he wouldn't want her now. Tyler surprised her by wrapping his arms around her and tugging her back to his front. His hands splayed across her stomach. "I'm sorry, *mon amour.* I know how much this hurts you. You love children. But never mind, we can adopt children."

Her heart jumped. "Then you still want to marry me?" It sounded impossible that he could be so understanding. Did he really care for her?

"Of course. Nothing's changed. I love you and I want to marry you. Children or not." He dropped his head and kissed her neck. Tiny shivers tracked down her spine.

Her spirit soared like an eagle carried on the wind. "You love me?"

"Of course I love you. Surely you knew? Haven't I told you time and again?" He rained a row of kisses along her throat. "I've done everything but take out an advertisement in the *Omega Herald.*"

"No, you never said a word." Her throat constricted

so she could hardly breathe. "You've never mentioned love, and you've never asked me to marry you."

"Of course I have. Over and over." He tightened his arms around her.

"You spoke to my father, to my stepmother, and *Dieu* only knows who else, but you have never properly proposed to me. You have never *asked* me to marry you. You've told me, ordered me, intimidated me, all but hog-tied me and dragged me to the altar."

His eyes widened in disbelief. "What an idiot I am. How could I expect you to accept when I'd never asked? No wonder you're so upset." He enfolded her fingers in his. "*Mon Dieu*, I'll do this right." Dropping down on one knee, he lifted her fingers to his lips. "Doctor Analise DeLery, will you do me the great honor of becoming my wife?" He kissed her fingertips. "I will love you forever. *Je vous aimerai pour toujours, volonte vous m'épousez?* If that doesn't convince you, I'll ask in Spanish: *¿Voluntad usted sea mi esposa¿* Or in German: *Willst du mich heiraten?* In how many other languages do I have to ask for your hand?"

Analise laughed, her heart on wings. "That's enough. I'm already confused. Yes, *oui, sí, ja*. I will agree to be your wife."

He stood and kissed her soundly on the lips. "Is that good enough for you?"

She cupped his face with her hands. "I love you, Tyler. I didn't want to admit it, not even to myself. But I do love you."

"All along I thought you knew how I felt. Knew how much I cared. I thought you were just being stubborn. It's you I love, *chérie*, and I want you for my wife. Now and forever." He brushed his thumbs across her lips. "To quote the Bard: Doubt thou the stars are fire, doubt that the sun doth move, doubt truth to be a liar but never doubt that I love."

Tears rolled freely down her cheeks. "Yes, Tyler,

this time I agree to marry you without a shotgun, or my father's threats." Without fear of rejection. An inner voice said she should reveal the whole story, but she couldn't. Losing her baby was too painful to admit aloud. It was her secret, locked away for all time with the pain in her heart.

"We have one problem, though." He kissed the top of her ear, her cheek, her eyes.

"I don't see a problem here," she moaned, the love bubbling up in her chest like bubbles in champagne.

Pressing his hips to hers, he settled his very male part to her female nest. He chuckled against her lips. "A very big problem. Millie wants us to wait until February for the wedding."

She fully understood his distress. Heat pooled deep inside her most feminine parts, a need that only his love could satisfy. "If that poses a problem, we can elope."

"Today?" Not giving her a chance to answer, he covered her mouth with his in a kiss that took not only her breath away but her will to refuse as well. Never had she experienced anything like Tyler's kisses. He knew how to touch her with hands, lips, tongue, and heart. Being in his arms, being loved by him was the most glorious feeling in her life.

The kiss went on and on, until they were both breathless with need. Tyler ended the kiss, and pressed his lips to her ear. "*Por l'amour de Dieu,* what you do to me is a sin."

"Why did we ever agree to such a long engagement?" She brushed her fingers along his jaw.

The answer came unexpectedly from downstairs. "Analise, are you up there?" Millie's voice rang loud and clear above the sound of hammers and saws.

Tyler groaned against her hair. "That is the reason we have to wait."

"I wonder if we will survive?"

He laughed. "I doubt it."

"I'm up here, Millie. I'll be right down." She took one step when Tyler tugged her back.

"We'll finish later. Meet me on the porch, after supper."

After a quick kiss to his lips, she raced down the stairs and halted before she ran over her stepmother.

Millie stopped her with her hands to Analise's arms. "You didn't have to rush, dear. Your cheeks are all red and you're flushed."

Analise cupped her hands to her face. Her cheeks were as warm as if she had scarlet fever. That same heat lingered deep inside her. "I heard your call, so I rushed to see if there was a problem. Is somebody hurt?"

Analise knew that Millie wanted only to discuss more wedding plans. After what had just happened with Tyler, she had new enthusiasm for the nuptials.

"Of course not. I have a new fashion magazine, and I want you to look at the latest designs."

Analise glanced up the stairs and found Tyler watching them from the landing. His wide grin shot a longing clear to her heart. "Later," he mouthed, with a shrug of surrender.

With renewed enthusiasm she nodded and obediently followed in the wake of her determined stepmother.


Tyler didn't meet Analise that evening as planned. Dr. DeLery, mayor of Omega, had called a special town hall meeting to which not only the council but everybody in town was invited. And particularly since he'd promised that refreshments would be served, the building was filled to capacity.

Some came to attend to the business at hand,

though nobody was sure what the emergency was; others came just for the free food and drinks.

With Analise on his arm, and hoping for some time alone with her later, Tyler entered the building and found seats at the back. Millie and Mrs. Hennessey manned the refreshment table, slapping hands to keep the children and hungry cowboys away.

Doctor DeLery and the council sat at the table in front, serious looks on their faces. At eight o'clock, the doctor called the noisy throng to order.

"Gentlemen, and ladies, I suppose you're wondering why I've called you here tonight."

"Yeah, what's going on, Doc? It ain't time for the annual budget meeting," came a shout from the audience.

"Morty, I'll get to it in a second," he addressed the shopkeeper. "I received notice today that Sheriff Rogers has retired. He's gotten married and moved to the next county."

A murmur raced through the crowd. Tyler grinned, and whispered aside to Analise, "He acted as if he had retired years ago. I've never seen a lazier sheriff."

"Hush." She pinched his arm playfully. "He was just slow, but he kept the peace."

Tyler shifted his chair closer to hers and caught her fingers in his. Her touch had such an effect on him that he almost missed what the good doctor said next.

"Now we are faced with a small dilemma. I know our charter calls for an election for the position, but the regular election won't be held until next year. Until then, we must appoint another sheriff to keep the peace in our fair town. Do we have any nominations?"

Heads nodded and whispers began all over the room. Jack Stuart, the owner of the Blackjack Saloon, spoke up. "I say we hire that Pinkerton man that caught those bandits. He sure can handle a gun, and looks like he'll stay awhile. Hear tell he plans to marry your girl."

All heads turned to Tyler and Analise. Tyler stood and held up his hands. "No, thank you. I am no longer interested in law enforcement."

Doctor DeLery ignored Tyler's protest. "Thank you, Jack. Do we have a second to the nomination?"

The blacksmith raised his hand. "I second the motion."

The whispers in the room grew louder. Analise tugged him back to his chair. "Don't you want a job? You're very good at law-keeping."

He leaned over. "I have enough savings to last quite a while, and if I decide to work, I can open a theater or teach acting."

The doctor pounded his gavel. "Do we have any other nominations?"

Everybody turned to face Tyler, but nobody spoke up. "Let's have a vote." This time it was Oliver Anderson from the hotel who spoke up.

Tyler sank deeper into his chair. Like it or not, it looked as if he was stuck. "I don't want to be the sheriff," he grumbled.

Doctor DeLery banged his gavel. "All in favor of appointing Mr. Tyler Morgan sheriff of Omega, please say 'aye.'"

Shouts from across the room were loud and sounded unanimous. "Any opposed, say 'nay.'"

Only Tyler's single, soft voice answered, "Nay."

"The ayes have it," called out his future father-in-law. The man knew how to wield a shotgun, literally and or figuratively. "If you will step forward, Mr. Morgan, we will pin the badge on you and swear you in as sheriff of Omega, Colorado."

At this point Tyler couldn't refuse. If he wanted to live peacefully in Omega and get along with his in-laws, it was best to agree. Maybe when election day came around he could convince somebody else to run.

Analsie leaned over and kissed his cheek. "Congratulations, Sheriff."

He shot her an agonized look and stood. Applause greeted him as he made his way to the front of the building where the mayor and council waited for him. After a pledge to uphold the laws of the City of Omega, the County of Omega, and the State of Colorado, and to defend the Constitution of the United States of America, he accepted the badge.

"The meeting is adjourned," announced the doctor. "Enjoy the fine refreshments the ladies have prepared."

Congratulations rang all around him. Like it or not, Tyler Morgan—actor, impersonator, and former Pinkerton agent—was now the legally appointed sheriff of Omega, Colorado.

Analise was waiting for him when he finally made his way back to her. "Looks like I have a job after all."

She slipped her arm in his. "And you'll be very good at it. We don't have much crime, but the way the area is growing, we need a peacekeeper."

"Let's get out of here. You can accompany me while I make my first rounds in town. Then I deserve more than a motherly peck on the cheek for being railroaded by your papa."

"I'll be honored to accompany you, but about the other, we'll have to see."

Tyler had been around long enough to have a feel for the responsibilities of a local sheriff. Many were lazy and incompetent, but, like cream, rose to the top when trouble started. Or ran and hid behind closed doors. Although the night air was chilled with the wind from the mountains, Tyler didn't mind. The walk down Alpha Street gave him the chance to be alone with Analise. Families and residents they passed greeted him warmly as "Sheriff," and he returned their greetings.

"Omega is a good place to settle, I suppose." He stepped away from Analise to check the lock on the general store door. He moved back to her side and glanced around. Here the street was empty, with dark shadows in the recessed doorways. He tugged Analise into his embrace. "About that kiss?"

Her hands snaked up his chest under his heavy coat and rested on the silver star pinned to his shirt. "Do you want me to corrupt our new sheriff on his first hour on the job?"

"It's the price you have to pay for stealing," he teased.

"I have never stolen a thing in my life."

"You stole my heart."

"Turnabout is fair play. You stole mine in return." She tilted her head and ran her tongue over her lips.

He sighed. "I'm going to have the council pass a law making it illegal for a woman standing in the shadows with a man to wet her lips with her tongue."

"And what will be the penalty?"

"This," he whispered, lowering his head and taking full possession of her luscious mouth. The kiss was long and sweet, filled with the love he had kept prisoner for so long in his heart. When he ended the kiss, they were both breathless with need.

"Ummm," she purred, "I think I'll wet my lips more often if I can get a kiss like that."

"I think it might be best to wait until after we're married. My poor body can't take this much torture."

Analise laughed, a sound that rang through his heart like the chimes of a Swiss music box. "You'll have to take the date up with Millie. And if I know her, she'll remind you that she's already set the date sooner than is proper or necessary for a successful wedding. She wanted us to wait a year."

"I'd never survive."

Arm in arm, they continued down the street toward her father's house. Analise stopped at the front gate and stared up at the house. "Did I tell you that Millie wants to take me to Denver to pick out material for my wedding gown? She wants to consult with a dressmaker, and I have no idea what all she has in mind."

"When do you leave?"

"The Monday after Thanksgiving, and we should be back by Thursday."

"Four days without you. How will I survive?" He crossed his arms over his heart with exaggerated emotion.

With a gentle laugh, she darted to the other side of the gate. "You're a much better actor than that. My being gone will give you a chance to cool your heels."

"It's not my heels that need cooling, *chère.*"

Pink touched her cheeks. "Watch it, Sheriff. My papa still has his shotgun loaded." She skidded away before he could reach over the gate. "*Bonsoir, mon ami,*" she called over her shoulder.

Tyler polished the silver star on his shirt, and smiled. Looked as if he was going to remain in Omega and become a part of the community. In his life as a performer and as a Pinkerton man, he'd never settled down. Even when Abigail had asked for a home, he'd refused. With Analise, he'd found a place, a home, a community, a family. Life sure was treating him good.

Onasis had followed a star and found a home. Tyler had followed his heart and found the miracle of love.

# Chapter 16

Thanksgiving had been a festive time for the entire DeLery clan. To Millie's delight her family had grown to include not only Analise but Tyler, Alex, Polly, Anna, and Manny as well. Of course the Hennesseys had always been part of her family.

A few days before the holiday, Tyler had taken Steven hunting. They had shot two wild turkeys, which had been the centerpiece of the feast. Later that evening, the entire town had gathered at the church for a special service and a pageant depicting the first Thanksgiving, written and directed by Tyler Morgan, of the famous Morgan Players.

Analise's heart swelled with love as she watched Tyler from the window of the train. They'd had little time alone recently, and she wished it was Tyler in the adjoining seat going to Denver with her for their honeymoon, rather than Millie, who had three full days of shopping planned for them.

As the train chugged away from the station, she waved to her fiancé standing on the platform. Every time she looked at him, her heart skipped a beat. Today he wore tight denim pants and a blue work

shirt under that long black coat that made him look
like an outlaw. His ever-present gun was tucked at his
hip. Tyler spent his days between being a very dedicated sheriff and supervising the renovations of the
clinic. As sheriff, he'd notified the railroad agent, the
bar owner, the blacksmith—and anyone else he could
think of who would come into contact with strangers—
to inform him about any newcomers to town. It was
his way of keeping track of trouble before it started.

"He certainly is a fine figure of a man," Millie said,
pressing her gloved hand to the window.

Analise nodded. "Tyler is a good man, and he's
been wonderful to all of us."

Millie laughed. "Him too, but I meant your father.
The first time he stepped into our store, my heart
flipped over so many times, I was dizzy with love. And
I didn't even know if he had a wife or family. I fell in
love with him that very moment. The same as you
with Tyler."

"I did not fall in love at first sight. I hardly even
liked him at first. Then I didn't like the way he had
fooled me into thinking he was a church official."
She settled back in the seat as the town disappeared
into the distance.

"You can't fool me. I saw your face when you
looked at him at the dinner table that night. Right
then I started making wedding plans. Now we're
going to Denver to select a dressmaker for your
gown." She smiled, satisfied at her insight. "I suppose
we should have a 'mother and daughter' talk sometime soon."

Heat surfaced to Analise's cheeks. She certainly
didn't need to be told of the relations between women
and men. Analise had learned firsthand all about
that. She lowered her voice to a whisper. "Millie, I am
a physician, a trained gynecologist. I am well aware of
the relationship between a man and woman. I've also

studied anatomy, so I will not be surprised on my wedding night."

Besides, she had already given herself to a man, and carried a child. The reminder brought a familiar twinge to her heart. At times she wanted to be able to confide in Millie and her father. But she couldn't disgrace them with her indiscretion. One thing that bothered her was her deceitfulness toward Tyler. He deserved to know the truth.

Her stepmother reached across the seat and patted her hand. "My dear, there is more to marriage than sexual relations. But we'll discuss it when we're alone. I don't want to shock our fellow passengers with a frank discussion about men and women."

Analise closed her eyes and refused to respond. Millie was much more sophisticated than she had ever imagined. The short conversation had her looking at her stepmother with new eyes. Perhaps Millie would understand what had happened to her in Paris. But she was certain her papa never would.


Denver was a bustling city. Nine years into statehood, the city was growing daily. With gold and silver mines working day and night, money flowed like water. Mr. Tabor had built an elegant opera house, and the city boasted several fine hotels. Electric lights had been installed two years earlier, and telephone lines linked Denver to Boulder, Colorado Springs, and Pueblo. A cab took them to the elaborate Windsor Hotel.

Bellmen and porters rushed to help with their luggage. The opulent hotel was as elegant as any in New York or Paris. Greenery and red flowers decorated the lobby in anticipation of Christmas. The desk clerk rushed from behind the wide mahogany desk to greet Millie.

"Miss Millie, uh, Mrs. DeLery, it is a delight to welcome you once again to our hostelry. We are full to the gills, but I have arranged a lovely suite for you and . . . your sister?" The older man with graying hair bowed elegantly over her hand.

Millie flashed a disarming smile. "Thank you. This is my stepdaughter, *Doctor* Analise DeLery."

The man's dark eyes widened. "A doctor, like your husband?"

"Yes. We're very proud of our daughter. Will you show us to our suite? We would like to rest before we go out." They started toward the elevator, escorted by the desk clerk. "Please send up a light lunch, anything from the dining room will suffice."

"Certainly, madam. I'll send some of your favorites right up."

Analise stared at her stepmother in surprise. "Millie, he acts as if he knows you. How many times have you been to this hotel?"

"Too many to count. Your papa and I come regularly to tend to our business affairs."

By then, they had reached their suite. The desk clerk unlocked the door and signaled in their baggage. He proceeded to open the draperies and light the gas lamps. "If you need anything, madam, just ring down, and someone will be right up."

Millie handed him a coin, and he bowed elegantly.

Millie removed her hat and flopped on a brocade chaise. "Relax, Analise. We'll have dinner after the theater. I hope you packed an evening gown."

"I packed a trunk, entirely too many garments for three days. I told you I can't stay away from my practice longer than that."

"You mean you can't stay away from your handsome sheriff for longer than that."

Analise responded with a shrug, not wanting Millie to know how right she was.

"Let him miss you for a few days. You don't want

him taking you for granted. We'll go to the theater, eat in the finest restaurants, and order your wedding gown. Your papa said I should select your trousseau—nightgowns, unmentionables, stockings, gloves, everything a well-dressed lady needs for her honeymoon."

Analise removed her hat and jacket. "Millie, I do not need all that. Papa can't afford such luxuries."

"How do you know? He's made a bit of money in his investments. Of course, so did I. You are our only daughter, and we can well afford whatever you need. We want this to be the wedding of the year, or even the decade."

"Tyler and I are thinking about eloping."

"Don't you dare. *I* want this wedding, *your father* wants this wedding, and *you* had better want this wedding."

She knew better than to argue with Millie when she made up her mind. After all, there she was in Denver obediently acting the blushing bride and spending her father's money.

"Does it matter what Tyler and I want?"

"No." Millie laughed. "Analise, relax. This is a special time for you. Enjoy it. It isn't often a girl gets to spend her father's money."

"Millie, I'm hardly a 'girl.' I gave up that distinction ten years ago. And I'm only twelve years younger than you."

"Hush. A lady doesn't reveal her age, her weight, or her past."

Analise narrowed her eyes. There was more to Millie than she knew. Until now, she thought of her father's wife as only a small-town shopkeeper, not the worldly woman who frequented theaters and fine restaurants. Analise wondered how much her papa knew. But then, Analise had her own secrets. Secrets she kept from her fiancé. "I agree. I believe I'll lie down for a while before we have to go out again."

"Of course, dear. Have a nice nap. I'll wake you up when our meal arrives."

They spent the next day in nonstop shopping. Millie selected the finest dressmaker in Denver to design and stitch the wedding gown. After minor arguments, Analise won on her choice of patterns. Even Madame Valcour, with her phony accent who did not understand a word of French, agreed that simple rose silk enhanced with only tiny pearls and beading was best suited for a woman of Analise's advanced age. One thing Analise refused to wear was a constricting corset. This time it was a major argument. In the end, the dressmaker agreed to sew boning into the gown for a proper fit.

Both were exhausted by the time they returned to the hotel. After a short nap, Millie insisted that they attend the theater again. The William T. Carleton Opera Company was at the Tabor Grand Opera House. The well-known baritone was performing in the Gilbert and Sullivan operetta *H. M. S. Pinafore.* Millie had gotten tickets from "an old friend of mine." As they stepped out of the cab and entered the opulent building, heads turned to stare at them.

Analise hoped they weren't making a spectacle out of themselves since they were not escorted by a gentleman. Millie wore a purple gown, cut very deeply in the neckline. She had tugged and pulled on Analise's gold gown to expose an overly amount of her full bosom.

All around them exquisitely gowned women, draped in furs, clung to the arms of men in elegant evening attire. The murmur of voices drowned out the clatter of horses' hooves on the cobblestone street. As they climbed the marble staircase, Millie waved to a gentleman or two, then allowed the usher to escort them to a private box. In her fur-trimmed cape, Millie was as elegant as the wealthiest matron.

"Whose box is this?" Analise asked. She removed her velvet cloak and draped it over the empty seat beside hers.

"The old friend who gave us the tickets. He is away on business and he didn't need them." Millie studied the patrons across the theater through her opera glasses. She lifted her hand and waved, and several handsome older gentlemen waved back. One threw a kiss.

Analise settled in her cushy seat and considered the opulent surroundings. Gold and gilt glittered everywhere, with marble statues reminiscent of the French Opera House in New Orleans. She had spent many evenings with her grandmother viewing a variety of performances. The orchestra played an overture, and she relaxed to enjoy the performance.

Several men stopped by their box and greeted Millie warmly. One was a state legislator, one a judge, and another a wealthy investor.

Millie appeared to know everybody, and they seemed very familiar with her. The strange thing was, it was all men who greeted her, no women.

The performance was all Analise had expected. She wished that Tyler was with her to share the experience. She laughed to herself. He probably knew Mr. Carleton and half the cast on a first-name basis. And at one time may have performed in the operetta.

At intermission, they wandered out for refreshments. A tall, dignified gentleman stopped Millie and offered champagne to both of them. "My dear Miss Millie," he said. Leaning closer, he whispered, "I have missed you since you left the boarding house."

Millie laughed. "Senator, I am now a happily married woman. May I introduce my lovely stepdaughter,

Doctor Analise DeLery. Analise, this handsome rogue is Senator Hardy."

He bowed over her hand. "My pleasure, Miss DeLery. You father is certainly a lucky man to have our Millie all to himself."

Analise nodded. "We're all fortunate to have Millie in our lives." She took one sip of the champagne and studied the elegantly attired crowd. Enough diamonds, emeralds, and other jewels were on display to fund a dozen medical clinics for years. Millie's only jewelry was a pair of diamond ear bobs, while Analise wore a cameo that had been her mother's. She shook her head at the waste.

Millie left the senator and wandered slowly toward the powder room. "Analise, I must powder my nose. Will you come with me?"

"No, Millie, I think I'll go back to our seats. The performance should resume soon." She lifted her skirt and mounted the first step. A tingling at the back of her neck caused her to stop. Somebody was staring at her. She paused and glanced over her shoulder. Several ladies stared, but turned away at her gaze. She continued up the stairs, but the feeling persisted. With another glance over her shoulder, she spotted a tall, slender man who slipped behind a marble pillar. Tyler, she thought. Had he followed her and planned another surprise? Then the man walked away. Her heart sped up a beat. He was much leaner than Tyler, but he carried himself with a haughty step that was vaguely familiar. The crowd returning to their seats filed around her and the man disappeared from her sight. Someone jostled her into moving. She put the man out of her mind and thought about Millie.

Her stepmother was an enigma. The loving, kind, generous matron who had married her father and gave quiet tea parties in Omega had shown to be a sophisticated woman of the world. A woman with a colorful past, if the men she'd greeted were any indication.

The houselights dimmed and the curtain rose on the second act. Millie returned to her seat in a flurry of skirts and subtle perfume. She leaned over and whispered to Analise, "I met the most charming Frenchman. He said he's recently arrived from Paris."

A chill raced over Analise. She forced herself to breathe deeply. There were millions of Frenchmen in the world. It was stupid to get excited that one had come to Denver. "That's nice," she said, returning her attention to the performance.

"There he is, in the Broadhurst box." Millie passed the opera glasses to Analise.

Hesitantly, she took the offered glasses and shifted her gaze to the box on the opposite side of the theater. She studied the six people in the box—three women and three men, all elegantly garbed and whispering among themselves. A fourth man sat in the shadows, his face hidden. Abruptly he stood, and disappeared behind the curtain. Her heartbeat sped up again. He looked too familiar. Too much like Victor. But it couldn't be her former lover. Victor believed that America was a total wilderness—even cosmopolitan cities like New York weren't worth visiting. Denver was so far west and rural, he wouldn't dream of venturing so far from civilization.

Analise returned the opera glasses and tried to concentrate on the operetta. But her mind was elsewhere. She longed to return to the safety of Omega and the arms of the sheriff.


At breakfast in their suite the next morning, Analise looked at her stepmother through new eyes. Millie was lovely, her red hair like a halo around her face. No wonder her father had fallen in love with the woman. With her full figure and sense of style, she could have been at home in New Orleans or San Francisco. Why had she settled in a backwoods town like Omega?

"Millie," she asked, unable to contain her curiosity. "What did the senator mean when he mentioned a 'boarding house'? And who are all those gentlemen who greet you whenever we go out?"

She laughed. "I was wondering when you would get around to asking." Taking a sip of her tea, she arranged her silk wrapper around her legs. "I was born and reared in Omega when it was the end of the line, and had fewer than a hundred residents in the entire county. My parents ran the general store." She moved to the window and pulled aside the velvet drapes. Morning sunlight streaked across the Oriental carpet. "I ran away when I was sixteen with a young man who was convinced he could find the biggest gold mine in history."

"Millie, if you don't want to tell me, you have a right to your privacy." And to her secrets, just as Analise had. She worried the lace edge of her wrapper, tracing the design with her fingertip.

"No, dear, I'm not ashamed of anything I did for survival. Johnny was killed not long after in a mining accident, but he had discovered a little gold. It was enough for me to buy a boarding house. I met a few young women in much the same predicament as myself, and we opened a house where gentlemen could eat, drink, play cards, and be entertained by decent women in a genteel atmosphere. I met the most important men in the state, and they helped me with my investments. By the time my parents died in Omega, I had quite a nice nest egg. I sold the boarding house and returned to Omega to run the general store." She returned to the chaise and refilled her teacup.

"No, I was not a prostitute," she continued, "though some of the girls did entertain in their rooms. They were providing a service and I did not object." With a smile she again sipped her tea. "Not long after I returned home to run the store, your father came to town. As I told you, I fell in love with him the minute he walked through the doorway. He was so handsome, and his voice, with that hint of a French accent, sent shivers through me. It still does, after all these years.

"And in case you're wondering, I told your father about my past within five minutes of meeting him. I have not kept secrets from my husband. In our visits to Denver, he's met every one of those men I flirted with last night." She gazed pointedly at Analise. "I have only one piece of marital advice for you. Do not keep secrets from your husband. Secrets have a way of jumping up and biting you on the butt, if you'll pardon the expression."

Analise nodded, a flush creeping up her neck. "I'll remember that. I can see how happy you and Papa are." She picked up her teacup to hide her discomfort.

"We are happy. There is only one dark spot in our marriage." A hint of sadness touched Millie's lovely face. "I wanted more children, but we were blessed with only one son." The teacup shook as she set it on the table. "Of course, Steven is a handful. I'm not sure I could handle another child. Your father and I are looking forward to grandchildren. I can't wait to see the beautiful babies you and Tyler will have."

Pain shot through Analise's chest. Tears burned behind her eyes. There would never be grandchildren from her. She cleared her throat in order to talk.

"Millie, I am so sorry to disappoint you." The tightness in her chest made speaking nearly impossible. "I cannot have children."

Eyes wide with shock, Millie stared at Analise. "What do you mean?"

There was no way she could confess all her sins. If her secret was to bite her on the rump, so be it. For now, it was her heartache to keep. "I'm a doctor, and I know when things are wrong. I've consulted with the best in Paris, and they agree." She turned away to hide her shame. "And I'm not keeping it a secret from Tyler. He knows, and he doesn't care."

Millie got up from the chaise and knelt in front of Analise. With the loving hands of a mother, Millie cradled Analise's face in her palms. "My dear, I am so sorry I upset you." She gently brushed away Analise's tears.

"You didn't. I'm glad to share it with you."

"Woman to woman, you know I wasn't sure I could have children, either. Steven was our little miracle, though sometimes I wonder." She laughed softly. "Never give up hope."

Analise let her tears flow. It was so good to share just a little of her pain with somebody who understood. Tyler might say he loved her, but he could not understand a woman's heart, or her desire for motherhood. "Millie, I'm so glad Papa found you. You've been such a good friend to me." She took the handkerchief her stepmother offered and dabbed at her eyes.

"Even though I'm domineering, pushy, and determined to get you married off?" She stood and kissed Analise on the top of her head. "Let's get dressed. We have another busy day, and I want to get a few more things for your trousseau and complete my Christmas shopping before we catch the train in the morning."

"I'm afraid you'll do your shopping alone. I need to order medical supplies. Then I have to select furnishings for the clinic. And complete my own Christmas shopping."

Analise thought of her feet hurting from walking from shop to shop, her body aching from the pins the dressmaker shoved into her flesh, and her mind spinning with decisions. "I trust you completely to select anything you want for me. But remember, no corsets."

On a long sigh, Millie raised her hands in surrender. "You and your modern ways. It isn't proper not to wear the correct undergarments."

"As a physician, I do not believe a woman should crush her ribs, injure her lungs, and distort her body for fashion. I would rather be comfortable and unfashionable, than locked into a device designed to torture and maim."

Millie waved aside her objections. "By the way, we have an invitation to tea from that handsome Frenchman I met last night and we'll have dinner with Senator Hardy at eight."

It took a second for Millie's plans to sink in. Tea with the Frenchman? That was one engagement Analise was not going to make. Chances were unlikely that she knew the man, but she didn't want any reminders of her time in Paris. Not when she had plans to marry a wonderful man like Tyler Morgan. "I'm afraid tea is out of the question. I'll be out until quite late."

"Not to worry. I declined the invitation to tea. I too will be out shopping. Just be sure to be back by six to dress for dinner with the senator. It doesn't hurt to have friends in high places. Especially since you're marrying the sheriff."

Relieved, Analise shook her head. "If we keep eating like that, I won't be able to fit into my wedding gown when Madame has it ready."

"If you wore a corset, it wouldn't matter." Having the last word, Millie retreated to her room to dress for the day.

Analise sagged back onto the chaise. Christmas was right around the corner. Everywhere she looked were reminders of the happy season. Yet she couldn't make herself rejoice in the holiday. Too many reminders of the past flooded her. She closed her eyes and blinked back tears. At this time last year, she was carrying her son and mourning her lost love. This year, she had a new love and was mourning her lost son. She wished she could go to sleep and wake up on January first, or better still, February fourteenth. On a long sigh, she stood and moved toward her bedroom to dress.

A chill raced over her at the reminder of Millie's warning. She should tell Tyler about her baby before the secret jumped up and bit her on the butt.

# Chapter 17

The train from Denver was a half hour late. Not bad for the Denver Southern, but Tyler paced the platform like a hungry cat waiting for a mouse to show his face. It wasn't unusual for him to meet the train; he met it every day. He liked to know who came to town and what their business was. If he was to make Omega his home, he wanted it to be safe for the residents and for his new-found family. This time he had a special reason for waiting: Analise was expected to arrive at any minute.

His fiancée had been gone for only four days, but it felt like four weeks. For a man who'd traveled the world and romanced any number of beautiful women, he'd never thought he'd settle in a small town with a lady doctor. There was no understanding the mysteries of love. He'd also found the peace of mind that had eluded him for so long.

In the distance the mournful whistle announced the imminent arrival of the Denver Southern railroad. He'd been tempted to board the train two days ago and meet Analise in Denver. Somehow, he had tamped down his desires and remained on the job. It was only a matter of minutes before he held her in his arms again.

The caustic smoke from the locomotive drifted down to the station along with bits of ash carried on the wind. The chug-chug of the engine announced the arrival of the train. He propped a shoulder against a post, feigning nonchalance. He waited until the train came to a full stop and the steps to the passenger car in place before he shoved away from the post.

Analise was the first off the train. She glanced around and when she spotted Tyler, she raced in his direction. He opened his arms to welcome her into his embrace—into his life, into his heart. His chest swelled with love for this woman. She leaped into his arms and planted a hard kiss to his lips. Laughing, he swung her off her feet in a wide circle.

"I missed you," they both said in unison.

He set her on her feet and gazed into her eyes. "You didn't meet some good-looking millionaire in Denver and decide to leave me, did you?"

Her blue eyes sparkled with laughter. "I met quite a few, and one I thought might be you in disguise. But his kisses couldn't compare to yours. I learned the truth just before we made love."

"Good thing that you did. I'd hate to have to shoot a man."

"You wouldn't, would you?"

"Remember, I'm a very dangerous man." He glanced over her shoulder. "Where's Millie?"

Together they looked back toward the train. Millie exited slowly, gracefully from the car. The sound of running footsteps alerted him to the doctor, who raced toward his wife. "Looks like your papa got here just in time."

"He was probably tied up with a patient."

Tyler locked arms with his fiancée. "Are you sure you don't want to jump back on that train and elope?"

"After all the trouble Millie and I went through to select a gown and trousseau, I wouldn't dare."

He gave a pitiful sigh. "I suppose we'll have to wait until Valentine's Day. If I survive."

"You will." She guided him toward her father and stepmother. "Let's see to our trunks, and then we can go home."

"I've already made arrangements for all your baggage to be delivered to your father's house. I want to show you what we've done at the clinic. Then Mrs. Hennessey wants us all to come to eat dinner together." He tugged Analise closer to his side. Now that she was back, all was right with his world. His life was back on an even keel, like a ship anchored in a safe harbor.

Over Analise's head, Tyler watched the remaining passengers disembark from the train. He recognized several of the Omega residents, a couple of men obviously peddlers with their large cases of samples. The last man to exit was tall and slender. He turned his head and addressed the station master. Perhaps somebody's brother or other relation. Analise spoke, pulling his attention back to her.

"I purchased some furnishings for the clinic—tables, chairs, and medicine cabinets," she said. "We can select the furniture for the living quarters together."

"Sounds good." He ushered her toward the opposite edge of town. Later he would check on the stranger. Better to be sure of who was in town than to deal with an outlaw later.

Analise and Tyler met early the next morning to work on the clinic. To her surprise, a large evergreen wreath had been nailed to the door in honor of the season. All around Omega, the stores and homes bore signs of the upcoming holiday. A time that should be joyous held a note of sadness for her. She smiled when Tyler greeted her by singing "Deck the Halls" as he entered the house.

Together they painted the downstairs rooms a pale green. At noon, she spread a blanket for a picnic lunch on the floor of their future bedroom. Mrs. Hennessey had packed the basket so that they wouldn't have to stop work to return home and eat. After they finished their cold sandwiches and lemonade, Tyler stretched out on the blanket with his head on her lap. He closed his eyes and within seconds he was asleep. A beam of sunlight filtered through the window, warming her back.

Analise studied him while he rested. She hadn't thought she could love a man the way she loved Tyler. Or that she could be so happy.

The only dark cloud over her was the secret hidden in her heart. Millie's warning resounded in her head, "Do not keep secrets from your husband." She shoved aside the admonition. There was lots of time to share her past with him. This special time was hers to enjoy. As sad as last Christmas had been, this one would be full of love with Tyler.

Fascinated by his long lashes, she brushed a finger along the soft tips. He wrinkled his nose, but his eyes remained closed. Unable to contain her happiness, a tear sprang up and plopped on his cheek.

"Is that a raindrop?" he asked. Catching her hand in his, he carried it to his lips. "Or is an angel kissing me with her tears?"

"Neither." With her free hand she brushed away the tears of emotion that choked her voice. "It is such a perfect day."

In their private quarters they were alone in their own paradise. "Only because we're together." He reached up and pulled her head down to his. "Want to make love?"

Tyler was such an accomplished actor, she didn't know whether he was teasing or really wanted to throw caution to the wind and make love. "I'm afraid we won't be alone for very long. The workmen will be returning from their lunch period, and if I know my stepmother, she'll be searching us out at any minute."

He kissed her briefly on the lips. "Can't blame a man for trying."

"You know, that elopement is sounding better every day."

From the hallway came the tap-tap of female footsteps. "Don't you dare even entertain such a thought. I have too much time and energy invested in this wedding for you to ruin it." Millie's shadow fell over them like an avenging angel. "You are our only daughter, and the entire town expects a big wedding. Not to mention the popularity of our sheriff."

Analise groaned. One never won an argument or discussion with her stepmother. "What do you need? We were just finishing our lunch."

Grinning down at the lovers, she picked up the now empty basket. "Come home early to dress for supper. We're expecting a guest." Without offering further information, Millie spun on her heel and returned the way she had come.

"A guest? I don't suppose a stranger can pass through town that Millie doesn't invite them to her home."

"After we're married, I intend to keep you all to myself for fifty years or so." He nibbled on her wrist and licked his way up her arm.

She swatted him away. "Let's get back to work. I hear hammering and sawing. Lying around won't get the clinic ready."

Tyler surged to his feet and tugged her up beside him. "As soon as the clinic is finished, we can start on the living space."

Hands entwined, they walked slowly down the stairs. He guided her toward the rear door. "I have a surprise I want to show you. Let's play hooky this afternoon and take a ride."

"I thought we were too busy."

"It will only take a couple of hours. I'll get you home in plenty of time to get ready for supper."

"How can I refuse?"

"You can't. I'll even let you drive."


A few minutes later, with Analise driving her father's buggy, they crossed Poseidon Creek, then turned north along the trail that took them out of town. The road was familiar, one they had traveled while going to visit Alex and Polly. In such a short time, he'd learned to love this country. The mountains cast their purple shadows over the plains, the valleys were fertile with grass for cattle grazing. Trees were sparse but grew in copses along the brooks. They crossed a stream and climbed a small rise.

"Are we going out to see Alex and Polly?" she asked.

"No. Turn down this path."

"Tyler, this is the way to the abandoned cabin. The one where the outlaws kept me captive. Why are we here?"

"I'll tell you when we get to the crest of this hill."

At the top of a rise that overlooked a small lake fed by an underground stream, he ordered her to stop. He jumped down and caught her by the waist and set her feet in the high, thick grass. The wind off the mountains whipped her cape around her legs.

"Look around. See that mountain in the distance?

That place where the river branches out, and over there, as far as you can see?"

"Yes. I've always thought this was a beautiful homestead. From the first time we were here, I've liked this land. But why have we come today?"

"This is our new home. I bought this at a tax sale. All five thousand acres. We'll build a house out here when we start our family."

"You really do intend to settle down," she said.

"With you. I thought we could build the house on this hill, where we can see the mountains, the lake, and the trees. Since our lands touch, Alex and I are forming a partnership to raise horses or cattle. We're still working out the details. For all I know, we could have a silver or gold mine running right under our land."

"Well, I won't allow anybody to dig it up. I like the land just the way it is." She spun around and laughed. "And it isn't too far from town, so I can still run the clinic."

He leaned back on the wagon to watch her delight. "When you have patients staying overnight, you can stay in the living quarters above the clinic. Or you can share the patient load with your father."

She stopped and stared at him. "Have you discussed any of this with my papa?"

"Yes, and I showed him this spot. He agreed this would be an ideal homestead for us. A place to plant roots, to start a dynasty."

Her heart constricted. "Tyler, I told you . . ."

"I know." He pulled her into an embrace and kissed her hair. "We can adopt kids. A dozen who need a home. We'll give them love and make them our own. A dynasty, sweetheart. They will be as much ours as if you'd birthed them."

Tears dimmed her sight. "Tyler, I love you."

He smiled down at her. "Let's get back to town, before we start the honeymoon here and now on our future home."

"You tempt me sorely, Mr. Morgan. But we had best get back to town before Millie sends out a search party. Besides it's much too cold out here to really enjoy ourselves."

"Just one kiss to warm me up?"

She knew one kiss would never be enough, but he was so loving, so wonderful, she wanted him as she'd never dreamed she'd want a man. "A little one," she teased.

Tyler lowered his head. The kiss was a quick nip, the barest touch of his lips on hers. Smiling, he ended the kiss and started to step away.

"Hold it, Sheriff," she said. "You call that a kiss?" She grabbed the front of his coat and pulled him flat against her. "This is a kiss."

She slipped her hand under his coat, pressing against the hard beating of his heart. With her other hand, she tossed his hat away. Twining her fingers in his dark hair, she tugged his head toward hers. His silky hair skipped through her fingers. She stroked her tongue along his lips, enjoying the taste of his skin. He remained perfectly still, not helping, not hindering, letting her take the lead, giving her control.

She pressed her breasts to his chest, brushing against his shirt. With boldness that surprised her, she fitted her mouth to his, moving slowly to increase the pressure. He smiled against her mouth and she thrust her tongue between his lips. He settled his hands on her waist, his fingers stroking gently along her back.

His surrender gave her a sense of power, making her the aggressor, the leader in lovemaking. Taking control gave her a heady feeling. Her tongue slipped past his teeth. She stroked, glorying in the texture of his tongue with hers. Her heart swelled with emotion. This was what love did to a woman—empowered her, made her want to merge her heart with another's. Their tongues met, tangled, and stroked.

Her legs weakened and she sagged to her knees, bringing Tyler with her. Thigh to thigh, chest to chest, mouth to mouth, they knelt on the cold damp ground. Being with Tyler—with the sun, the clouds, and the birds overhead as witness to their love— filled her with happiness beyond her wildest dreams. Her spirit soared on the wings of his love.

Tyler tightened his grip and lowered them both to the ground. Analise lay sprawled atop him. She wanted him, and his desire for her was evident even through layers of clothing. Her hands shifted down his arms, the muscles hard under her fingertips.

His touch sent shivers of delight through her. For now, all that mattered was being with him and enjoying the moment. He shifted under her, showing her what other pleasures awaited them. But not yet. Deep in her mind, Analise realized she was playing with fire, a flame that could easily burst out of control. Some things were better left for marriage. She ended the kiss and lifted her head. His eyes were glazed with passion, and the same heat that burned her cheeks, reddened his under a day's stubble.

She smiled down at him, again taking control. "*That* was a kiss."

A touch of a smile drifted over his mouth. "*That* was a kiss." He continued to lie flat on his back on the grass. "Are you going to leave me like this?"

Her gaze drifted slowly over him, stopping for a second on the very male and very aroused part of him.

"I'm dying here," he groaned.

Analise smiled. "I think you'll live for another two months."

He rolled over onto his stomach and buried his face in his arms. "Two months, three days, and four hours. Can I survive the torture?"

"You're a strong man, you'll make it."

Laughing, he rose from the ground. "You are a cruel woman, Doc. Does that oath you took allow you to leave a man suffering mortal pain?"

"I didn't bring my bag, so I suppose you'll have to suffer until we get home. Then it might be best that my father treat you, him being a man and all." She loved having control, of finally having things going her way. "Let's get back to town before Millie comes looking for us."

Tyler groaned and lifted her up to the high seat of the wagon. "I'll get even, just wait and see. If you think that kiss was something, wait for our wedding night. I'll kiss you so many ways and in so many places, your eyes are going to roll back in your head, your toes are going to curl. Then you're going to beg for more."

Her hands rested on his shoulders. "Is that a threat?"

He pinched her side. "No, *chère*, that is a promise."


Angry voices assailed Tyler the instant he entered the Olympia Hotel a short time later. He walked across the worn carpet toward the manager's desk to see about the confrontation. A tall, slender, and impeccably dressed man shook his fist at Oliver Anderson. Tyler recognized the man as the stranger who'd arrived on the same train as Analise the day before.

"*Mon chamber*, . . . that room, is not sufficient for my needs. I desire *un appartement*, a suite." Under his breath, the man called the desk clerk a foul name in French.

"I'm sorry, sir, our only suite is currently occupied." Oliver tugged the tight collar of his shirt and sent a pleading glance at Tyler.

After another string of French curses, the man glared at Oliver. "Then have the party removed. I insist."

Oliver's unspoken plea begged Tyler to intervene. He stepped forward, asserting his authority as peacekeeper of the town. "Problem, Oliver?" He propped his hip against the oak desk. With the cuff of his sleeve, he polished the tin star on his chest.

The stranger glanced at him and dismissed him as unworthy of notice. "Is there another hotel in this plebian village?"

"No, we're the only one." Oliver's Adam's apple bobbed up and down, and his face turned American-flag red. "Sheriff, can you help us? This gentleman wants the suite, and you have it. Would you mind moving? Please?"

At the request Tyler would have gladly moved to another room, for any guest other than the arrogant Frenchman. "Sorry, Oliver. I'm all settled in, and I like all that space." He turned to the Frenchman, taking an instant dislike to the fellow. "Take what you can get, mister. Either that, or you can sleep over in the livery with the other jackasses."

Pulling himself up to his full height, the man curled his gloved hands into fists. "Monsieur, in my country I would call you out for such an insult."

Neither giving an inch, they stared eye to eye. The stranger had a straight, aristocratic nose, and pronounced cheekbones. Though the same height, Tyler was far more muscular. There was no doubt that Tyler could beat the man in any battle, or duel. He was sorely tempted to take him up on the challenge.

"Then I'm thankful we're here in America so I won't have to shoot you." Tyler turned on his heel and strolled toward the stairs. "Oliver, when you get finished with his majesty, the king of France, send up some hot water. I have an important dinner to attend."

Leaving the obnoxious man spouting off a string of French expletives at his back, Tyler laughed, refusing to let an overbearing Frog ruin his good mood. Tyler took the stairs two at a time, eager to get to the DeLery home and Analise.


The tap-tap at the window drew Analise from her vanity mirror. Since returning from the outing with Tyler, she'd washed and dressed in a pretty lavender afternoon gown, one unlike her usual gray and brown. She had found the dress in Madame's shop and had it altered to fit to perfection—though she had to admit the seamstress cut the neckline a bit low for her personal taste. She smiled at her image. Tyler would like it. In the short time that she'd known him, she'd changed her hairstyle and clothing to please him. Well, maybe not to please him, but to assert her femininity and show off some. Looking her best gave her confidence and a bit of power over the man she loved.

More tapping drew her gaze toward the window that overlooked the rear garden. A face was pressed against the pane and fingers rapped on the glass. Tyler.

"What are you doing up here?" she asked. "Do you believe you're back on the stage playing Romeo?"

"Open the window before I fall to my death."

She slid the sash up and stared at the man hanging onto a trellis. He clung to the sill. "But, soft! What light through yonder window breaks? It is the east, and Analise is the sun." She laughed at his antics.

With a charming smile, he flung a leg over the sill and entered her room. She stuck her head out the window. The drop was more than twenty feet, enough to break a limb or two. "What do you think you are doing?" She set her hands on her hips and glared at him. "You could have killed yourself."

He shrugged, as if it was nothing. "That trellis was about to break under my weight. You saved me just in time."

"Tyler, what are you doing in my boudoir?"

His devilish smile would tempt even a saint to sin. "You sure look pretty, Doc. It would be worth a broken bone or two if you took care of me."

The man was impossible. "Why are you sneaking into the house? You could use the front door like an ordinary person." What a foolish statement, she thought. Tyler Morgan never did anything like an ordinary man.

"I wanted to know if you were ready to elope. How about it? We can still make the evening train." He opened his arms and she went willingly into his embrace.

"I believe I already explained why we need to wait until February."

He kissed her softly on the lips. "I may understand, but I don't have to like it." With gentle hands, he stroked her back. "Do you need help with all those tiny buttons and ribbons women use to torment men?"

Her lips tingling from his tiny kisses, she stepped away. "No, I have been dressing myself for years, and I'm ready to go downstairs."

Not to be put off, he caught her hand and tugged her back to his chest. "We still have a few minutes. The clock hasn't chimed. We don't have to go down just yet." He dropped onto a brocade chaise and pulled her onto his lap. "Besides, I have something to give you. I wanted to give it to you this afternoon, but it didn't arrive until a few minutes ago."

She brushed her fingers over his freshly shaved jaw. "Tyler, you've already given me more than I deserve. The clinic, the homestead . . ." She hesitated before continuing. "Your love." Deep in her heart, Analise believed she didn't deserve any of it. Especially since she hadn't been completely honest with him. Not about her past, her affair, or that losing the baby had ruined her for having his children. Secrets.

*"Mon amour, mon coeur,* just a *petite* token of my affection." He tugged a small package from his coat pocket and set it in her palm.

"Couldn't you wait until Christmas to give me a gift? It is only two weeks."

"No. This is not a Christmas gift. I want to seal your fate now, today."

Her hands trembling, Analise tore away the white paper and opened the velvet-covered box. She stared wide-eyed at the lovely emerald ring, mounted in gold, surrounded by sparkling diamonds. Emotion tightened her throat. "Tyler, it's much too expensive."

Ignoring her protests, he pulled the ring from its confines and slipped it onto her finger. "I want everybody to know that you belong to me. If some handsome stranger comes to town, I want you to flash this at him and tell him you're already spoken for by a very dangerous man."

She flung her arms around his neck and kissed him fully on the mouth. The kiss was salty with her tears. "And an incredibly generous man. *Je t'aime.* I love you—now and forever."

Tyler increased the pressure of the kiss, falling back onto the lounge with Analise prone on top of him. Nothing had ever felt better, safer than being in

Tyler's arms. He was strong, and protective. She loved the security she felt when with him. Could her chest even hold all the emotions swelling inside her at that moment?

The clock in the downstairs hall chimed, and Tyler broke off the kiss. "We still have time to make that train," he said, his breath coming in short gasps.

Overwhelmed with happiness, Analise planted one last kiss on his mouth. "We had best get downstairs. You don't want to upset Mrs. Hennessey by being late for supper."

Laughing, he rose, with Analise lifted high in his arms. "And Oscar is likely to fill me with buckshot if he catches me in your boudoir." He set her feet on the floor, but kept his arm around her waist.

"Besides, I want to show off this beautiful ring. And to brag about my generous fiancé."

"And I can show off my beautiful wife-to-be."

Mrs. Hennessey was placing the meal on the dining room table when they exited the rear stairs. She looked up and smiled. "It's about time you both came down. Millie's been looking for you. Seems we have a guest and she wants you to meet him."

"How did you know Tyler was up there?" Analise asked, surprised at what the housekeeper knew.

"I saw him wrestle with that trellis. The man liked to fall and break his fool neck." She swatted at Tyler with a small towel. "All he had to do was come in through here and mount the stairs like a normal person. I could have told him you was up there." She lifted a hand and pointed to the doorway. "And I would have shown him the mistletoe."

He laughed. "I apologize for putting you through any sort of distress. Next time I want to be alone with my beautiful lady, I'll do it the proper way, by asking

your permission." Tugging her hand, he pulled
Analise into the center of the doorway and planted a
quick, noisy kiss on her lips.

A flush darkened Analise's cheeks. "Let's go see
what kind of evening Millie has planned for us."

Hand in hand, they moved through the dining
room, the table set for six. Looked as if there was one
additional guest for supper. Laughter and voices
came from the parlor. Millie's bright chatter, her father's deep tone, and a heavily accented, oddly familiar voice.

Analise stopped, afraid to go farther. A vise tightened around her chest. The conversation shifted
from English to French, as often happened when her
father found someone to converse with in his native
language.

Tyler continued to tug her toward the parlor. It
was too late to stop. Millie had already spotted them.

"Come in, you two. I want you to meet our guest.
Analise, remember I told you about the young Frenchman I met in Denver? He showed up today, on his
tour through the West."

The tall man turned toward them—his smile that
of a feral predator. He was the last man on earth she
wanted to see—her worst nightmare come to life.

Millie had been right. Secrets had a way of jumping up and biting you on the rump when you least
expected it.

"Analise, Tyler, may I present our guest, Monsieur
Victor LaBranche, recently arrived from Paris.
Monsieur, our daughter, Doctor Analise DeLery, and
her fiancé, Sheriff Tyler Morgan."

# Chapter 18

Her world exploded around her. Analise clutched Tyler's hand for support. Icy fingers tightened around her chest as she faced the man who could destroy her life. Who could ruin everything she loved and had worked for. Who had nearly destroyed her over a year before.

Why was Victor here? He hated the States. To him America was uncivilized and filled with savages. He'd once accused her of being bourgeoise and unrefined. Now he stood in her father's parlor accepting Papa's "gauche" hospitality. As always, Victor wore a smug and superior look on his handsome face.

Confronted by her shameful past, her first instinct was to run, to keep going where nobody could find her—not Tyler, not her family, and not Victor. But Analise was not a coward. She summoned her courage and faced her nightmare head on.

At her side, Tyler tightened his grip on her chilled hand. "What the hell are you doing here?" he rasped, his voice hard and demanding. Anger masked his face, his eyes narrowed to tiny slits.

Analise stared at him. "You . . . you know him?" The

words came out in a squeaky croak, like a sick frog. Her stomach clenched and she nearly doubled over.

Tyler pulled her closer to his side. "This *gentleman* caused a ruckus at the hotel today. He wanted my suite. I told him to go to hell."

"*Sacrebleu!*" Victor clenched his chest in exaggerated horror. "I meant no harm, monsieur. I am *tres* . . . very sorry to cause you distress. I did not know you were acquainted with Madame and Monsieur DeLery and their family." He bent at the waist, that elegant gesture meant as a courtesy, but was as haughty as a sneer. "*Pardon moi*, forgive my boorish behavior."

Millie rushed forward and shot a quizzical gaze at Tyler. "I'm sure there was no harm done. Analise, I told Monsieur LaBranche that you spent time in Paris. Perhaps you know some of the same people."

Numbed at the turn of events, Analise could only stare at Victor. How had she ever thought he was special, that he could love her? That she could love him? Love was what she shared with Tyler. And what Victor could snatch from her. "I doubt it," she said around the constriction in her throat.

Bold as brass, Victor stepped forward and nodded to her. His ebony eyes issued a challenge. "Have you ever been to the delightful Café de la Monde on the Left Bank? It is one of my favorites."

The reminder of the place where they had met and spent many hours together tore at her heart. "No, I do not recall the place."

Not to be undone, Victor shrugged. A sly smile curved his lips while his eyes dropped to the center of her chest. The touch of his gaze felt like worms crawling on her skin. "Your mama tells me you are a *docteur*. That is most unusual for a woman, *n'est-ce pas*? Especially one so young and lovely." For some reason of his own, he hadn't revealed that they were acquainted. She was certain it wasn't to protect her reputation. Everything Victor did was for his own purpose. He turned to Tyler. "You are a very fortunate man, for a *gendarme*."

At her side Tyler gritted his teeth at the implied insult. "I sure enough am." To make his point, he wrapped his arm around Analise's waist. His touch bolstered her courage.

A thousand questions assailed her. Why was Victor here? What did he want? Had he followed her from Denver? Her mind shifted to the night at the Opera House and the man she'd spotted in the distance. It *had* been Victor, and he'd seen her. But why not approach her then? She had nothing he wanted. She wasn't wealthy, she wasn't a beauty; she was a country doctor. Even in their lovemaking, he'd accused her of being too naive and provincial for his tastes. Yet he'd taken advantage of her innocence and stolen her virtue.

In the awkward silence, Millie stepped forward. "Let's continue our discussion at the table."

Victor offered his arm to Millie. She allowed her guest to escort her to the table and seat her at the end, opposite her husband. Footsteps dragging, Tyler and Analise followed behind Steven and her papa.

Tyler leaned down and sneered, "The king of France sees fit to honor the peasants with his company."

His hint of humor eased a bit of the chill that had numbed her. She prayed for strength to get through supper without making a complete fool of herself.

Exercising supreme control, Analise forced her hands not to tremble, while every organ in her body quivered like a leaf in a windstorm. She squared her shoulders, and allowed Tyler to escort her to their customary seats at the table. Victor sat across from her, a calculating smile pasted on his lips. Too often his gaze dropped to the deep neckline of her gown.

She was sorely tempted to snatch Tyler's gun from his holster and shoot the despicable man between his beady eyes.

Analise wished she had taken Tyler up on his offer and eloped on the evening train. In the distance the long, low whistle of the train rang with the lost opportunity. She fingered the beautiful ring on her hand. By evening's end, she supposed Tyler would demand its return and banish her from his life forever.

At her side, Tyler relaxed, completely at home. Or was he putting on another act for Victor's benefit? He devoured his food and asked for seconds. Analise shoved her food around the plate; her stomach churned, preventing her from taking a single bite. Victor merely picked at the plain, hearty food, far different from the rich French cuisine with which he was acquainted in Paris.

The conversation around the table ran from gossip in town to literature and theater performances they'd seen. Tyler was amazingly quiet, never mentioning his own career in the theater. Victor began a story in French, and was halfway through the description of Paris in winter, when he glanced over at Tyler.

"*Pardon moi* . . . I am sorry, monsieur. I sometimes forget myself and lapse into my native tongue. It is very rude to converse in a language that others do not comprehend." Victor made an apologetic gesture with his long, elegant hand, his large diamond sparkling under the chandelier. "I must remember to practice my American English."

Analise wanted to slap the smug look off his face. As if he could ever be near Tyler's equal, much less his superior.

Tyler shrugged. "Don't you never mind, Vic. I may not polly-voo like you folks, but I sure do like this French wine." He lifted his glass. "Bun appetite."

Victor's face reddened at the shortening of his name. Why was Tyler feigning complete ignorance and acting the fool? Well-educated, worldly, and intelligent, Tyler was fluent in at least four languages that Analise knew of. French being one.

Victor sipped his wine. Analise caught the distaste on his face. Even the wine wasn't up to his standards. *"Oui, c'est bon."*

Tyler grinned and wiped his mouth on the back of his hand.

Analise barely bit back a snort, and Steven buried his laughter in his napkin. She fully expected Millie to bop all of them on their heads. Her father took control of the conversation and questioned Victor on the latest happenings in Paris. Analise ignored all of them. Her thoughts drifted off to how she was going to get out of this horrible predicament. Telling Tyler was the right thing to do. But she couldn't. Not when the clinic and her life depended on keeping her secret.

She reached for her glass with her left hand. The emerald and diamonds sparkled in the candlelight. She'd completely forgotten about the lovely jewel.

"Analise!" Millie exclaimed. "What is that on your finger?" She snatched Analise's hand and studied the ring. "An engagement ring? When did you get this? And you didn't even show it to me!"

Bombarded with her stepmother's enthusiasm, she wanted to slink away and hide. "Tyler gave it to me today," she whispered.

Millie gripped Analise's hand. "Look, Etienne. I suppose this makes the engagement official. Tyler, you have exquisite taste."

"Thanks, Millie. Nothing but the best for ma li'l ol' gal." He caught Analise's fingers and kissed the tips. "She's worth a whole lot more to me. It sure will be handy being married to a doc. Just in case I get into a duel or gunfight." Laughter glittered in Tyler's eyes, but Analise saw no humor in the entire situation. If only he knew the truth, he wouldn't think it was so funny.

Victor's gaze locked on the ring. "May I congratulate you, monsieur? To have won the hand of such a *belle femme* is quite a feat."

"For a gen-de-army, you mean, Vic? Mercy boo-coop."

Millie and her papa laughed softly at Tyler's mispronunciation. If the situation wasn't so serious, she would have enjoyed the byplay, and the way Tyler managed to insult Victor without the Frenchman realizing he was being ridiculed.

With supper finished, her father invited the men to his study for brandy. Victor agreed, while Tyler refused. "It's time for my rounds. I like to make a last pass through the town before I turn in." He tugged Analise from her chair with him. "Want to walk out with me, my little sweet patootie?" he asked, laughter in his eyes. His rough finger touched her ring. His callused touch was so different from Victor's hands, which were as smooth as a woman's.

She glanced at Victor, who had hardly taken his gaze off her during dinner. This was her chance to be alone with Tyler, and to share the secret that had her stomach upset and her life in turmoil. Before she could react, her brother jumped up. "Can I come with you? I want to learn all about being a lawman."

Tyler ruffled her brother's red hair. "Sure, if it's all right with your papa and mama. I need you to start learning the ropes. When I'm away on my honeymoon, you can take over for me."

The boy puffed out his chest. "I'll do a damn . . . darn good job."

"Shall we get your shawl?" Tyler asked.

Relief flooded Analise. She was grateful for the reprieve, especially with the way guilt gnawed at her gut. "I have a terrible headache. I'm going right up to bed," she offered as a lame excuse. She reached up and kissed Tyler quickly on the cheek. "I'll see you tomorrow." Not giving him a chance to question her, she spun on her heel and found Victor staring at her. His hard black eyes glittered with malice. A shiver raced over her. He had come to cause trouble—trouble for her. She knew it as surely as she knew the sun would rise in the morning.

Tyler escorted Steven back home after he finished his rounds. Most people were safely in their homes, with the only activity at the local saloon. At the DeLery home, the lamp burned in the study, while Analise's room was in darkness. For a moment Tyler considered joining the doctor and the Frenchman for brandy. He just as quickly dismissed the idea. One evening with the obnoxious man was all he could abide.

He walked around the house, checking for prowlers. From the window of the study, he heard the male voices chattering away in French. He listened for a moment. They were talking amicably about literature and history. French literature and French history.

His instinct about people had been honed over years in the theater and as a Pinkerton agent. LaBranche bothered him. The man was a snake, a predator, and Tyler felt that Analise was his target.

She had been ill at ease since they had entered the parlor and she'd spotted the Frenchman. Something was up, though he didn't know what. Had something happened in Paris? Had they known each other? Yet they had acted as if they were strangers.

He remembered her telling him of the man she'd

loved in Paris. Could this be the same man? From
her strange behavior at supper, he suspected La-
Branche was her former lover—or acquainted with
her lover.

Though he hated eavesdropping, sometimes it was
necessary to gather information. He paused when he
heard LaBranche mention Analise. Her father revealed that his daughter had studied in Paris, and
was now ready to set up a clinic in Omega. The doctor shifted the conversation to his own visit to Paris as
a young man. Tyler ducked behind a hedge and continued to listen. He didn't trust the Frenchman, and
he intended to learn as much as possible about the
man, and perhaps his motives. Especially if his
scheme concerned Analise.

Tyler learned little about the man other than that
he was a pompous ass. He remained hidden until he
heard the Frenchman bid the doctor *"adieu,"* and
walked out the door. Tyler followed at a distance, slipping into the shadows. LaBranche marched boldly
down Alpha Street, turned at Pandora, and strolled
into Blackjack Saloon.

Not wanting to be noticed, but needing to keep
tabs on the man, Tyler hurried to his hotel room, and
minutes later, an old prospector rushed down the
rear hotel stairs. It was amazing what a false beard,
wig, and ratty clothes could do to change a man's
appearance. To appear authentic, he stopped behind the hotel and rubbed dirt onto his face and
hands. He doubted that even Analise would recognize him. But he wouldn't bet money on it.

Tyler sauntered into the saloon and sidled up to
the bar. With a shaking hand, he dropped a coin on
the long mahogany bar and signaled for a beer. Jack
Stuart glanced at him, and without a sign of recogni-
tion, he slapped a mug in front of Tyler. Neither spoke
as Jack went about his business. A battered hat low on

his eyes, Tyler scanned the room. The Frenchman had wandered over to the table where four half-soused cowboys were involved in a game of poker. Two of the bar girls tagged behind him, each vying for LaBranche's attention.

The Frenchman snapped his finger. "*Garçon*, barkeep, bring me a glass of your finest whiskey."

Jack stopped wiping and looked up. "Mister, I ain't no 'garson' and I ain't no 'barkeep.' If you want a drink, walk your lazy butt over here and get it."

Tyler bit his lip to contain his smile. The aristocrat was just another customer to the crusty bar owner. Ducking his head, Tyler watched the color surface to Vic's face. He liked calling the man by the shortened name, knowing it irritated him. The Frenchman surely had a lofty opinion of himself. In a few angry strides Vic slammed a coin on the bar and again demanded the best whiskey in the house.

Jack reached under the bar and pulled out a bottle of premium liquor. He filled a glass and slid it to the man. Picking up the glass, Vic returned to the poker game in progress.

"Do you have room for one more?" he asked, his voice cajoling and smooth.

Brett, a cowboy who worked as a wrangler at a ranch west of town, shrugged. "If you want to lose that Frenchie money we'll be glad to take it from you." He grinned up at the newcomer and gathered the pile of money on the table. "Dealer's choice, one buck to ante."

Vic set his drink on the table and settled on a vacant chair. "I am not familiar with American rules. However, I am a fast learner."

Tyler sauntered over to the table to keep an eye on the gathering. Various cowboys won the first few hands, then it seemed as if Vic's luck changed. After losing a few small pots, he started winning the larger ones. Tyler watched closely as LaBranche dealt, as he handled his cards, and as he raked in the money. Tyler had spent years with sleight-of-hand artists, and he knew a cheater when he saw one. Vic was palming cards, dealing from the bottom of the deck, and marking cards with his large diamond ring—fake diamond, if Tyler knew anything about gems.

To expose Vic would be to expose himself, but Tyler couldn't let the cheater get away with his scheme. A couple of the cowboys dropped out, having lost all of their money. "Mind if I sit in?" He flopped into an empty chair. "Say, Jack, kin we'uns have a new deck?"

The bar owner tossed an unopened deck of cards from behind the bar. Brett reached up and caught it one-handed. "Let's see if your luck is any better than mine, old timer," he said.

If Vic thought he knew tricks, Tyler could teach him a thing or two about handling cards. He dug deep into the pocket of his ragged canvas pants. "Don't got much, just a couple coins. But I feel lucky tonight."

Vic looked at him as if he was a pile of horse manure. Yes sir, Tyler thought, this man needed to be brought down a notch or two. "Frenchie, mind if I deal first?" he asked, in an aged, gravelly voice that projected weakness and vulnerability.

"It was my deal," the Frenchman protested. "And these cards are still good."

"Yeah, yeah, but a new deck is always lucky for me."

The other cowboys dropped out, leaving Brett, who was almost broke, to face the Frenchman and the old prospector. "Let the old guy deal. He won't be in the game for long," the young cowboy stated. He lit up a cigarette and blew the smoke into the air. The former players gathered behind their friend, urging him on.

"Thanks, bud." Tyler took the new deck of cards from the package and started to shuffle them. He fumbled with the cards as if he couldn't quite move his stiff fingers. Finally, he began to deal. "Five card stud, nothing wild." On the first hand, he let Brett win, throwing in his hand. Next, the Frenchman dealt and took the hand. Tyler spotted right off how he'd managed to cheat, even with a new deck.

Winning went back and forth for another half hour. It was getting late, and Tyler grew tired of playing cat and mouse. It was time to get serious. Tyler won the next two hands. On Vic's next deal, Tyler spilled his drink, and mopped up the liquid with a dirty handkerchief. "Sorry, Frenchie," he said, switching the cards with the skill of a stage magician.

Vic shifted away from Tyler as if offended by his nearness. "Get away from me, you oaf."

"Don't get your pants in an uproar." Tyler settled back into his chair and studied his cards, his winning cards. "Say, Frenchie, is it true that Frenchmen wear lace drawers?"

Laughter spread around the table; even the girls giggled at the insult. Victor's face reddened, and he grunted between his teeth. "Are we going to play cards? I feel my luck changing."

Tyler chuckled. "For the worse."

Brett folded, and Tyler raised the bet. Since Vic's hand was good, nearly as good as Tyler's, both men stayed in, continuing to raise until a huge pot sat in the middle of the table. Finally, Tyler called and tapped his card with a grimy finger. "Well, looks like you got quite a hand staring at me—two pretty little ladies and a pair of treys." And that was all he had, as Tyler had set him up with the cards. "Ya might have another pretty lady hiding. All's I got showin' is two deuces and two fives. Now, the question is, do you have a full house that can beat mine?" Tyler turned over another five—his full house beating Vic's two pairs. He laughed, scooping the money over in front of him. "Winner take all."

The Frenchman's face turned red with fury. He leaped to his feet and knocked over his chair. "You cheated. You are a scoundrel and a rogue." He let out a string of French expletives as he pulled out a Colt revolver from under his coat.

Tyler lifted his hands. It wasn't time to pull out his own hidden gun. He glanced over at the bartender. "Jack, you reckon Frenchie just insulted me in that foreign tongue?"

"Could be. Did you cheat?" Jack pulled a sawed-off shotgun from under the bar and aimed it at LaBranche's back.

"Didn't need to. Frogs don't know nothin' about poker. I won fair and square." He gestured toward the bar and the shotgun. "Frenchie, ya had better put away that little pea shooter. Jack don't like blood on the floor of this fine establishment."

LaBranche growled and spun toward the bar. At the sight of the ominous weapon, he tucked the gun back under his coat. "I will not stand for this. I should go to that incompetent sheriff and report you."

Tyler slouched down. "His office is down the street. But I saw you marking that ace on that other deck. It's like the pot calling the kettle black."

"Hey," Brett called out, "Frenchie cheated us?"

Victor eased toward the door. "I did not. It was this degenerate, this reprobate." Like the coward he was, LaBranche hurried from the bar, leaving a string of curses floating in the air.

"You guys can dig out what you lost to Frenchie. I'll take the rest. Looks like Lady Luck was smiling on me and frowning on Frenchie."

Brett shrugged and gestured to his friends to leave.

"You won fair and square, old timer. You bested us. It's your winnings."

Tyler hated taking the money from the hard-working cowboys. But to insist would cause suspicion, and he might need this disguise again. He shuffled over to the table and retrieved his winnings. "Thanks for the grubstake, fellas. I'll cut you in when I hit that mother lode."

They laughed, knowing that few prospectors ever struck it rich. "Sure, we'll be waiting. Let's get back to the ranch. If we don't get up in time tomorrow we'll lose our jobs."

After shoving his winnings into his pockets, Tyler shuffled out, heading toward the hotel. As he neared the alley that ran between the bank and haberdashery, a shot rang out. He dropped to the ground and pulled out his gun. Another bullet whizzed past his head. He rolled over and over until he reached the alley and ducked into the deep shadows between the establishments. Footsteps pounded on the board-walk, running away. When he stuck his head out, the street was empty.

Tyler gripped his gun and stared at the direction from which the shots had come. He didn't have to search. Instincts told him that Victor LaBranche had tried to kill him. It was either revenge or to steal the money. Or both.

Whatever his motive, or his reason for being in Omega, the Frenchman was a dangerous man. Tyler vowed to keep a close watch on Vic. And to keep him far away from Analise.

# Chapter 19

After a long, sleepless night, Analise entered the medical office the following morning before the rest of the household stirred. Worried about Victor, she'd given up the idea of rest and decided to get to work. As she walked through the doorway, the first thing she saw was a pair of large booted feet propped on her desk.

In spite of the gray Stetson hat covering his face, she recognized Tyler by his long legs and muscular physique. "Sheriff Morgan, to what do I owe this visit? Are you ill? Do you require the services of a physician?" Seeing Tyler brought both happiness and anxiety.

With one finger, he shoved back the hat. "Just wanted to spend a little time with my sweet patootie before we get busy."

In spite of the fear that had settled in her chest, she smiled at his antics. "Since when did I become your 'patootie'? Whatever that is."

He swung his feet to the floor and strolled slowly toward her. "Now darlin', don't you like being my sweetie?" She darted out of his reach and slipped behind the desk.

"Tyler Morgan, you definitely should go back on the stage. That performance last night would do your father proud, if he liked seeing you act the fool."

He laughed, hitching a hip on the edge of the desk. "How about a good morning kiss?"

Unable to resist, she moved between his legs and wrapped her arms around his shoulders. She pressed a quick peck to his lips and backed away before he could deepen the kiss. "I'm glad you came. It saves me looking you up later."

His eyes widened. "Couldn't wait to see me?"

All night she had thought about Tyler and how to handle the situation that was stickier than taffy. "I'm thinking of taking you up on your offer." She stroked a finger along his freshly shaved jaw.

"What offer? You mean the elopement?" His voice deepened to a husky growl.

She nodded. "Is the offer still open?" Getting out of town was the perfect solution to her predicament. They could leave, and not return until after Victor had continued on his tour.

Tyler tightened his arms around her waist, drawing her closer between his legs. "We can leave on the evening train. But what about Etienne and Millie?" A hint of suspicion glittered in his eyes. "What changed your mind?"

Wanting to distract him, she cupped his face and pulled it closer. "This." She planted another quick kiss on his mouth. "I'm tired of waiting. Two more months seems like a lifetime."

He smiled like a fox that had just caught a fat, juicy hen. "I'll make the arrangements and pick you up at six."

"I'll be ready." Her heart swelled at the thought of being with him, loving him, and spending her life with him. If only she could quiet her conscience. That inner voice spoke loud and clear that it was wrong to marry Tyler without telling him the truth about her past. He deserved the chance to make his own decision. But she couldn't take the chance of his rejecting her here. She would tell him the whole sordid story on the train, once they were away from Omega. That way, he could make his choice before they married. If he rejected her then, she could continue to Denver, or another city, and remain until Victor resumed his tour.

"Hmmm, can I seal our bargain with a real kiss?"

Analise pressed her lips to his, putting her entire heart and soul into the kiss. When he pulled away, they were both breathless and shaking with need. "I suppose you had better go. Papa will be coming in at any minute."

Tyler set her away. "Be ready on time. We don't want to be late starting our honeymoon."

She smiled. "By the way, what was the real reason you showed up so early?"

"I needed a moment alone with you. I wanted to warn you about LaBranche. The man is trouble, and I don't want you anywhere near him."

Her stomach flipped at the mention of the name. "What . . . what do you know about him?"

Tyler gathered her hand in his and touched his lips to her palm. "Other than being an arrogant ass, he's a liar and a card cheat. He stopped at Blackjack's last night and swindled some cowboys out of their week's wages."

She wasn't surprised at anything Victor would do. "What did you do?"

"*I* didn't do anything. But an old prospector wandered in and taught him a thing or two about cheating."

"An old prospector just happened to wander in?" She shook her head, certain that it was simply another of Tyler's many faces. "One who knew how to outwit a card shark?"

Tyler laughed. "Just a little sleight of hand. Like this." He touched behind her ear and showed her a shiny silver coin.

She snatched it from his fingers. "You are just full of surprises."

"Life with me will never be dull." He gave her another quick kiss.

Footsteps from the hallway announced her father's arrival. Tyler headed for the door. He whispered, "Stay away from LaBranche."

"I will." And after tonight Victor LaBranche would be out of her life forever.

The morning passed quickly for Analise. A number of patients asked for her, finally accepting her as a physician. The practice was growing, and when she opened the clinic, it would grow even more.

When the office was free of patients and her father was at the bank, Millie wandered in. "Analise," she whispered, looking around surreptitiously. "Are you alone?"

Analise nodded. She opened the door to the private examining room and invited her stepmother in. "More wedding decisions? Or Christmas plans?" With so many plans to make, Analise was glad she and Tyler had decided to elope. They would return in plenty of time to assist with the Christmas celebration.

"No." Millie paced the floor and wrung her hands together. Usually calm and composed, she paced like a caged animal.

"Is something wrong? With Papa? Steven?" Her breath caught.

"No, no, nothing like that. It's me." The older woman's eyes glittered with unshed tears.

Analise wrapped a comforting arm around her beloved stepmother's shoulders. "Are you ill? Did something terrible happen to you?" Her first instinct was that Victor had done something to hurt the woman who wasn't much older than he.

"No. Yes. I'm late."

Wide-eyed, Analise stared at her stepmother. "Do you mean your courses?"

"Yes. I've only been this late once before, and that was when I was pregnant," she whispered the last word as if it was a curse.

Millie buried her face in her stepdaughter's shoulder. "I wanted a baby so badly, but now I'm afraid. I'm too old. Etienne is too old."

Analise smiled into Millie's red hair. "Have you told Papa any of this?"

"No. I don't want to get his hopes up if it isn't true, if I'm simply going through the 'change.' You're a gynecologist, you should be able to tell for sure."

She set Millie away from her. "How late are you? When was your last monthly?"

Wiping her eyes on a handkerchief, Millie sniffed loudly. "Before you came home. Four months ago, I think. I just got so wrapped up in making everything comfortable for you, and then so much has happened to all of us, I lost track. Then this morning, I was dizzy and lost everything in my stomach. Thank God your father had already left our bedchamber."

"It sounds very much as if I'm going to have a little brother or sister." She thought about the implications, of the stress on Millie. "Do you want to have a baby?"

"More than anything. But I have to be sure before I tell Etienne."

"Let me examine you, and we'll have a good idea."

All the signs pointed to a pregnancy, including the physical examination. "I'd say we're nearly a hundred percent sure. I'd guess we'll know for sure sometime in May."

Millie threw herself into Analise's arms. Her tears flowed freely. "Of course you will be my doctor. Etienne was so nervous with Steven, I had to get a midwife to assist in the delivery."

Analise laughed. "Certainly. The clinic will be operational, and you'll have the best care in the world."

"I only worry about what Etienne will say."

Setting the older woman away, Analise wiped away Millie's tears with the hem of her apron. Her throat burned with unshed tears. "He'll be delighted. Nothing makes a man feel more masculine than to know he can sire a child. He'll love you more than ever."

When Millie smiled, her face glowed with joy and contentment. "I'll tell him tonight. I'll prepare a special dinner with candlelight and wine. A romantic interlude."

Her own heart filled with emotion, Analise offered, "Tyler and I have plans for the evening, and I'll send Steven home with Oscar for the night. That should give you and Papa time alone." And she and Tyler could leave without anybody getting suspicious and looking for them.

"Thank you, darling. Thank goodness I didn't invite that self-important ass, Victor LaBranche, to supper tonight. Once with that man was all I could stand."

Analise felt her mouth drop. "I thought you were enthralled with him and his European manners."

"Please, dear, I have better sense than to be taken in by some pretentious fool. Tyler certainly put 'Vic' in his place. Actually, your father met him on the street and invited him to dinner. I saw through him when we were in Denver—for an impoverished aristocrat who's in America to latch on to some unsuspecting heiress. Stay away from that man. He's trouble."

"Oh, I will." Analise couldn't believe how perceptive her stepmother was. It had taken her one evening to see what it had taken Analise months to discern. Her respect for Millie's intelligence and cunning continued to grow by leaps and bounds.

"I must go and get things ready for tonight. Pray that this dreaded nausea stays at bay until I tell Etienne the good news. What a delightful Christmas gift this will be for all of us. I told you miracles can happen."

"As your doctor, I want you to take it easy, get lots of rest, and eat properly."

Millie practically floated to the door. She winked over her shoulder. "Certainly. I'm accustomed to doing what the doctor orders."

With her stepmother gone, Analise let her own tears flow. Millie hadn't thought she could have children, yet she'd gotten a miracle. A Christmas miracle. Analise touched her stomach with both hands. Was there hope for her? Was there a miracle somewhere in her future?

After lunch, Analise took a list of additional renovations and walked over to the clinic. Earlier Tyler had informed her that he was on his way to the Barry farm to settle a dispute between Mr. Barry's milk cow and Mr. Sinclair's bull. He had promised to return in a few hours.

The renovations were progressing nicely. Tyler had purchased only the best lumber and hired the finest craftsmen in the county. She rejoiced to know that the project meant as much to him as to her.

She discussed the placement of bookshelves and

the arrangement of the kitchen with the carpenter, then wandered into the backyard to think about her garden. Although it was the middle of December, she looked forward to spring when she could plant her herb garden. Deep in thought, she didn't hear the man approach until he spoke.

"*Ma petite*, I have been searching for you. Have you been avoiding your old lover?" Victor stepped from behind a tree, a long slender cigar clamped between his lips.

Her heart slammed against her ribs and her stomach clenched into a hard ball. "Victor, what are you doing here?" She hugged her cloak closer to her chest.

He leaned nonchalantly against the wide oak, his gaze narrowed on her. Victor's hand snaked out and caught her arm in a hard grip. He tugged her deeper into the trees and overgrown shrubs. "I wanted to see you. We have much to discuss."

She shook off his grip. "Do not touch me again. Tyler will be here soon."

"The simple-minded sheriff? He is off somewhere seeing about a cow and a bull." He laughed. "That is the proper pastime for such a tiresome fool."

"Don't think that you know anything about Tyler. He's twice the man you've ever been or ever will be."

"Does he know about us? How we were lovers in Paris? How you leaped into my bed at every opportunity?" He backed her against a tree, crushing his body to hers. His arousal pressed into her stomach, bringing with it a wave of nausea.

She shoved him away with her hands at his chest. "Liar. You pursued me because you thought I was a wealthy heiress. You seduced me." The words tore from her throat like sandpaper.

Humorless laughter poured from his mouth. As he drew on the cigar, the tip glowed and dimmed.

Then he dropped it on the ground and smashed it under his heel. "I only gave you what you wanted, *chère*. You wanted me. You cried for me."

"I cried when you rejected me."

He braced a hand on either side of her head, effectively blocking her in. "You were *tres chaud*, very hot. For a virgin."

Anger flooded her. "You are despicable."

Lowering his head, he aimed his lips toward hers. She turned so that his mouth brushed her cheek. The very idea of his touching her turned her stomach. "You are more desirable than you were a year ago."

She shivered at the sound of his voice. With a bravado she didn't feel, she tilted her chin. "I can scream and a half dozen workmen will come running."

"But you will not." He twisted a stray lock of her hair around his finger, tugging painfully. "I will be forced to tell your papa and stepmother about your sins—your indiscretions, shall we say?"

"It isn't unusual for a woman to be seduced and to give in to temptation." But she knew if word got out, she would be ruined.

"What about a young, unmarried doctor who gives birth to her lover's child? A woman of morals so low, she had a child out of wedlock? What would your virtuous papa think if he learned his precious daughter got rid of her child?"

The heat drained from her body, shivers racked her. With each word he distorted the truth and tightened the noose around her neck. "I carried the baby for seven months. He was born before his time. He died in my arms."

"How am I to know that is true? How is your papa to understand? Will he still claim you as his daughter? Will the good women in this town respect you as their doctor if they learn you are a woman of ill repute?"

"Victor, why are you saying all this? You didn't want me or the baby."

He brushed a long gloved finger over her cheek and down her neck. "What I want is quite simple. You said you had no money, now I learn you received a large reward for the capture of some outlaw. If you do not want your papa to know about your wicked life in Paris, you will pay me for my silence."

"I don't have the money. It is all going into the clinic." Her words dropped to a harsh whisper.

He snatched her hand. "Go to your papa. I understand he and his wife are well-to-do. Until then, I will take this as a down payment."

"No." She curled her hand into a fist.

"Give it to me, Analise. Or I will go to the sheriff, and to every citizen in this town and tell them that you are a fallen woman, one who will corrupt them and their daughters."

"You wouldn't."

"Do not dare me. I met the man who writes the newspaper. He would be eager to learn the lady doctor is nothing but a fraud."

She dug her nails into her palms. "How did you find me?"

"The marriage announcement in the *New York Times*. I decided to come west and seek my fortune." He grabbed her hand and tore the ring from her finger. "I want a thousand dollars by the end of the day. Meet me back here with it at five o'clock."

"And you'll give me back my ring?"

He studied the stones on the ring. "I will think about it." Twisting his fingers in her hair, he pulled her face to his and covered her mouth with his. Caught off guard, Analise was too shocked to move. Too shocked to do anything.

She pulled away and swiped the back of her hand over her mouth. "Remember, *petite*, five o'clock."

He disappeared into the thicket of the trees, leaving Analise weak and scared and more alone than she'd ever been in her life.

Her knees gave out and she sank to the cold, hard ground. The pain in her chest ached as if she was suffering heart failure. She folded her arms across her body and bent double. A tidal wave of hot tears poured down her face.

She had lost everything.

First her baby, now Tyler.

Stolen from her by a faithless predator who cared for nothing and no one but himself.

# Chapter 20

"Have you seen Doctor Analise today?" Tyler inspected the finished work as he entered the room that was to be Analise's office. The work was proceeding nicely, and the clinic should be ready for patients in another month.

The carpenter removed the nails from between his lips and glanced up at Tyler. "The lady doc was here a while ago. Showed me where she wanted those new bookcases." He whacked the hammer one more time to set the nail. "Then she left."

Tyler nodded and moved toward the stairs. He'd spent the better part of the day west of town, settling a dispute between the two farmers. It took a while, but he had managed to get control of a randy bull and docile cow. For a man trained to track and capture outlaws, he was ill prepared to settle such mundane disputes. But it sure beat getting shot at every time he turned around. Like last night. If there had been better lighting, he was certain LaBranche would have hit his target: Tyler.

The painter slapped the brush on the wall and glanced at Tyler. "I think she went out into the backyard. Over there by the trees." He returned to his task, leaving Tyler staring at the rear yard.

Another workman stopped him at the rear door to discuss another detail of the renovations. He had never owned a home or any kind of building, so it surprised him to learn of the number of small details that needed his attention. Another problem solved, he jumped down from the porch and strolled toward the tree line. There was no use calling for Analise. The saws and hammers would drown out the sound.

He glimpsed movement among the thick copse of trees. Wanting to surprise her, he moved in a circle to come up at her side. As he neared the spot where she stood, he stopped cold. Somebody was with her. With the background noise, he couldn't hear what they were saying, but he saw it all perfectly clear.

Analise was kissing a man. She pulled away and he recognized Victor LaBranche. His woman was in the arms of another man—the snake who had tried to kill Tyler the previous night.

It took all his willpower not to draw his revolver and shoot the bastard where he stood.

In an unexpected silence LaBranche's voice rang out, "Remember, *petite*, five o'clock." Then he disappeared into the overgrown shrubbery.

Analise dropped and was hidden from sight. For several long minutes Tyler struggled to control his temper. He took deep breaths, curled his fingers into his palms, and counted to one hundred. Finally in control of his emotions, he stepped through the bushes.

He found her slumped down on the ground, her face buried in her hands. Her shoulders shook and harsh sobs racked her body. His anger quickly dissolved at the sight of her anguish.

He squatted beside her and touched her arm. Startled, she jumped, lifted her head, and stared at him through a veil of tears. This was the Frenchman's fault. Now he was sorry he hadn't shot the rat.

Hurriedly, she wiped away the tears with the hem of her skirt. "Ty . . . Tyler, what . . . what are you doing here?" She hiccuped loudly.

"Looking for you, sweetheart. What's wrong?" He gritted his teeth to control his temper.

Her face was blotchy and her eyes red-rimmed. She blinked, then turned away from him. "I tripped and fell. I think I sprained my ankle."

Tyler easily saw through her lie. She'd been crying as if her heart was breaking, not her ankle. Analise was a strong woman who now appeared on the verge of an emotional breakdown. She'd been agitated since the minute she'd seen LaBranche the evening before. Yet she hadn't admitted she'd known Vic or that he had been her lover. Was she still in love with him, while she'd claimed to love Tyler? Betrayal cut like a knife into his soul.

Yet, in spite of his pain, he didn't want to upset her any further than Vic had. Using all his well-honed acting skills, he went along with her story. He dropped to the ground beside her and reached for her foot. "Let me look at it."

She shoved his hands away. "No, I'll be all right. I'll go home and soak it." Her breath came in harsh gasps.

"We don't want anything to stop us from leaving this evening, do we? I think we ought to sneak away a little early. I'll pick you up at five. We can have supper at the hotel, then take the train."

Her face paled. "I can't."

"Why not?"

She hesitated as if trying to come up with a reasonable excuse—a lie. "I have a patient coming in at five. I can't possibly be ready before six." Her voice trailed off into a whisper. Analise would never make it on the stage. Every emotion showed in her eyes, including the anguish of her lies.

What were her plans with LaBranche? Was she planning to run away with him? Pain arced through his chest. This was worse than when Abigail had died. He snatched her hand and kissed her fingers. The ring he'd given her was gone. The rejection tore his soul apart. "Where's your ring?"

She stared at her hand as if seeing it for the first time. "I . . . I must have forgotten to put it on after I washed my hands."

Lies and deception. His heart wrenched at the thought that she would play him for a fool. He loved her, she'd said she loved him. Something was very wrong. If she didn't want him, he had to know now, before they married and made a mockery out of that love. If she wanted another man, he would never stand in her way. He loved her enough to want her happy at any cost. Even at the cost of his heart.

He picked her up into his arms and strolled deeper into the trees. "Tyler, put me down. I want to go home, I'm freezing."

"I'll take you when I'm darn good and ready." It was time for a showdown, and he wanted privacy when he laid out his heart for her to stomp on.

"Tyler, why are you acting so strangely?"

"*I'm* acting strangely?" His control snapped. "You didn't catch *me* kissing another *woman*, did you?" he spouted off, unable to hold back his temper. "Or crying as if my world was ending."

She shoved at his chest and he set her on her feet. They were far enough away so that nobody could hear or see their confrontation. The winter wind whistled through the trees. She shivered. He clutched her arms and forced her to face him. "I . . . I don't know—"

"Don't lie to me, Analise. I saw you kissing La-

Branche." Unable to control his distress, he shook her slightly.

"Let go of me, Tyler," she said between heart-wrenching sobs. "I tried to tell you that I couldn't marry you, but you insisted. Now do you believe me?" She squared her shoulders. The pain in her eyes belied her words. "I'm not good enough for you or any decent man. I release you from the engagement."

Those were the hardest words Analise had ever had to say. But she had to, she couldn't string Tyler along any longer. It wasn't fair to tie him to a woman whose reputation was in tatters—whose entire life was a lie. She knew that no matter how much she paid Victor, it would never be enough. He would never leave her alone, and Tyler didn't deserve that kind of torment.

"Are you planning to leave with LaBranche?"

She stepped back as if she'd been slapped. "Lord, no. I hate him, but I will be leaving, soon."

"What about your plans for the clinic?"

Not only was she losing the man she loved, but the clinic she'd dreamed of. "Papa will take over, or he'll call for another doctor to assist him. Unless you take back the house and close the clinic."

He tugged off his hat and raked his fingers through his hair. "Why, Analise? Why are you doing this?" Pain glittered in his gray gaze. Her heart ached for him, and for her, for their love, for what they could have had, and what was never to be.

"I have to. If I don't he'll ruin everything. Papa and Millie will be humiliated, and I'll never be able to practice medicine. You'll be the laughing stock of the town." The words burst from her like water from a broken dam.

"I don't give a damn what the town thinks about me." He reached out and tugged her into the shelter of his chest, wrapping his arms around her against the cold. "Tell me, what's going on? What happened between you and LaBranche? Did you know him in Paris? Was he your lover?" His voice hardened. "Is he threatening you?"

She nodded, her heart in her throat. "How much do you want to know, Tyler? Victor was my lover. He seduced me, but I went to him willingly time after time. The man used me and threw me away like an old shoe." How could Tyler help but hate her for deceiving him?

"That isn't so bad. Few women remain a virgin at your age. Unscrupulous men seduce innocent young women all the time."

"But as a doctor, I must have an impeccable reputation. And if my papa knew, he would be devastated."

"You're a wonderful physician. Nobody will care about that once we're married. That isn't a reason to give up everything you love."

"There's more." She buried her face in his chest. "I thought I was in love with Victor. When he learned I'd spent my entire inheritance on my education, he stopped calling on me, he started seeing other women."

Tyler gently stroked her back for comfort. "You were better off without him."

He deserved the truth, the whole truth. "That was when I learned I was carrying his child." She bit her lip to control her tears.

That revelation nearly knocked him off his feet. Tyler struggled to remain calm. After all he'd seen in his life, he'd thought nothing would shock him. He was wrong. "What was his reaction?"

"He wanted me to . . . He said as a doctor I should know how to do it." Her fingers clutched his shirt. "I couldn't. I wanted my baby. He disappeared. I didn't see him again until yesterday."

"And the baby?" he rasped around the constriction in his throat.

"My son was premature and he died in my arms."
Now her tears flowed freely. "My baby died, and now I
can never have another child. You see why I can't marry
you. I'm a fraud. A liar and a cheat. I'm a fallen woman,
no better than the whores who walk the city streets."

Tyler's heart broke for her, for her lost child. This
wonderful woman, who'd dedicated her life to healing the sick, was hurt far beyond what a woman
should have to bear. He knew firsthand the heartache
of losing a child. And of losing the woman who held
your heart in her hands. "Hush, darling, you're a
good woman, a wonderful doctor." The light dawned.
"Is LaBranche blackmailing you?"

She nodded. "He threatened to tell my papa and
the entire town if I didn't pay him a thousand dollars
by five o'clock." A hard sob ripped through her. "He
took my ring."

Tyler bit back a string of curses. "Leave everything
to me. I'll take care of good old Vic." The words
nearly choked him.

Analise clutched his jacket. "No. I have to pay him.
I couldn't bear for him to add his lies to what happened in Paris. No woman in this town would ever respect me if she knew I was such a wicked woman."

Tears pooled in the corners of his eyes. He loved
her so completely, he felt her pain as acutely as if a
knife had stabbed him in the gut. "Sweetheart, you
aren't wicked. And the only way to stop a blackmailer
is to call his bluff. LaBranche is a lousy poker player,
a cheat, and a coward." A wicked smile curved Tyler's
lips. He was going to enjoy bringing the snake down.

"Tyler, please don't get involved. I don't want anybody to know."

He had made up his mind. Nobody was going to
threaten the woman he loved. First he would get rid
of LaBranche, then he would settle his relationship
with Analise.

"I'll take you home, then I'll take care of LaBranche. Believe me, he'll never bother you again after today."

After wiping her face of the tears, he escorted her to her father's house. He wasn't sure how he would handle the blackmailer, but after today, Vic would never bother Analise again.

With every step Tyler took, his temper rose another notch. After escorting Analise safely to her father's home, his next stop was the hotel. All around him were signs of the Christmas season. Homes and businesses boasted evergreen wreaths and swags of greenery. People greeted him with a cheerful, "Merry Christmas." The holiday spirit was lost on him. For the past twelve years, he had dreaded the season. Without Abigail and David, he'd felt he had nothing to celebrate. This year he had Analise. And he was determined not to lose her to anybody or anything. Losing one love was enough for a lifetime. He wasn't going to be a two-time loser.

In the hotel lobby, Oliver Anderson stood on a ladder hanging a large wreath over the fireplace. When asked about the Frenchman, Oliver gestured toward the restaurant. Tyler found LaBranche sipping tea with several women. Tyler nodded to the banker's wife and daughter, then he pulled a chair up to their table and turned it backward, resting his arms across the back.

"Having a nice tea party with the ladies, Vic?" he asked, forcing a smile just short of a grimace.

LaBranche shot an angry glare at him. "*Gendarme*, I do not recall inviting you to join us."

"Hey Vic, don't get your lace drawers in an uproar. I just wanted to talk to you for a minute." Tyler glanced at the ladies. "You don't mind, do you, ladies?"

"*Sacrebleu!* I have taken all a civilized man can take of your barbaric manners." The Frenchman leaped to his feet, knocking his chair over with a bang. "I demand satisfaction."

Slowly, Tyler got to his feet. "Sorry, Vic, you won't get satisfaction from me. You've got to look at a woman for that."

"Monsieur, you are an infidel and a reprobate."

"I've been called worse." He caught the Frenchman by the arm. "What say we *marchez* over to the jailhouse and talk this over privately." He nodded to the women and the other diners in the restaurant. *"Pardon nous, madame, et mademoiselle, s'il vous plaît."* His French was impeccable and his enunciation perfect. He was finished acting the fool.

Victor shrugged off his grip. "Unhand me. I also wish to speak to you. We have something in common, or is it proper to say *someone* in common?"

Tyler struggled to ignore the man's smug attitude. With supreme effort, he managed to control his temper. *"Après vous."* He gestured for Vic to lead the way, following at his heels. Vic was surely a snappy dresser. His expensive suit fit his slender body to perfection and was covered with an equally costly coat. He wondered what kind of woman had paid for the Frenchman's clothing.

They entered the jail and Tyler set the lock on the door behind them. "Have a seat, Vic. This might take a little time."

"I will stand. You have no right to treat me like a common criminal."

"The way I see it, a blackmailer *is* a common criminal." Tyler leaned against the desk and crossed his feet at the ankles.

"You are insane. You are merely jealous because *I* was Analise's first lover. You are angry because *I* took her virginity, not you." The man's gaze touched Tyler with complete disdain. "A cowboy cannot measure up to a Frenchman in the boudoir."

Tyler set his jaw in an effort to remain calm in the face of the man he wanted to kill. "No, that isn't why I'm angry. I'm angry because you hurt a wonderful woman. Because you treated her like garbage, and because you're a self-serving bastard."

Victor laughed. "I see we understand each other. We are both men of the world. We should not be enemies."

"By the way, how did you find Analise? Why look for her now?"

"I saw in the *New York Times* that the daughter of the wealthy Doctor DeLery was to marry. The writer said that she had received a large reward for the capture of an outlaw gang. I hoped she would be sympathetic with an old friend and share her good fortune."

Tyler pushed away from the desk and set his hand on the revolver at his hip. "Well, it's like this, Vic. She isn't sharing anything with you." He pointed a finger at the other man's chest. "Not her money, not her jewelry, not her time, and definitely not her bed."

Victor backed up until he hit the wall. "I will go to the editor at the newspaper and tell him what a whore the lady doctor is. I will tell him she paid for her education on her back."

That did it. Tyler wouldn't take that kind of talk about any woman, much less the woman he loved. It took only two punches to drop LaBranche. He fell like a tree at a lumberjack's axe. Tyler stood over the man, feet braced apart, and hands clenched into fists.

"Get up, you sniveling coward."

Blood spurted from the Frenchman's nose. "You broke my nose, you brute." His string of curses would have made a French sailor proud. "I will have you arrested."

Tyler laughed. "You forget, I'm the law in this town. And that is just a small taste of what you'll get if you ever even think of coming near this town again. Or if you contact Analise or anyone in her family." He tugged the man to his feet. "Where is her ring?"

"She gave it to me." He pressed a handkerchief to his nose.

"I am running out of patience with you, Vic. Hand over the ring, or I'll have you strung up for stealing."

Reading the determination in Tyler's face, the man thrust his hand into his pocket and brought out the ring.

"Thanks." Tyler dropped it into the front pocket of his denim pants. "Now, Vic, I have something for you." He gripped LaBranche by the arm and shoved him roughly into a cell and slammed the door.

"You cannot lock me up. You have no cause."

"Stealing, blackmail. That's just two charges against you. I could add impersonating a human being. But no jury would believe that. You can just stay here and cool your heels. I'm going to make arrangements for your return trip to New York." He tucked his thumbs in the waistband of his trousers. "You'll be on the evening train out of Omega. Don't look back. And forget you ever heard of Analise DeLery or Omega. But never forget Tyler Morgan."

"I hope you and that bitch are miserable together. You deserve each other."

"*C'est la vie*, Vic. When you reach Denver, a Pinkerton agent will escort you to New York. You can look for a rich woman there."

Tyler left the jail and locked the door behind him. With the Frenchman on the evening train, Tyler changed his plans for the elopement. Like he'd told Vic, that's life. It was more important to get rid of the pestilence before he and Analise settled down in marriage.

*   *   *

At loose ends, Analise didn't know what to do. She'd promised Millie she would stay away from the house in order to give her parents privacy for the evening. Steven had gone home with the Hennesseys. There was no use packing to leave; she wasn't going anywhere with Tyler. If anything, she would be forced to pack her trunks and leave Omega forever. She'd hoped this year things would be different. Thanks to Victor, it looked like another lonely Christmas for Analise DeLery.

Left alone with her thoughts, she struggled to control her emotions. She'd been hurt when Victor had rejected her. Losing the baby had devastated her. But to lose Tyler tore her asunder. She didn't believe she would ever heal from this latest heartbreak.

Tears rolled unbidden down her cheeks. Where was the Christmas miracle when she needed one?

She returned to the clinic that would soon be snatched away from her. The workmen had left for the day, and the building was as quiet as a grave. How appropriate, she thought. Her dreams had died here where Victor had killed them. She would be fortunate even to be allowed to practice medicine in the most remote outpost in the country.

The long wail of the train whistle brought more tears. She'd thought she'd already cried an ocean dry. She should be on that train with the man she loved, instead of standing in the middle of a near-empty building lamenting what would never be.

For once, the train to Denver was early, a few minutes before six. It stayed only long enough to disembark passengers and freight, and to load people and goods. She walked around the office and stopped at the spot where she'd planned to put her desk.

She hadn't seen Tyler since he'd left her alone

that afternoon. In fact, after what he'd learned, she doubted he would want anything more to do with her. For all she knew, he could be leaving on that train without her. With no place to go, she wandered up the stairs to what was going to be their living quarters. From the window of the proposed bedroom, she watched the smoke from the steam engine and listened to the chug-chug of the train wheels leaving the station. She continued to stare as the smoke disappeared into the distance. The train was gone, and with it her hopes, her dreams, her life.

Lifting her gaze to the sky, she watched as the stars came out one by one. High above, one star, her special star, blinked as if mocking her. She'd lost everything. There was no use wishing on the Christmas star. Miracles just didn't happen.

Tyler had said he would handle the situation with Victor. But if she knew Victor, he had already spread the stories of her indiscretions all over the county. The man had no ethics or morals. Tyler was right. Her former lover was a scoundrel of the worst sort.

In the room that was to be her and Tyler's special retreat, she sagged to the floor, her back braced against the wall. The bed Tyler had ordered for them had arrived earlier, along with a soft feather mattress and a lovely patchwork quilt. But she couldn't bear to touch it. They had made so many plans. Millie had filled her hope chest with the finest linen—goods she would never use. She hugged her cape around her body against the cold, but nothing would melt the ice in her heart.

Exhausted from worry she closed her eyes for a minute. It was really funny. Victor had found her because of her engagement announcement in a newspaper. And his interference had ruined that betrothal. Analise was alone once again.

# Chapter 21

Tyler remained at the depot until the last whiff of smoke disappeared into the distance. Victor LaBranche was out of his hair for good. To ensure his departure, Tyler had personally paid for the train fares all the way to New York City. He'd bribed the conductor to keep an eye on the man and not allow him to exit the train at any of the local stops. So unless Vic hopped off the speeding train, he would reach Denver by morning. In Denver the Frenchman would be met by a Pinkerton agent who would escort him all the way to New York.

Since he and Analise had missed their elopement, Tyler needed to talk to her about trying again soon.

He wanted to marry her, but he sensed she would be reluctant to go through with it. LaBranche had humiliated her and disgraced her and made her feel unworthy of love. Every time Tyler remembered her heartbreaking tears, his chest ached for her.

Now it was up to him to encourage her and re-assure her of his love and of her own worth. Analise meant more to him than his own life.

Stopping at the hotel, he washed up and dressed

in clean denims and a shirt. He arranged for the restaurant to prepare a basket of cold chicken, bread, cheese, and a bottle of wine, with plates, glasses, and silverware for two. Since this should have been their wedding night, he aimed to share it with his intended bride. Showing his love was the surest way of easing her anxiety.

After all the pain they had both endured because of Vic, he would make this the best Christmas of their lives. Starting tonight.

Knowing she wouldn't be home, he hoped she would be at the clinic. After searching the downstairs, he lit a kerosene lamp and slowly climbed to the second floor, listening for any sign of life. He found her in their bedroom, their private sanctuary. Slumped against the wall, she was sound asleep.

For a long moment, he watched her there on the floor. Her chin rested on her chest, but tracks of tears marred her flawless cheeks. He should have shot the man who had made her cry, who had broken her heart.

No, shooting was too good for him. LaBranche deserved to be strung up by his toes.

The room was as cold as a tomb, and he watched her shiver in her sleep. When the bed had been delivered, he'd carried up wood for the fireplace. Quickly, he struck a match to the kindling and blew on the flame until the wood caught. With the fire started, he glanced over at Analise, asleep on the cold floor, lost in her misery.

Tyler settled down beside her. Slipping his arm around her shoulder, he rested her head on his chest. She felt so good in his embrace. No matter what her past, or how she felt about it, he wasn't giving her up. Any real or imagined transgression in her past paled next to those in his past. Thanks to her love, he'd stopped blaming himself for Abigail's death. Now he hoped his love could convince her to forgive herself for what had happened in Paris.

He planted a light kiss on her forehead. She swatted at him as if at an insect. Night had fallen and through the bare windows the full moon cast its light in the room while the stars glittered in the black sky. "Wake up, sleepyhead," he whispered, his mouth at the curve of her ear.

She woke with a start and jerked away from him. "What happened?"

"It's all right, sweetheart. I'm with you now."

"Tyler? What are you doing here?"

He laughed softly. "We were supposed to elope tonight. Sorry, but something came up, and I couldn't make the arrangements."

"Please let me go." She shoved out of his embrace. "What did you do with Victor?"

Her concern for her tormentor tore a hole in his heart. "Don't worry about him. The Frenchman won't bother you again."

Eyes wide with terror, she trembled. "You didn't . . . kill him, did you?"

"Why should you care? I got rid of him—that's all that matters."

She wrapped her arms around her chest as if to ward off a chill. "I didn't want you to hurt him."

"I didn't hurt him, if that's what you're worried about. We just had a man-to-coward talk, and I put him on the train back to New York. Maybe there he'll find his heiress to take care of him."

"Then it's over?" She closed her eyes and dropped her head to her chest. "Everything is over." A large tear rolled down her face. Tyler wiped it away with his thumb.

His heart ached for her, and for himself. He hadn't known she still loved LaBranche. He hardened his voice. "He isn't worth crying over. The man was a reprobate. He would have left you sooner or later."

She jerked her head up and glared at him. "I wouldn't shed a tear for that bastard. He never loved me, he just used me as a man uses a whore. And that's all I am."

He reached for her, but she fended him off. "Analise, sweetheart—"

"No, Tyler. I . . . release you from all your p . . . promises and obligations." She hiccuped, then continued, so softly that he struggled to hear her. "I c . . . cannot hold you to the engagement. You deserve a woman who is pure and . . . good. Not some sullied woman who gave herself to a man like Victor La-Branche."

His skin grew cold. She blamed herself for what had happened and now she was punishing herself. "I don't want to be released. I want to marry you."

She shook her head and jumped up, backing away from him. "No. You can't. Nothing can ever stay a secret. Millie warned me of that. I should have told you the truth weeks ago."

"Do Millie and your father know?"

"Not yet. I realize I was wrong not to confide in my family. I had best tell them before they read it in the newspaper."

"It will never be in the newspaper. But I agree, you should share your heartache with your parents."

"They'll hate me, like you must hate me." She ducked her chin and lowered her eyelids.

With a finger under her chin, he forced her to look into his eyes. "I could never hate you. I love you. We're going to be married."

"No, I can't marry you. I'm soiled. I had another man's baby, and I can never give you your own child."

"Sweetheart, I don't want a baby. I want you." He softened his tone as if speaking to an injured child.

"No, Tyler. As much as I love you, I can't. You'll always wonder if I still have feelings for him."

He tucked her into his embrace. "Will you always wonder if I still have feelings for Abigail? Listen to me. I admit, I'll always love her. She's a part of my past, and I'll always remember the love we shared. But my love for you is different. That was the love of a young man—a first love. My love for you is of a mature man for a mature woman. A love that will last through trials and tribulations, into eternity. Nothing in your past affects the way I feel about you."

"I'm sorry to put you through this. I'm not good enough for you."

He set her away from him with his hands on her shoulders. "Look at me, Analise. I've killed men. I would have killed the Malone gang if you hadn't been there. I didn't have to bring them in alive to get the reward or my bonus, or to fulfill my assignment. I'm an itinerant actor, a nomad. I've never stayed in one place for more than six months at a time. I can understand if you reject me for those reasons, but never, never think you aren't good enough for me. I'm not worthy to brush the dirt from your shoes."

She caught his face in her hands. "Don't say that. You're a wonderful man. You'll make a wonderful husband. Any woman would be fortunate to have you marry her. It just can't be me."

"If we're both so wonderful, we deserve to be together. That was Vic's last blessing. He said we belonged together. See, even he could see the truth."

For a long moment he stared into her eyes. When his words didn't work, it was time for action. "Sweetheart, if you don't believe what I say, I'll have to show you how I feel." Reaching into his pocket, he pulled out the engagement ring and slipped it onto her finger. "Analise DeLery, will you marry me?"

Without giving her a chance to respond, Tyler pulled her hard against his chest. His mouth settled on hers, soft and coaxing. Her body felt so right, he vowed never to let her go. She tasted of the salt from her tears. He was certain some of those tears were his own. He loved her, and she was his. It was time to show her, to make her his woman in every sense of the word.

He stroked his tongue along the seam of her lips. Her soft moan told him the second she stopped resisting and submitted to his love. She opened to him, inviting the sweet invasion of his tongue. Her eagerness fueled his passion, and he was lost. He swept her up, pressing her close to his body, letting her feel through the layers of clothing how much he needed her. Hands shaking, he removed her cloak and dropped it to the floor. He shrugged out of his heavy wool coat.

Analise was lost the instant his tongue touched hers. Desire surged through every inch of her body, pooling in the middle of her belly. His hands stroked her back, making her skin tingle. Her breasts pressed against his muscular chest; the tips tightened into needy buds. With eager hands, she tugged his shirt from his trousers, wanting to feel his warm flesh under her fingertips. She needed his warmth to chase away the chill that fear had dug deep into her heart.

His kiss turned hard, demanding, met by her own demands and needs. He ended the kiss and continued to rain tiny nips across her chin and down to her neck. "I need you, *chère*, like I need air to breathe. You're my life, Analise. Be mine. Now. Tonight. I can't wait two months, or until we can elope, I need you now."

She threw back her head to give him better access

to her throat and chest. His day's stubble increased the sensations of his lips on her sensitive skin. "This was supposed to be our wedding night. Let's not be cheated out of it."

Desire burst like an inferno in her. Never had she wanted, no, needed, a man like she did Tyler. Love was the difference. Love that made a woman want to be one with a man, and made that man cleave to the woman. She knew this was right. Nothing had ever seemed so perfect. She and Tyler belonged together.

He continued his exploration of her neck. Somehow the tiny buttons of her blouse loosed and the garment slipped from her shoulders. His shirt followed hers onto the floor. With eager hands, determined mouths, and hearts full of love, they touched, stroked, and kissed.

Lost in the wonder of it all, Analise wasn't aware she'd shed her skirt and petticoats, or that Tyler's trousers and boots lay discarded on the floor until he lifted her nude body high in his arms and lay her gently on the mattress of the bed.

He fell beside her and stared down at her. "*Mon amour*, I wanted to make love to you our first time on silk sheets, with rose petals and perfume instead of a rough mattress with the smell of paint and sawdust lingering in the air."

She touched a finger to his lips. "We'll have that soon enough. Now we're in our very own bed. With you, this is as wonderful as the finest hotel in the world."

"Are you sure? We can stop now, but in about ten seconds, I'll be committed." He threw his leg over hers, giving evidence of his need.

She brushed her fingers through his hair. "As long as you're committed to me."

"Now and forever, I make my vows to you. I love you, Doctor Analise DeLery. Be mine for eternity."

She smiled up at him, her finger brushed unexpected dampness from his cheek. "Now and forever, Tyler Morgan. I'll love you, into eternity."

The full moon was high in the sky when Analise woke with her head nestled on Tyler's shoulder. After they'd made love, he'd thrown the lovely quilt across them and they'd fallen asleep.

"Finally awake?" he asked in a voice groggy with sleep.

She rubbed her arms. "I'm cold."

He wrapped her in his arms and covered her with his body. "I know an excellent way to warm you."

Smiling, she returned his embrace, pressing her bare breasts to his equally bare chest. Never had she felt better, more alive, or happier. "True, you had me on fire. But now I'm hungry. Didn't you carry a basket in with you hours ago?"

With soft laughter, he released her and swung his legs to the side of the bed. "A well-planned seduction needs a fine meal to top it off."

She sat up and tugged her chemise over her head. It did little to cover her body, but she wasn't sure she could walk around completely nude. "So you admit you planned to seduce me."

"Ah ha." He turned and patted her cheek. "I don't believe in leaving anything to chance. And who knows when we'll get this opportunity again?"

"How about tomorrow?"

"I'll be busy. I might have to settle another dispute between a bull and a cow." He picked up the basket and set it on the bed between them. Boldly naked, he stretched out on the bed. "But I have another idea. The new preacher will be here in a few days, and we can be married for Christmas. How does Christmas Eve sound for a wedding?"

Analise opened her mouth to protest, when he pressed lips solidly to hers. "Don't argue. I have no intention of waiting until February. That's like telling me I can't take another breath, or eat another meal for two months. I need you, and I want to live with you. With or without the sanctity of marriage."

Shocked, she wasn't sure if he was serious or just forcing the issue. "Tyler, you can't mean that. Think about our reputations."

"Hang our reputations. We said our vows to each other a while ago, right here, in our room. I feel as if I'm already married to you."

"Fine."

"Fine? You aren't going to argue?"

"*Non, mon ami.* You hold my heart and soul. Christmas Eve, we'll be married. If we eloped Papa and Millie would be hurt. They want so much to give us a lovely wedding. Christmas Eve is a perfect time for our celebration. Millie will have the house decorated and tables laden with food. And she's already invited half the county to a midnight supper. We've even convinced Alex and Polly to celebrate with us."

"That's perfect. Alex and Polly can stand up for us. But I think we should keep it a secret until after the pageant. We don't want Millie and Etienne to protest or try to change our minds."

"I agree. We can be married with all our friends and neighbors to wish us happiness."

Tyler pulled out a bottle of wine from the basket. "Let's toast our engagement." Filling two glasses, he passed one to her. "To you, Doctor Analise DeLery Morgan. May all your dreams come true."

Tears blinded her eyes. Happiness filled her heart. "To Mr. Tyler Goodfellow August Morgan, who has made all my dreams come true."

And a year ago she'd thought miracles didn't happen.

# Chapter 22

"Analise, please hold still so Madame can fit the gown." Millie tugged on the neckline of the gown. "Christmas is only four days away, and Madame was kind enough to come to Omega to fit our gowns for the holidays."

"Millie, it isn't good for you to get upset. I will allow Madame to make me into a pincushion, and I will even wear the corset, if it will make you happy."

The modiste laughed. "*Petite*, you will not need the corset. Your sheriff made it clear when he ordered the gowns that you do not need the assistance of the undergarment."

A sly smile crossed Millie's lovely face. "I believe I will lie down for a while." After taking a few steps from the room, she turned back to the dressmaker. "And Madame, I wish to order enough gowns to last through my entire . . . confinement." She laughed. "Not that I plan to be confined for one moment."

Analise sighed. Now that Millie's pregnancy was common knowledge, she planned to take full advantage of the situation. Etienne was walking on air and treating his wife as if she were made of fine porcelain. As she well deserved.

"You will be lovely in the rose silk, *chèrie*. Your sheriff is a lucky man. And so generous." Madame Valcour set aside her pincushion and helped Analise out of the dress.

The dressmaker had arrived the previous day at Tyler's invitation with six new dresses in tow for Analise's final fittings. To her surprise, Analise learned that her fiancé had selected the patterns, colors, and fabrics, and given the instructions to Millie to take to Denver. The dressmaker had even brought the rose silk that was originally to be her wedding gown. She would wear it on Christmas Eve.

When Madame had measured and poked at Analise in her shop in Denver, Millie had indicated that the gowns were part of the trousseau from her papa. She had never expected that Tyler was behind the project.

"Are all the men in this little village as handsome as your fiancé and your papa?" the dressmaker asked.

With a laugh, Analise stepped out of the silk gown. "Yes, they are. You will meet many of them at Christmas, if you wish to celebrate with our family." She glanced down at the black-haired woman who was about Millie's age, and very attractive. A list of the town's bachelors raced through her mind. The idea of playing matchmaker made her smile.

Once in her everyday gown, Analise headed out of the sewing room. "I have to get back to my patients." She hurried down the stairs and entered the office.

The new minister, Jeremy Leonard, and his wife, Sally, had arrived a few days earlier. The young minister was delighted to be conducting his first Christmas service, but he didn't know it would also be his first marriage ceremony in Omega. Tyler had agreed to direct the children's pageant.

Everything was falling into place for both the wedding and the clinic. More than once Analise had to bite her lip to keep the planned nuptials secret. To make things even better, Sally Leonard, who was a trained nurse, had agreed to work in the clinic. It was just one miracle after another.

Analise greeted a waiting patient and started to usher the mother and child into the examination room, when Tyler burst through the doorway. She paused and stared at him. Looking like an outlaw with his handgun at his hip, a rifle in his hand, and saddle-bags thrown over his shoulder, Tyler halted midstride.

"Excuse me, ma'am, I have to see Doctor Analise for a moment." Without giving her a chance to an-swer, Tyler gripped her arm and guided her into the hallway that joined the office and the house. A shiver raced up her spine. Something was wrong. Tyler's face was a mask of anger and agony.

"You want to call off the wedding. You're leaving me." Her worst fears tore her heart in pieces.

He shook his head and tugged her into his chest. "No, sweetheart, never. But I have to leave for a few days." He kissed the top of her head. "Harvey Malone escaped from jail. I have to join the posse to track him and take him back to prison."

Analsie trembled. "How did that happen?"

"Harv complained of chest pain, and when the doctor went into the cell to examine him, he man-aged to escape. He killed a guard and the doctor. The Denver police tracked him as far as Castle Rock and lost him. I have to go. I can't let Harv get any-where near Omega."

She looked into his determined face. "But Tyler, that's dangerous. Can't the local authorities track him?"

He shook his head. "Harv is dangerous and tricky. When I was appointed sheriff, I promised to uphold the law and protect the citizens of this state against men like Malone. I have to go, to protect you."

"But the wedding is in four days." Analise felt her miracle melt away like snow in the sunshine.

"I'll be back in time. This should only take a day or two. I won't let anything or anyone stand in our way. Have faith, sweetheart." He bent his head and kissed her hard on the mouth. "I have to go. I'm not even waiting for the train. I'm riding out and hope to meet the posse south of Castle Rock. We'll find him, and I'll be back."

Tears rolled down her face. "Be careful. I love you."

"I love you too. And we'll get our miracle." With another kiss, he raced through the office and out the door.

Analise covered her lips with her fingers to hold in the warmth of his kiss. She sagged against the wall. Tyler was only doing his job, and he was very good at it. But why so close to the wedding, so close to Christmas? So close to her finally getting a miracle.


Tyler knelt in the newly fallen snow and placed the flowers on the grave. If he was to start a new life with Analise, he had to say good-bye to the old one.

Harvey Malone had been a tougher opponent than he'd expected. The outlaw had been cornered, but hadn't given up. He had wounded three lawmen before he'd been killed. Tyler had caught a bullet in the shoulder, a flesh wound that didn't mean a thing. He hadn't notified Analise, not wanting to frighten her or upset her.

On the spur of the moment, he'd felt the need to pay his annual visit to the cemetery. Instead of heading toward Omega, he'd hopped the first east-bound train and he'd jumped off at Abilene. If he hurried, he would be able to catch a train to Denver within the hour. The telegraph operator had reported a blizzard moving in from the west. He hoped it held off until he could make it back to Omega.

He touched the headstone, remembering the past year, when he'd believed there were no miracles for him.

In the newly darkened sky, the brightest star blinked down on him. He closed his eyes and let his tears fall. As much as he'd loved Abigail, it was past time to get on with his life. Behind his eyelids he pictured his late wife smiling at him. A voice whispered in his head, a voice that sounded very much like Abigail's. "Be happy." The words were as clear and resounding as the bells from the nearby church.

He looked up into the sky and let the snowflakes touch his face. Words of thanks came from his heart. His spirit soared, knowing that after twelve years, he was on the right track. "Good-bye, Abigail," he whispered. "I have to go, but I'll always love you and David."

In the distance, the mournful whistle of the train cut into his reverie. He felt as if a huge weight had been lifted from his shoulders. His spirit soared clear up to that star. He had a wedding to attend.

In twenty-four hours, he would marry the woman he loved and start a new life.

This year, he was going to get his miracle.

All of Omega was decked out for Christmas. Everywhere she looked, Analise saw happy faces, homes decorated for the holiday, and nobody was happier than Millie.

Her stepmother's pregnancy didn't slow her down one bit. She and Mrs. Hennessey had spent days making cakes, cookies, and colorful decorations. She'd even set up a large fir tree in the parlor with piles of brightly wrapped packages underneath. Analise and Sally had also decorated the clinic with greenery, holly, and lots of ribbon. They planned the grand opening soon after the new year.

And every night she prayed on the Christmas star that Tyler would return home safely to her.

Analise awoke early on Christmas Eve, to find freshly fallen snow blanketing the ground. Outside, Steven and several boys were running and tossing snowballs. She had not heard a single word from Tyler since he'd left. Several times each day she'd rushed to the telegraph office, hoping to learn that he was fine and on his way home to her. She was frightened, as scared as she had been the previous Christmas when she lost her baby.

She'd told Papa and Millie everything that had happened in Paris. Everything. Neither parent condemned or faulted her in any way. They only regretted that they hadn't been present to support her and help in her time of need.

Hoping for good news, Analise hurried downstairs. She expected to see Tyler seated at the table enjoying Mrs. Hennessey's elaborate breakfast. She rushed into the kitchen and spotted only Oscar at the stove, pouring a cup of coffee.

He turned to her with a sad look on his face. Her heart raced. "Oscar, is something wrong?"

"Missy, I'm sorry."

She sank into a chair. "Is it Tyler? You've heard from him?"

"No, not yet. The telegraph operator got word from up the line. A blizzard has everything stopped between here and Denver. We just got the tail end of the blizzard, but places like Colorado Springs and Castle Rock were blasted. If the sheriff is still there, he'll be stuck until the tracks are cleared or the roads are passable."

Her heart sank. Now she was certain Tyler wasn't going to make the wedding. Millie rushed into the kitchen, Mrs. Hennessey on her heels. "Oscar told us about the blizzard. If Tyler isn't able to return in time for Christmas, we'll celebrate again when he returns."

"What if he isn't coming back? What if he can't? Anything could have happened to him. He could have been shot, he could have had an accident, he could have gotten lost in the mountains."

Millie brushed her fingers along Analise's cheek. "He will be back. He loves you. Your love will lead him back." She grabbed Analise's hand. "Madame wants you for the final fitting on your lovely new gown."

"Why bother, Millie? I won't wear it tonight."

"You most certainly will wear it. Madame Valcour and I went to entirely too much trouble to let it go to waste. Even if Tyler isn't here, you will wear the gown for Christmas."

They were halfway up the stairs when the rear door flung open. Her father stomped the snow from his boots and hung up his hat. "I've just come from the telegraph office." He looked up at Analise, sadness in his eyes.

Analise raced back down to her father. "Have you heard from Tyler?"

He caught her warm hands in his cold ones. "Not directly. The posse caught up with Malone, but several men were wounded."

"Tyler?" She groaned, afraid of the answer.

"I don't know. With the storm to the north, the telegraph lines are down. We only got half the message. We'll keep praying for him." Her father took her into his arms and hugged her as he had when she was a child. "*Chérie*, he will be fine. Tyler is a strong man. He'll come back to you."

"Papa, I have a bad feeling. I should go look for him. He may need a doctor."

"My child, if he needed you, he would send for

you. There is nothing we can do until the train is again running. We will celebrate Christmas as we always have, and rejoice that we are together as a family."

She nodded and shoved away from her father. Analise DeLery was a woman, not a child to cry and whine on her father's shoulder. She refused to be defeated, to give in to her fears. If Tyler was late, they would just have to live with the situation. Whenever it happened, they would marry and have a life together.

She would not give up on her miracle.


At six o'clock that evening, Analise stood at the window and looked at the sky. The clouds had gathered and it looked like there'd be more snow. Not a star or moon could be seen in the darkness.

She studied the lovely rose silk gown on the bed. Madame Valcour had already dressed Analise's hair in the latest style, and in a few minutes, she would assist her with the gown—and all the tiny buttons Tyler liked to complain about. She ran a finger along the beads and pearls that outlined the neckline. Should she wear the gown tonight, or wait until she was certain the wedding would take place? Tyler had made it clear, he wanted her to wear the rose silk on Christmas Eve. For their wedding. Wearing the gown would show her faith in their love. If worse came to worse, she would wear the gown twice, three times if necessary.

The Christmas Eve celebration at the church was to begin at eight, and the DeLerys had invited a number of friends to their home for a late supper after the service. Alex, Polly, Anna and Manny had arrived earlier, and the couple had agreed they would all spend the night at the DeLery home.

A light knock on the door drew her out of her reverie. "Enter," she called, not surprised when Madame Valcour stuck her head into the room.

"Your family has gathered downstairs. I must assist you into that beautiful gown. You will be magnificent for your sheriff."

"If he returns," she whispered.

Madame laughed. "Have faith. He will return." The dressmaker removed Analise's wrapper and picked up the gown.

On a long sigh, Analise allowed the woman to help her dress. In its simplicity, the gown was stunning. Tyler had excellent taste and an eye for design. She supposed it was because of his years on the stage working with costumes. Unfortunately, he was not going to see her in the gown. Tyler was not going to make the wedding.

First Harvey Malone escaped, then the weather conspired to keep Tyler away. As much as she wanted him with her on this special night, she hoped he had the good sense to remain in a protected location until it was safe to travel.

With all the tiny buttons hooked, Analise glanced at her image in the cheval mirror in the corner. She touched her fingers to her lips, barely recognizing the woman staring back at her. The gown was magnificent, her face aglow, and her hair like a dark halo about her head.

She squared her shoulders. The lovely gown showed off her figure to perfection even without a corset. The sheer yolk over the deep neckline of the gown preserved her modesty while allowing the cleavage to show. Tyler would love it. If he ever saw it.

"You are exquisite, doctor." Madame tugged at the seams, adjusting the fit of the gown. "Your guests are arriving. Let us go and greet your friends." She tapped her finger on her chin. At some point, the French accent had dropped. "Tell me, does that handsome Mr. Anderson from the hotel have a wife?"

Analise smiled at the woman. With an hourglass

figure many women would envy, nearly black hair, and plump cheeks, the modiste was a very attractive woman. "Mr. Anderson is a bachelor, and he owns a fine establishment. Mr. Henry, the bank clerk, is also single. And if I'm not mistaken, he is actively looking for a wife."

Madame Valcour waved a hand in dismissal. "I was just curious, that is all. I may decide to leave Denver, and set up my little shop in this lovely town."

Analise easily saw through her. "Omega is growing daily. A fine fashion house would be a delightful addition to the town. I am opening a clinic for women and children, and several other businesses are looking for locations on Alpha Street."

"Perhaps I will speak to Mr. Henry. I have a bit of money saved, and he can advise me on the advantages of relocating." She hooked her arm in Analise's. "Let us go down and greet your guests. You must introduce me to your friends."

Analise bolstered her courage. It was Christmas Eve, and her family and good friends had come together to celebrate the best holiday of the year. With or without Tyler, with or without a wedding, she was wearing a beautiful gown, and she would enjoy herself.

The Christmas service was scheduled from eight to ten, then the families would return to their homes. Tyler had planned the pageant and expected the children to perform even without him. To everybody's delight, they were doing an admirable job, with Sally directing the action. Everything was going smoothly in spite of the youngest angel falling asleep, while another little girl raced up and down the aisle flapping her wings trying to fly. Both Steven and Manny stood tall and proud as Wise Men.

By the dim candlelight, the Winters's youngest

girl, playing the Virgin Mary, cradled her doll, the baby Jesus, and around her the shepherds sang "Silent Night." Analise allowed the tears to roll down her cheeks. Last Christmas, she was alone burying her infant son, tonight she was surrounded by loved ones. She glanced at Polly rocking Anna in her arms. The young woman wore a pretty worsted gown, and Alex wore a new black suit and looked very uncomfortable. From time to time, he ran his finger under the tight collar of the shirt. Two pews ahead of them Madame Valcour was sandwiched between Mr. Anderson and Mr. Henry.

As the last note of the carol rang in the air, Analise felt movement at her side. "Move over," a voice whispered.

Tingles raced over her. A large body slid into the pew, pressing indecently close to her. "Tyler?" she whispered.

"I had better be. I won't have you marrying another man."

At her other side, Millie caught her hand. "I told you he would be here."

"But, but the snow, the blizzard."

"A little snow couldn't keep me away from the woman I love."

Tears gathered in her eyes. "How?"

"I merely followed the star and it led me directly to you."

She cupped his face with her hands. His cheeks were chilled, but his tears were warm. "The stars are hidden by the clouds."

"No, I'll show you our special star. It's shining bright and clear. A miracle in the sky."

Through a veil of tears, she noticed his left arm in a sling. "You've been wounded."

"Just a scratch." He lowered his head to whisper, "It's good that I'll have a doctor to look after me."

Analise was suddenly aware that the song had ended, and by the dim candlelight all eyes were on her and Tyler.

Abruptly, Tyler stood. "Pastor, I see my little thespians did a wonderful job." The children still on the platform in the front of the church giggled, while the younger ones dashed for their parents. "Now I have a special favor to ask." He reached down and tugged Analise to her feet.

"My lovely fiancée and I wish you to perform our marriage ceremony tonight. With the entire congregation as witness to our vows."

Analise glanced at her father and saw the surprised look on his face. He looked to Millie who smiled as if she'd known all along. Analise didn't doubt that her stepmother suspected, and that that was why she had insisted on the new gown.

"Go," Millie urged. "Your father and I give our blessings." She reached for little Anna. "Polly, you will be the matron of honor. Alex, go. You're Tyler's best man."

Analise gaped at her stepmother. She glanced at Tyler and saw that he wore an evening suit as elegant as any gentleman at any theater in Denver or New York. She was totally confused. The only thing that mattered was that he had come and they would be married.

Around them the congregation whispered and smiled. Tyler lifted her hand and kissed her palm. "Let's get married."

Tears dampening her cheeks, Analise tucked her arm in Tyler's and walked down the aisle.

She loved him, he loved her. Love was the true Christmas miracle.

Only the stars knew what other miracles were in store for their future.